DOC'S CODICIL

And the Christmas Pageant That Went Awry

GARY F. JONES

Virginia

Doc's Codicil and the Christmas Pageant That Went Awry

This is a work of fiction. All of the characters, names, incidents, organizations, and dialogue in this novel are either the products of the author's imagination or are used fictitiously.

Published in the United States by BQB Publishing
(Boutique of Quality Books Publishing Company)
www.bqbpublishing.com

Printed in the United States of America

978-1-939371-83-6 (p)
978-1-939371-84-3 (e)

Library of Congress Control Number: 2015941806

Book design by Robin Krauss, www.bookformatters.com
Cover design by Ellis Dixon

CONTENTS

Chapter 1

Codicil: a document that amends a previously executed will.

The Heirs' Story

Rockburg, Northern Wisconsin, September 2013

Al finished tying his tie and looked at himself in the mirror. A halo of wispy, white hair edged his shining pate; his back was stooped; and his face lined and creased. *You're kind of an old fossil for this nonsense,* he thought. He reached for his suit coat, hesitated, and left it where it was. "Too damned hot today," he grumbled. "I wouldn't bother with a tie if I knew these kids better."

His wife Jan, white haired and dressed in her robe, looked at him from the master bathroom and mumbled something as she brushed her teeth.

He snorted quietly. *Together forty-five years, and she still thinks I can understand her when she talks with a toothbrush in her mouth.* "What was that, dear?"

Jan set the toothbrush aside and rinsed her mouth. "How do you think your meeting will go?" she asked.

"I do not know. You can't play games with bank stock and not expect consequences, even if you are dead." He scanned his dresser and the bed. "Where the hell are my socks? I had 'em in my hand a second ago."

Jan sighed. "On your left shoulder, Al," she called to him, "where you put them while you tied your tie."

He saw her roll her eyes. *I guess I deserved that.*

Thirty minutes later in the bank's board room, Al Huss watched Seth, Doc's oldest son, pace back and forth at the other end of the conference table. Six foot tall, frowning, muscular, and shaved bald, Seth looked intimidating. Al followed Seth's eyes as they lingered over the dark wainscoting, wide moldings around the doors, windows, ceiling, and the wood flooring that groaned as he paced. Al had seen the look before. *Kids move to a big city and think our bank is a museum piece.*

Seth's sister, Julie, an attractive, willowy brunette, the youngest of the family, was dressed casually in shorts and blouse and sat halfway down the mahogany conference table to Al's left. Her pixie haircut set off a wicked grin. Al saw her flick something, maybe a paper clip, across the table at her brother Jed. Jed, in jeans and T-shirt, had a beard, thinning auburn hair, and was slightly shorter and leaner than Seth. Whatever Julie had aimed at him, Jed deflected toward his cousin Mark, a thin, dark-haired young man sitting next to him. Mark, the only one wearing a suit, gave a start, and looking puzzled, glanced around the room. A smile flickered across Jed's face; as with studied innocence, both he and Julie used magazines from a rack by the wall to fan themselves. *Both have graduate degrees and families, and they get home and act like fourth graders,* Al thought. *Just like Doc said.*

Yellowed curtains behind Al fluttered pleasantly in a light breeze from an open window behind him. Wally picked up a newspaper and began to fan himself. *Apparently natural ventilation isn't enough for a generation raised with air conditioning,* Al thought. *They don't look happy that I haven't turned the lights on, either.*

The light from the windows was enough for Al. He drafted the will years ago and reread it after the funeral last week. Al had agreed to do this as a favor for Doc. That was before the codicil. *Crazy bastard, I told him not to do this. Just like him, though, the stubborn SOB.*

He looked at Doc's sons. Both appeared to be in their mid-forties, Seth slightly older. Jed whispered something to Wally and smiled. Al recognized something of old Doc in that smile. *Ah, hell, I owe it to him. We had some great times, but for Christ's sake, squirrel fishing?*

Al glanced at his watch and the door. *Late*, he thought. *Doc warned me.*

The pendulum clock on the wall struck ten o'clock. Al looked over his glasses at it, then toward the heirs lining the table. "Julie, Jed, and Seth, thank you for coming. Do any of you know if Josh plans to be here?"

"He's coming," Julie said and shrugged her shoulders. "At least, that's what he said, yesterday."

Seth took a chair, sprawling more than sitting. "Josh hasn't been on time in twenty years. Let's get started."

Al, elbows resting on the table, pressed his fingertips together in front of him. It was an old habit, a pose he struck to make it clear he was in charge. "That's what your father said. He also left instructions I was not to begin until all of his children were present, barring accident or catastrophe."

He turned his attention to the cousin. "Mark, as . . ."

Mark looked up from his newspaper. At thirty-three, he was the youngest in the room. "I stopped using my first name—too much confusion with my dad's. I go by M. Wallace for legal documents, otherwise, call me Wally."

"I'll make a note of that. As you know, there is not a financial settlement for you and your family in the will, but all of your grandmother's descendants share equally in properties covered by the codicil. Will the rest of your family be joining us?"

"Nope," Wally said. "Mom isn't well enough to travel, and my brother and sister were detained by business. They asked me to represent them."

The door opened, and Josh, a harried-looking man in his late thirties, with a beard and ponytail, and dressed in cutoffs, sandals, and T-shirt, peeked into the room. He looked toward Julie and grinned, "Guess I'm in the right room. Sorry I'm late."

Al introduced himself and got down to business. He explained that they had three items on the agenda: the will, the safety deposit box, and the codicil. He passed out copies of the will to each of Doc's children. Wally busied himself with his cell phone while the will was read. The terms were straightforward; all assets, except the farm and those covered by the codicil, were to be divided equally.

The bank president, another old friend of Doc's, brought in the safety deposit box, and behind him came his secretary with her laptop. They sat on either side of Al; the president opened the box and gave it to Al, as his secretary booted her computer.

Al went through the contents—insurance policies, stock certificates, deed to the family farm, certificates of deposit, outdated contracts—naming each item aloud, accompanied by the soft clicks of the secretary's keyboard, as she prepared the inventory. The routine was broken when Al came to four sealed envelopes.

Al paused a moment. He hadn't expected this. Probate could be a legal nightmare if the envelopes contained valuables and the kids fought over something. "These envelopes have your names on them. I will assume they are yours and are not part of the estate. I suggest you open them later." He passed them out to Julie, Seth, Jed, and Josh.

Only a brown envelope remained in front of Al. He put it aside earlier, hoping to get the bulk of his work completed before the fireworks, just as he turned off the air conditioning before meetings to encourage people to leave rather than argue. Al planned ahead.

Doc had given Al the envelope five years earlier. It still mystified him. It resembled a standard business envelope, but was heavier and made of card stock rather than paper. "Buy War Bonds" was printed in large blue letters across the front, and in the upper corners were an eagle to the left and an American flag on the right. It was an antique in its own right, a survivor from World War II. Doc insisted the codicil be stored and delivered to his children and his sister Linda's children only in this envelope.

Al didn't recognize the name "Tim Wilson" or the handwriting on the front. Maybe, it had something to do with the final request in the codicil. Al glanced at each of the heirs and hoped Doc had passed on his sense of humor. *Guess this is when I find out.*

"Doc and Linda inherited two properties. One is the family farm, now being managed by the son of your grandmother Elspeth's, ah, grandmother's . . ." Al was a bit prudish, and finding the right words with the lady's granddaughter in the room came hard for him. "Ahem, ah, your grandmother's companion."

"You mean Grandma's boy toy," Julie said.

The heirs giggled, and Al felt himself turn red. At least, they had a sense of humor. "Whatever. The codicil states that the farm is to be sold at a discount to the current manager. The proceeds will go to fund the codicil and your expenses incurred in discovery."

"Discovery?" asked Seth. "What's that all about? And why does the manager get a deal?"

Al remembered Doc had warned him about Seth. "Your father recommended the young man to your grandmother and helped her hire him away from another farm decades ago. It was only later that they discovered the relationship to, ah, the relationship. Doc and Linda have, or had, great respect and affection for the young man."

"There's a property other than the farm?" Wally asked.

"Stock in this bank. It was purchased by your grandfather in 1950, when he served on the board."

"Grandpa was on the Board of Directors? Here?" Julie asked.

"He was the Chairman of the Board. There were two factions on the board, and the only person in town who could get along with both of them was your grandfather. Board members sold him bank stock at a discount to get him on the Board. He left the stock to your grandmother, and she put it in trust until Linda was fifty. Apparently, neither of your grandparents thought people under fifty should be trusted with money. Doc and Linda agreed to set the stock aside for the next generation. They saw it as a means to bring you together, bring you back to their home town, and to teach all of you a lesson."

Al knew he'd made a mistake as soon as he finished the sentence.

Seth came out of his chair. "What? Teach us a lesson!"

Al tried putting his fingertips together again and looked over his glasses at Seth. This was not going well, and he hadn't even gotten to the hard part. "Doc was one of my best friends. Wally, your mother Linda is another. Your mother and Doc prepared this codicil together, against my advice, and over my objections."

Two crazy bastards, Al thought, but immediately regretted it. *No matter how crazy Doc could be, Linda was always a lady,* Al thought. He looked at the heirs again. They were staring back at him. He took a deep breath and forged ahead.

"Doc, with the approval of Linda, requested I read the following: 'Linda and Mark and I and Mary are proud of all of you. You are honest, hardworking, and bright. That's a good start in life, but we are asking more of you.

'We would like you to laugh and sing, loudly and often. Be kind to others, help your fellow man, love those close to you, study for the sheer joy of learning, seek out difficult tasks, and go at them. Do not fear failure; it happens.

'Your checking accounts will be empty before the end of the month from the time your kids are in high school until they're out of college, maybe longer. Buck up; it will pass. Enjoy them while they're with you.

'Be honest, be truthful, and always, always remember to take Doofus squirrel fishing.'"

"Squirrel what? With who?" asked Seth.

Al ignored him, and without pause or looking up to check the other heirs' reactions, he went straight into the financials.

"The bank stock is to be sold within five years, or as needed, to allow the estate to get the best price. The proceeds will be deposited in the bank as long-term CDs until they are dispersed. The initial CDs will be given to each of you when one of you answers the first question."

"What's the question?" asked Jed.

Jed was the only one of the heirs who was smiling. Al remembered Doc had told him Jed was a puzzle fan.

Al swallowed hard. He'd be lucky if he weren't committed for psychiatric evaluation after this meeting. "The first question is, 'Would you like to go squirrel fishing?'"

Silence. Al had never seen five such clueless people. Make that six, counting himself. He had no idea what the answer was. That was in a smaller envelope.

Al continued reading the codicil. "The second set of CDs will be given to those of you who take Doofus squirrel fishing, and—"

Seth snorted, stood, and resumed pacing the floor. The squeaking floor was the only sound in the room, until Al resumed reading.

"The last CD will be given to the person who returns this envelope to its rightful owner. If any of you do not take Doofus squirrel fishing, your share of the proceeds will be given to your issue upon your death."

Seth scowled, Josh looked at Wally and shrugged his shoulders, and Jed dropped his pen. The soft clatter sounded like an overturned garbage can in the quiet room.

Jed retrieved his pen and broke the silence. "Who is Doofus, and where does he fish?"

"I do not know. I suspect it is allegorical," Al said. "The answer for each question—"

"I think Doofus was a character Dad invented for his stories," Josh said. "I'm not—"

Al coughed. "Allow me to finish, please. The answer for each question is in a sealed envelope. There are three. Each is to be opened only when necessary."

"How much is the bank stock worth?" Wally asked.

The heirs nodded in agreement.

"Yeah, what's the payout on this dizzy game?" Seth asked.

This is where it gets unpleasant, Al thought. *Maybe nasty.* "My guess, which is only a guess, as shares in the bank are sold infrequently, is somewhere between 150 and 200. Sale of the farm could add over ten times that, depending on the appraised value."

Seth made a quick calculation. "So, 2,000 bucks divided between seven of us?"

Al fidgeted. Even with the breeze from the window behind him, he was sweating. "You misunderstood me; 150 to 200 is 150 to 200 *thousand* dollars. With the proceeds of the farm, that could be 350 to 450,000 dollars for each of you, with a possible $100,000 bonus CD."

Josh whistled. The rest of the heirs looked, in turn, incredulous, happy, and upset.

"Why in hell tie everything up in bank CDs?" Seth asked.

"None of you are fifty yet. Linda and Doc agreed with their parents about young people and money," Al said.

The heirs, some scribbling on scraps of paper, some looking into space, each quietly calculated how the money would affect them.

Al interrupted their reverie. "I didn't mention it before, as the value is uncertain, but your father's book is due to be published in November. Proceeds from the publisher's contract will add $2,000 per heir to the CDs. That figure could be increased substantially, if the book sells well."

Wally looked surprised. "Unk wrote a book?"

"It was a fantasy," Jed said. "That's the story about Doofus. He talked about it a lot after Mom died, but I never paid attention."

Julie thought for a minute. "I did. So did your kids. All our kids did. Dad told those stories every Thanksgiving, silly stories, stories about the family and his work. The kids ate it up."

Seth nodded. "Marcie learned a bunch of new words from Dad's stories. Martha was furious. That's why we cut back on holidays with the family."

Josh snickered. "Yeah, Dad's language could be salty."

Seth stopped his pacing. "I'll be damned if I'm going to—"

Al interrupted. "One of the reasons I mentioned the book was that Doc and Linda signed the codicil before he wrote the book and negotiated with the publisher. I would suggest you contest the codicil were it not for that, as the sums involved and the bizarre requests bring Doc's sanity into question. I don't think that's open to you now."

Seth wasn't mollified. "Well, I'm not going to give up that kind of money. He wanted an answer? Okay, I'll go squirrel fishing."

Al already had the appropriate envelope in hand. He had hoped someone would answer the question, today. It gave him a chance to look at the response Doc wanted, which might give him an idea of what the hell the old fool had been up to.

A small piece of paper fell from the envelope. *Handwritten. Great.* Doc's handwriting was nearly indecipherable. Al read the answer, straightened a crease in the paper to see if that would help, pulled out his handkerchief, and wiped his glasses. The answer remained the same.

Al reevaluated his friendship with Doc, trying to remember if there were reasons Doc would deliberately torture him. The last time he'd seen Doc was after Doc's retirement. They'd been having a beer on the deck at Doc's. A couple of squirrels had been in a tree above them.

Al remembered. He tried not to, but he started to laugh. He gave up any pretense of self-control and let loose, howling with laughter. Tears were running down his face by the time he regained his composure. *God, I loved being around that guy.*

Al turned to Seth. "No. That is not the correct answer."

Seth's face was dark. The other heirs were silent; the men, other than Jed, were sullen.

Al decided he'd better do something. "Doc didn't say I couldn't give you a hint. Remember the backyard of your parent's home. They were inveterate gardeners. One structure was unusual. That structure is the key to your father's question, 'Do you want to go squirrel fishing?'"

Silence, again. Al felt a trickle of sweat running down his back. He held his breath as the trickle turned into a stream.

Julie started to laugh. "Dad, you crazy . . ." Grinning, she looked at Seth. "Will I go squirrel fishing? Freshwater or marine?"

Al exhaled. "I believe we are done for today. With your permission, I'll sell 30 percent of the bank stock and have the initial payment for the question mailed to each of you."

He began to gather the papers before him. "There are no limits on the number of answers you submit or the time you require to take Doofus fishing. You are to discuss this amongst yourselves, as Doc and Linda did this, in part, to ensure continued communication between the branches of the family. Contact me if—"

"What the hell. That was the answer?" Seth asked. "A question was the answer?"

"Yes. Congratulations, Julie. You read your father's mind." Al stood, put the brown envelope in his briefcase and moved around the table, shaking hands.

Seth's handshake was uncomfortably firm.

As they left, the heirs passed the door to a cloakroom. It was a long, narrow room of a type common in public buildings built before 1920. Seth energetically waved the others over and held a finger to his lips when he was next to the door. With exaggerated care, he turned the doorknob, stepped to the side, and jerked the door open.

What the hell is he up to now, Al thought, and watched in consternation as the heirs behaved as though they'd been teargassed.

Josh slapped a handkerchief over his nose. "Wheeuww. For God's sake, close it. Smells as bad as when they clean Grandma's barn."

"What possessed you to open that?" Julie asked.

Seth didn't answer. He took a gulp of air, flipped the old-fashioned light switch next to the door, and quickly explored the windowless room. "I heard somebody in here," he said, as he came out. "He was listening to our meeting. I heard him laughing."

The room was empty, and Seth was standing in the only door.

Chapter 2

The Heirs' Story

Rockburg, September 2013

Julie and the other heirs stood on the street corner outside the bank and looked up and down Main Street for a place to talk. The town, population 926, *wasn't as much a town as a hamlet with pretensions*, Julie thought. Main Street itself was only two hundred yards long. Other than the bank behind her, she could see five stores, four taverns, a barbershop, two feed mills, and a café on Main Street. Several commercial buildings displayed their 1880s date of construction, molded in concrete and set in the false front, while the narrow storefronts and small size belied the age of the remaining stores.

Seth stood in one place, but his hands, fingers, and elbows were in continuous motion.

"We need to talk. This codicil crap. God! If Dad had something to say to us, why didn't he just say it? He was never shy before." He looked at the signs above the nearby taverns.

"Where can we get a cold drink and go over this?" he asked the others.

Julie looked up and down the street again. "You know, I didn't appreciate this street when I lived here. I'll bet it hasn't changed in seventy years. There isn't a parking lot in town. The storefronts are out of the nineteenth century—all dark brick and wood-framed glass. It's like a Hollywood set."

"It was one for a couple of months," Jed reminded her.

Julie remembered. She'd been away at college when a Hollywood director used the town to film a period movie. Letters from Josh had kept her informed. The backdrop for the climactic scene of the movie was to have been the hand-carved 1882 vintage bar in Johnny's Tavern.

The director's mercurial temperament was ill suited to working with the locals who didn't do lunch and whose weekends lasted four hours, from the end of Sunday services to the start of evening chores. Their outlook on life was unfathomable to the director, and California-speak indecipherable to them. Alcohol and pharmaceuticals helped the director cope with the novelty, until the studio pulled the plug and he went into rehab. His prolonged treatment became the town's dubious claim to fame. Even girls on the same floor at Liz Waters, her dormitory at the UW-Madison, had asked Julie about it the following year.

Wally announced he was more hungry than thirsty and led the group to the Coffee Cup Café across the street. The dining room was small and narrow, with stools and the counter on one side and booths on the other. The heirs slid into a booth where Julie rediscovered how different small-town life was to what she'd grown used to.

Dinner was served at noon, and widowed and bachelor farmers had already taken their places on stools at the counter. Julie was the sole female patron in the restaurant. The only waitress, stout, white haired and ancient, took the orders and traded insults with her regulars before attending to the heirs.

Finished at the counter, she moved to the booth. "I haven't seen you kids in, gosh, it must be twenty years."

Julie was taken aback at being called a kid. She was about to object, when she recognized the lady as the same waitress who served her when she was in kindergarten. The lady had looked a lot taller to her then, younger, too, with smooth skin and dark brown hair.

"The special today is an open-faced beef sandwich, gravy, mashed potatoes, and string beans, or you can have it with chicken or ham. Coffee, pumpkin pie, and whipped cream goes with the meal. Who wants to start?"

Seth gulped. "Could I get a garden salad with—"

"This is the noon rush, kid. I don't have time for special orders. I didn't take any guff from your grandpa or your dad—my condolences by the way—and I'm sure as the daylights not going to take any from you. Beef, chicken, or ham?"

"Ah, start with him," Seth pointed to Wally.

The waitress pivoted to Wally. "How's Linda? Haven't seen her in ages." She turned to answer a question from one of the men at the counter, told him to stuff it, and yelled something to the cook, as her regulars guffawed. The cook nodded, and she turned back to Wally. "Tell your mother that Gert said hello."

Wally was speechless for a moment. "How did, ah . . . Mom isn't well. She—"

"Sorry to hear that. Beef, chicken, or ham?"

"Chicken. Can I split it with Julie?" he asked.

"You look just like your mother, Julie. Your dad talked about you all the time. Coffee?"

"Um, yes."

The orders were taken, and the food was promptly delivered—bread covered by slabs of meat crowded mountains of mashed potatoes, all swimming in what seemed like lakes of gravy. The plates were so full the vegetables had to be served on a side dish. The waitress talked as she handed out the plates. "Just let me know when you want the pie. I figure you want to talk about your dad's will and that stupid codicil, but this is my rush hour, and I can't let you tie up the booth." She nodded toward the back of the café.

"We'll serve your pie in the back room, first door past the restroom. Your dad always got a kick out of eating there; it was where old Doc Rohr did surgery until 1925, or so I was told." She didn't wait for an answer.

Seth leaned toward the middle of their table. "Goddamn it! How the hell does she know about—?"

Julie glanced around the crowded room, put her hand on Seth's and a finger to her lips. "Shh. We can talk about it later in the private room."

As they ate, Jed put into words what Julie thought. "Isn't it freaky?" he said. "It seems everyone recognizes us, and I haven't recognized anyone. I wouldn't have known Al if I'd met him on the street."

The others agreed and hashed it over as they ate. Twenty minutes later, Julie felt stuffed on her half-portion of dinner. The other heirs sat behind plates that were cleaner than she suspected any of them had intended. The canned and reheated vegetables were largely untouched, but the meat and potatoes had disappeared.

Josh looked at Seth. "I thought you weren't hungry?"

Seth glared at him briefly and suggested they take their meeting to the private room. The heirs left the booth, the men stretching as they stood. A few groaned softly as Julie led the group into the back room. The room was modest and the table an old, nondescript folding table, *possibly from a church or school,* Julie thought. A window at the rear of the room looked out over railroad tracks a few feet away. The coffee and slabs of pumpkin pie slathered with mountains of whipped cream arrived as soon as they sat down.

"Is there an extra charge for the private room?" Julie asked.

Gert, on her way out of the room, paused at the door. "No. Your dad took care of that before he died. Paid your bill for lunch, too. He said you kids would be upset about the codicil and come over here to whine. 'When they do,' he said, 'tell them to quit bellyaching and start working together.'

"Now, if you kids have what you need, I've got customers to serve. You've got the room until closing if you need it." She closed the door behind her as she left.

Jed was already eating. "This pie is great, and the whipped cream, it's real. My god, it's good."

Seth gave him a disgusted look. "Isn't anybody else bothered that we're the only ones who don't know what the hell is going on? The waitress knew about the codicil. She's even been paid ahead of time for our meal and this room."

Julie was chewing thoughtfully on the pie. "Jed's right. This is the best pumpkin pie I've tasted since Mom died." She kept her face a mask as she checked Seth's expression. His face was red, his brows furrowed, his jaw clenched. *Knife inserted, wait . . . wait . . . twist,* she thought. "I wonder if she'd give me the recipe."

Seth dropped his fork, picked up his napkin, and threw it on the table. "Goddamn it. Will you guys pay attention? I don't have time for this shit. How the hell do we satisfy terms no sane man can understand?"

Josh and Wally exchanged smirks, irritating Seth even more. "What the hell do you guys think is so—"

"Seth, take it easy. Think a minute," Julie said. She toyed with the pie and whipped cream with her fork. *He needs to learn patience.* "Dad and Aunt Linda set up an elaborate game to bring us back home, bring us together, and make a point."

Seth slouched in his chair. He pushed the dessert plate away and held his cup of coffee in both hands.

Julie continued. "Since they both loved us, let's just ride with it, and see what happens. You can take some time off for $400,000." She had another bite of pie. "I earned the first 50,000 for you, so you have nothing to gripe about. None of us have even opened our envelopes."

Jed, Seth, and Josh brought out their envelopes and tore them open, as Julie fished for hers in her purse. She pulled out the letter, opened it and took a moment to read.

Another riddle, she thought. Jed and Josh scowled at their letters. Seth slammed his letter on the table. "Aw, Christ. More damned riddles. Mine says, 'Ideas are important, but most of them are bullshit.' What the hell is that supposed to mean?"

"You're the big city detective, Seth," Josh said. "Quit your bitching, and let's put these together. Mine is, 'Truth doesn't depend on the profit to be made or the number of people who believe.'"

"I've got, 'Grow a large garden, but weed like hell, and thin the growth often.' That sounds like Dad." Julie giggled. "He didn't like vegetables, but Mom made him eat them to set a good example. Remember how he'd take a tiny helping and push it around his plate?"

"According to mine, 'Your most important tools are the measures by which you test truth, and they will always be wrong, sometimes, especially at the extremes.'" Jed put his letter down, sat back in his chair, and looked at the others. "Did you notice that each of these fit the recipient? Seth's used the language Seth uses. Julie, a plant scientist, was given a clue couched as advice about gardening. Josh's fit business and marketing, and mine is true for every lab test I ever developed or used."

Julie reread her letter and looked at her brothers. "These seem to fit together, but—I'm not sure how. Let's sleep on it and compare them again tomorrow."

The others agreed, though Seth continued to sulk.

Jed and Josh finished their desserts, and Julie saw them eye Seth's abandoned slice. They glanced at each other and nodded almost imperceptibly toward Seth. Julie shook her head and silently mouthed, "No," at Jed. She'd seen this act before. *Over a million dollars at stake and these guys are angling for a free piece of pie.*

Seth slid the untouched slice of pie across the table to them.

"Jesus, you guys are garbage hounds. Don't you think of anything but your guts?"

Josh intercepted the plate, split the pie, and gave half—well, almost half—to Jed.

Julie guessed that Wally missed the nonverbal communications between the brothers, as he looked, in turn, confused and thoughtful.

"What are you thinking, Wally?" she asked.

"Remember the attorney's expressions when we asked questions about the codicil?" Wally asked. "He was clueless, if I read his face right. Our waitress knew more about the codicil and what Mom and Doc meant than he did. I say we cultivate the old lady and see if she can help us figure this out."

Josh finished his half of Seth's pie. "Right, and the first thing we need is a copy of Dad's book. It's the key to this puzzle and these letters." He shrugged and looked at the others. "So let's check Dad's computer. Who has the keys to the house?"

Jed raised a hand. "I do." He wiped whipped cream from his upper lip and pushed himself away from the table. "Let's go."

Wally didn't move. "Guys, IT is my job. Every computer I've ever seen has a password. How do we figure out your dad's?"

Julie looked at her brothers and Wally. All but Seth were looking blankly at each other. He was looking at the table in front of him. "I know where the list is," he said, quietly. "Dad told me where it'd be if I ever needed it."

"And you've been sitting there feeling sorry for yourself? Ugghh." Julie took a breath and closed her eyes. *I don't bug him as much as he deserves.*

Wally stood and grabbed his jacket. The others followed suit, as though on signal. Julie was the last to leave the room, right behind Jed and Josh. Josh caught Jed's arm at the door. "What the hell's gotten into Seth? He's on a hair-trigger today."

Jed looked ahead to Wally and Seth, who were already leaving the café, before he turned to Josh and Julie. "He doesn't want anyone to know, but Martha found a lump. She's scheduled for a biopsy next week."

Fifteen minutes later, they were in Doc's house, the home that all but Wally were raised in. It felt strange for Julie to walk into the house without calling out to her father. She gathered from her brothers' faces that they felt the same. *Concentrate on the job at hand,* she thought. *Now isn't the time for grief. Dad was seventy-one and tired of living without Mom.*

Seth turned on the computer, rummaged through the top drawer of the computer desk, and extracted a yellow pad.

Julie slid into the chair in front of the keyboard and waited for Seth to decide if he had the right paper.

"Try '25Walter.' See if that gets us anywhere," he said.

Julie typed it in. "Wrong password" popped onto the screen.

Seth thought a moment. "Okay, try '2stanley.'"

Again, the computer refused the password. "What are you reading?" Julie asked him.

"Dad's clues. He was too cautious to write his passwords down. He described them. We're looking for 'anniversary of the old fool.'" Seth showed her the pad.

"So, who's the old fool, and when was his anniversary?" she asked.

Silence.

Josh's face lit up. "I'm ready for another piece of pie. How about you guys?"

Seth snorted, but for once didn't gripe. "Let's wait until after two. The noon rush will be over, and the old lady might have time to talk." He groaned and hit himself on the forehead with the flat of his hand. "Did anybody leave her a tip?"

The heirs walked into the Coffee Cup Café at two fifteen. The only customers in the place were two gray-haired ladies having coffee. Gert, now wearing a sweater over her white blouse, was resting in one of the booths, eating a bit of pie.

She smiled wryly. “Back so soon, kids? Was the pie that good?”

Josh, apparently not trusting Seth’s temper, took the lead. “The pie was fantastic, but we wondered if you’d have time to help us out? Dad’s computer passwords are riddles about the town and people he knew. We’ve been away too long to know the answers.”

The old lady nodded slowly. “I’ll try to help, but my heart medicine wipes me out in the afternoon. Your dad was a crafty old geezer.” She sat up and took a sip of coffee. “What’s the first riddle?”

Julie took the seat opposite her. “We think it’s ‘the old fool’s anniversary.’”

“Everybody calls me, ‘Gert,’ by the way.” Gert buried her face in her hands and thought. “There was a couple your parents vacationed with a few times. She was a nice lady, older than her husband and rich, at least for this area, but not very bright and too trusting. Suzy, yeah, her name was Suzy. Your dad never forgave her husband for dumping her for a younger woman, a little gold digger from a farm on the hills south of town.

“What was that jerk’s name? Anyway, he took half of Suzy’s money, married the little hussy, and left town.”

Gert stared into space, straining to remember. “Suzy fell for some creep who took the rest of her money. Left her broke and sick. She crawled into a bottle and died in a mental hospital five years later.”

Gert massaged her temples, took another sip of coffee, and thought. “Andy, that was her first husband’s name. Andy’s new wife took him the same way he took Suzy, only faster. Miserable goddamned jackass, and it served him right. He was back in town and broke in ten years.” Gert nodded to Julie, “Andy, Andy’s the name you’re looking for.”

"How does 'anniversary' come in?" Julie asked.

Gert pursed her lips and stared at her empty dessert plate for a few seconds before looking up in triumph. "That's it. That's what pissed your mom and dad off so much. Andy walked out on Suzy on their thirtieth wedding anniversary. Try the number thirty and 'Andy' or 'Andy' and 'thirty'. See if that does it."

The heirs looked at each other. Seth nodded to Jed and Josh, and the four men started for the door.

"That sounds like Dad," Julie said. "Can we give you a tip for your help?"

Gert shook her head, emphatically. "Nah. I always liked your parents. Your mom was only a year ahead of me in high school. She set me straight about a soldier at the base who was sweet-talking me, the lying bastard. Your mom and grandma were the only women in town who didn't turn their backs on me when I showed up pregnant. Just get out of here for a while, and let me take my nap. Come back around five, and let me know if it works."

Gert put her feet up, leaned back, and closed her eyes without waiting for a response.

Chapter 3

The Heirs' Story

Rockburg, September 2013

Jan set the dining room table as Al relaxed in his living room. He read the paper, one eye on the six o'clock television sports news.

This was the home Jan had always wanted. It was open and spacious. Al could see the big TV from the kitchen or dining room, and she could interrupt his game from the same rooms.

"How did the meeting go?" Jan called. She popped another packaged dinner into the microwave. It hardly paid to cook for the two of them, which was a waste of a beautiful kitchen, but she had put in her years at the stove.

There was no response. Jan asked again, louder, as carpet and drapes in the living room absorbed sound, and Al was next to the television.

"What's that, hun?"

"Dinner's ready. Come to the kitchen, so I don't have to yell." *Someday, I'll tell him he can fix his own dinner,* Jan thought. *Maybe, he'd appreciate what I do.* She put the dinners on a small table in the kitchen. *Nah. He's never given me credit for the information I dig up. Why would he start now?*

"What were you mumbling about?" Al stood right behind her.

She told him to sit, put two cups of decaf on the table, and took a seat. "I asked you about the meeting with Doc and Mary's kids. How did it go?"

"Fine, I had everything under control." Al turned to peek at the sports show. "Why'd you ask?"

He deserves this. "Oh, no reason." Jan took a bite and waited until she judged the timing right. "I was in the Coffee Cup this afternoon talking to Karen Jensen, when the heirs came in. They sat right behind me, with Gert."

She stopped talking until Al took his eyes off a touchdown replay and turned to face her. "Gert and the kids were talking about the codicil and their dad's book. Sounded like Gert had information for them."

Al stopped in mid-chew and stared at Jan. "How does Gert know about it? Did you hear what she said?"

"Of course not, dear. That would be eavesdropping." Jan pretended to be engrossed in removing a bit of shell from a shrimp on her plate. *Let him steam a little,* she thought.

Al watched her warily for a couple of minutes before going back to his meal and the sports news.

Jan was quiet until she served dessert. "Hank at the hardware store asked about the codicil, too."

Al dropped his fork. "What? This was confidential. I haven't said a word about it to anyone." He drummed his fingers on the table, absently staring at the butter dish.

Yeah, never said a word. That's rich. Complained to anybody who'd listen! "I might be able to learn what's going on, if you'd tell me a little more about the codicil and Doc's book."

Al seemed lost in thought. "I wonder what Gert and Hank know?" he muttered. Could be more than I do. Doc ate at Gert's, and he played cards with Hank."

Jan coughed, cleared her throat, and waited. *Rolling pin? Frying pan? Do I have to hit him upside the head to be noticed?*

"Oh, sorry, dear." Al paused and glanced around the table. "Hmmm, ah . . . yes, please," and held out his empty coffee cup.

Rolling pin, hell. Meat Cleaver. Jan gritted her teeth and repeated her request for information as she poured the coffee.

Al sat back in his chair and looked in the distance. "I think, I think Doc started on the book and the codicil about the same time. It was after he retired. The book was about something that happened to him between Thanksgiving and Easter the year before he left his practice. Linda and Mark had problems over Christmas that year, too."

"Financial problems?"

"No, no. Whatever it was, Doc grew a lot that year. By the time he left practice for research, he was more confident in himself than I'd ever seen him—and we started kindergarten together. Linda seemed happier, too, although I rarely saw her. She and Mark were already living in New Orleans by then."

Jan sipped her coffee. "What does the codicil have to do with the book?"

"I, ah, I'm not sure. Doc and Linda wrote the codicil while Doc was working on the book." Al pursed his lips and rubbed his chin. "When did I first hear him mention Doofus? That was . . ."

Jan saw Al's eyes begin to glaze and decided to intercede before he left again for that happy land his mind wandered to when she was talking. "Al, Al! Who is Doofus?"

"Uhh, yes, dear?"

"Who is Doofus?"

"Oh, I, I don't know. I don't even know if he exists. Doc said he'd introduce me to him once, but he didn't show up. I think, yeah, it was the same day he told me about squirrel fishing."

"Squirrel fishing?"

"Some fool game Doc played after he retired. I think he did it to irritate one of his neighbors, or maybe it was the squirrels. I couldn't tell when he was pulling my leg."

"Do his kids know Doofus?"

"No. They were emphatic on that." Al absently pushed a crumb around his dessert plate with his fork. "Something strange happened at the end of our meeting this morning. Doc's oldest son claimed he heard someone laughing in the cloakroom, and when he opened the door, the kids complained about a smell."

"And?" Jan knew the cloakroom was used for storage. Old papers get musty.

"I didn't smell a thing." Al rubbed his chin again, "Strange."

Jan ignored this. She knew what Al's fishing tackle smelled like, and that never bothered him. She returned to what she'd heard. "It sounded as though the kids are trying to get into Doc's computer files. They figure his manuscript will be there."

"I hope so, and I hope they figure this out. Interpreting that codicil could land me on a psychiatrist's couch. I can picture that crazy bastard stuffing his answers in the envelopes, thinking how this would drive me nuts, and cackling about it."

Jan gathered up the plates. "Why would you expect that?"

"We used to play tricks on each—"

"Oh, Lord. I'd forgotten. Juvenile doesn't—"

"The last time I saw him, he was talking about ideas, especially wacky ideas. That could open the door for all kinds of Delphic answers, knowing him. I just hope the kids figure it out quickly."

"They might. Gert answered their question for them. They're probably reading his book now."

Doc's Manuscript

PART I

Chapter 4

Doc's Manuscript

Rockburg, Wisconsin, 1987

Prologue

It was late November, and every breath turned to fog, as I waited and watched a five-hundred-pound calf sniffing a trail of cow patties leading from his pen to a narrow chute. The chute, fifty feet long and bordered by steel rails, curved gently to the right and ended in a head gate that would catch and hold the calf. Once we released the calf, another alley would return him to his pen.

We'd been trying to turn a group of calves into the chute, and they'd been deftly avoiding it. I stood quietly, getting cold and hoping "Sniffer" would decide he'd found a trail used by other cattle and follow it. Two other calves watched their companion and lunged to get ahead of him. They weren't sure about the alley, but they'd be damned if they'd let Sniffer go there, or anywhere else, ahead of them.

Sniffer bolted toward the chute to stay in the lead. Now, we had three calves stuck in an opening two calves wide. All we wanted to do was vaccinate them and send them back to their pen, which should have taken ten seconds per calf, but we'd been working for half an hour and hadn't vaccinated one. This is why cattlemen learn to weave torrid tapestries of profanity.

A few minutes of prodding and profanity and Sniffer pushed

warm, and comfortable in a thick robe. It was the perfect time for my favorite treat.

The house was dark except for the pool of light thrown by a lamp behind my chair and small multi-colored Christmas lights surrounding the window on my left. The lights gave a dim but cheerful glow to the edge of the room. The crystal, silver, and pastel globes on the Christmas tree standing against the opposite wall reflected that light, and as the furnace kicked in, the reflections danced across the wall, betraying currents of warm air moving gently about the room.

Heat, wonderful heat. I gave my wine glass a twist to celebrate feeling my toes again. The liquid ruby swirled round the glass, as I offered a silent toast to Mary, may she sleep soundly tonight.

On the second glass, I was startled by a swoosh of air exhaled by the cushion of a wing-backed chair to my left. I glanced at the chair, but couldn't bring it into focus. *Contacts must be dirty,* I thought and returned to my book. I'd barely read a paragraph when I caught a whiff of cows, a stench, really. I didn't mind it, but Mary would have my hide if I'd tracked anything from a barn onto the carpet. I hauled myself from the recliner and checked the carpet all the way to the front door.

Clean. No problem there.

Nose must be playing tricks on me. I returned to my chair and poured a third glass. *This had to be the last. Tomorrow would be another fourteen-hour workday.* I took another bite of Stilton, crumbly yet creamy, a pungent and savory blue with a background of cheddar, when I heard a throat clear. I put my book down and looked around the room. Empty.

It had to be one of the kids. Nobody but veterinarians and dairy farmers go out in weather like this, but we're not rational. Ask our wives. The only crimes committed in this weather are done in a warm office with an electric heater under the desk. I hadn't even locked the doors tonight. Never did, in this weather.

"Josh, is that you?" I called softly. Our youngest son was a light sleeper and up at odd hours. More to the point, he knew this snack was off limits, and he wasn't above blackmail.

The silence unnerved me. A shadow moved in the dining room to my right. "Who's there? What the hell is going on?" I whispered.

A man's voice came from the kitchen. "Cripes, some host you are. Ya wouldn't have a cold beer and some cheese curls, would ya?" A clunk and squish came from the kitchen as the refrigerator door closed and a beer can opened.

I hustled to the kitchen on tiptoe and turned on the lights. The room was empty. A six-pack of beer, sans one can, sat on the counter, and a trail of cheese curls and brown stuff—cow manure—led from the refrigerator, through the other doorway, and back to the living room.

"Where ta hell did ya go? How can I talk to ya if ya don't stay put?" came from the living room.

I grabbed a kitchen knife from the counter and hastily put it back. I wouldn't know how to handle a knife in a fight, and I cut myself every time I do belly surgery on a cow. I'd be safer without it. At six four and two hundred fifteen pounds, I felt confident I could handle anything.

Let's see who this insolent bastard is. I zipped round the corner to the living room in a fury and skidded to a stop in the doorway.

"Who . . . who the hell . . . ?" In front of me was a man in a torn, brown-spattered pink tutu, a matching top, and dirty western boots. He was six feet tall with a muscular build and the start of a beer belly. His chubby face and smile were set off by a bushy mustache. He looked like a licentious cherub. About thirty, he reeked of cows. I stood in the doorway, uncertain if I were drunk, hallucinating, or having a stroke.

"Here, want some?" He offered me my own cheese curls. "They're kind 'ah stale, but if this is the best ya got . . ." He finished the sentence with a shrug, smiled, and arched his eyebrows, making him look like a kid with an idea his dad would hate. "Say, ya wouldn't have any pretzels, would ya? And while you're looking for the pretzels, how about another beer?" He belched loudly and handed me his empty.

"What—" I bellowed, before remembering Mary asleep and the Stilton on the end table. I whispered, "the hell do you think you're doing in my living room?"

I've never been in a fight; then again, I was bigger and in better shape than this jerk. I was sure I could whip him, but I didn't want to get a grip on any guy in a skirt, and if I tried, the cow-flop decorating his tutu would act like grease. It would be more farce than fight. If I won and called the cops, our local newspaper would run the story for a week. If I lost and filed a police report, they'd think I was nuts and run the story even longer. I couldn't afford either. Bored women at the hairdresser are models of discretion compared to dairy farmers, working alone, often miles from their neighbors. I'd have to explain the story on every farm call I made for the next year and listen to my clients as they tried to be witty. The time lost would cost me more than anything this character could steal tonight.

"Why don't you take what you want and get out of my house? I have insurance."

"I didn't come here to steal stuff."

"Go ahead. Take what you want and leave."

"Listening sure ain't your strong suit, Doc. Did ya ever try shutting up for—"

"Grab what you want. I'll help you carry it to your car."

"Never had a car. Got no use for 'em."

"Take mine. I'll get the keys for you, but leave. Go! Now!"

"You're weird. You been drinking?"

"I'm weird? I'm not wearing a skirt in my living room and telling me my cheese curls are stale. Take something and get the hell out of my house."

"You oughta see a doctor."

I pointed to the door. "Listen, you shit-covered weirdo, steal something, and get out of here, or I'll beat the crap off you."

"Take a deep breath. Calm down, for gosh sakes."

"By God, I'll, I'll . . ." I ran out of steam. This was ridiculous. "Okay," I sighed. "Let's start over." I sat back in my recliner.

"That's better, but ya shouldn't have said that stuff. I feel hurt."

I stared at him, my muscles tense. "You feel hurt?"

"You called me a weirdo. That hurt my feelings. You should apologize and get me another beer."

That was too much. I lunged at him from the chair. I went for his knees but only caught air, branches of the Christmas tree, and a mouthful of pine needles.

"Where are you?" I hissed, spitting pine needles.

"Okay, I'll get my own beer. Want me to get one for you?" I heard the refrigerator door shut in the kitchen, followed by the "spoit" of a beer can opening. "Ya want a Bud or one of these imports?"

He returned, a beer in each hand. I jumped from the floor and swung for his gut.

My fist went through him. "What the devil?" I looked at my right hand: wrist, palm, five knuckles—the usual. I normally only fight with cows, but even after several glasses of port, I was sure a punch wasn't supposed to go through a guy. I took another swing. It went through his chin. The momentum carried me in a circle, and I came to rest leaning against the wall, panting and bewildered.

He handed me a beer. "Can we talk now?"

I was still leaning against the wall, catching my breath and shaking my head as I tried to make sense of what happened. I came to life as he started to sit in Mary's favorite chair. "Whoa, that's—"

"Aw, don't worry about Mary's precious furniture." He waved his hand dismissively. "Others can't see or smell me. They can't see these clothes ya gave me, you bastard, and they can't see the cow sh . . . Oh pardon me—the cow-flop on 'em either." And he sat.

"What do you mean, clothes I gave you?" I tried to remember how much port I'd put away while reading.

He glared at me. "You're the son of a bitch who stuck me with these clothes and this stupid name."

"What name? Who the devil are you?"

"Well, geesh, allow me to introduce myself." He stood, straightened to his full height, and announced, "I am Doofus, Doofus the Cow-Flop Fairy, counselor to kings and advisor to presidents." With that, he did a broad and clumsy curtsy and loudly broke wind.

I staggered out of my chair. "Warn a guy, will you." I gasped, fanned the air, and backed away. "How come other people see pink elephants or UFOs, but I get you? Jimmy Stewart's mentor was an avuncular six-foot rabbit, but me, I get a flatulent, transvestite cowboy with a grudge."

"It's only what ya deserve." Doofus fixed me with a scowl. "You're the guy who figured I was out there, gave me a name, and described me. According to the rules, that's what I'm stuck with. Now that I got some spare time, I thought we should get acquainted, you whining, liberal, over-educated ass. You're a goddamned communist, if ya ask me."

"What? When did I name you, and what rules?" I felt as though I'd followed Alice down the rabbit hole.

Doofus took a long swig from his beer, leaned back in the chair, and stretched his legs out to get comfortable. "Remember the tale you told your kids to explain the dumb decisions and bad behavior they saw on the evening news? You told them that when people worked cattle for vaccinating, the easiest way to get calves to go where you wanted 'em to was to make it look like cattle had walked that way before. That meant not being fussy about cleaning up; nothing says cows to a cow more than a trail of cow-flop, you called it."

He pulled a folded paper from his waistband. "Here, I was so pissed off I wrote down what ya said." Doofus opened the paper, glared at me over the top of it, and read, "'Follow the cow-flop' is to take the well-trodden path, to follow a leader without question, and to do it on a damned dirty trail. Nothing recommends it save simplicity; however, it is not the road less traveled. It is the most commonly used system to make decisions, although by its use millions of bulls become steers, and thousands of sheep are shorn."

I cringed. It sounded pompous even coming from Doofus.

Doofus waved the paper at me. "So you 'invented' a new fairy to explain the arrogance and greed your kids saw on the news. You told 'em it was all the fault of 'Doofus, The Cow-Flop Fairy. '" He returned to reading. "You called me 'that shy, malodorous sprite of the pasture who lurks just out of view whenever horoscopes are read, wishful thinking is substituted for planning, and profit is the measure of truth.'"

"Thanks a heap, jerk," Doofus growled. "Anybody who'd talk to a kid that way is an arrogant ass."

I was in Wonderland. I was talking to a fairy, and he wasn't happy. I guzzled my beer before I tried to answer. "I, ah, I—I didn't know you existed. I was only trying to explain things to my kids."

"Doesn't matter," he said. "Your description was close enough for the Council, so I'm stuck with it. I mighta got out of it, but ya nailed it when Julie asked ya about me. So here I am, along with the Tooth Fairy, Santa, and the Easter Bunny. We're all stuck with physical forms we hate. Hell, the Easter Bunny was a handsome guy humping half the bar maids in Europe a couple hundred years ago. He gave painted eggs to a young widow's kids, to cozy up to her, don't ya know, and she told everybody about it. First thing he knows, he's got floppy ears, a fuzzy tail, and all girls do for him is scratch his chin and trip over his basket."

I remembered, at least a bit of it. Julie had been four and sitting on my lap, upset and sniffling after an argument with Josh, the youngest of her older brothers. "Daddy, is Doofus mean?" she asked.

"No, honey. He's simply impulsive, a little careless, and awfully clumsy."

She smiled at this. "Oh, he's just like my brothers, isn't he?"

"Not quite." And that's when I had described Doofus, the Cow-Flop Fairy, as a cowboy dressed in boots and a manure-spattered pink tutu.

"Ya remember now, Doc?" asked Doofus, bringing me back to the present.

"Parts of it, but what are these rules and Council, and where did you get the idea I'm a communist?"

Doofus adjusted himself in the chair. "About the rules and Council, I am not at liberty to say. The only reason I let ya see me is so you'll think before ya speak next time. That's what you're always telling others, isn't it?"

"I am not always—"

"Your yammering about origami beer steins didn't get anyone in trouble, but this stupid idea did, and it was Old Fred who told me about your politics. That pissed me off, an' I thought I'd let you know how I felt about it."

"Fred, my client on county B? Doofus, Fred's a John Bircher. He told me Eisenhower was a Commie sympathizer."

Fred was a lonely, twice-divorced dairy farmer who had three favorite topics to rant about: taxes, former wives, and veterinary bills. When I arrived on his farm, Fred would lumber up to my pickup, glowing with ebullient belligerence. His greeting would be curt and to the point, after which he'd begin gnawing on me, unless I turned the conversation to taxes or perfidious women.

"So, what do you want of me?" I asked.

"Nothing. I figured you ought to know it wasn't just politicians and presidents I helped. I nudged you into action, too, when ya couldn't get your sorry butt moving on an idea."

"Helped me? On what?"

"Remember that hundred-twenty-pound wheel of Jarlsberg ya

got for 25 percent off?" Doofus sat up in the chair and pointed a finger at me. "And the stock in the silver mine you bought?"

"You . . . ?"

Doofus leaned on the arm of his chair, arched his eyebrows, and cocked his head toward me. "I helped ya make up your mind on those, too. Ya never woulda had the guts to get that first date with Mary if I hadn't kept on your butt."

"You're right about my first date with Mary. I owe you on that one, but those other decisions were the dumbest things I've ever done. The Jarlsberg lasted two years and took up most of the refrigerator. Mary was ready to kill me over it, and I lost my shirt on the silver stock."

"Well, it wasn't my fault ya screwed up almost every time I got ya to move. Matter 'ah fact, it's gotten hard to get ya to move on any idea, lately. Even when ya do get going, you're damned eager to drop stuff, if it doesn't work perfect."

"Doofus, I'm spending part of my time in research now. Clients expect me to be right all the time in my vet practice, but I'd be stunned if I were right twice a year in my research. Science lives with the Huxleyan tragedy of the beautiful and innocent theory, torn to shreds by a gang of ugly facts.[1] Most of our ideas die that way. The most important thing I do is recognize when an idea is dead, drop it, and move on before I waste more time. I wish I dropped bad ideas faster."

Doofus stared at the wall behind me, a glazed look in his eyes and his mouth wide open, which gave me a view of half-chewed cheese curls and beer foam.

"Well, I don't give a rat's ass about Huxa-whatever. You're wimpin' out on me every time I give ya an idea. Get some persistence, goddamn it. Ya can't give up every time ya hit a bump!"

---

1 "The great tragedy of Science—the slaying of a beautiful hypothesis by an ugly fact." Thomas Henry Huxley, Presidential Address at the British Association, *"Biogenesis and abiogenesis"* (1870).

"Okay, I'll work on it." Explaining proof of principle studies would take all night, and the discussion was close to fitting the "don't argue with a fool" adage.

"Good. I'll expect to see some results soon from ya, then, and I'll expect ya to speak more kindly of me in the future. Matter of fact, I've got a new project that looks real good."

I froze. "This doesn't involve another war or slashing education funds, does it?"

"Naw." He shook his head. "I'm takin' a vacation from politics. The crop o' politicians we got now is worse than you. They gotta look at everything from six sides, and that last group . . ." Doofus rolled his eyes toward the ceiling. "Cripes! It didn't take much to convince 'em to do something, but I'd no sooner get 'em moving on a great idea than they'd screw up."

"This isn't another round of deregulating banks or cutting environmental regulations is it?"

"I told ya," Doofus explained patiently, as though to a slow learner, "I've given up on those yahoos. I have to wait until we get a bunch 'ah politicians in office that knows how to make a decision without studying it to death 'afore I start helping out on big projects again. This project is a small job, but kinda cute."

I relaxed. "What is it? Or is it a secret?"

"Oh, heck, no," said Doofus, as he warmed to his subject, "but I have to watch my language on it." He glanced nervously to both sides and leaned forward. "This is a living Nativity scene at one of those mega-churches down south. Thought I'd help the Big Guy out on one. I found a gent with balls, unlike you, who really wants to get this project moving. Me an' Charles are going to expand a living Nativity scene, kick the little kids and elementary students out of the program, use live animals to make it realistic, and put adults in all the big roles."

I'd seen this kind of pageant before. "Doofus, Nativity scenes and Christmas pageants are for kids. Things go badly if you forget that."

"Aw, you're just being negative again," he said, "but I'll keep ya posted on it, so get ready to eat crow, and it's about time you started working on your projects. Get to work on them, or I'll start 'em up for ya." He laughed, drained his beer can, and vanished.

My projects? Good God! I shuddered, put the port away and poured myself a brandy, a double. *How could he? Oh, damn!* I tossed back the rest of the brandy in a gulp. If he meant the project I'd been daydreaming about lately, my marriage, professional reputation, and bank account were on the line; Lord knows what would happen to his Nativity pageant, but at least, I could stay out of that.

I arose early the next morning to clean up the living room and make sure I'd put the Stilton away. I could have slept longer. No beer was missing from the refrigerator, the tree was undamaged, and nothing was out of place in the living room.

A nightmare. That was it. Last night was a nightmare from exhaustion, port, and a *Three Stooges* movie I'd watched with Josh last week.

Chapter 6: Linda's Problem

Happiness and Beauty are by-products. Folly is the direct pursuit of Happiness and Beauty.
—George Bernard Shaw

Doc's Manuscript

New Orleans, December 3, 1987

Doc wouldn't have felt so confident if he could have eavesdropped on his mother and sister six hours later at Les Deuxelles, a restaurant in New Orleans.

The waiter put menus before the two ladies and waited. Linda, the younger of the two, tall and willowy, wore her dark hair short. Elspeth, her mother, was still a handsome woman, but matronly and gray. Her square jaw, softened by a ready smile, suggested a woman of determination. She absently fingered her pearl necklace as the waiter hovered over them.

"Would you ladies like to order something to drink now or wait for your meal?"

"Is the bar open?" asked Elspeth.

The waiter glanced at his wristwatch. "It will be by the time I give them your order."

"Good. I don't know about you, Linda, but 'tis the season, and I'm going to be jolly, if it kills me. Brandy Manhattan, straight up, with a dash of cherry juice, please."

"Mother, it's barely noon."

The waiter jotted down the order. "And what is someone from Wisconsin doing so far south? Visiting family for Thanksgiving or fleeing the cold?"

"How'd you know I'm from Wisconsin?"

"Wisconsinites are the only people who ask for brandy in drinks civilized people take with whiskey." The waiter smiled and looked to Linda for her order.

Elspeth glared at the waiter, saw the smile, and relaxed. "Cheesehead yourself, eh?"

"Born and raised in Eau Claire—and what will the young lady have?"

"Hot tea."

Elspeth made herself comfortable; she liked it here. "Your father and I ate here often on our honeymoon. Food and drink were excellent and the staff impertinent; we loved it."

The ladies ordered lunch. Linda talked about the children and plans for Christmas as Elspeth surveyed the old restaurant. Elspeth listened halfheartedly to Linda rattle on; Elspeth was more interested in memories than her daughter's chatter at first. But something began to nag at her, like a stubborn shred of pot roast wedged between her teeth. She didn't place the source until the food arrived.

Linda's conversation was superficial, skipping from topic to topic, circling something, but never getting to the point. It reminded her of the times she'd been trapped in conversations with a neighbor lady who did the same. Elspeth detested it when she couldn't find a polite way to excuse herself, and now her own daughter was doing it to her.

"Cut to your point. Why did you turn cold when Mark came home yesterday, and why did you ask me to meet you here instead of at your house?"

"I . . . I don't know what you mean."

"Bull. I'm your mother, remember? You hardly spoke a word after he came home. Even the kids noticed."

Linda looked at the place setting in front of her, sighed, and faced her mother. "I don't know how to start. It's just a feeling. Mark isn't paying as much attention to me as he used to. Maybe it's the kids, age, or his work. I don't know, but I'm not happy."

"Honey, happiness is something you'll never find by looking for it. It's what you discover when you're doing other things: working on a project, playing with the children, or helping someone. Searching for happiness is like a dog chasing its tail."

"But, I'm . . . I'm afraid Mark might be looking around."

Elspeth thought a moment. "Have you seen anything, anything at all to make you suspicious?"

"No."

"I thought not. From what I saw of Mark yesterday, I'd say you have nothing to worry about."

"How can you say that?"

"The way he rushed into the house, his expression, his body language, how he greeted you and the kids."

"That's easy for you to say. You and Dad were married forty years."

"And we were in marriage counseling four times. Neither of us are, were, shy about speaking our mind. It wasn't easy, but we'd be married yet if the old goat hadn't died on me." Elspeth turned away and pretended to examine a portrait hanging above her on the wall. "God, how I miss him."

The drinks arrived, and Elspeth sampled her Manhattan. "Ahh . . . they always made wonderful drinks here. Did I ever tell you what your father did on our honeymoon?"

"Mom, I don't need—"

"It was at a table over there." Elspeth pointed to a secluded corner of the restaurant. "It was our regular table that week. He ordered a drink with an orange rind in it, brandy old fashioned, I think. Several old fashioneds, actually. He was tipsy, bored, and punching little holes in the orange rind with a cocktail straw. Made a mess, orange rind and shreds of wet cocktail napkin all over the table, worse than a toddler. The barmaid looked at the mess and told him he should have better things to do on his honeymoon. Without missing a beat, he held up the straw and said, 'Yeah, but this stays stiff.' I could have killed him. The poor girl never came back to our table."

"Mother!"

"Knock off the Southern belle delicacy, dear. We were both raised in Wisconsin on a farm. We know too much about biology, and you have a master's in genetics, for gosh sakes." Elspeth sipped her drink and looked at Linda. "If you and Mark have a problem, and I don't think you do, it probably stems from what I call 'Dick's Law of Biology'."

"What is—?"

"Give a male of any species too much food, wealth, power, or free time at any age between puberty and death, and the damned fool will do something stupid with his dick. Poor devils can't help themselves. You're Mark's wife, and it's your job to make sure that doesn't happen."

"How?"

"The same way women have done it for the last ten thousand years. Keep him busy. If you can't do that, use your credit cards to make sure you look good, and there isn't money to fund such nonsense."

"But, but . . . how do I keep him busy?"

"Have him paint the living room, wallpaper the bedrooms, landscape, rearrange furniture. You belong to a church, don't you?"

"Yes. A large one. How will that—"

"There you go. Every church I've known has programs during the Christmas season, and they can never find enough people to run them. Volunteer him. There's no way he'll be able to back out gracefully, and he'll know it." Elspeth tapped her fingers on the table, thoughtfully. "Look for something with high school kids and men, though. Men work better with teenagers, and you don't want to throw him in with a gaggle of women."

"There's the 'Living Nativity.' They need a director."

"What's that?"

"The church has a Nativity program every year before Christmas. They rent the amphitheater in the park, dress kids in costumes, and have them walk through the Nativity story. It's cute, and the kids don't get stage fright, because there aren't any speaking parts. They've changed it this year, though."

"How?"

"They've put adults in all the roles and contracted with an animal park to provide calves, donkeys, and lambs. The Three Wise Men will ride in on camels."

Elspeth scowled. "Bad move. Christmas pageants are for kids."

"A lot of parents agree. Many are angry about the way the kids were excluded."

"It's a complex project with a good chance of crashing, and half the church is already unhappy. It's the perfect job to keep Mark busy. He'll have his hands full, and you'll have a chance to work with him: hem costumes, make phone calls, and help coordinate. Spend time with him."

Elspeth paused and looked hard at Linda. "Sweeten up though. Honey catches more flies than vinegar."

"Mother, you can't fix problems with old aphorisms."

"Those aphorisms lasted for a reason. Trust me. Your troubles with Mark are over. You'd better start looking for another church, though."

"Why?"

"Fights in churches are the nastiest fights you'll ever see. Now, where's that cute waiter? I could use another Manhattan."

Lunch lived up to the restaurant's reputation and Elspeth's memories. She turned serious as the valet brought Linda's car around. "Before you rope Mark into this fiasco, think about why you married him, and reread first Corinthians 13."

"Doesn't ring a bell, Mom. And I thought you were agnostic?"

Elspeth's shoulders sagged. "I thought you had a better education. A story doesn't have to be true to be instructive, and I'm a skeptic, not a fool. I still know beauty and wisdom when I find them. That's a problem with life; we don't recognize wisdom until it's too damned late to do us any good."

Elspeth looked at Linda and made sure she was listening. "You're still young enough, though. Look it up. Read it. Read it aloud, as you would the sonnets, and don't ever forget that passage. It was your father's favorite." Elspeth fumbled for a handkerchief, blew her nose, and remembered. *Though I speak with the tongues of men and of angels, but have not love . . .* "Lord, he read it beautifully."

Mark stayed an extra hour at work and was late again that night. Fit, trim, and about six feet tall, he came through the front door and took the stairs two at a time as he came up to the main floor of the house, grabbed seven-year-old Wally, tossed him in the air, caught him, and gave him a kiss on the forehead. Five-year-old Bobby and three-year-old Sophie demanded the same. Over dinner, Elspeth pulled out the brochure for the cruise she booked. Passed around, it didn't make it past the boys. The adults chatted about the holidays, while the boys poured over pictures of the cruise ship.

Mark got a rise out of Elspeth, after he asked how Doc was doing.

"He's finally given up his search for a research position at a vet school and settled back into practice. He's doing research in his practice, collecting data and samples on the cattle he sees every day. He is so fixated on bovine medicine and immunology that he can't talk about anything else. And Lord, he will talk about it until your eyes glaze. He's my oldest child, and I love him dearly, but with people, he's the most stupendously obtuse man on the planet. He couldn't be more at sea if he were an engineer. I don't know how Mary puts up with him."

"It can't be that bad. I'm an engineer, and Linda and I understand each other, perfectly," Mark objected.

Elspeth was bent double by a spasm of coughing, apparently choking on a piece of chicken or celery. Between hacks, she managed to sputter something that sounded like, "Oh, my God, two in the same family."

Mark thumped her on the back until she recovered. "What was that you said?" he asked, as her coughing subsided.

"I said, ah, hmm, I said, 'Oh, but you haven't spent an extra five years in graduate school.' Linda, don't let him even think about going back to school like your brother did."

The ladies laughed nervously and, as they finished with the entrees, cleared the table, and served dessert. The adults talked as the kids concentrated on their favorite part of the meal.

"Are you taking the cruise to get away from the snow and cold in Rockburg, Mom?" Linda asked.

"No. I'm getting away from an empty house and eating alone every night. The days are long and lonely, and the nights are worse. I still have my hand in running the farm, but my manager only meets with me twice a week, and I know he'd like to cut it back to once a month." She paused and absently shoved a piece of pie around her plate. "I need to talk to people, play cards, flirt, maybe even dance again."

Mark thought the cruise was a grand idea. Linda was less sure. The conversation turned to the kids and how they were doing in school. The boys joined in with their views on that, until Elspeth clanged a fork on her water glass and said she had an announcement.

"I'll be back about the time the boys get out of school for

Christmas. As my Christmas present to you, I'll watch the kids during the day and for two nights before Christmas. I don't get to spend much time with them, and it will give you two a chance to get away by yourselves for a weekend."

"Why, that's . . . that's very nice," Linda stammered. "Are you sure you can . . . "

Mark put down his fork and looked at his mother-in-law. "That's a lovely idea, Elspeth. You're on, if you can handle the kids."

Elspeth smiled, reached over to Mark, and patted the top of his hand. "Oh, I can handle the kids, but we have a lot to do between now and Christmas, a lot to do."

Mark liked Elspeth, but there was something in her smile tonight. It played at the corners of her lips and eyes. She knew something he didn't, and it wasn't something she was going to share.

Chapter 7: Nativity Rehearsal

Doc's Manuscript

New Orleans, December 4, 1987

Befuddled, Mark looked at Linda. "Why? Why can't I say no?"

Mark had been getting ready for bed when Linda came in. He sat on their bed and kicked off his shoes, trying to figure out where her latest idea came from. They took Elspeth to the dock that morning to see her off on her cruise. Her departure trailed a string of surprises, and this was the biggest.

"The whole church will talk if you back out after I volunteered you," Linda said. "It can't be that hard." She snuggled up to him and started to unbutton his shirt. "Or is it?"

"I don't care, and I don't know a damned . . ." Mark reconsidered her comment as Linda undid another button. She'd been distant and cold since Thanksgiving. What was she up to now? He tried to remember what he'd been about to say; " . . . a damned thing about directing."

He kissed her lightly on the nape of her neck.

"Oh, stop being a baby. Besides, I can help you with costumes, phone calls, and coordinating. I can be talented." She undid his belt buckle, gave him a quick kiss, and pushed him back on the pillow. "Don't you want to work with me? Hmmmm?"

Mark recognized blackmail when he saw it. His choices were to spend the holidays in the dog house or say "yes" and take the consequences. He thought of the consequences and smiled as he wrapped his arms around Linda while she slowly unzipped his fly.

And it came to pass . . .

A week later, Mark was in the church gym, a great barn of a room, placing tables and chairs to represent the Nativity set. He looked at his watch and wondered where the cast was.

A bigger mystery was why Linda had volunteered him to direct a Nativity pageant. She had scolded that it would only take a couple of hours, and all he would have to do was tell some old guys and teenagers where to walk. It'll be the easiest job you'll ever have, she'd said.

Yeah. Easy. He'd spent the last week learning that getting things done for the Nativity pageant required diplomacy and tact. No one was paid, and orders didn't work for anyone over seven years old. Everything was a request, really more like a desperate plea, when working on this project. He put the last chair in place and, from an office off the gym, called the lumberyard to see if the sets would be ready by Saturday.

Cast members wandered in a few minutes later. Three middle-aged guys entered together from the lobby, across the gym from the stage. Their dress was casual: jeans and sneakers. John and George, the taller two, wore light jackets. Bill, shorter and stockier, wore a sweatshirt. Holes in the sleeves attested to its age. The three men and Mark had been friends since high school.

"Hi, guys. Have you seen Charles?" Mark asked. "He is coming to the practice, isn't he?"

"Coming? You couldn't keep him away," said Bill. "Putting adults and livestock in the pageant was his idea."

Mark, hands on his hips, looked around the room. "Good. I just learned the sets haven't been built yet. The guys at the lumberyard said they can't lift a hammer until Charles gives his approval. Why—"

The double doors to the gym burst open and Charles made his entrance, removing his coat and tie as he came. "Sorry I'm late. George, Bill, Mark, how is everyone this evening?"

In his late fifties, Charles was heavyset, paunchy, and over six feet tall. His girth, height, erect carriage, neatly trimmed white beard, serious expression, and insistence on being called Charles or Chas—never Charley—gave him indisputable *gravitas*, which he took pains to cultivate.

"Evening, Charles," Mark said. "We're just getting organized. I'll work with the shepherds while you guys look over the program for the show." Mark left the programs with Charles and moved to the other side of the gym where several high-school boys had draped themselves over folding chairs. The acoustics in the open gym made it difficult for Mark to concentrate. He could hear everything said in the room, even as he talked to the boys.

Charles passed out the programs to the other men. "I tell you, George, ever since I had the idea to expand the pageant and bring in the camels and livestock, it's as though an alter ego, a voice, is urging me on, guiding me. This is going to really put me, ah, us, that is, the church, of course, in the news.

"Now, Bill, and you, too, George—we will be the Magi. All you'll have to do is follow my lead. You're familiar with the amphitheater in the park. We'll ride the camels onto the stage and . . ."

Charles looked at the chairs representing the manger. "John, who's playing Mary?"

"Betty Schmitz. One of her boys will be a shepherd, and she wants to make sure the kids don't screw around."

Betty entered the gym as they spoke, but Charles's back was to the door.

Charles frowned. "With three children, Betty playing a virgin is a stretch. Although with her looks and personality, I'd believe they were all virgin births."

"It will be no more difficult for me to play a virgin than for you to play a wise man, Charles, and I'll have the advantage. I was a virgin once," retorted Betty. She patted Charles on the cheek and waved to the other men, as she swept past on her way to the stable.

Charles's ears turned red and his face flushed.

Mark hurried to intercede. *No spoken lines*, Linda had said. *What could go wrong?*

He was making a mental list for her: sets that weren't ready, the feud between Betty and Charles, Charles and his ideas. For now, he warned everyone, "People, keep the chatter down. It's like an echo chamber in here. Even small sounds can be heard all over the gym."

The other men put their backs to Mark and Charles and acted as though engrossed in reading their programs. Their shoulders shook, and Bill and George leaned on each other for support.

Mark clapped his hands to get everyone's attention. "Okay folks, listen up. We'll just walk through it tonight. The Magi will walk in single file from stage right to the stable, stop at the stable door, and go through the motions of dismounting the camels."

Charles cleared his throat. "Will we continue in single file at the manger, I mean, should we kneel in single file?"

"We'll do it however it looks best."

"I really think it will look best with us in single file and all of us in profile," Charles said. "I'll be the first in line, on the camels, as we approach the manger. Am I to search the heavens for the star or turn to the other Magi and point to the stable? What is my motivation?"

"Your *what*?" asked Mark.

"My motivation. As I lead the Magi on stage at the amphitheater, are we still searching for the right town? Should I point toward the star or toward the stable? Should I turn toward the others as though giving orders?"

Mark looked at his feet, looked at the shepherds and Joseph, put his hands in his pockets, turned to Charles, and spoke softly. "Charles, there are no lines; there is no dialogue. You have no experience riding camels, so your hands will be gripping the saddle. Your motivation as you ride is to stay on the camel without getting sick. Your motivation when you get off the camel is to avoid tripping on your robe; your motivation when you kneel to offer your presents is to avoid kneeling in calf poop or tipping over the manger. The audience will be too far away to see subtle expressions, and no one here has the training to carry off broad theatrical gestures from a camel."

Charles flushed. He stood straight, glared at Mark, and glanced toward the others. None of them seemed to have heard the exchange. The muscles of his jaw twitched, but he said nothing.

Mark turned to the others. "Okay everybody, the worship committee wants audience participation, so there will be several Christmas carols. The cast will not sing. Sue Bilshot will lead the singing, but only the congregation, er, audience will sing. Got that?"

Mark reviewed the rest of the program with the adults before going back to the teenagers.

"Shepherds, shepherds—come on, guys, pay attention. Put the darned Walkman's and cards away. Now!" Mark put his hands on his hips and glared. "There will be no cassette players, Walkman's, or chewing gum while I'm talking to you or while you are on stage, and certainly no card games here in church. Save that stuff for later."

Several sheepish shepherds picked up their cards and avoided Mark's gaze.

Mark had a hard time keeping a straight face. He liked the boys and had taught a couple of them how to play the card game Sheepshead. "Okay, guys, the spotlights will be on you while you hear the word from the angel. Where's the angel?" Mark scanned the faces in front of him and did a quick look around the gym. "Dave? Dave? Dave! Where the heck are you?"

A tall boy lounging across a couple of chairs, reading a paperback, and oblivious to the world, looked up. "Huh, time for the angel? Where do you want me, Mark?"

"Pay attention, Dave. You'll stand on a platform set in a Styrofoam rock. It'll have a support for each of your arms, so you can hold them outstretched over the shepherds while the audience sings a carol. The spotlights will make it look as though you appeared miraculously. You will not scratch, pick your nose, or make faces while the lights are on you. Understand?"

Mark waited for Dave to nod. "You can get off the stand when the lights move to the stable. For tonight, stand by that chair and pay attention.

"Shepherds!" Mark raised his voice a notch. "Pay attention. The lights will move slowly from Dave to the stable. Walk toward the stable so you stay in the light. There will be sheep and calves in front of the stable. They are not housebroken, so watch where you step. If you do step in it, ignore it. Clean it off later. Got that?"

Mark looked at each kid to make sure they'd paid attention. "When the camels and Magi get to the stable, stay away from the camels. Move if a camel handler tells you to. Do not surprise the camels, and don't come up behind them. They are big. They could hurt people or tear the set apart just stepping away from you."

One of the boys raised his hand. "Mark, will we—"

"Let me finish. Everything will be strange to the camels, including you. We don't want them spooked on stage. Camels can spit, and they can kick. What they spit is cud, and it stinks to high heaven, so stay away from the darn camels."

Bill and George looked at each other uneasily.

Charles leaned forward and caught their attention. "Don't worry, guys. We'll be on the camels most of the time, and I'll be in charge. Nothing will go wrong."

Bill and George didn't look convinced. Neither they nor Charles, had ever ridden anything wilder than a lawn mower. Betty smiled broadly and waved to the Magi.

Mark pretended to ignore the body language of the others. "After the Magi leave, a spotlight will focus on Jim Peterson. He will be the mature Christ figure. A crane will lift him. In the dark, it'll look like Christ is ascending into Heaven, as he gives the blessing."

Betty was showing a tall, young man how a wig and beard were to be worn. Hearing his name, he turned to Mark.

"Hey, Mark, how high is that crane going to lift me?"

"Oh, hello, Jim. It shouldn't be more than ten, maybe fifteen feet, if you speak slowly. Why?"

"I'm not afraid of heights, but I could lose my dinner, if there's a wind and I start to swing."

"Have you seen the harness they have for you?" asked Mark. "It's safe, but I'll talk to the pastor and make sure it's a short blessing."

The cast, in fits and starts, walked through their paces twice before Mark called it a night. He thanked everyone for their time and approached Charles. "Charles, could we talk about the Nativity production?"

Charles forced an unconvincing smile. "Happy to. As a matter of fact, I'd like to propose an idea. Usually, we have a choir sing during the collection. Nothing's on the program for that, and my daughter and niece do a beautiful rendition of *Oh, Holy Night.* It would fit perfectly, and they've had a lot of experience singing in public."

Mark had heard them sing a duet once in church. The girls had been supremely confident and absolutely tone deaf. He tried to look as though he was considering the proposal. "I'll talk to Sue. She's the music director and should make that call. By the way, the lumberyard told me the set couldn't be delivered until you approve it. What's that about?"

"I'm the chair of the Finance Committee. I have to approve all expenditures for special projects. It's my fiduciary responsibility."

"The approval for the Nativity budget was given three months ago. We need those sets at the amphitheater for the dress rehearsal on Saturday," Mark said. "I can't keep this production moving forward with delays like this. Does anything else in the budget need further approval from you? Is everything still okay for the insurance, the advertising, and the rental on the camels and the crane?"

Charles glared at Mark. "I will look into that tomorrow and let you know."

As the practice broke up, Charles walked quickly from the gym, grabbed his coat and tie from a chair, and roughly shoved the lobby doors open. He heard his inner voice, as he walked to his car. As the voice assured him that he was the man in charge and urged him to put Mark in his place, Charles didn't question why his inner voice used substandard English and spoke with a Southwestern accent.

Although he usually never drank anything but scotch or merlot, Charles stopped by his club for a beer on the way home. The barman had to hunt to find the cheese curls that Charles requested, and they turned out to be stale.

The sets were delivered two days later. An e-mail from Charles informed Mark that funding was insufficient to cover the advertising budget and the cost of the camels and crane crew for the dress rehearsal. The money would go to advertising. The Magi would practice with the camels at the animal park, but the camels and the crane would not be available for the dress rehearsal.

Chapter 8: *Ventum Mingit*

Vir prudens non contra ventum mingit,
—Nielsen, S. 10th International Congress on
Mycobacterium avium subspecies
paratuberculosis, 2009

"A wise man does not pee into the wind" (data not shown).

Doc's Manuscript

Rockburg, December 12, 1987

"I don't know a damned thing about camels. What brought this up?"

It was six in the morning. I'd been at home and in the middle of breakfast when Mark called. I like Mark. Anybody who can put up with my sister has my admiration—but camels? He's an engineer and doesn't have anything to do with animals. And six in the morning?

"Linda roped me into a Living Nativity: camels, donkeys, sheep—the whole menagerie. They've kicked the little kids out of the pageant and put in animals and adults. Nobody in church knows anything about large animals, so Linda volunteered me to be the director because she was raised on a farm, and you're a vet. Go figure . . . I guess I should be happy you're not a proctologist, or I'd be manning a shovel, in charge of scooping."

"I'm sure an engineer could come up with something better than a shovel."

"Not in this time frame. What advice can you give me on big animals, church pageants, and teenagers?"

"Avoid them."

"I'll tell Linda. What else?"

"Make sure whoever provides the animals also provides professional handlers. The rest of you should keep clear of 'em. The animals won't know you, and your people won't have a clue how to behave around them."

"Already covered that, but I'll give the lecture again," Mark said. "Anything else?"

"The 'anything else' is your problem. The only time I saw a Christmas pageant switched from kids to adults, the pageant went down the tubes." I didn't tell him it was three years ago and it was my kids that sunk it. "Inserting adults could mean one of the adults wants the stage. That—"

"That would be Charles. This whole thing was his idea. I'm the director, but he's kept control."

Mark gave me a thumbnail description of the program. *This is a recipe for a fiasco*, I thought. "All I can tell you is to take every chance you get to tell your people to move slowly, speak softly, and never come up behind an animal without a warning—hum a tune, talk quietly—anything, but be sure the animal knows you're there. Startled animals kick first and think later. People could get hurt, even killed. You'll be lucky if any of your advice sinks in, so have somebody there who's trained in first aid."

Linda should have been able to tell him as much, and Mom was there.

Oh, hell! I should have seen it before. Mom and Linda together can cook up some cockamamie ideas, and Mark was trying to stumble through it and keep his sanity. Mom and Linda, I love them dearly, but those two!

Four hours later, I was in trouble. *How do I get myself into such stupid, stupid situations?* I listened to the tires of my pickup spin and cursed myself again. Even with the thousand pounds of fiberglass and steel of the veterinary practice unit, four-wheel drive, and ten minutes of shoveling, I was stuck. I debated calling for help on the two-way radio, wondering how I'd explain to the office dispatcher why I was on a back road five miles off my route between the morning's farm calls.

Every morning, I got up, had two mugs of tea with breakfast, stopped by the office to pick up supplies and a list of calls, and had a Diet Coke or two while I gassed up the truck. I don't recall having a problem when I started in practice, but now I seemed to spend most of the late morning looking for a place to take a leak. Which wasn't always easy.

Only the two largest farms in our practice had toilets in the barn: After all, when you're standing in a barn surrounded by a gutter filled with tons of manure, why look for a facility? Farm wives, that's why. Farm wives have always helped their husbands in the barns, but I'd never seen them in the barns as often as I did lately. One seemed to be standing behind me every time I turned around.

A few weeks earlier, I'd thought I was alone in a barn and was relieving myself in the gutter when I heard a giggle. Looking behind me, I saw the farmer's wife, red-faced, giggling, and trying to hide behind a post. She was two axe handles across at the hips and the post was only eight inches wide; so that didn't work well. She broke into giggles and guffaws every time she tried to talk about the sick cow, the bill, or the weather.

So this morning, when I felt the urge of nature and cursed myself for drinking too much, I took a detour down a tree-lined side road. The trees had acted like a misplaced snow fence during the storm the day before, heaping the blowing snow on the road, and molding it into ridges and swales like a disorderly blanket on an unmade bed. I didn't worry because I had four-wheel drive, a heavy truck, and a different problem on my mind.

I pulled off the road a foot or two, as there wasn't much of a shoulder, hopped out, and relieved myself. Getting back into my truck, I put it in gear, gently pressed the accelerator, and listened to my tires spin. Shoveling snow from in front of the tires didn't remove the snow under the truck, which was packed up to the axles.

Damn it! How could I have been so stupid, so thoughtless? How could I? How could I?

I heard papers sitting on the passenger seat next to me rustle.

Was there more than alcohol and a Three Stooges movie to my nightmare? I thought. Not daring to look to my right, I whispered, "Doofus, are you here? Have you been 'helping' me this morning?"

"So?" came a voice from the passenger seat. "Ya feel more comfortable now, don't ya?"

Obviously pleased with my predicament, Doofus, handlebar mustache, tutu, and Western boots, had appeared and was lounging in the passenger seat.

"I think ya should call in and have 'em send out a tow truck to get ya outta here, don't you? If ya don't get moving pretty quick, you're gonna be working until midnight to catch up. Say, do ya think they'll ask about the yellow snow? Ya know, a guy with any flair would 'ah writ his name in the snow while he was at it."

He clapped me on the shoulder and laughed.

I began to growl an answer, but a tap on my window cut me short. Amos Yoder, one of my Amish clients, was standing in the road in a heavy, homespun coat and tall boots. His reddish-blond beard was stippled with frost, and a few small icicles clung to the edges. Behind him, his team of Belgian draft horses blew clouds of fog with every breath. Their winter hair coat made the big, tawny horses look shaggy and even bigger than they were.

The bobsled they pulled was twelve feet long, with a set of four-foot-long runners in front and back supporting a bed of rough planks. Two-by-four upright stakes in the planks made a frame for the sled's sideboards. Sleds like this were used to haul manure from the barn every morning in the winter, and Amos and his son were returning from the field. I rolled down the window.

"Ah, ya got yourself stuck here, Doc?" Amos asked.

"Looks like it. Can you help me out?"

Amos stroked his beard and appraised the truck's track in the snow. "The snow ain't that deep, Doc. Ya should 'ah had enough momentum to keep moving, wouldn't ya think?"

I didn't question how a man whose religion didn't allow him to drive a motor vehicle or go beyond eighth grade knew it had taken special talent for me to get stuck. "The office girls called on the radio with some questions, and I wasn't paying attention to the road."

I was stuck so often on back roads, in winter snow and spring thaw mud, that I bolted hooks to the front of my truck and carried chains for a tow. Amos looped one end of a chain over the stakes on the bobsled and the other over one of the hooks on the truck. He climbed on the bobsled, clucked to the horses as he slapped one on the rump with the reins, and the truck was moving again.

Amos stopped the team, got off the sled, and unhooked the chains. According to long established practice, I gave him a box of medication I knew he used for his horses.

"Thanks, Doc. Remember the story my boys gave me when they wrecked the buggy racing the Hauser twins last summer?" Usually dour, Amos was smiling broadly.

"Yes, and?" I remembered watching his sons working on the buggy. They'd been a quiet crew. The three teenaged boys kept their heads down and avoided eye contact as they pieced the wooden buggy back together. Amos, out of sight of the boys, laughed as he told me how his boys had gotten into a buggy race on a back road. Both drivers had to head for the ditch when a milk truck came around a corner. Amish teens pulled the same stunts all kids do, but there's less damage when your top speed is fifteen miles an hour and every accidental pregnancy ends in a marriage, a marriage the whole community celebrates.

"Well, ya know, Doc, sometimes it's better to just tell the truth, and maybe drink less 'afore ya go out on farm calls than try to blame the office girls and your radio." He winked and walked back to his sled.

I felt like a first-grader who'd been laughed at by the whole class. I put my forehead on the steering wheel as Amos and his horses moved away. *When will I learn?* I didn't ask Doofus why he was the one wearing a tutu and I was the one who felt stupid.

I let the truck idle until Amos and his bobsled broke through the snowdrifts on the next hundred yards of road. There were no trees beyond that, and the wind had swept the road clean. The truck was moving easily, as we turned onto a black-topped county road, freshly plowed.

That's when it struck me that Amos hadn't said anything about Doofus.

"Doofus, how come Amos didn't, I mean, you're not the usual—"

"For a guy with your education, ya sure don't remember much, do ya Doc? I told ya, nobody sees me unless—"

"Okay, I forgot, but what brings you back to this neck of the woods? I thought you had a big project down south."

"Well, I thought I'd drop by to fill ya in on how it's going, just to let ya know what someone with ability and persistence can do with my help. It makes a nice contrast to your own work. Hell, today we've proven ya can't even take a leak without getting into trouble." He smiled and waited for me to answer.

I didn't look at him. "Oh, just, just, ah, how is your project going?"

"Oh, my man on the scene is taking charge. Charles has control of the finances for the pageant. He's got clout in the community, so he has lots of ways to keep things moving. The camels and livestock are all lined up, and he's even gettin' a big role for his daughter." Doofus watched the snow banks roll by. "You really oughta take lessons from him." He relaxed, took a deep breath, and added, "Not that you haven't got a few good points yourself, leastwise, if a guy doesn't look too close." He untangled one of his boots from an empty fast-food bag I'd tossed on the floor of the truck, " . . . and ain't too picky."

He watched me closely, as though waiting for a response. "If you was to ask real nice, I could arrange for ya to meet Charles, maybe learn firsthand from him." He thought a minute. "That'd be good for ya, and I could tell the Big Guy I'm doing some charity work, too, so it'd be a feather in my cap. I'll have to work on that."

Charles, Charles in control. Was Mark . . . ? Nah, there must be a million guys named Charles, I thought. I didn't dwell on what my life must look like if a chubby guy in a manure-spattered pink tutu thought helping me was charity work. "Sounds fascinating," I lied.

"Well, I'll be in touch," Doofus said. "We wouldn't want ya to miss out on how great the pageant goes in the hands of a guy who can make decisions instead of looking at every side of a problem until—"

"Don't put yourself out for me. I'm doing okay."

Doofus lightly punched me on the shoulder. "By golly, Charles and me will make a man outta ya yet. I know just the projects, too. It's those ideas you've been dreaming about on cold days."

Oh, damn. I stared at Doofus. *How could he know?* "What plans?"

"One is that daydream ya been mulling over every winter. The other is the one you've been modeling on your computer."

"I, ah, I don't know what you're talking about."

"God, Doc. If you're going to lie, get good at it. I understand wanting to spend a winter day in a heated pool with a strong drink, but damned if I know why you'd want to hear a lecture first. Now, the dairy farm, that looks good to me, but you don't have enough time to set it up, so I found a group you can hook up with. How does that sound?"

I opened my mouth, but I was so scared I couldn't speak. A large dairy farm could cost millions. Anything I said would probably make things worse. I looked at him again and unconsciously turned the steering wheel to the right. I corrected in time to stay out of the ditch. "How did you know about—"

"Get some balls, Doc. Ed will rent ya the pool, and you know the guy ya want to hear. Do something about it. I'll introduce ya to your partners on the farm after Christmas."

"But—"

"Don't ask me how. You're a big boy. Quit your damned daydreaming and get to work on it."

Doofus made sense. That scared me. I worked in cold, wet weather every year from late November until April. Sometimes the temperature didn't get above zero for a month. I spent my days driving from farm to farm. I slid into ditches; I changed flat tires in snow banks; I worked on animals in cold sheds and paddocks; I gritted my teeth and drove through blizzards. I spent whole days unable to feel my toes. Always, I dreamt of going to a meeting that would be half medical seminar and half playtime in a warm, indoor pool, and me with a snifter of brandy.

It was time I got off my butt and worked on it, but there had to be a downside if Doofus liked the idea.

"I'll think about it, but the farm coming up on the left is my next call," I said.

"Doc, the difference between thinking and daydreaming is whether ya got the balls to act. I'll have Charles show ya how, but get to work on the pool and talk. You get that moving, and I'll get the other one ready for later. Don't wimp out on me, now."

He slapped me on the shoulder and was gone.

Chapter 9: Costumes

Doc's Manuscript

New Orleans, December 13, 1987

"What do you mean, the costumes won't be ready?" Mark asked.

He'd gotten home from work, checked on the kids, and walked to the den. Except for floor-to-ceiling windows on two walls, he didn't recognize the room; the collapsible sides of Linda's cutting table were up, and three sewing machines were surrounded by mounds of multi-colored fabric. Parts of costumes, bolts of fabric, and skeins of heavy cording covered every horizontal surface, including the floor.

Linda held up a dark red fabric. "Look at this. Just look at this stuff! Charles bought drapery and upholstery fabric! It's been murder to cut and hem the Magi's robes. Marge and I worked for hours. We've broken so many needles on the serger, we'll have to stop until I can pick up more. What was that man thinking?"

Marge, a short woman twenty years Linda's senior, looked up from a chair in the corner, where she was tacking two pieces of fabric together by hand. "I heard Charles say the heavier fabrics would look rich. I don't know where he got the idea, but it's only for the Magi's costumes." She looked at the material in her lap and shook her head. "This must have been expensive."

Mark leaned against the doorframe. "Charles again! That, that . . . ahhhgg. It's been a long day, and I'm whipped. Figure out what to do, and do what you can. I don't know a damned thing about fabric." As he started to leave, he turned back to the ladies. "I need a drink. Either of you like one?"

He headed for the kitchen and got to the liquor cabinet before they could answer.

The ladies put their work away and joined Mark in the kitchen.

Work went faster after Elspeth arrived the next afternoon and kept her grandchildren entertained. She ordered pizza late in the afternoon when the children complained they were hungry. While they waited for the pizza, Elspeth and the kids looked through the costumes in the den. Elspeth held up one of the Magi robes. "Good grief, this fabric is heavy. It's beautiful, but Lord, they'll be sweltering in these costumes. Why on earth did they buy this?"

Linda leaned back and stretched. "Charles, his ego, and blind ignorance. He doesn't know anything about fabric, and he's too proud to ask a woman. I heard that a clerk told him this stuff would look impressive. That was enough."

Elspeth hefted the robe again. "Maybe it won't be too hot, if they don't wear much under it." She picked up a white costume of thinner material. "And what's this?" She hefted it and rubbed it between her fingers. "This is sensible, feels like an old sheet."

"It is," Marge said. It's for one of the high-school boys, the one who'll play the Angel of the Lord. Charles only spent money on the Magi's costumes."

Elspeth shrugged. "He's a consistent twit, I'll give him that." She folded the costumes and put them back on the cutting table. "I'd like to meet this Charles. He sounds like a pluperfect a—"

"Mother," Linda said quickly, "not in front of the children."

"I think 'Ass' was the word you were looking for," Marge said.

Elspeth harrumphed. "Well, you know what I mean, Linda."

The pizza arrived, and shortly thereafter, Mark got home for dinner. Linda and Marge called it quits on their work. The kids were fed, the pizza boxes disposed of, and the adults relaxed around the table after the kids were in bed.

"So, how was your cruise?" Mark asked Elspeth.

"It was okay," Elspeth conceded, "but I've never met so many shallow, conceited old duffers. There were five women for every available man, and all of the old fools knew it. If Presbyterians had convents, I'd sign up today."

"Sorry it turned out that way," Mark said. He turned to Linda. "How goes it with the costumes?"

"We'll finish tomorrow, but many of the seams will be tacked, not sewn. The cast will have to be careful with them."

Chapter 10

The Heirs' Story

Rockburg, September 2013

Julie, her brothers, and Wally took their seats around the square oak table in the dining room to compare notes on what they'd found. Doc and Mary's dining room was comfortable: oak paneling, a worn, tan carpet, and double patio doors on the south wall. The north side of the room was open to the living room, giving the room a spacious feel.

Wally leaned against the paneling and heard a click. Two cabinet-sized doors opened in the wall behind him as he stepped away. Julie smiled. "That's the built-in china cupboard. Dad got a kick out of blending the doors into the paneling and using pressure latches."

"He did a good job. I didn't see the doors until they opened," Wally said.

"Dad wanted to try it with the bathroom door in the hallway, but Mom wouldn't let him. She didn't want guests thumping on the wall, desperately looking for the bathroom door."

Wally closed the doors as Seth dropped a bundle of papers on the table. "He had a sense of humor, but God, Dad was a pack rat. I think Jed and I waded through every piece of paper that crossed Dad's desk in the last fifteen years. Not a scrap was relevant to the codicil."

Elbows on the table, Seth held his head in his hands. "Tomorrow has to be better than today." He looked at Josh. "Did you get anything more from Gert?"

"She told me a few things I hadn't heard about Mom's car accident. Mostly, I concentrated on getting to know Gert. She's quite a lady." He slid back in his chair and looked at Julie and Wally. "What did you guys find?"

Julie slouched in her chair. "The Doofus story is weird. The story sounds autobiographical for Dad, biographical for Linda and Mark, but the Doofus character stumps me. I don't know whether he's supposed to be allegorical, an alter ego, or a fantasy."

"Same here," Wally said. "Parts that take place in New Orleans have a few lines that suggest Doofus was involved. He had to be pure fantasy, yet the rest fits with stories Mom and Dad told us about an old Christmas Nativity pageant." Wally dropped a sheaf of papers on the table. "I don't know what to make of it."

Julie stood and paced back and forth along the table. "Dad always tried to be rational, careful, scientific, but he had a wild sense of humor, and I guess, you'd call it an 'active imagination.' Is that how you'd put it?" she asked her brothers.

Jed and Josh nodded in agreement. Seth leaned back in thought.

Julie continued. "In Dad's story, his imaginative side takes on a persona, Doofus. Maybe it's an alter ego. Anyway, 'Doofus' is in conflict with Dad's rational side, and Dad is goaded to action when Doofus makes sense."

"So what the devil is squirrel fishing?" Wally asked.

"Squirrel fishing was a game Dad played to tease the squirrels. What I told Al was all I knew, and half of that was a guess." Julie yawned and leaned on the table.

"Does anyone else have ideas about the letters?" Jed looked around the table; he saw only shrugs and befuddlement. "While I was going through Dad's papers, I remembered Julie's comment about them seeming to be on the same topic. There were similar themes in the letters. You could organize them into ideas and truth, testing, and exclusion. One interpretation could be, 'Develop many ideas, test them, and discard the weak, false, and uninteresting ideas.'" Jed looked around the table again. "Does that sound reasonable?"

Heads nodded and smiles replaced the yawns and frowns around the table. They agreed to continue working for two more days and to eat that night at the nearby Oak Grove Supper Club. As they prepared to leave for the Oaks, Julie asked Josh to help her with a box she'd found in Doc's closet. "You guys go ahead. This won't take long," she told her older brothers.

Josh watched Seth and Jed turn onto the main road and head west on the highway. "Okay. They're gone. What's up?"

Julie sat at the table. "Something odd I found in the first chapter of Dad's book." She looked at Josh. "How'd you know I was lying?"

Josh pulled out a chair and sat next to her. "I looked through Dad's closet before. There aren't any big boxes in it." He leaned back in his chair and absently played with a pencil Seth left on the table. "Why didn't you want to bring this up with Jed and Seth?"

"This is silly, and it can't mean anything, but well, it's weird. In the book, Dad describes the smell of cow manure seconds before Doofus materializes. I—"

"Materializes?" Josh put the pencil down and looked closely at his sister.

"Yes. Doofus materializes in the kitchen and tracks cow manure around the house, but only Dad can see or smell it. It reminded me of the closet at the bank, as—"

Josh sat up straight. "Yeah, as we were leaving. Seth thought he heard someone laughing at us."

"Did you notice how Al and the bank staff looked at us, when we complained about the smell?"

Josh shrugged. "So?"

"People in small towns are touchy about anything that makes

them look like hicks. They would have been apologizing and explaining, if they'd smelled anything. But—"

"They didn't! You could tell by their expressions. They thought we were nuts." Josh stood and began to pace, "and there wasn't anyone in the room."

"Now, do you see why I didn't say anything to Seth and Jed? There's no logical explanation."

Josh stopped his pacing and looked at his watch. "Let's go. We can't find an answer sitting here, and I don't want Seth and Jed thinking we got lost. We'll come back to this when we know more."

At the Oaks, Julie and Josh found their brothers at the bar, waiting for a table. They were seated within ten minutes. None of them was very hungry after their "lunch" at the Coffee Cup, but dinner gave them an excuse to take a break and have a few drinks. Julie made notes and the four agreed on a structure for tomorrow's search as they ate dinner.

The restaurant's dance floor cleared, and the band struck up an old waltz as the group prepared to leave. As Julie stood, a tall, thin man in his late fifties approached their table. Like most of the other diners, he wore a sport coat and tie. He extended a big, heavily calloused hand toward Seth.

"Allow me to introduce myself. I'm Justin Hampshire. I farm a few miles up the coulee from here. Until he left practice, your father took care of my dad's dairy herd. I always enjoyed talking to your father. He had a unique way of looking at the world and a blunt and honest way of expressing himself. My condolence on your loss."

Seth stood and shook his hand. "Thank you, Mr. ah—"

"Your dad was terrible when it came to names, too. My wife and I saw him here often, until he became sick." He nodded to the rest of the heirs at the table. "Again, my condolence on your father's death, but I'd better get back to my wife. She loves to dance. Let me know if there's anything I can do for you. Your dad told me there were things you might want to know if you got stuck on the codicil." He nodded goodbye and walked back to his table.

"Goddamn it!" Seth exploded. "Even the cows here know about the codicil. I feel like a sideshow freak. I hardly know anybody, but everybody knows me and comes to gawk."

"Sit down. People are looking," Julie said. "Apparently, Dad knew these people had information he wanted us to hear." She paused. "It looks like he didn't tell them what we would need."

"How do you figure that?" Wally asked.

Julie leaned forward. "Justin didn't volunteer specifics. He said Dad told him we would have questions, but he acted as though he wasn't sure what we would want, and Gert—we had to tell her what we needed, and she had to work to dredge up the details."

Jed thought a moment. "So with Dad's friends, our task is to come up with the right questions, right?"

Seth was near the end of his tether. "I'm getting thoroughly pissed off."

Jed put a hand on Seth's shoulder. "Don't get mad. Think."

"This crew is damned near as slow as you were, Doc. I never met a guy who needed as much help as you."

"Put a cork in it, Doofus."

"Doc, they ain't going to get anywhere if I don't help."

"Not yet, Doofus. They have to work at it, or it won't sink in. Julie and Josh, you can, oh, give one of them a nudge in a couple of months."

"Ya think a nudge will be enough? I could—"

"No. A nudge. No more."

Doc's Manuscript

PART II

Chapter 11: Dress Rehearsal

Doc's Manuscript

New Orleans, December 18, 1987

Mark swore to himself. Dressed in jeans and light jackets, he and George stood on the stage of the amphitheater, looking over the stable set. "I wish this rehearsal was at night, so we could get the lighting right and let the cast get used to moving in the dark."

"Could we go through it again, tonight?" George asked.

"Nope. Charles said he couldn't arrange it. Hell of a lot of good it would do, anyway. We don't have the camels or a crane crew today, because Charles spent the money on advertising." Mark kicked a stick off the stage. "The two riskiest parts of the performance and we can't practice them because of Charles and his goddamned advertising budget."

"Better keep it down, Mark. Sound really carries here." George put his hand on Mark's shoulder. "There's no point in saying something that'll get back to Charles."

George worked with Charles and knew he had the ears and memory of an elephant.

"We wouldn't need an advertising budget if Charles hadn't cut the little kids and junior choir. We'd fill the seats with family members," Mark put his hands in his back pockets, "but we're stuck with it. Let's check the rest of the set." Mark and George walked to the platform and faux rock for the "Angel of the Lord" on the far right of the stage.

The amphitheater in Memorial Park was sunny but empty, except for George and Mark. A frame of two-by-fours covered with canvas and cardboard made a presentable stable at the center of the stage. Two panels painted to look like rough stone walls framed the stable doorway. A small wooden manger, partially filled with hay, sat in front of it. Rows of short sections of yellow tape on the stage floor indicated where actors were to move.

Mark remembered Doc's advice as they passed the stable. "George, would you give tickets to your friend—the one who's an EMT. I want to have first aid on site. "

"Makes sense. I'll put him in the front row and make sure you have his name."

"Thanks. That's a load off my mind. Now, let's see if this platform will hold an angel."

The Styrofoam boulder of the "Angel of the Lord" set, several paces to the right of the stable, fit well with the amphitheater's backdrop of shrubs, trees and rocks. Eight feet tall, the boulder hid the bottom three feet of the Angel's platform and would put Dave well above the shepherds.

Mark gave the platform a push and felt it give. "The carpenters said this will hold Dave?" Mark gave it another push. "We'd better tell him to go easy with it."

George tried pushing it. "Ahh, it only gives a couple inches. All Dave has to do is stand there, arms outstretched, two minutes, max. It'll be okay if he doesn't dance on it."

"You want to try it out?" Mark asked.

"I'll take a pass. I had too many rum toddies at Charles's party last night. Charles is so darn proud of his drinks that he won't take 'no' for an answer." George sat on a bale of straw. "The drinks did make it easier to put up with his bragging."

"It isn't just his bragging," Mark said. "That guy really gets to me."

Betty, in dark slacks, sweatshirt, and walking shoes, arrived with her son Rob, a tall, gangly kid in jeans, a jacket, and baseball cap. He trailed a few steps behind Betty, as though looking for a chance to put more distance between himself and his mother.

Rob headed for the faux rock, climbing on the platform as Mark explained to Betty that there wouldn't be a night practice. Betty was stunned. "How will we coordinate the movement of the Magi and shepherds with the spotlights?"

Mark chose his words carefully. He couldn't afford a fight between Charles and Betty. "We'll be okay if people stay on the taped marks and move with the spotlights. The lighting crew will adjust."

"That's not—"

"I know. I'd feel better if we could practice with the camels, the crane, the duet, and the lighting and AV crew."

Betty's face looked like a thundercloud. "Aren't the camels and crane here? And what duet? I thought only the audience and Sue would sing."

Mark had a sinking feeling that he should have kept his mouth shut. "The crane is here, not the operator. The animals won't be here until the performance. Charles said we couldn't afford to have them here for the rehearsal."

"That's insane. Is the budget really short, or is Charles throwing his weight around?" Betty glanced around the stage, looking for Charles.

"I don't know, but I don't think you're the one to change his mind," Mark said. "Maybe, we can practice with the crane and camels before the show tomorrow."

"And the duet?"

Mark looked around for something urgent he could attend to. No luck. "Charles's daughter and niece. Charles volunteered them, and Sue agreed to it."

Betty glared at him and bustled off to help Linda distribute costumes.

The rest of the cast and the AV and lighting crews came on stage. In small groups, they explored the set and checked out the crane, the dressing rooms and facilities to the side and rear of the stage. The stage faced seats set into a hillside. Pine and spruce trees and tall shrubs flanked the stage on each side. The line of trees curved toward the rear of the stage, hiding the support facilities and lending the stage a rustic appearance.

An earthen mound crowned by low shrubs provided the backdrop for the stage and screened a parking lot and loading dock from the audience. The Magi would mount up at the loading dock and ride the camels on a path over the crest of the mound to the stage and stable.

As Mark watched Betty and prayed Charles wouldn't arrive until she'd cooled down, he walked back toward the changing rooms behind the stage. When he neared the corner of the building, he heard Rob talking on a pay phone mounted on the wall. "Ted, yeah, meet me at the Styrofoam rock when you get here. Are you in with me? We'll . . ." Rob hung up when Mark came around the corner.

"Come on, Rob. There will be no pranks during this program. What do you guys have planned?"

"What do you mean?"

"Don't play games with me. What are you and Ted up to?"

"Nothing."

Mark decided to chance a bluff. He'd heard that Rob had done something to embarrass Dave at the public swimming pool the previous summer, but he didn't know the specifics. "Rob, I'll tell your mother what I heard about the pool, if you guys pull anything, anything at all. Got that?"

"Got what?"

"I know what you did to Dave at the pool last summer. Betty will ground you for the rest of the year if she makes the connection. You guys pull any crap, and your ass is toast. That's a promise. Now get into your costume."

Unsure how much Mark knew, Rob sulked, but went to change without further protest. Mark watched him and tried not to smile. Rob was a good kid and smart, but he had a wicked sense of humor and a knack for identifying sensitive issues. Betty and her husband had their hands full riding herd on him.

Mark stationed himself at the faux rock and intercepted the rest of the boys cast as shepherds and sent them in to change. He hoped that meeting him instead of Rob would keep them in line.

Mark checked in with the AV crew as they set up a black control panel with slides, dials, and digital displays. "I'm glad you guys understand this, because I'm lost when I get past 'on' and 'off.' You guys have everything under control?"

Kurt, a balding, heavyset man in his late thirties, sat back in his chair behind the console. "Don't worry. Everybody who speaks or sings will be assigned a wireless mic. We'll adjust the volume settings to their voices once they get in costume and decide how they'll wear their mic."

"You've given them the lecture about turning microphones off when they aren't on stage?"

"Yup."

"Did any of them listen?"

Kurt was silent. Mark had heard inappropriate broadcasts at amateur plays. "Kurt, I've heard it all, and I don't want it happening on my watch."

"We can isolate the microphones on the board and turn them off here. It's more complicated, especially at night, but we'll do what we can."

Satisfied, Mark picked up a microphone and called the cast on stage. "Everybody get into costume," Mark said. "And be gentle with the costumes. The seamstress ran out of time, so some costumes are only tacked together or held together with safety pins."

The cast dressed and walked through the pageant. Mark identified and corrected likely problems in moving the shepherds and Magi on stage, as best he could. Without the livestock at the rehearsal, he warned everyone that adjustments might have to be made on the fly during the performance. The cast went through most scenes once and had time to go over rough spots a second time, but there could be no practice of the final scene without the crane crew.

The cast agreed to meet at the amphitheater at four thirty the following afternoon for the evening's performance. Volunteers were assigned to bring a light supper for the cast, and final arrangements were made for that essential event in all amateur productions—the cast party. With those issues settled, Mark and Jim examined the crane.

"Did you try on your harness?" Mark asked.

Jim tilted his head back to look at the end of the crane's boom, fifty feet above them. "Uh-huh. Betty helped me put it on and get the costume over it. But what connects the harness to the crane? Is it on that pulley?" Jim pointed to a bundle attached to a pulley midway to the tip of the boom. "Why'd they put everything up there?"

"They lift everything off the ground so it doesn't walk off overnight. Darned if I know where your cables are. I'll ask the crane operator to come early so you can work it out with him. Charles said the crane operator has done this before. Come to think of it, this whole 'ascension' scene was another of his 'inspirations.'"

"What's that about?"

Mark became brusque. "Too long a story. Have Kurt assign you a mic and do a voice test. I have to check on the Magi."

Mark dropped Jim at the AV control panel and walked over the mound to the parking lot where the Magi were discussing where to go for lunch.

"Charles, are your camel-riding lessons all set?" asked Mark.

"Right after lunch. It's two o'clock, and we're famished. We thought we'd get lunch on the way."

"While you're there, would you make sure the animals will be here by five tomorrow?"

"Will do," replied Charles. "I'll take care of everything. You have nothing to worry about," Charles gestured expansively. "What can go wrong? See you tomorrow."

The Magi piled into Charles's Mercedes. Mark swore quietly to himself and watched the Mercedes drive out of the park. "Camels, a crane, teenagers, yeah. What could go wrong?"

Chapter 12: Camel Riding

Doc's Manuscript

New Orleans, December 18, 1987

Charles swaggered to his car. He would not have done so had he realized the swagger of a fat man looks like a waddle. He opened the car door and dismissed Mark with an imperious wave. As the trio roared out of the parking lot, they joked, laughed, told whoppers, and argued about where to go for lunch, acting more like high-school kids on a class trip than old guys working on a church project.

Charles heard his inner voice as he drove. In soothing western tones, it told him he was in charge, and if the media did their job, after this pageant he'd be able to branch into politics, consulting—anything he wanted to.

Bill, shortest of the three, ran his hands over the supple leather covering the back seat of the Mercedes and wondered if he and George could get Charles to pick up the tab for dinner tonight. He thought it best to approach the topic obliquely. "How about stopping at Murry's after the camels?" he asked. "Carol isn't expecting me home until late. Charles, George, what about it?"

Charles glanced at Bill in the rearview mirror. "Sounds perfect. Let's grab some burgers on the way to the lessons. We can watch the end of the game at my club after the camels. The bar has a new TV with a huge screen over the bar."

"Dinner there or go to Murry's?" asked George.

Charles knew that the meals and drinks would be on his tab at the club, but he might dodge paying for it all at Murry's. "Great idea, George. Haven't eaten at Murry's in ages, and the chef at the club is on vacation this week," he lied. "Murry's it is."

They inhaled lunch in order to get to the animal park on time, but Charles drove slowly, giving himself time to lecture George and Bill on the finer points of camel riding. Charles had skimmed a magazine article on the subject and was proud of his new knowledge. He wished he'd read the book the article was based on, unaware that the author had never ridden a camel, never even touched one. The author had once stroked the neck of a llama in a petting zoo and regularly read the essays of a Texas camel aficionado, camel breeder, and more to the point, camel salesman.

Charles wouldn't have indulged himself in lecturing George and Bill had he ever noticed that men freely dispense opinions on subjects they know nothing about, but in public are reluctant to speak of things in which they have expertise. Any woman who's been on a date could have told him that, but Charles had never been good at listening.

The "boys" arrived at the animal park at three thirty. A lean man of medium height was pacing back and forth in front of the office. He pushed his beat-up Stetson back on his forehead and hooked his thumbs in his belt as Charles parked in front of him. "You the camel jockeys from the church?" he asked.

"Yes, indeed, that's us." Charles puffed out his chest, as he shook hands with the man.

"I'm Jerry, the manager. Hoped you'd be here earlier. The staff leaves early on Saturday, and we close around four. We'll only have enough time for each of you to ride once around the paddock. That should give you an idea of what to expect tomorrow, if you pay attention." Jerry looked at each of the men. "If you're ready, let's get to it."

In his faded jeans, denim shirt, and worn western boots, Jerry looked like the quintessential wrangler to the Magi. Pleased, Charles said, "That's what we're here for. Lead the way."

The Magi followed Jerry to a barn. The shaded interior offered respite from the summer sun, but today it kept the barn cool and uninviting for the redoubtable Magi. They hesitated, as Jerry slid the wide door open and walked in, covering their angst by examining the door, the walls—anything that would give them an excuse to stay in the sunlit doorway and watch as Jerry walked down the smooth clay floor of the barn's center aisle.

A row of wooden box stalls lined the aisle on each side. The Magi could see the interiors of the first stalls, as the upper half of the stall doors were open except for vertical metal bars. A few stalls were empty. In others, dromedary camels watched the men, tore mouthfuls of hay from racks hanging from a wall of each stall, or chewed their cud with a pronounced elliptical movement of the lower jaw.

Jerry, now fifty feet away from the Magi, grabbed a lead shank and halter from pegs on the door of an empty stall. Charles stared absently and listened to his voice. "Okay, Charles; here's where ya show 'em who's in charge, who's got the balls and talent in this here outfit."

On the far end of the barn, a camel lifted her nose regally, rolled the food around in her mouth, paused to look through her long eyelashes at a bird flying past the window, and resumed chewing. Content, she considered the pleasures of the mundane and congratulated herself on the life she led. Opportunities are limited if your brain is the size of an orange. She had long ago narrowed her options to being a radio talk show host or chasing grass, and chasing grass seemed more respectable for a lady.

The sound of the door sliding open at the end of the barn disturbed her reverie. She rocked forward, as she lifted her hind quarters, and from side to side as she extended her left and then her right front leg. She was standing when the door to her box stall opened.

Damn! This means work, and just when I'd gotten comfortable. She turned her rump to the door, buried her head in a corner, and laid her ears back. She wanted to make it clear she wasn't an easy camel. A lady has to have standards.

"Whoa, now! Stop it, Gladys, you miserable old bitch." Jerry ignored her threat, slapped her on the rump, and moved to her head. There he slipped a halter over her head and nose. "Behave or I'll have camel burgers for lunch." He scratched her behind the ears and adjusted the halter.

Gladys grumbled, and Jerry pretended to be tough on her, but the tone of his voice didn't match his words. They'd settled into this greeting long ago. Gladys knew Jerry always picked her for training sessions; *they were a pair*, thought Gladys, and woe to the camel or horse that came between them. She sensed he trusted her more than other camels. Or his students.

"Eeeungh, eeeuunghh," rumbled down the center aisle as Gladys complained. Jerry saddled her and led her past the Magi and into the waning light of the December day. She noticed he hadn't put the nylon bosal on her, the equivalent of a hackamore bridle for horses. That meant Jerry would have control, and she wouldn't have to put up with reining from first-time riders.

That suited Gladys. She may have known the students would be safer if they had no control over her, but student safety was lower than a bale of moldy clover on her list of priorities.

Jerry walked Gladys into the paddock next to the barn. The paddock, a rectangular patch of dirt in a sea of manicured grass, was ringed by now leafless shade trees and a fence of white posts and two-by-six, white-washed planks. A wide gate facing the barn was open. The ground in the paddock, a mix of topsoil, clay, and wood shavings, was well tended and soft. Gladys would be comfortable kneeling for students to board her, and the students wouldn't get hurt if they couldn't stay in the saddle.

Jerry stood next to her head, tapped lightly on her shoulder with a polished show stick, and whispered, "koosh, koosh." Gladys dropped to the ground, resting on her sternum, her long legs tucked beside and under her.

"Okay, who wants to be first?" Jerry asked.

Bill watched Gladys as she and Jerry walked from the barn. Bill had seen llamas at the zoo. Nice, small llamas. He knew they were related to camels, so he wasn't concerned when he'd volunteered for the pageant. He hadn't considered what it would be like to ride a camel, to roll with its movements, or how far off the ground they would be. Bill assumed it would be like sitting on a hairy chair that wanted to please him.

He reconsidered this at the first sight of Gladys.

She was not small. At five feet nine inches tall at the shoulders and seven feet at her hump, Bill had to look up to look her in the eyes. Those eyes scared him. When he looked at her, she looked back. Bill recognized with a shock that there was an independent mind under that mountain of hair, and the way she laid her ears back was not a friendly greeting.

Bill looked to George on his right, Charles on his left, and back at Gladys. He edged away from Jerry and Gladys and, imperceptibly, drifted to a place behind George. This turned out to be a complicated maneuver: George was trying to get behind him.

Charles stepped forward. "Jerry, you don't know how long I, or we, have waited for this, or the keen anticipation we've felt. I'm sure this will be—"

"Just step this way," Jerry said. He made a sweeping gesture with his hand, from Charles toward Gladys, trying to get Charles to move. Windbags always irritated Jerry.

Bill and George relaxed and stopped their slow waltz to the rear as Charles leaned toward Gladys. He raised a foot to take a step toward her.

"Eeeungh," Gladys complained, broke wind in a spluttering whoosh, and glared at Charles.

Charles paused in mid-stride. His foot reversed its forward arc, and he pivoted toward the other two with surprising grace. Pretty damned fast, too. "Bill, you're the lightest of us. Why don't you go first?"

Jerry motioned to Bill. "Step over here and throw a leg across the saddle. Time is limited. Get yourself centered, and we'll take a walk."

Bill eyed Gladys warily. He nodded agreement but did not move.

"Bill, wake up! Get moving or the rest of us won't have time on the camel." Charles pushed him forward.

Bill stumbled toward the camel, cursing Charles under his breath. He glanced toward Charles and George as Jerry helped him into the saddle. He tried to act assured but would have been more convincing if his hands hadn't quivered. He looked at Charles again, not quite pleading, not quite threatening, as Jerry gave him his instructions.

"We're just going to teach you enough to mount a camel and stay in the saddle long enough for your pageant." Jerry tapped him on the knee to make sure he was paying attention to him, not Charles. "Now, and in the pageant, let the handler leading your camel do the talking. Okay?"

Bill nodded assent. He would have agreed to anything Jerry said, as long as he didn't leave him alone on Gladys. The preliminaries settled, Jerry took a step away from Gladys and gently tugged the lead rope. "Hut," he said quietly, and Gladys stood as Bill closed his eyes.

"Oh, my God! Where . . . ahh, what . . ." Bill hadn't believed his world could go in so many directions at once. He was pitched forward, backward, and from side to side. He stifled further exclamation and clung to the saddle with white knuckles, as Gladys arose and started forward.

Riding wasn't a problem, once he survived the gyrations as Gladys stood. Bill adjusted to the rolling motion after Gladys walked the first hundred feet. He loosened up a bit but was careful not to take a second look at the ground, far below.

They made a circuit of the paddock; Jerry spoke quietly to Gladys, and Bill slowly got the hang of it. Returning to the others, with a "koosh, koosh," Jerry ordered Gladys to drop to her knees for Bill to dismount.

Jerry adjusted the halter and scratched Gladys behind the ears. "Now, that wasn't so bad, was it?" He gave Bill a hand as he dismounted, steadied him a bit, and turned toward the others. "Ok, who's next?"

Bill's first steps on the ground were unsteady, but an ear-to-ear grin lit up his face, partly from relief, partly as he thought of the dinner he was going to stick Charles with tonight.

Charles stepped forward and mounted Gladys. Jerry gave him the same instructions he'd given before. Chin up, Charles sat erect in the saddle. He turned and saluted Bill and George before giving Jerry a condescending nod to indicate he was ready to begin. Charles was in charge.

Gladys stood. Charles pitched violently in every direction. Unlike Bill, who was trim and physically fit, Charles could go in three directions at once; his head pitched forward, his gut went to the left, and his butt swung in a graceful arc to the right. He would have yelped, but air and lunch were fighting for space in his throat, and it was some time before air won out. Gladys had to be content with a muffled gurgle. Camels are given a variety of audible commands: Koosh (down), Hut (up), and Muffled Gurgle (way to go, girl!).

George nudged Bill in the ribs, "I'd give up my time in the saddle to see that again."

Bill grinned, "I'd let you."

Charles paid attention only to his stomach, the distance to the ground, and his grip on the saddle. He ignored the repetitive and predictable movements of his mount and did not adjust to her gait. He was, as a result, a delicate shade of apple-green as they returned to the starting point.

Charles moved incredibly fast for a chubby, old guy as he dismounted, so fast he stumbled and fell to one knee on his first step away from Gladys. He caught himself with the heels of both hands, scrambled to his feet, and as he brushed black loam and wood chips from his knees, he glanced at Bill and George.

Yup, they'd seen it. On solid ground and aware of his audience, his courage and voice returned. "By golly, guys, I might be a natural at this."

As Charles turned to Jerry to explain that he'd tripped on a loose shoelace, Bill leaned toward George. "Do 'naturals' always turn green?"

Gladys recognized the dichotomy between the tone in Charles's voice and the fear she'd sensed during his ride. *Heavy as a hippo and dumb as a horse.* She snorted, blowing chunks of half-dried mucus toward the retreating Charles. Gladys had a low opinion of horses, and Charles was a target too big to resist.

She watched George approach. His stride was longer than the other two; he didn't dither as he approached, and a sniff didn't detect any sweat. Gladys listened to the drone of Jerry's voice as he gave instructions and felt the added weight as George climbed onto the saddle. *I hope this is the last of these loads.* She extended her prehensile tongue, and, being a tidy lady, carefully cleaned each nostril with a delicate swirl of the tongue.

This is a normal part of the well-groomed bovine's toilette, but it's rare for camels. Gladys had watched a cow clean her nose at a fair and saw its effect on a group of boys who'd just consumed hot dogs, bratwurst, deep-fried cheese curds, deep-fried Twinkies, cotton candy, and watermelon, all washed down with fruit drinks of vivid hues and uncertain provenance.

It was time to reset to empty, anyway.

Gladys added it to her riding lesson repertoire on the spot.

George mounted, and they followed the course taken before. Gladys didn't mind George. *At least he doesn't sway back and forth or dig his heels into my ribs like Tubbo. This one I can take . . . if Jerry's here.* All the same, she gave Jerry a gentle push in the shoulder with her nose to speed him up so she could get back to her stall.

They returned to the starting point, and Gladys knelt. She felt the weight leave the saddle as George dismounted and was surprised when he stroked her neck. She watched him walk toward his friends. She noticed he still walked in a straight line and regretted she hadn't swayed more.

The Magi left the park at five, watched the football game at the club, and dined at Murry's. Charles, in a celebratory mood, surprised even himself by insisting that dinner was on him. Innocent of any knowledge of camels, other than that gained from the dubious essay, he allowed his imagination free reign, as he regaled George and Bill with advice on camel riding, camel nutrition, camel psychology, and camel history.

The harangue didn't sputter to an end until dessert. Sloshing with wine and overcome with the urge to sing during the drive back to the amphitheater, Charles launched into songs that made him think of camels. It was a regrettably extensive list. He was braying through "The Sheik of Araby" when he drove past the entrance to the amphitheater.

He wasn't in a hurry to correct course until Bill said he was feeling nauseated and hoped the leather seats would be easy to clean. Charles whipped the car through a U-turn and had them back at the amphitheater to pick up their cars faster than Bill could say "woofing cookies."

Bill watched the tail lights of Charles's car fade in the distance. He thought a moment and turned to George. "Is your brother still practicing law?"

"Yeah. Why?"

"I'll need a lawyer if I hear Charles say another damned word about his 'inspiration' for this pageant or how to ride a camel."

"He's not easy to take. But you made him pay for it. Where'd you put all that food?"

"I promised myself this would cost him, even if I had to have my stomach pumped." Bill let out a burp that echoed across the parking lot.

George shook his head. "What was he singing? I recognized 'Lawrence of Arabia,' but what was after that?"

Another burp. "Not sure. It was god-awful, something from *Le Cid.*"

"The movie?"

"No. The opera. Wife dragged me to it once."

"Charles could make a music lover homicidal. Imagine the headlines, 'Tone-deaf baritone slain by retired piano teacher.'"

"Don't suppose that could happen by tomorrow, could it?"

"Dream on. See you tomorrow." George waved and got in his car.

Bill fumbled for his keys and unlocked his car. "Inspiration, my ass."

Chapter 13: Plots & Pranks

Hope springs eternal in the human breast;
Man never Is, but always To be blest . . .
—Alexander Pope

Doc's Manuscript

New Orleans, December 18, 1987

Ted and the other boys cast as shepherds sauntered into the Burger Shack. They still wore the jeans and sweatshirts worn at the rehearsal, but their hair was now carefully combed and anointed with gels and oils advertised to be irresistible to nubile females. Although the ads were silent on what else might be attracted, the fruit flies that formed a permanent part of the Burger Shack décor were not immune to the lure. A haze of flies buzzed about their heads.

A quick sniff would have detected a variety of scents: cheap cologne here, father's aftershave there, and occasionally a combination of odors in uneasy coexistence. Their progress through the burger stand was irregular as each teen tried to imitate the swagger of college jocks: three confident strides, a surreptitious glance to see if the girls were watching, two crestfallen shuffles, and repeat. They had the hair, the bouquet, the covered pimples, and the gait of inexperienced, but hopeful testosterone on parade. Even the oft rebuffed and acerbic Pope would have smiled.

Rob waved to them from a booth. Justin, a freckled kid of medium build and height with curly red hair, waved back. The group joined Rob and slid into the booth, three opposite and one next to Rob.

"Been here long?" asked Justin.

"Nah. I had to walk, but it gave me time to think."

Ted nodded. "I'll bet you had stuff to think about. Mark was really ticked today. He kept scowling at us—totally weird." Ted, as tall as Rob but more muscular, had a thicker neck and thin face. The combination gave him a feral look, reminiscent of a weasel.

Rob considered how much of Mark's comment he should share. "He thinks we're up to something."

A short boy with mild acne slid into the empty seat next to him. "Hi, guys. I don't have to start work for a couple of minutes. Mind if I join you?"

"Sam, my man. Just the dude we need. How about an employee discount on the chocolate shakes?" Ted asked.

"I'd like to, guys, but no way will old man McFurdy let me get away with that. What are you guys up to?"

Seizing the opportunity, Ted launched into his topic for the evening. "Men, we are here to help Rob plan his revenge on Dave."

"Or at least decide who's with us," said Rob, glancing at the other boys. "Did you guys talk it over? Are you in or out?"

Ted waggled an eyebrow. It gave him an expression of inept calculation. "I don't know about them," he nodded to the boys next to him, "but I'm in. It's been long enough for Dave to drop his guard."

Sam looked confused. "What are you guys talking about? I thought you and Dave were buddies."

Rob folded his hands on the table in front of him and attempted a wide-eyed, innocent look. "We are. Dave's the best friend I have, and as his best friend, it is my duty to see that he doesn't get too cocky. It would be bad for his character if I let last fall pass without payback."

Justin, sitting next to Ted, frowned, thrust his hands in the pockets of his denim jacket, and shook his head. "Guys, the pageant is too public. We can't pull something with half the church and our parents watching. Do what you want to, but count me out." He picked up a menu. "I'm going to get a burger, shake, onion rings, and walk home."

"Holy cow! You just ate dinner," Ted said. "Did they short you on dessert?"

"That was an hour ago. See you tomorrow, and thanks for reminding me." Justin slid out of the booth.

"Reminding you of what?" asked Ted.

"The cookies here are great. I need some of those, too." Justin headed to the counter to place his order.

Ted watched him walk away before returning to the topic. "Justin has a point. Mark's already suspicious. It has to be quiet, something the audience won't notice."

Steve nodded in agreement. "Justin's totally right. We gotta add cookies to our order."

Ted punched him lightly in the shoulder. "Forget your darned gut for a minute. How are we going to get anything done? We need something quiet that'll make Dave squirm, something that'll get even for the bowling party, but won't get us in trouble."

Sam leaned forward, all ears. His parents believed that keeping him busy with a job, homework, sports, and chores around the house would keep him out of trouble. The plan was working, but he had no social life and felt left out when friends talked of parties and games. "What bowling party?"

The boys bowled in a league, and a grudge match developed between Rob and Dave when they discovered they both intended to ask the beguiling Marcy to the next school dance. Dave put a drop of oily hair cream in the thumb hole of Rob's ball and proposed that the loser of the game cede Marcy to the winner, at least for that month.

He crushed Rob in the game and made condescending comments all night about Rob's bowling, his imaginary love life, and his bleak and celibate future.

Ted, not yet understanding the social status of a snitch, chimed in to take credit. "Rob wouldn't have figured it out, if I hadn't told him how Dave did it."

Sam ignored Ted's remark. He'd perked up when Marcy's name was mentioned and now went back to it. "Was that the Marcy who works here?"

"Yup," Rob said. "Dave thought he had a date with her, but she called it off at the last minute. She said her grandmother died."

Ted looked closely at Rob. Nothing in Rob's expression suggested disbelief, and Ted realized Dave probably believed her, too.

"Are any of you guys dating her now?" Sam asked.

"I don't think either of them had the courage to ask her again." Ted looked across the table at Rob, "Or have you?"

"I've, ah, I've been busy, and I don't think Dave has either." Rob looked at Sam suspiciously. "Why?"

"I, I thought, maybe," Sam shrugged and looked at his watch. "Oops, my shift is starting. I have to get to work. Talk to you later." Sam's step was lighter, almost jaunty as he headed to the back of the shop and work.

Ted leaned across the table, "So, Rob, what are we going to do to help you even the score?"

"Sometimes, I think you're more interested in me getting even than I am. Do you push Dave to get back at me, too? I know you've helped him."

Ted looked away and sat back in his seat. Silence settled around the table, until the shakes and food came. Ted tried a new tack as the boys dug in. "I don't think you'll ever beat what you did to him at the pool last summer. That was a work of art."

It was more temptation than Rob could resist when two of their number confessed ignorance of his pièce de résistance, and he was soon recounting the story. Rob used a toenail clipper to cut and fray the drawstring on Dave's swim trunks as Dave was showering before going into the public pool. Ted started trash talking in the pool in front of a group of girls they knew and told Dave he didn't have the guts to go off the high dive.

Dave was proud of his diving skill, he was on the diving team at school, and he invited the girls to watch him.

"Dave went to the end of the board, got everyone's attention, and palms up, motioned for applause with his fingers. He made a high spring from the board and did a pretty good jackknife."

"So what?" asked Steve. "He's good."

Rob loved interruptions like this, as they accentuated the ending of his story. "The drawstring broke when Dave hit the water. He came up in front of all the girls with his trunks around his ankles." Rob leaned back. "Never underestimate what a man can do with toenail clippers and an imagination."

Ted snickered. "It was the perfect prank, until he caught up with you. I wasn't sure he was going to let you come up for air."

Rob glared at Ted. "Yeah, I paid for that one. He wouldn't have known it was me, if you'd kept your mouth shut."

"But what are you going to do for this one?" Ted asked.

"I have an idea," Rob looked at the others, carefully examining the face of each. "I want to think about it overnight. If it works, Dave will have to sweat out the whole performance without moving, and Mark and the audience won't see anything." Rob refused to elaborate, but he asked Steve to bring six tubes of superglue and Ted to bring a camera to the Nativity.

Chapter 14: Pageants and Plans

Doc's Manuscript

Rockburg, December 18, 1987

"Ya started on your seminar yet?" asked Doofus.

His sudden appearance in the passenger seat scared the daylights out of me, and I almost put the truck in the ditch.

I was on an ice-and-snow-covered back road. Most of the roads in our practice area were back roads, and some more backward than others. Two had fords across rivers instead of bridges, and there was an unmarked bend in mid-river on one of them. All but a few of the 200 miles a day I drove were on gravel roads.

"Gee, Doofus, give me a little warning next time, will you? I see too much of ditches as it is."

"Touchy today, are we? I forgot about your delicate nervous constitution and lousy driving skills. Ya want me to give ya some driving lessons?"

Doofus was easily pleased by his own wit. He sat back and grinned. It was probably meant to irritate me, but it only made him look more comical.

"Well? How ya doing on your homework? We agreed you'd work on your dream."

"I checked on facilities, prices, airfare, and got Professor Rodger's phone number."

"Ya still haven't made any commitments, have ya? You're just daydreaming, but this time you had a pencil in your hand. Big deal. Ya might as well have shoved it up your butt."

He was right, and I hated that. I'd been a busy coward. I'd carefully avoided doing anything. "I'm, ah, I'm getting there. I have to assume every penny will come out of my pocket."

Doofus gave me a disgusted look and changed the topic. "So, what ya got against adults in Christmas pageants?"

I remembered Mark's phone call and looked at Doofus. Nothing in his expression suggested subterfuge or guile. Maybe they were different pageants—must be a thousand going on across the country. I decided to play along with Doofus and find out what he was up to. "I don't have anything against adults in Christmas programs for adults. It's just, well, adults taking over the kids' program often doesn't work out."

"Why do ya say that?"

"Experience."

"Experience?"

"I've lived through it. When Julie was a baby, the lady who directed the children's Christmas pageant at our church was a frustrated musician. She'd tried to find places to perform, but there weren't any in our area. So, she tried to use the kids' Christmas pageant as an artistic vehicle."

"What do ya mean?"

"She staged the pageant as a musical event: adult soloists and instrumental pieces—the whole shebang. High-school students were cast for all parts that put kids at center stage, and younger kids were relegated to a children's choir kept off to one side."

"Sounds like a smart move ta me. Kids screw stuff up."

"Boy, can they, but this was the children's Christmas pageant, not the director's. Anyway, Julie was six months old that Christmas, and we let them cast her as Jesus."

"What's wrong with that?" Doofus asked.

"The girl who played Mary kept Julie pacified, mostly. We could hear every coo and whimper Julie made, because somebody forgot to turn off the pulpit microphone.

"When the director launched into a soprano solo, Julie chimed right in. She sang with joy, and she sang loudly—no words, just a happy-baby "Ahhh, yahhh, ahhh."

Doofus shrugged. "That's better 'an having her crying."

"Yeah, but it was a small church, and Julie was next to the pulpit and the only microphone. The louder the director sang, the louder Julie sang. It was no contest. When it's baby versus adult, the baby wins every time, and this time the baby had a mic. The congregation was in stitches.

"Julie's mood changed when they put her in the manger. For 'authenticity,' there was real hay in the manger, and it was mostly weeds, stems, and sandburs.

"Julie whimpered at first and started crying softly. Nobody paid attention until she launched into a full-throated howl. She cried full volume through the director's next solo and continued when it was over. The girl playing Mary was rattled, and the director was tight-lipped and seething."

Doofus sat quietly, shaking his head, as I continued. "They finally came to a carol by the children's choir. The director stood in front of the kids, scowling. Josh was three, almost four, and in the first row, right in front of the director, sucking on his pacifier. The pacifier seemed to push her over the edge. She lunged at it two or three times before plucking it from his mouth. Big mistake."

"What do ya mean? I hate to see kids, walking around, sucking on those durn things."

"Spoken like a true bachelor, Doofus. You've never tried to get a night's sleep with a screaming baby.

"No one heard what Josh was singing while he had the pacifier. Good thing, too. The only song he knew was a dirty version of *Jingle Bells* that Seth taught him. Josh started yelling his song as soon as the director pulled his pacifier. 'Jingle bells, shotgun shells, Santa laid an egg . . .' The director tied herself in knots, leading the choir with one hand and trying to stuff the pacifier back in his mouth with the other.

"She no sooner replaced the pacifier than he heard Julie crying and turned to go to her rescue. Seth, standing next to him, was always eager to keep his younger brothers in order. He grabbed Josh by his coattails and held on. They started fighting, right in the front row of the choir. My money would have been on Josh, but the teachers were fast, and it didn't come to much."

Doofus looked ill.

"Jed, on the far left of the choir and farthest from the manger, ignored his brothers. He didn't sing; didn't believe in it. He didn't hold it against his friends if they sang, as long as no one made him do it.

"Jed's nose started to run early in the program. He ignored his handkerchief and took care of the problem with a few passes of the back of his hand and sleeve. Having established his 'theme,' he improvised a set of variations, almost like Baroque ornamentation. It was virtuoso nose picking.

"Mary tried to stop him with hand signals and waving a handkerchief. She finally gave up and pretended she didn't know him.

"A Sunday school teacher handed Jed a handkerchief. He examined it, unfolded it with care, and held it up for public view. He inspected the hem, turning the handkerchief over and over, like an anthropologist examining a strange artifact. He smiled at the congregation, and when he noticed a pattern woven into the fabric, he held it up for everyone to see. He grinned at Mary and put the handkerchief over his head.

"By this time the Director's eyes glittered, one eyebrow was twitching, and her mascara was running. She quit the church a week later.

"So it's all about motive. I'm not against adults in pageants, but their motives and the objectives of a children's pageant often don't mesh, and it comes back to bite 'em."

Doofus sat in silence, looked at me, and shook his head. "Good gawd, with your kids, no wonder you've got a twisted picture of Christmas."

He felt so sorry for me he reached over and patted me on the shoulder.

"Doofus, think of it as the difference between *haute cuisine* and hamburgers, between art and charm. Each has a place, but they aren't the same. With kids and animals, unless you're a professional, you might as well relax, watch the screwups, and enjoy them. Something will always go wrong and have to be fixed on the fly. Odds are, the fixes will make the problems worse, if the adults are in it for themselves. Children's Christmas pageants are about love and kids. It's beauty, but it's not art."

"Ya, but that's your family. Let me tell ya, my production is goin' great. We don't have no little kids in the show, and we've got professional animal handlers, so there ain't gonna be a problem in that area."

"Is it coming up soon?"

"Yup. Sunday night. And let me tell ya, it's gonna be a humdinger. We'll have a donkey, calves, a couple 'ah goats, and the wise men will all ride in on camels." He clapped me on the shoulder. "Tell ya what, I'll bet I could arrange for ya to see it somehow, maybe get TV coverage so you can watch it on the news."

Oh, Lord. Mark said his pageant was this Sunday night. I did my best to act nonchalant and probed further. "Boy, Doofus, with that menagerie, I have to hand it to you: You have more guts than I'd have. Animals are worse than kids."

"I don't know 'bout that, but I tell ya, Charles and me have balls. Ya ought a get yourself a set. Like I said, after this is over, I'll have time to help ya develop a personality and spine. Maybe me and Charles can help on your project, and I'm going to send you that other idea, too. Ya got a lot of good points—well, maybe only two or three—but it's a shame to see 'em go to waste."

Charles! Oh, cripes. Mark mentioned a Charles in a pageant. The pageants are the same.

Doofus didn't seem to know of my connection to Mark. I decided to keep it that way. "Gee, Doofus, I didn't know you cared. Thanks for the offer, but this is my busy time of the year."

"Well, don't say I didn't try to help out." Doofus smiled, oblivious to the sarcasm. "Say, I got to go, but I'll be back to let ya know how great it went." He was gone in a shimmer of air.

I shuddered to think of the problems Doofus, his protégé Charles, and Mark and Linda might be headed for. The advice I'd given Mark was sound and all I could do to help. Gnawing at the back of my mind was Doofus's critique of my project.

I'm a veterinarian and a scientist, and a guy I wouldn't trust to tell me the time of day nailed it. I hadn't done a damned thing. My so-called planning amounted to dodging any commitment. It was more than my ego could take when I saw it that way.

I thought about my dream: a veterinary seminar centered on an indoor swimming pool. My fingers were cold, and I could barely feel my toes, but I could feel that warm water lapping around me.

I had to do something, but with one screwup, I could empty my checkbook and ruin any goodwill and reputation I had with the veterinary faculty. I couldn't take that, either.

My dithering reminded me of Doofus's comments, and I decided to call Professor Rodgers in the clinical pathology department when I got back to the clinic.

The office was empty when I arrived. I dug through my desk to find his phone number and thought of what I'd say. I couldn't focus, because there was too much riding on this. I called Mark first.

Mark answered on the first ring. The dress rehearsal was over and hadn't gone well. I wanted to warn him about Doofus, but how could I tell him that the patron fairy of bad decisions was sprinkling cow-flop on his pageant? And I knew, 'cause I talk to fairies! Daily.

I stopped procrastinating and took a crack at it when Mark again mentioned Charles. "Mark, this Charles, he, ah, well, if he wants all the credit, give it to him. Keep a low profile and keep your name out of it, in case this turkey tanks."

"Sounds like good advice. I'd have to wrestle Charles to get any credit, anyway. You should see the draft program. Charles has his name on everything. We're printing them tomorrow at church. I'll put my name in eight-point font, if it's on the program at all. Thanks for calling, but I have to go. Linda's calling for dinner."

I said goodbye and returned to thinking about Rodgers. He was out of the office when I called. Of course he was: it was Saturday.

Weekends and weekdays were a blur when we were busy. *I was out of my fricking mind*, I thought, as the phone rang and rang and rang. Thank God, an out. I could just hang up.

Before I could put the phone down, a recording asked me to leave a message. Cripes, I hadn't arranged my thoughts. I was about to babble incoherently, but pulled myself together. "Ah, this, this is Jack Wilson, and I'm the secretary of a local veterinary group. We've read your papers on electrolyte and enzyme profiling in dairy herds and their use in diagnosing herd problems. Would you be available to speak at our next meeting?" I left my telephone number and address and hung up.

Chapter 15: Professor Rodgers

Doc's Manuscript

Rockburg, Evening, December 18, 1987

I got home from the clinic at a reasonable hour that evening. Mary and I talked while we washed dishes after dinner. The rambling message I left for Rodgers and the whole dizzy idea was eating at what ego I had left.

"You're the secretary of a local veterinary group?" She shook her head and sighed.

"That's what I told him."

"What's the name of this group?"

"Name?"

"Yes. Groups have names. It's an old custom. When does your group meet? Is this an annual meeting, your winter meeting, or do you meet monthly?"

I felt sick. "Meet?"

"Meet. People get together, greet each other, and discuss their plans. You should try it sometime. You could start with the family you rarely see from October to March."

"I'm sorry, but—"

"Who's in this group without a name that doesn't meet?"

"Me."

"That explains it. You could hold a two-hour meeting and not hear five words spoken. Anyone else I might know?"

"I don't know. I have to call some of the local vets."

"Did one of the farmers give you a glass of high-octane Christmas cheer today? I hope you weren't driving in this condition." She put her towel down and looked at me. "You weren't, were you?"

The phone rang. I leapt at it, hoping it would save me from more questions that made me look dumb and feel sick.

It was Professor Rodgers.

"Hi, Jack. This is Bill Rodgers. I just returned from a conference, and I'm catching up on my phone mail. What is your group and what do you want me to present?"

"Ah," I said, putting down the phone, looking dumb and feeling sick seemed like a wonderful option. It was not available. Delay, I had to delay. "Thanks for returning my call so quickly." *You couldn't wait for me to get my lies in order, could you? A name, I need a name for the group. What—*

"You said you'd like me to present my work on herd serum enzyme profiling. When is your meeting and how long would you like me to speak?"

I scanned my calendar for open weekends in January. Rodgers was busy on each of them. Here was my out. I'd apologize, thank him for calling, and say goodbye to my worries. Heated swimming pools and saunas were lovely, but . . .

Relaxing, I heard myself say, "What Saturdays do you have open in February? If it will help, we'll fly you and your wife here, so you don't have to waste a Friday and Sunday driving."

I clapped my hand over my mouth. My God, was I nuts?

We settled on a two-hour presentation at $300 an hour on February 12. Airfare would be $580.

I had a $150 in my checking account. Mary was going grocery shopping tomorrow to stock up for Christmas. All four kids would be home, and the three boys could make whole steers disappear before lunch. I could be in the poor house before I got off the phone.

"It's certainly been nice talking to you, Jack."

"Yes, it was a pleasure. Thank you for calling. We'll be in touch."

My knees were shaking. If I was quick, I might get the handset in the cradle before I defaulted on my mortgage and Mary had me committed.

"I apologize, Jack. I've already forgotten the name of your group. What was it again?"

A warm mental institution, that's where I should be. Name, what? What's in a name? No, not that, not now. The Lying Bastard, that would fit. Names, think! "It's the Central Wisconsin . . ." *Milkers? Don't be an idiot.*

An empty Burger King wrapper in the wastebasket caught my eye. *Burger King, Queen, Dairy Queen? Dairy what? How did anyone as dumb as me get into Vet school?* "Dairy Veterinarians."

"The Central Wisconsin Dairy Veterinarians. I haven't heard of that group. Is it new?"

Oh shit. Why doesn't the battery on this phone die? "Yes, very. We are very new, but very active. Very active." *If digging holes with my mouth counts as active.* "Oh, shoot. I have a call I have to take on the business line. Thanks for calling, Bill, and I'll, ah, I'll be in touch after the holidays. Bye."

Mary looked at me with a quizzical smile. "Nice save. You sounded more disturbed than the Marx Brothers and just short of The Three Stooges. You might not have to talk to Rodgers again if he has caller ID.

"By the way, I saw Ed at the grocery store today. He said fuel oil has skyrocketed, and he has to charge more for heating the pool and building. You can talk to him about the price tonight, and . . ."

Why not more money? I'm spending like a Senator on steroids. Christmas bills, spring semester tuition for the two boys, cost of the meeting—all due at the same time. Why not throw another 200 or 300 dollars in the pot? Damn you, Doofus.

"You have mentioned this to Ed, haven't you?"

"Huh?" I looked blankly at Mary.

"Have you talked to Ed about renting his pool?"

"No. I just set the date a few minutes ago."

"Good God! How do you get through a day on your own? I hope the pool isn't already reserved the day you need it. You'd better finish your dinner and clean up while I get Jenny."

What if I can't get the pool on the . . . Jenny, what? "You're picking up Jenny? What for?"

"We accepted the invitation to Ron's birthday party, remember? You made the Charlotte Malakoff for it last night. You'd better plan on going; it took me all day to clean up the kitchen after you. You get ready. I'll get the sitter."

I'd forgotten. Ron's wife rented Ed's pool for the evening for a surprise birthday party for Ron and invited everyone they knew who made a dessert Ron liked. It was twenty below zero tonight. Drinks, great desserts, friends, and a warm pool sounded fantastic, and I had to talk to Ed about reserving the pool for the seminar.

With my luck . . . I didn't want to think about it.

We arrived at Ed's and parked in a gravel parking lot between the farmhouse and the building that Ed built for his pool. He'd done well at farming, but was never able to leave the farm for a vacation. Instead, he built a big indoor swimming pool.

His first two marriages ended in divorce, other romances were short, and now he was a lonely seventy-year-old bachelor. Mary thought he rented the pool to his friends just to have people around.

I followed Mary as we walked toward the pool entrance. The penetrating squeak of our boots on the packed snow sent shivers up my spine. That sound always irritated me, but it fit how things were going for me. Every obstacle I overcame on this crazy project only uncovered new problems.

Buildings in seriously cold climates are entered through an air lock. The air lock was a small, enclosed porch, just large enough for four people to enter and close the door to the outside before opening the door to heated rooms.

The north and west walls of the pool room were concrete blocks painted a light green, while the south side was a row of patio doors. Tonight, each door was covered in frost and ice except for a clear oval in the center. The changing rooms, showers, and sauna were on the east end, a few steps from the pool. The bare concrete floor, heated by hot water pipes beneath it, was always warm. A few guests were already in the pool. The rest lounged in lawn chairs by the pool or were bending over a table, putting the final touches on the desserts they had brought.

Floodlights outside lit the snow-covered garden to the south of the building. The snow, heaped in banks by the wind, pine trees, and bare branches of shrubs covered in ice and snow were beautiful in the lights. Usually, it was wonderfully relaxing to sit in the warm pool, watch the drifting snow through the patio doors, and sip hot drinks. But I had too much on my mind to enjoy it tonight, at least until I could talk to Ed.

It took awhile, but I was finally able to get Ed alone. I told him about the seminar and pool party. He looked at me in slack-jawed wonder.

"You pretended to, ah, and hired a speaker at 300 an hour? You've got more guts than I have. Are you going to hold it at the Holiday Inn in town?"

"I was hoping I could rent your pool. Is it available?"

"I close the pool for February. It's too damned cold to heat it then."

At least nobody else reserved it. We discussed how much extra it would cost to keep the pool open until I needed it.

"I'll have to pencil it out, Doc. Hmmm, have to get the snowplow in to clear out the parking lot, and you should get insurance. Somebody might trip, drown, or step on glass."

The dollar signs were spinning past my eyes when Ed pointed

out that there wouldn't be any way for Rodgers to project slides at the pool.

"Why don't you try the country club? It's only two miles from here, and they might rent a room to you for a couple of hours." Ed stroked his chin and stared at the floor. "Probably have to buy everyone lunch, too, to get the club interested." He nodded, almost as though to himself, before turning to me. "You better talk to 'em soon, or they might be taken."

More expense, more obstacles, more worries. "Sounds like a good idea," I said. My voice cracked, and I went from bass to alto in mid-sentence. "I'll call them next week."

I went straight to a table set up as a bar. My worries were inconsequential after a couple of brandies and disappeared entirely with more lubrication. It's difficult to tell the difference between inspiration and brandy on evenings like that, but I had a great idea. Mary walked by, and I mentioned it to her. She nodded in agreement, or maybe it was in response to something one of the other ladies said.

With her approval secured, I invited everyone to our house for Sunday dinner the following week, a few days before Christmas.

Ed brought me his estimate for opening the pool in February an hour later. Another $200. I swallowed hard, said I'd check with an insurance agent, and told him he had a deal.

"Doc, were you serious about having everybody over for dinner?" he asked.

Why is it I've never been able to shut up? I thought of a joke, and just had to tell Ed. "Sure. Mary would never get the house cleaned if I didn't invite people over now and then. She's probably checking now to see how tall the tallest person here is."

"Why?"

"To see how high she has to dust. She says there's no sense cleaning what no one can see. Dinner should be ready around one."

Ed promised he'd be there and I wandered back to the dessert table. Giving in to temptation is a delightful way to spend an evening. It's one of the few things I do well.

The Charlotte, my favorite dessert, is made with dark chocolate melted in strong coffee and slowly beaten into sugar, almond extract, powdered almonds, butter, and lightly whipped cream. The batter is poured into a mold lined with ladyfingers dipped in orange liqueur and refrigerated overnight. It's light and fluffy on the tongue, with a slight crunch from the powdered almonds. I love its subtle mix of flavors.

I'd put the seminar out of my mind, and, oh, was I mellow as we started home. I didn't even mind the cold as we got into the car. Mary set the remains of the Charlotte between us. "Dinner next Sunday, for everyone? I hope you're planning on spending tomorrow and next Saturday helping me clean and cook."

"No problem. Work tomorrow should be light, and I have next weekend off." I rubbed my gut. "My stomach is a little upset, though."

"How much did you eat?"

"I had a piece of each dessert. Just a taste—didn't want to offend any of the cooks."

"You've always been careful about that. I wish you were as careful about other things. What else did you have?"

"The chocolate cakes were pretty good. I had seconds on each."

"And?"

"An extra piece of each strawberry pie. I couldn't remember which one was the really good one."

"And?"

"I think I had a little more of the Charlotte."

"Three times. I counted. A normal person would be in cardiac arrest."

I changed the subject. "You know, I can't figure out why a nice guy like Ed hasn't been able to maintain a relationship. He's alone again, just broke up with his lady friend."

"Yes. I had a nice talk with Ed tonight. It was very informative. He had interesting observations about cleaning. We should revisit the high points tomorrow. We don't need to cover all of them, only those the tallest person can see."

The rest of the ride home was chilly and silent.

Chapter 16: Emergency Calls

Doc's Manuscript

Rockburg, December 19, 1987

I normally don't consider lectures breakfast food, but it seemed safest to take it as it came the morning after the party. It was Sunday, our kitchen island was her pulpit, and Mary had a lot to say. She made it clear the only thing I was to do was listen.

"What in the name of heaven made you think I agreed to a dinner party just before Christmas? Are you nuts?"

"I thought—"

"I don't care what you thought. Now, you're supposed to cover emergency calls for the clinic today, but you are going to help clean this house every minute you aren't on call. Do you understand?"

Apparently, Ed asked her if my invitation to everyone was real and told her my little joke about the house only being cleaned when company was expected. That's how I learned never to share a confidence with a man who's been divorced more than once.

Puppies that people are eager to give away and men who are free after their second divorce are available because they've never been housebroken. They've never learned the rules. Tell that guy anything—a joke, a wisecrack, a story—and he and the puppy will dump on you.

I cleaned and polished, straightened and tidied, from seven until noon. Mary informed me I would be cleaning and cooking next Friday night and all day Saturday. I agreed. It was the only safe thing to do. That's how a man who's housebroken handles these things. We're smart, we're savvy, we're cowards, but we're still married.

The business phone rang. I turned off the vacuum cleaner, feigned annoyance at the interruption, and answered the phone.

"Hi, Jack, this is Steve, Steve Brown. I hate to bother you, but I have a couple of horses that are going downhill fast. Could you take a look at them?"

I drew a blank on Steve Brown, scribbled a note, and shoved it toward Mary. "Could you be more specific?" I asked.

"I have three mares and a gelding. Two of the mares and the gelding have been losing weight since it turned cold."

"That would be mid-October?"

"Yeah, I guess so. They're nothing but skin and bones now. We're going on vacation next week, and I was wondering if you could look at them today?"

It was a typical backyard horse weekend call: a chronic condition that's an emergency because the owner has plans. I looked at Mary.

"He's a dentist. Your receptionist takes her kids to him," she whispered.

Even Mary saw I couldn't dodge this call. The problem could probably wait until Steve got back from vacation, but there's no way to determine that when you're talking to an owner who doesn't know much about his animals. I asked Steve to have the horses inside and haltered, grabbed a hasty lunch, and drove out to look at his horses.

The horses were in the barn when I arrived. Steve said he fed them hay outside and grain in the barn. The horses preferred being outdoors and came inside only for the grain. He left one of the double doors to the barn open so the horses could wander in and out at will.

Three of the horses were rail thin, and the fourth was a tub. I slapped the old girl on the butt to get her to move over, so I could listen to her lungs. My light slap caused a wave of fat to ripple under her skin from her rump to her ears.

None of the horses had bad teeth, respiratory infections, or lameness. Worms were unlikely as Steve treated them regularly for internal parasites.

"Is the fat mare the dominant one?" I asked.

"What do you mean?"

"Which horse goes first when they head to pasture or go to the hay rack?"

"Old Betsy, the fat one."

"Do you watch them as they come in for grain?"

"No. One of the boys feeds them when he gets home from school. He makes sure the door is open and heads to the house to do his homework."

I had Steve turn the horses out and put grain in each manger, as his son normally did. I rattled the feed bucket to get the horse's attention, and we watched out of sight as the horses returned.

Old Betsy trotted up to the door, turned around, and blocked the entrance. She laid her ears back and tore into the gelding, biting and striking with her hooves when he tried to get past her. The attack was savage. After that, she ate most of the grain before letting the others in.

"There's your diagnosis. Any questions?" I didn't add that any alert twelve-year-old could have made the diagnosis.

"I'll be damned. That mean old . . ." Steve put his hands on his hips and scowled at the mare before turning to me. "Sorry to drag you out for this, Jack."

I pretended to believe him and suggested he move the three starving horses to a local stable where they could be fed properly while he was on vacation.

Another call came in on the truck radio on my way home. A cow on a small farm owned by Carl and Judy Border was unable to stand the day after her calf was born. Most of these cases were a lack of blood calcium. It's easily corrected if the cow is in a well-bedded stall and hasn't injured her legs.

Judy and her daughters supplied most of the manual labor and all of the management on the farm. Carl's parents lived with them and made sure Judy kept her nose to the grindstone, while Carl went fishing, hunting, and trapping. Smaller farmers in the area often supported themselves by farming in the summer and poaching deer and cutting pulp wood in winter to sell to nearby paper mills. The sons followed their father into the woods.

I pulled up to the small barn and from my truck got my bag, a pail for hot water and disinfectant, and a bottle of calcium solution. A path through the snow led to a milk house attached to the barn. I was surprised to find Carl, his two older brothers, and his father standing next to the six-hundred-gallon stainless-steel milk tank. Judy usually met me here and provided the information I needed about the cows.

The men were in a bad mood, and their therapy of choice today was beer. They were working their way through a case and asked if I cared to join them.

"Can't. I'm handling emergencies alone today. Where's the cow?" I asked.

Carl told me his problems as he guided me to the cow. He was about to join his brothers as an ex-married man. Judy and the kids moved out yesterday, and Carl was served with a restraining order. This was bad news for the cows, as Judy had been a good herdsman and a careful manager. Carl didn't know one cow from the other.

His brothers and father followed us and discussed their domestic problems, while I treated the cow.

Carl's younger brother began the lamentations. "I don't know what my wife wanted," he said. "I took her trapping, hunting, fishing, and snowmobiling." He sighed, nursed his beer, and vacantly watched the recumbent cow. "She didn't seem to mind the fishing."

Carl was near tears. "Same here." His lips quivered. "I did

everything for that woman. We went fishing, hunting, and trapping. I even took Judy winter camping with my buddies, so she could cook and wash up for us. She came home to do the chores and milking twice a day, but we didn't complain none."

Carl leaned against the cow's stanchion, ignoring the cobwebs clinging to a beam above it. "That was only last week." He took another drink. "That's when she got the restraining order and moved out." He drained his bottle, opened another, and looked at me. "Doc, what the hell do women want?"

The cow stood as I finished treating her, and I hurried to leave the farm while I could keep a straight face.

It was dusk when I reached home and turned into my driveway. A thin curl of smoke rose from the chimney; the kids must have set a fire in the fireplace. A copse of leafless maples to the west and south cast deep shadows over the house, accentuating the Christmas lights around the entry and the warm yellow light from the kitchen windows that fell on the snowdrifts surrounding the house. I was glad to be home.

I parked the truck in the garage, plugged in the truck's block heater, and hung my coat on the wall. I sensed a familiar presence.

"Doofus? What are you doing here? I thought you were busy with your Nativity?"

The air next to the truck shimmered, and Doofus appeared. "Oh, I was, but it's going fine by its lonesome. It don't need my supervision 'cause I got a talented guy helping me—not like when I work with you. I tell ya, me and Charles are putting on the best damned Nativity that city, hell that state, ever had. People will be talking about it for years."

Doofus grinned; his eyes danced. He was leaning against a workbench along the wall of the garage. "How's your project coming? Got a speaker and swimming pool lined up?"

"I try not to think about it. I've set a date, hired a speaker, put the airline tickets on my credit card, and rented the pool. All I need now is a place for the seminar, a veterinary group to listen to it, and money to pay for it." I shuddered, thinking about the bills I was running up. "I can't believe I let you talk me into this."

"Ya wanted to do this for years. I prod ya to move on it, and all ya do is whine. Just get to it. You'd be all set now if ya had the balls my buddy Charles has."

Doofus talked while I picked up the trash in the cab and wondered how things were going for Mark. I listened to him brag as long as I could take it. "Boy, Doofus, I wouldn't have the guts to walk away from a crew this close to the show no matter how good they are."

"Now, don't you go worrying on my account." Doofus waved his hand dismissively. "Everything should go just perfect."

"Yup, and teenagers should behave, and politicians should be honest."

"God, but you're a pessimistic son of a bitch. Don't ya ever relax? Haven't ya had a time when ya knew ya did the job right and it's time to celebrate?"

"Sure." I worked to get my boots and coveralls off. Getting out of coveralls is a struggle when you're over six feet tall and wearing multiple layers of clothing, including a hooded sweatshirt. Bald guys like me need cover on top in cold weather. "I would hate to count the number of times I felt confident, only to have everything fail disastrously."

"Ah, that's—"

"That's the way it is in science, Doofus. Things go wrong. You have to be ready to laugh at yourself."

"It can't be that bad. Hell, ya—"

"I'm being realistic. A lot of scientists have a paper they published that they'd rather forget. That's why it's so important that experiments be replicated by others. A single study doesn't prove a point, in science or in life. It's the accumulation of information from many sources, as it was with cigarettes as a cause of lung cancer, evolution by natural selection, and Einstein's theory of relativity."

"Getting back to the pageant. I tell ya, I don't have any worries. Charles and his crew are saddling up to show 'em how it's done. Charles, now, he's a guy with guts and balls, not like some yahoos I know who just talk forever. He knows how to stick to a project an' push it through."

Doofus licked his lips. "Ya wouldn't have a cold beer around, would ya?"

"Sorry, I'm out. Drop by after the pageant when I'm off duty. You can tell me how the show went, and we can both have a beer."

"Yeah. You can fill me in on your plans for the seminar, and we can start lining up those partners for the dairy farm that you're gonna buy."

That scared me more than the seminar. Part ownership of a dairy farm would be six figures or higher. "Ah, I'm not sure I—"

Doofus looked at a nonexistent wristwatch. "Oh, look at the time. Son of a gun, I gotta go, but tomorrow ya better be ready to eat crow, 'cause Charles is gonna do great tonight. The next time I'm here, save that science stuff for one 'ah them snow banks ya land in. It might be interested." He disappeared in a twinkling shimmer, like an indoor snowstorm.

Chapter 17

The Heirs' Story

Rockburg, 2013

Julie yawned as she took a chair at the table in Doc's dining room at noon the next day. The rest of the heirs looked as tired and dispirited as she felt. No one seemed to have any energy or enthusiasm. Jed even appeared to be dozing in his chair.

Josh walked in, late as usual. And just as irritating for Julie, he looked wide awake and eager to get to work.

He took a chair across the table from Julie. "I had breakfast at Gert's this morning. She asked me if we wanted her to cater Thanksgiving for the families here, at the house, or somewhere else."

Seth rolled his eyes toward the ceiling. "Christ, more surprises. This is getting disgusting," he said and threw a pencil on the table. It slid across the polished oak top and hit Jed in the chest, eraser-end first. "Why would she think we'd—"

"Same thing I asked her," Josh said. "She just smiled and served me breakfast. I've never had so much butter, salt, bacon grease, and coffee." He belched loudly. "The estate owes me a gym membership."

Julie frowned. "You said 'families,' not 'family,' right?"

"Yup. She even asked how many kids everybody had so she'd know how much to prepare." Josh leaned back in his chair and held his stomach. "My God, you should have seen the size of the portions."

Julie polled the others for their results. She'd seen Seth throw the pencil and went clockwise around the table to put him last. Wally had nothing new, and when asked, Seth shrugged and nodded toward Jed.

Jed's report was short. "We found correspondence from Dad's publisher. He had the same questions about Doofus that Julie had yesterday. If the issue was resolved, it wasn't in the correspondence we found." Jed looked at Wally and Julie. "You guys find anything?"

Wally shrugged his shoulders.

Julie pretended to look at a notebook in front of her. *Should I mention the odor at the bank and the odor associated with Doofus?* she thought. *It sounds crazy, and this isn't the time. Seth will lose his temper. The rest will ignore it or wonder if I've lost my mind.*

Jed asked her again, "Julie, did you find anything?"

"I discovered that our copy of the book isn't complete. Wally and I read almost all that's available. Dad deleted the rest. We'll have to wait for the book to be published to go further."

Seth threw another pencil on the table. "Aw, shit. This is taking forever. What the f—"

Jed blocked the pencil, this time, and Julie threw a wad of paper at Seth. "Do you listen at all? For a detective, you sure don't—"

Julie glanced at Jed, raised an eyebrow, and nodded slightly toward Seth.

"Seth," Jed said. "Josh said that Gert expected our families to be here, with our kids, for Thanksgiving. Somebody asked her to cater it. That had to be Dad."

"My mom must have been in on it, too," Wally said. "I'll call her this afternoon." He picked up a pen to make a note, thought a moment, and tossed the pen on the table. "Oh, damn. We might not have access to the stuff Doc blocked until after Thanksgiving."

"Why 'after' Thanksgiving?" Seth asked.

"Doc and Mom wanted the families to get together, to socialize. Working on the codicil would get in the way." Wally shrugged, "I could be wrong, but it seems logical."

Damn, Julie thought. It made sense. She felt as though a blanket of gloom settled over the group as Wally's observation sank in.

Josh broke the silence, "Anybody else want more pie? Who wants to go with me?"

Julie nodded agreement, as did the others, but only Wally moved to leave, and he stopped in the kitchen to look for a snack. Julie yawned and sat back in her chair, unable to work up the energy to move. She noticed Jed, sitting to her left, absently thumb through the local phone book from a counter behind him. Less than an inch thick, it included five small towns and the yellow pages for two counties.

Jed turned to her. "Justin—Justin, what? Do you remember the last name of the farmer who introduced himself last night? We should talk to him, too."

"Hampshire, I think," Julie said.

Jed went back to the phone book. "Uh–oh. I've never seen so many Hampshire's. Worse than Petersen's in the Twin Cities. Three of them are Justin's: Justin E., Justin G., and Justin M." He looked at Julie and his brothers. "What do we do now?"

"Call Jim McMorrison," Seth said. "He's the manager on Grandma's farm. He knows every dairy farmer in the county." Seth stood, fished a slip of paper from the front pocket of his jeans, and handed it to Julie. "Here's his cell number. You call him. I might say something I shouldn't."

"How about taking his family to dinner at the Oaks tonight?" Julie asked as she walked to the phone. "If I can get Justin's phone number, I'll invite him, too." She remembered Al's comment about expenses and the codicil. "We can probably bill the estate for the dinner."

That appeared to improve outlooks around the table. Julie made the contacts and the heirs met at the Coffee Cup late that afternoon, where Gert was snoring peacefully in a booth. The five watched her, fidgeting and whispering.

Gert spoke before she opened her eyes. "For God's sake, you couldn't make more noise if ya had a marching band. Can't you let an old woman get her sleep?"

She yawned, adjusted her sweater, and sat up. "What do you need now?"

Julie slid into the booth across the table from Gert. "Didn't mean to wake you. We were wondering if you knew anything else Dad arranged for the holidays? Thanksgiving dinner was a surprise."

"Lord, girl. It's September. You've got better 'an two months to ask me that. You could have mailed a letter from Timbuktu, and I would have had time to mail you my answer. Your Dad's plans are getting to be a pain in my keester."

"But we're only here for another day," Julie said.

"Okay, okay." Gert rubbed her eyes again. "What do you want to know?"

"Could you tell us what Dad told you about his plans for the holidays?" Julie asked. "We don't know anything about them. Did he make plans for Christmas?"

"You don't know about Christmas?" Gert asked.

Julie and her brothers exchanged glances and shook their heads. "We took a guess," she answered.

Gert pursed her lips and raised her eyebrows. "I don't know anything about it either."

Seth started to fidget. "Do you know if Dad arranged anything else for Thanksgiving?"

Gert looked at him. "I heard you're on a police force somewhere, a detective in a big city. Is that right?"

"Yeah, I—"

Gert snorted. "And you're asking an old lady in a small town how to check this out? And I thought Agatha Christie was full of bull."

Seth turned red. "What do you mean?"

"Whenever I've made reservations, I had to use a credit card, and the motel notified the card company, sometimes even insisted on a deposit. The only card I ever saw your dad use was his bank card." Gert took a sip of her coffee. "You've got your dad's bank statements, and I'll bet you can check his phone records, too. Look at 'em." She gave Seth a forced smile. "Or do I have to teach you to read, too."

Julie cringed. Seth was behind her. She heard him stomp out of the café.

"Doesn't take advice well, does he?" Gert said. "He'd better learn to, if he's going to get cooperation from people in town."

"You'll have to excuse him," Julie said. "He's under pressure from home. His wife is ill."

Gert shrugged. "Sorry about that." She took another sip of her coffee. It was cold. "Ach, people pay for this?" She wiped her lips with a napkin. "Your dad arranged for the catering with his bank card, said it was set up so the estate would be billed. He knew how to do it, as though he had practice."

She dismissed them with a wave of her hand. "Would you turn that 'Open' sign on the door as you go? I'm getting too old to work this late."

Dinner that night was at eight. Their guests were fashionably late, though fashion wasn't the issue; it was the milking schedule on the farms. Jim and Justin told Julie they couldn't leave until after their work was done.

That evening, Julie rode to the Oaks with Josh again. The restaurant and golf course was on a county road that wandered back and forth across Fish Creek, the stream that created the narrow valley, locally known as a coulee. The drive was relaxing. Fields of corn and hay and small dairy farms dotted the valley, while the surrounding hills and the banks of the stream were still forested. Five hundred yards after a tight corner on the road, the first tee and the clubhouse of the Oaks relaxed in the deep twilight shade of the oak and maple trees that flanked the parking lot and separated the fairways.

Julie and the other heirs sat at the restaurant's bar while they waited. She sat between Jed and Josh. "Why so tense," she asked Jed.

"I'm tired, frustrated, and thirsty, but I shouldn't drink anything but soda because we all should have our wits about us. We have to interrogate Jim and Justin without seeming to do it."

Julie nodded and ordered ginger ale.

Jed turned from the bar and looked out at the first green, 550 yards away.

"What are you looking at?" Josh asked.

"At the spot where I gave up golf when I was in high school." Jed swiveled his bar stool to look at Josh. "I drove the green in two and six putted. I couldn't handle making two incredible shots and blowing it with six awful puts. I walked back to the clubhouse and sold my clubs." Jed took a sip of his ginger ale. "I've never regretted it. I don't have the temperament for golf."

Justin Hampshire and his wife arrived first. Jim and Helen McMorrison came a few minutes later, shortly before their table was ready. Introductions were made and drinks and dinner ordered. Jim brought up the codicil as soon as the waitress finished taking their orders. "Doc told us you'd have questions about the codicil. How can we help you?"

Seth buried his head in his hands. "It's so frustrating. Nothing makes sense, and everyone seems to know more about the codicil than we do." He looked at Jim. "Did Dad tell the whole town about it?"

Justin answered for both of them. "No. I think Jim, myself, and maybe Gert were the only ones he confided in. Your dad was a good friend of Al's," Justin paused, shoulders hunched, "but I got the impression he thought Al would try to make it easy on himself and you kids by spilling everything he knew." Justin looked around the table at Doc's children. "Your dad was a cagey old bird."

"Yeah, we know," Seth said.

It turned out that Jim and Justin had no idea what squirrel fishing was, nor did they know anything about Doofus. Julie mentally wrote the dinner off as a bust. The other heirs seemed to also, as they stopped trying to grill their guests and relaxed with them over after-dinner drinks.

Justin, sitting next to Julie, started to reminisce. "You know, Julie I owe a lot to your Dad."

"Dad always—" Julie started.

Justin raised his hand to stop her. "Your dad was good, but there were other vets around who were just as good. What I'm talking about is how he looked at life."

He took another sip of brandy. "Your dad thought out loud a lot his last year in practice. He'd mumble to himself, as he tried to make up his mind whether or not to leave his veterinary practice and go into research full time. It was the same time I was deciding what direction to go with my farm. Do I sell the herd and crop the land or take out loans and expand the herd? If I expanded, should I just get bigger or look for new approaches to dairying?"

Justin put his hand over his wife's hand and gave it a squeeze. "Listening to your dad work through his decisions helped me work out mine. He took his time, organized the facts, and set goals to measure progress. He struggled, and things went wrong. They always do, but he acted when he made a decision. He said the difference between daydreaming and planning was action."

Jim nodded in agreement. "Same here. I was younger, so he felt free to lecture me, and I worked for him, so I had to listen when he did. I hated the lectures, but I learned in spite of myself." Jim leaned forward, elbows on the table. "He told me once that there is no progress without a vision, a dream, and you can't dream if you bury your head in your work. There'll always be more on your plate, but your life will have no direction, if you don't keep one eye on the horizon."

The dinner broke up shortly after that. Jim and Justin had to be up and working by five in the morning.

Julie was in Doc's office at his computer when Wally walked in the next morning.

"What should we work on today?" he asked her.

"Josh is going to explore Rockburg and the family plot at the cemetery. We are going to look into this." Julie held up a flash drive she'd found on a shelf of the computer hutch. "It's a file of e-mails from your mother, and it looks like it may have more of the New Orleans chapters of the manuscript. I call it 'the Linda File.'"

During the day, Wally tried to call Linda several times without success. He returned to the office after a call made in the late afternoon and tapped Julie on the shoulder.

"I have to leave," he said.

"Going for dinner?" Julie asked.

"No. I have to go home. My sister Sophie answered the phone when I called. She asked me to grab the first flight home. Mom has seemed confused the last couple of days, and she stumbled and was unable to walk when she tried to get up this morning." He explained that his mother had been hospitalized for tests, but her physician thought she was stable.

"Oh, Wally. I'm so sorry," Julie said. "Go home. I and the boys will take care of things here."

Wally left for his hotel room and then for the airport. Before he left, he told Julie he was still confident he could wheedle the information they needed out of his mother.

Julie and her brothers met around the dining room table again that evening. Julie told them about Wally and Linda and the extra chapters she'd discovered. "Has anyone found anything else?" she asked.

"I've dug up some information. Dad paid for Thanksgiving dinner and a block of rooms at the Westphalia, a motel twelve miles from here. It has an indoor water park for the kids, a spa for our wives, and downhill and cross country skiing starting in December. The motel reservation office said we have the rooms for four days and three nights over Thanksgiving and for five days and four nights over Christmas. Dad only paid for half the cost over Christmas."

"Great job, Seth," Jed said. Josh nodded agreement.

Seth leaned back in his chair and smiled. "I've learned something about getting information after seven years as a detective."

"So you checked Dad's bank statements, like Gert suggested?" Julie asked.

Seth sat up and looked through some papers in front of him. He seemed to avoid looking at Julie. "Ah, I checked a variety of things."

"Including Dad's bank statements?"

"Yes, they included Dad's bank statements. I would have done that even if Gert hadn't said anything."

Wally called the next afternoon, as Julie was picking up the last of her things and getting ready to drive home to the Twin Cities. Linda had suffered another stroke that morning and slipped into a coma. He called Julie again at her home on October 3, the day after his mother had died.

Julie, her husband Todd, and Josh rode together in Josh's rental car a few days later in Linda's funeral cortege.

"Dad and Linda, both gone within a month," Julie said. "Everything comes to an end. It makes me want to hug my kids and not let them go."

"It made me realize how quickly families grow apart," Josh said quietly. "Mom and Dad had cousins they grew up with, but we rarely met. Someday our grandchildren will do the same."

Julie watched the houses by the road slip by as the cortege worked its way to the cemetery. "I wish I had a job that let me work at home and take time for the family when I needed to."

Linda was buried next to Mark. Julie and her brothers, with the other mourners, returned to the church for a light lunch. Julie didn't discuss the codicil, and she didn't hear her brothers say anything about it. She wasn't free to stay long, and discussing the codicil at the funeral seemed inappropriate. There were other relatives to talk to, some she only saw at weddings and funerals now, and might never see again.

Julie, Todd and their two children joined the rest of the family at the Westphalia for Thanksgiving. Dinner at Doc's home, catered by Gert, was a hit. Julie and Wally's sister, Sophie, pitched in and helped, although Julie found herself tearing up when she polished her mother's silver and laid the table with the china and crystal she remembered from her childhood. The three women got on so well that Julie asked Gert to cater Christmas Eve supper, Christmas dinner at the house, and hire a housekeeper to get it ready.

The heirs and their families played in the indoor water park, partied in the evenings, and drove through the valleys and small towns of their youth. Julie drove her family on these outings because she knew the roads. A mile from the family farm, she parked near a bridge over a small stream and asked Todd to stay in the car with the kids for a minute.

She walked to the bridge, leaned on the railing, and looked over the stream and pasture south of the bridge for several minutes. She dropped a couple pieces of gravel into a pool a few feet south of the bridge, watched a fish dart into the shadows, and returned to the car.

Todd asked, "What was—?"

"We used to fish here, and sometimes Mom and Doc would have a picnic lunch with us in the pasture," Julie explained.

Todd peered at the stream. "Ever catch anything? It doesn't look six inches deep."

"I caught a few small trout south of the bridge. I always threw them back."

"What about north of the bridge? There must be deep pools under the big trees on the bank."

"Very deep," Julie said. "Mom and Doc never let us go to that side of the bridge." She buckled her safety belt and started the car.

"Why couldn't you go on the north side?"

"Mom said it was too dangerous," Julie said. She checked the road behind them and pulled onto the black top. "I tried to get more information, but Doc wouldn't talk about it and Mom wouldn't say any more. I asked Elspeth once, and she started to cry. I didn't have the nerve to ask more questions after that." Julie looked at the clock on the dashboard. "It's getting late, and there are still things I want to see again."

The sightseeing and socializing didn't leave time for serious discussion of the codicil. That's what Doc and Linda intended. Doc's book went on sale the Monday *after* Thanksgiving. Serious study of the e-mails between Doc and Linda and of the book began in early December with the story of the Nativity.

The kids slept in the car as Julie and Todd headed back to the Twin Cities and their home. They drove north in silence. On their left, the sheer limestone bluffs carved by the Mississippi soared 200 to 400 feet above them. Trees and shrubs, skeletal and grey in a cold December wind, climbed the slopes of the bluffs, bordered the backwaters and covered the sandbars on the other side of the highway, where the river rolled through the main channel to mingle with the La Crosse, the Ohio, and the Missouri farther south.

Julie wiped condensation from the car window and watched gulls wheeling overhead as they passed the Dresbach lock and dam. "Waters from all the rivers of the Midwest come together, but no matter what we do, our great-grandchildren are likely to be strangers to each other. Even while we have the kids with us, we spend more time at work than we do with them."

Julie turned from the bleak scenery. "I'm beginning to understand why Dad and Linda set up the codicil. At Linda's funeral, I felt so sad thinking how children grow up and move across the country. Even close families grow apart. I want to find a way for us to spend more time with our kids while we can."

"How can we do that in today's economy?" Todd asked. "We need two paychecks, and I thought you loved working in the seed lab?"

"There is more to horticulture than testing conditions to break dormancy for seeds. I know the economics, but it seems such a waste to mold our lives around economics rather than the reverse. We'd have to have a business of our own—something the kids could work in, too, like a restaurant or a farm or the nursery we've talked about."

Startled, Todd looked at her. "Honey, you know the investment a farm would take, and the nursery and truck farm is something we've talked about doing when the kids finish college. I'm not sure we can swing it before then."

Julie put a hand on his knee. "Let's work on it in more detail after Christmas. I'd like to complete the computer model and plug current costs and prices into it. That will tell us if it's feasible. Set a goal of mid-February to complete that and it can be our Valentine's gift to each other."

Doc's Manuscript

PART III

Chapter 18: Last-Minute Preparations

Doc's Manuscript

New Orleans, Afternoon, December 19, 1987

Jerry stroked the neck of the sick camel and gently squeezed the animal's trachea. The camel extended its neck and coughed.

"That's what I thought. You're not going anywhere tonight. Damn! And I was counting on you." Jerry gave the camel injections of an antibiotic and left the box stall.

He walked along the line of stalls, checking the other camels to see if they were eating and continued to the big double doors at the end of the barn. The waning light of the December afternoon cast his shadow down the middle of the barn. He stood in the doorway, stared at the dirt floor, and considered his options. The crunch of footsteps on the gravel drive interrupted his train of thought.

Jerry nodded at the wrangler walking toward him. "Pete, we've got problems. Rufus has pneumonia. We'll have to watch him for the next few days. A couple of the others are off their feed, too. We can't use camels from this barn for the show tonight. What does that leave us?"

Pete swore. "I guess we could use Misty, Gladys, and Topper, but I don't know if those three have worked together before, and I got more bad news. Jason called in sick, so it's just you and me tonight."

Pete was a wiry man in his mid-fifties. He'd spent his life working with cattle, horses, and big circus animals. A wild youth and constant exposure to the sun and weather, deeply lined and tanned his face. He had dreams, once, and a few too many girlfriends. At least, that's what his first wife thought. Damned if his second wife didn't think so, too. Women were plain unreasonable, as Pete told anybody who listened after she had filed for divorce and moved to Minnesota with their son, Jim.

Between alimony and child support, all he could afford was an occasional beer and the faded jeans, nondescript long-sleeved shirt, and old western boots he wore every day. He didn't mind. The animals he worked with were his family now. Like the other wranglers he played penny-ante poker with on Friday nights, he took better care of the animals than he did himself. That made him invaluable to Jerry.

Jerry frowned. "Gladys and Misty worked together a couple years ago, but they haven't even been in the same paddock since then, and Topper is new."

"And it's just you, me, and three newbies in the saddle?"

"Yup. Do you think we can do it, safely?"

Pete put his hands on his hips, looked at the ground, and pushed the dust around with his foot. "Yeah, maybe. Gladys is an old trooper, and Misty is usually pretty levelheaded. I don't know about Topper. Do any of the riders have experience with big animals?"

"Not that I know of, and one of them is too confident," said Jerry. "I'll call the guy in charge and see if they'd be willing to cut back to two camels. If they won't go for that, how do you think it would work if I lead Misty in front, we put Gladys in the middle without a wrangler, and you lead Topper in the rear, far enough back so he can't start something with the other two?"

"It should work, as long as whoever rides Gladys doesn't let her get too close to Misty, until we're sure they get along."

Jerry rubbed his chin and thought. "If the riders can't follow orders, the worst we'll get will be a couple camels spitting at each other."

Pete shrugged. He didn't like arrogant novices. "They wanted camels and authenticity. That'll be authentic for 'em."

In a suburb ten miles away, Charles dropped by the church an hour before the cast was to get ready for the show. George and Bill were to meet him there, pick up the costumes for the cast, and drive to the amphitheater in his minivan. The phone in the church office rang insistently, and the answering machine didn't kick in. Charles let himself into the office and answered the phone.

"The church office is closed. This is Charles van Kalden. Can I help you?"

"Mr. van Kalden, this is Jerry Baldwin. I gave you the camel riding lessons yesterday. We have a problem. One of our animal handlers is sick, and so are a couple of our camels. We only have two wranglers to lead the camels. We can make do with two handlers and three camels, but there could be problems if a camel gets spooked in front of the audience. Would you consider doing the show with two camels?"

Charles listened in silence, his brow furrowed, and his face slowly flushed. He heard his inner voice. *Charles, are ya gonna take that lyin' down? It's time to let 'em know who's boss. They promised three camels and, by God, you're going to have three camels. Straighten this guy out, pronto!*

Charles tightened his grip on the phone. "No, definitely not. It's three camels or none. Let's go ahead with the staff and the camels you have, unless you can't keep your animals under control."

Jerry stood straighter, and the muscles of his jaw tensed. "My camels are well trained. We can do it with three, as long as you're aware that it will take longer to get the camels under control if something goes wrong."

Charles relaxed and allowed himself to smile. "Good, good. See you in an hour at the amphitheater. This is going to be a magnificent pageant."

Preparations were well underway at the amphitheater. Mark was scooping shovels of wood shavings and sawdust onto the stage near the stable when Charles, Bill, and George arrived. The boys cast as shepherds wandered around the set, checking the taped lines that marked their path to the stable and clearing stray sawdust from them.

Rob arrived with Betty, who set about collecting Walkman's and getting the other shepherds in costume.

Ted waved to Rob. "Yo, Rob, how's it going?"

As Ted approached, Rob looked around to make sure no adults were nearby and waited until Ted was next to him before speaking, "According to plan."

"Here's the superglue and the latex gloves." Rob passed a small paper bag to Ted, "Don't put the glue on the armrests until Dave heads toward his stand. Spread it where his costume will touch, but don't put it anywhere he'll touch with his hands."

Ted nodded. "Got it. Who's going to spill the stuff on his pants at dinner? This won't work unless he's naked under his costume."

"Steve and Justin. But Justin," Rob shook his head. "What a wuss. He's still scared about getting caught." Rob remembered another problem, "You covered us, like I asked? If Dave makes a break for it and a spotlight catches him running bare-assed—"

"Not to worry. Everything's covered." Ted nodded to Rob's left, "Shh, Dave's coming. You talk to him. I have to get into costume." Ted headed to the changing rooms with a wink to Rob and a friendly wave to Dave.

Dave saw Betty collecting cassette players and other distractions as he walked onto the stage. He removed a pack of gum from his shirt pocket, slid it into his pants, and walked past her toward Mark.

Dave dug a toe into the sawdust and shavings, "What's all this for, Mark?"

"Hi, Dave. It's a precaution. These animals aren't house broken, so it helps to have something absorbent on the floor."

"Oh, wow. I didn't think about that. How big is a camel?"

"I'm not sure, about the size of a horse or cow, nine hundred to fifteen hundred pounds, I guess. Ask one of the wranglers."

Dave thought for a minute. "So if they take a whiz, it could be gallons, huh?"

"I don't know, but don't forget to check your gum with Betty."

"What gum?"

Mark pointed at Dave's pocket. "The pack you put in your pocket. Hand it in."

Jim was at the AV console, trying to concentrate while Al helped him attach the wireless microphone and transmitter to his costume. Al was giving him his final instructions when Mark approached.

"Jim, listen up. The controls and transmitter are in this." Al held a black box the size of his hand in front of Jim. "This knob slides back and forth. Slide it this way, and the green light goes on, and the audience hears everything you say. Slide it the other way, and the red light goes on, and the microphone is off. Got that?"

"Yeah, green, on; red, off," Jim said and flipped the knob back and forth.

"Good. Now count slowly to ten, so we can readjust the sound at the control panel."

Jim counted, the sound was adjusted, and he counted again while Al double-checked his settings. Satisfied, Al repeated his instructions. "Remember, do not . . ."

Jim grinned and looked around the set. He spotted Dave and waved.

Al put a hand on Jim's shoulder. "Jim, look at me. This is important. Do not, I repeat, do not turn this on until you need it, and be damned sure it's off, if you're backstage and talking to your buddies."

"Sure. Got it. Nooo problemo." Jim put the control box in a pocket at his waist and glanced back toward where Dave had been.

"Looks like you're all set for sound. Have you checked out the harness and lift equipment with the crane operator?" asked Mark.

"Yup. The cable was too short to keep the gear out of the spotlight. They rigged an extension to fix it."

"Extension?" Mark asked.

"Yeah, a bungee cord. Carl, the guy in the crane, said he's done this before. It should work, if he takes it slowly."

Mark frowned. Anything with a bungee cord in it sounded unpredictable, but Carl should know. He looked at his watch. "It has to work, but there isn't time to test it. You'd better eat and have Betty help with your makeup. Hustle."

Mark trotted off to inspect the camels, and Jim ambled toward the dressing rooms and dinner.

At the loading dock behind the mound and stage, Bill and George helped Jerry and Pete, who were busy with the camels, unload the tack and feed from the trucks. Bill nudged George. "Look who's coming."

Bill watched a procession worthy of a Caesar move toward them. "Good Lord. Charles must have half a dozen people with him, and he's already in costume."

"That's one way to make sure no one puts you to work. He struts around like a prince. Let's disappear, or we'll have to listen to him." The two moved behind a truck.

Charles loudly held forth on the intricacies of camel handling, as he and his coterie approached the camels.

Behind the truck, Bill listened and shook his head. “Those guys are probably the only people who know less about camels than Charles. Listen to him. You’d think he’d spent his life riding camels.”

George held a finger to his lips.

The camels were tied to the sides of a large truck, the type often described as a “straight job.” The tethers were tied high and short on the truck to keep the camels’ heads up, making it easier for Pete to saddle them and brush them down.

Charles, taking care not to step on his robe or in camel doo, waddled and hopped toward Pete. “Say there, my good man, which camel will be in the lead?”

Pete adjusted Topper’s saddle and glanced over his shoulder at Charles. “The one tied to the end of the truck,” Pete said, and tried to get on with his work.

“Which saddle will be on that camel, and when will you saddle it?”

Pete ignored him and tightened Topper’s saddle girth.

Charles moved closer and asked in a louder voice, “I say, which saddle will be on the lead camel?”

Topper, startled, swung his rear around so he could look at Charles. The movement slammed Pete into the side of the truck.

Bill grimaced at the sound of Pete hitting the truck. “That had to hurt. How far do you think Charles will push it?”

George craned his neck around the corner of the truck to get a better view. “I don’t think Pete puts up with much. Charles might get himself decked.”

Pete recovered his balance and rubbed his ribs. “You’ll have to ask the boss. He’s at the stable, tying up the calves.”

Bill and George looked at each other. Jerry was leaning over them, listening to the exchange. All three watched as Charles led his followers across the mound to the stable. Mark arrived just as Charles disappeared over the mound.

Jerry, his face flushed, walked around the truck and introduced himself. "Hi, I'm Jerry. I'm in charge of the camels tonight. Are you Mark?"

"That's me."

"You're in charge of this show, right?" Jerry took Mark by the arm and walked a few steps away from the others.

"Yes, I'm the director."

"Good. I wonder if you could do something for me. It would help avoid problems with the animals," Jerry said softly.

"Shoot."

"Until the show starts, keep that domineering, fat-assed son of a bitch away from my camels, away from my truck, away from my people, and out of my hair."

"Ah, you've met Charles, then? I came to tell him it was time he ate and had his makeup put on. That should keep him away for now, but he'll be riding the lead camel in the pageant. How can I help you on that?"

"Tell him we are short-staffed tonight. We need to keep the camel's attention focused on the handlers. When he comes back, he will speak only to Pete or to me. He will speak quietly and only when necessary, and he will listen to us and do as he is told. Pete and I are the only ones who will speak to the camels or say a word during the performance." He tightened his grip on Mark's elbow. "Make damned sure it sinks in."

"I'll do my best."

"'Best' is not what we need. We need that prick to shut up and follow directions."

"I'll do what I can," said Mark.

The cast dinner was fast food, ample but nothing special. People ate, chattered, put on their makeup or had Betty or Linda help them.

Final details of the cast party were announced and maps to the party passed around.

Mark took Charles aside after dinner as the three Magi headed back to saddle up.

"Charles, from the time you and the camels are visible until the Magi are kneeling at the manger, all eyes will be on your group. No one else in the tableau will be moving. That will be the high point of the night."

Charles beamed and nodded in agreement. "That's just as I—"

"This is important, Charles. Jerry is shorthanded tonight. The three of you must speak softly, only when necessary, and only to Jerry and Pete when you are near the camels. Once you are in the saddle, nobody but Jerry and Pete are to say a word. Got that? Jerry wants the attention of the camels solely on the wranglers."

"That's exactly what I told Bill and George." He clapped Mark on the shoulder. "I'll remind them about it again. Don't worry, I'll keep them in line. You can count on me."

Charles excused himself and led Bill and George back to the camels. Mark watched the trio, shook his head, and said a prayer.

Chapter 19: The Living Nativity

Any effort that has self-glorification as its final endpoint is bound to end in disaster.

—Robert M. Pirsig,
Zen and the Art of Motorcycle Maintenance

Doc's Manuscript

New Orleans, Evening, December 19, 1987

With more competing agendas than a Republican Presidential Primary, the cast, the support people, and the wranglers completed their preparations. The camels saddled, Jerry and Pete led the other livestock to the stage. They tethered the donkey, calves, and lambs near the stable, each with enough feed to keep them quiet during the performance. Jerry saw one of the shepherds, caught his eye, and motioned the teen to him.

"Hi, I'm Jerry. I'm in charge of the animals tonight. Do you know who will be near the calves by the stable?"

"Uh, I guess that would be me and the other shepherds," Ted said.

"Good, then you're the one I need to talk to. A couple of the calves have diarrhea." Jerry motioned toward two calves tied next to each other. "Diarrhea can be explosive at their age. Tell the shepherds to stay away from the calves, and whatever you do, don't get close behind them."

"Yeah, we wouldn't want to get near that. I'll let everybody know."

Jerry and Pete headed back to the camels, and Ted walked over to the other shepherds, considering his options. With a calculating smile, he stood in costume at the edge of the group, his hands clasped innocently in front of him. He said nothing.

The AV crew sent word to the cast members that the audience was filing in. Lights visible from the seats were turned off. In the dark, Betty and John took their positions at the manger, and the shepherds hid behind bushes, ready to come on stage. Dave and Jim made a trip to the men's room as the first carol signaled the start of the performance. A dim light glowed green on the wireless mic control box in Jim's pocket.

Charles's daughter Robin and niece Cindy surprised everyone with a passable performance of the first chorus of "Oh, Holy Night." A barely audible baritone hum intruded on the second chorus.

The amplified sounds of a heavy stream hitting a toilet and a tenor voice joined the baritone. The tenor's words—a ditty about a drafty costume—were garbled. He sounded like a strangled squirrel or a boys' choir trying to yodel. The baritone chuckled, stopped his humming, and burst into song.

Jim, like many older teens, was no longer a boy and not quite a man. He was a good-natured bundle of insecurity and improbable dreams wrapped in boundless energy and questionable judgment. Inchoate man, he faced the world with a silly grin, a stupid joke, and a set of goofy assumptions about life that would give an adult a coronary.

He'd taken an interest in Handel, of all things, largely because he didn't need to know much about the composer to be considered an expert by his peers. Besides, humming a few bars of *See The*

Conquering Hero[1], while standing at the urinal, impressed his friends and always made him feel good.

Baroque conventions allowed Jim to adapt any risqué ditty to the music. His latest favorite was a limerick about a fortunate young man named Handy, and he launched into it to amuse Dave.

"There once was a young man named Handy, who's . . . (sounds of a second stream hitting still water and the tenor yodel) . . . a dandy, big strapping and hung . . . (sounds of flatulence and laughter) . . . the ladies . . ."

The sound system was balanced so that the girls singing on stage could hear their music and what the audience heard, only better. The two made a game attempt to ignore the voice-over, but twice turned crimson, and Cindy once put her hand to her mouth and turned toward Robin in shock. The ribald lyrics, audible to attentive listeners in the first ten rows, were at last drowned out by the deep-throated growl of a flushing toilet.

The young ladies conceded defeat, took a quick bow, and ran off the stage.

The audience, many of whom had been chatting, thought their inattention and boorish behavior had upset the girls. They made up for it by giving them a standing ovation. This dumbfounded those who had heard the limerick and sent Robin and Cindy into paroxysms of sobbing. "What kind of people are these?" Robin wailed.

The AV crew didn't cut the feed from Jim's microphone until after what became known as Handy's Water Music had ceased. Less public was Handy's Royal Fireworks Display, which took place when Jim's mother cornered him.

Dave had to hustle to get in position behind the faux boulder in

---

1 Handel, George Frideric. "See The Conquering Hero Comes," *Judas Maccabaeus*, 1746. I know. You were about to object that Handel's march was too slow for Jim's limerick. Jim used the livelier melody from the third movement of Beethoven's *Variations* on Handel's march.

time. The shepherds took the stage, a second spotlight came on, and Dave appeared as the Angel of the Lord. The shepherds mimed fear and shock, but one look at Dave and several of the shepherds turned away from the audience to hide their laughter. Dave whispered, "Hey, what's up? Something wrong with my costume?"

That convulsed two of the shepherds. From the seats, it looked as though they were overacting their awe of the angel.

Dave hadn't detected the superglue when he put his arms on the arm rests. His questions unanswered, he didn't notice that his costume was firmly attached to the armrests and other parts of the stand.

Jerry and Pete helped the three wise men mount the camels. Charles was put on Misty, with Jerry guiding, and George was on Gladys. The lead rope for Gladys was tied to a ring on the back of Misty's saddle, and Pete, at the rear, led Topper with Bill on board.

Jerry whipped out a soft rag and wiped gobs of sticky mucus from Misty's eyes. Gladys watched and waited for Jerry to clean her eyes. It didn't happen.

Jerry whispered to the Magi, "Stay quiet and let us do the talking. Relax, stay loose." He stepped to the side of Misty that wouldn't be visible to the audience. "We're on, gentlemen."

Jerry and Pete led the camels and their riders over the mound toward the stable. Floodlights backlit the Magi as they crested the rise. The camels and Magi appeared in silhouette, as though on a hill with the setting sun behind them. The effect was dramatic, and all watching the scene became quiet.

Gladys was not happy. Jerry was concentrating on Misty, and she was in the lead. Gladys snorted, blowing gobs of camel . . . well, she cleared her nasal passages. Jerry was her buddy. She watched him attend to Misty through eyes narrowed by jealousy. Unable to endure the betrayal in silence, she raised her head and vented. "Eeeuuggh, eeeuggh."

Misty smacked Gladys across the nose with her tail for the fourth time, then raised her tail and passed a potent cloud of gas.

Gladys snorted and laid her ears back. Her nostrils flared with rage, and she brought up a mass of stinking cud. It was time to settle the pecking order. She squinted against the glare of the stage lights and watched for a chance to make her move.

Topper was not used to being at the end of a line. Then again, he was following a female, and she might be willing. Well, probably not, but how could she resist a studly dude like himself? He wasn't sure if he should make a move on Gladys or resent being third in line. Like many males, his brain wasn't built to handle two thoughts at once and walk in a straight line, especially if one of the thoughts was about sex. He stopped.

Pete felt Topper's lead rope tighten. He turned to see what his charge was doing and, with a jerk on the rope, put Topper in motion again.

Topper decided Gladys wasn't his type. On the other hand, Topper wasn't sure what his type was. Oh Lord, another question; Topper stopped, and Pete put him in motion again.

Topper's observations blended seamlessly with his daydreams, something males of all species have a talent for. He blew his soft palate out his mouth and exhaled loudly around it—the male camel equivalent of bedroom eyes and expensive cologne.

Pete saw Topper's display and realized he had to get Topper under control. He jerked on the lead rope to let him know who was in charge and wished he'd put a nose peg in the idiot.

Topper sucked his soft palate back in, but decided he'd ignore Pete and give Gladys a playful nip on the rear when he had the chance. As they descended toward the stable, he watched for a chance to make his move.

Charles heard the gasps of the children in the front row when the Magi and camels were seen at the top of the rise. He savored the oohs and ahhs of the audience, and congratulated himself for having the guts, talent, and inspiration to create the pageant. He sat erect and tried to look stern and wise, as he composed a toast to himself for Bill to give at the party that night. In profile, with his chin up and his turban slightly askew, he looked oddly like a caricature of Topper.

Jerry halted Misty when they came to the calves tethered at the stable. He dropped Misty's lead rope, reached toward her rear, and with a jerk untied the slipknot that linked Gladys to Misty's saddle. At that moment, he was not in control of either camel.

Gladys launched her attack as Misty dropped to her knees for Charles to dismount. Gladys hadn't counted on Misty dropping. She might have adjusted her aim, but Topper nipped her in the butt at the same time she spit at Misty.

Charles had eaten a spicy barbecue for dinner, and the way he rolled in every direction as Misty lowered herself for his dismount had a dramatic effect on his stomach. He was barely holding his dinner down when he was struck in the ear with a stinking gob of camel spit. Charles did not recognize it as camel spit, but Misty did.

This was war. Misty bounced from the ground, reversing all the movements that had so disturbed Charles's stomach. She swung her rear and pivoted on her front feet to face Gladys. Her rear quarters knocked Jerry over and crashed into the side of the cardboard and canvas stable, buckling it and scattering Mary, Joseph, and the shepherds.

Gladys kicked back at Topper, missed, and swung to spit at him. Misty let fly with a wad of cud when Gladys turned, but Misty had a famously bad aim. Her first shot caught George in the side; her second and third caught him in the face and chest when he turned to look at the collapsing stable.

Ignorance of what hit him did not impede the reaction of Charles's stomach. He launched his dinner. It did not cut through the air in the majestic arc traversed by the camel spit. His dinner gushed down his front, pooling in the folds of his costume. He doubled over, clutching his belly.

Gladys saw Charles lose his dinner and misread it as an amateurish and inept attempt at spitting. She aimed a wad at him because it was easy.

This must have marked Charles and the other Magi as combatants in the eyes of the other camels. Charles, Bill, George, and anyone near them were henceforth targets for all three camels. Each of the Magi became soaked with camel spit, and each thought the camels had singled him out as a target.

The excitement and the turning and dodging camels prevented the audience from following the play-by-play action after the initial moves of the engagement. This was a shame, as connoisseurs of camel fights say it was one of the best.

Misty stumbled. Charles pitched head first off her, slid like a torpedo toward one of the calves, and smote the rear of the calf with his face. The startled calf bleated, raised its tail, and anointed Charles with a generous splash that made camel spit smell like perfume.

George managed to dismount from Gladys, but he slipped and fell in the sawdust behind the calves. He did not meet the calves as intimately as Charles did, but his costume was almost as soiled. Bill tried to dismount from Topper, but was hit by cud from both Gladys and Misty and thrown off balance as Topper dodged a shot from Gladys. He landed in donkey doo, which he didn't notice until later.

The fighting camels trashed the stable set. A donkey, possibly a pacifist, broke his tether and bolted toward Dave's Styrofoam rock. Dave still stood on his platform, acutely aware that his costume was glued in place, and he was naked without it. He didn't know how few stitches held his costume together.

The platform had little in its center. The donkey crashed through the faux rock, bumped into the supports of the platform, and ran between Dave's legs. The platform crumbled. Dave lost his balance and his costume and fell astride the donkey, facing the animal's tail. The terrified donkey doubled back toward the camel fight with Dave riding backwards, bare-assed and screaming for help.

He fell off the donkey when the poor beast ran past the camels and through the spotlight. Dazed, Dave scrambled up and stood nude in a spotlight, surrounded by chaos. He made a break for what remained of the stable, but the camels moved and blocked his path. Changing course, he ran toward the audience to get around the fight, skirted the front edge of the stage for twenty feet, and doubled back toward the screen of pine trees behind the stage where he was finally out of the spotlight.

Dave's streak caught the interest of a certain demographic in the audience. Most teenagers would rather die than be seen in public with parents and younger siblings. The thirty-five girls between thirteen and sixteen years old in the audience were no different. They were forced to attend and hadn't looked at the stage prior to the camel fight, lest an acquaintance see them and think they were enjoying the show. The camel fight got their attention, and Dave's *au natural* dash brought them out of their seats.

Pubescent curiosity and parental censorship have rarely been so exquisitely timed. As the girls lurched forward to take advantage of the "unobstructed view from every seat" for which the amphitheater was famous, fifty protective parents hastily tried to block that view by placing a hand over the delicate teenage eyes.

Although not the audience participation planned by the worship committee, it was impressive. A resounding "smack" was heard across the theater as the protective hands met faces well forward of where the parents thought they were, followed quickly by thirty-five disappointed teenage drama queens howling in unison in surprise, pain, and anger.

Mark grimly watched the destruction of his pageant. He helped Betty, John, and the shepherds get out of harm's way and offered to help Jerry and Pete. They didn't want amateurs in the way and brusquely told him so. As the wranglers got the camels under control, Mark told the AV crew to cut to the last carol and bring the program to an end, then jogged over to Jim and the crane crew.

"We're closing this pig down after the next carol," he told Jim and Carl. "When can you be ready for Christ's ascension?"

"Give us four minutes to hook the bungee cord to Jim's harness," Carl said.

Mark turned to Jim. "Turn on your mic and get ready to go before somebody gets hurt."

Sue Bilshot, who led the audience in the carols, wasn't informed of the change in plans. She recognized the intro to *Silent Night*, but thought the AV guys had gotten it wrong again. She tried to correct them by singing a couple bars of *We Three Kings*, but transitioned to *Silent Night* when they didn't take her hint. The audience joined in fitfully, as it was the lyrics for *Oh, Little Town of Bethlehem* that were projected on screens around the stage.

While Jim prepared for his ascension, Mark visited the Magi, who were recovering behind the remains of the stable. Bill and George were standing, scraping foul-smelling cud off the rags that remained of their costumes. Charles sat nearby on a bale of hay, silent and immobile.

Charles stared at the sawdust between his feet. At the moment of his greatest triumph, his dreams had turned into public humiliation and filth in a downfall as rapid as that of Sejanus.[2] Coherent thought was beyond him; his mind flinched from it as if from a hot iron. For the moment, he was numb. Anguish, self-recrimination, shame, despair—these would come tomorrow.

Mark, assaulted by the stench surrounding the Magi, covered his nose and asked, "How are you guys doing?"

---

2 Lucius Aelius Sejanus, a confidant of the Roman Emperor Tiberius and commander of the Praetorian Guard, Sejanus controlled the Roman Empire. Accused of treason, Sejanus was condemned by the Senate. He, his children, and associates were murdered that same day.

"Ahh! This stuff reeks!" said George, trying to clean his costume with a handful of fresh sawdust.

Bill agreed. "I've never smelled anything this bad in my life. I feel as though I've been swimming in a sewer during a cholera outbreak. Charles, how are you doing? Can I help you clean up that costume?"

Charles tried to speak. "I, ah, I," he choked back a sob, lowered his head, and waved a hand in lieu of speech, just as the music of the carol ended.

On the other side of the stage, Carl waved to the AV men, they turned on the feed from Jim's microphone, and a clamp, holding the bungee cord and Jim to the ground, was released.

In the haste to prepare for Christ's ascension, the bungee cord was stretched a tad more than planned. Jim, as Christ, exploded into the air, flew out of the spotlights, and higher than the crane's pulley.

Christ's second coming was as abrupt as it was brief, as were his third, fourth, and fifth through eighth. His screams and pleas, amplified by the sound system, drowned out the last noises of the camel fight. The fight was dying down anyway, and the camels didn't seem to mind being upstaged.

No one confused Jim's broadcast comments with church doctrine. His first words as Christ were "Whoaaaa, whaaaat, noooaaaaa, [string of expletives], get me, aaahhhh, down," and a final "Aiyeee," as the bungee cord came free from the crane and Christ took flight. The final scene was memorable for the number of times the "F" word was broadcast at a church function.

Mark heard the commotion and looked toward the crane as Christ flew over, headed for the pine trees. "Oh, my God, was that Jim?"

Mark pointed to the trees, and called to the shepherds. "Hey, guys, get over there and look for Jim." He pulled out the note from

George with the EMT's name. "Rob, get on the sound system and ask John Wheeler to come backstage, now, please. Ask if there's a doctor in the house, too, and have someone call an ambulance, just in case."

Mark turned to George. "If you guys are okay, there's a hose back by the changing rooms. It'll be cold water, but you can hose yourselves off while I find you a ride back to the church."

George shivered. "Kinda cold tonight to use a hose, isn't it?"

"I'll get a blanket for you, and there are hot showers at the church. You can clean up there before you get into your street clothes."

Mark trotted off to get the blanket and make sure an ambulance was called. On the way, he crossed paths with John Wheeler, the emergency medical technician. "John, have you found Jesus?"

"No, but we haven't checked all the trees yet."

Chapter 20: Officer Williams

Never ascribe to malice that which is adequately explained by incompetence.

—N. Bonaparte, peripatetic *bon vivant* and French agent famous for securing a century of British hegemony over Egypt.

Doc's Manuscript

New Orleans, Evening, December 19, 1987

"You want us to ride in the back, in the open bed of a pickup, on a cold night?" asked Bill. Hosing off with cold water removed the chunks of filth, but the Magi were soaked and they still reeked. Now they were frozen, and their costumes were falling apart.

"There isn't room for all of ya in the cab, and I'd never be able to use the truck again. I know ya tried ta clean up, but the stench of you three together could peel paint." Tom looked sheepish, but held his ground.

Tom Petersen loved his truck and kept it in immaculate condition. Elaine, Tom's wife, complained that he spent more time on his truck than he did with her.

"Maybe it won't be too bad if we toss a bale of straw in the back to sit on and wrap ourselves in the blanket. It's only a couple of miles to the church," said George. "Let's get rid of these stinking rags, too. They're still filthy, they're wet, and they'll just keep us from warming up."

"Yeah, get the blanket, and to hell with what people think. Let's d-d-do whatever it takes to g-get dry and warm," Bill said.

Charles didn't argue. He sat on a bale of hay, silent, eyes focused on the ground by his feet.

Tom brought his truck to the Magi. Mark threw a bale in the back and set it behind the cab. He helped the three bedraggled and nearly naked men climb into the pickup and tucked his blanket around them.

Charles, sitting on the bale in the truck, finally took note of what they were doing. "God, I-I'm wet and co-cold. Let's g-get going and get a hot shower."

The three shivering men huddled together under the blanket. Tom carefully edged into gear and started for the church. He was soon on the highway and accelerated to the minimum speed for the freeway to avoid drawing the attention of the police.

Back at the amphitheater, Dave thanked his lucky stars that he was still wearing his sandals. Otherwise, he'd be scampering naked in the dark from one pine tree to another with sore feet, too. Only one more tree to cover his approach before he made a dash to the door of the changing room through a dimly lit clearing. His troubles would be over, and Rob's would start.

He made it to the last pine and caught his breath. Even running, he was so cold he shivered. At this temperature, everything that could had shriveled to insignificance. If a spotlight hit him now, he wouldn't have anything to hide.

His only source of warmth was a nascent plan for revenge. Dave gathered himself, made sure the coast was clear, and sprinted for the changing room door. He made it to the door in seconds. Gratefully, he grabbed the door knob, twisted it, and pulled, and pulled, and swore. All the billfolds and Walkman's were in the room, and the door was locked.

"Hey, Dave! Got anything to say to your public?" Rob called out.

Dave whirled around—oops, big mistake. Three flashes blinded him as a shutter clicked. Rob laughed and handed Dave his clothes. The other shepherds formed a cordon around Dave, in case anyone else came along before he got his pants on.

Dave went after Rob as soon as he was dressed, and Rob, laughing, hightailed it. Rob got away easily: Dave's heart wasn't in the chase. He wasn't in a rush. His retribution would take months to plan.

The pickup with the Magi had only gone a half mile down the road before Mark's blanket was lost to a crosswind and frozen fingers. The biting cold wrenched Charles out of his funk and he reverted to character.

"D-damn it George, you let go of the blanket. Now, we-we'll free-freeze our butts off."

"Hey, you h-had a chance to h-hold onto it. Don't blame me for everything. This whole d-damned night was your idea."

"Yeah," said Bill, "you haven't h-helped a whole bunch, since we, we . . . oh my God, look at that," and he pointed toward the road behind them.

Flashing blue lights were rapidly overtaking the truck. A siren wailed and the Magi made out the markings on the squad car. Tom pulled the pickup onto the shoulder, came to a stop, and waited.

Sheriff Robert Lapham, when talking to his children, always referred to patrolman Williams as "your mother's nephew," or "your cousin on your mother's side," although when reporters were around, Williams was "the relative you don't know, not now, not ever."

Patrolman Earl Williams was not one of the brighter lights of the department, but he was Mrs. Lapham's favorite nephew, and Mrs. Lapham was a determined and forceful woman. The Sheriff, under pressure at home, rationalized that, as Williams was deeply religious, if not polished or bright, he wouldn't embarrass the department if they kept him on night duty from Sunday to Thursday, and used him to fill in on family holidays like Thanksgiving and Christmas.

Patrolman Williams got out of his squad car, put on his hat, and walked to the back of the old Ford F-150. "Son of a bitch! What the Sam Hill is going on here? Who the hell are you guys, and Jesus Christ, what in God's name do you mother-suckers think you're doing?"

Earl normally did not use profanity; but he'd taken to watching police shows on cable, and he thought a little salty language made him sound more professional. He was not entirely sure what some of the words meant and occasionally put them together in unique combinations, to the amusement of other officers and the befuddlement of civilians.

The cold and the profanity brought Charles back to life. He was deeply offended by the abrupt manner of address and crude language. He firmly believed those words should never be used off the golf course, where he used them frequently himself.

Charles summoned all the dignity he could, sucked in his gut, stood ramrod straight, and registered his objections: "Sir, you w-will please keep a civil t-tongue. We are the three wise men, and you sh-should know b-better than to address anyone so rudely."

Standing to deliver a rebuke gives it more force—usually. The speech might have chastened Williams had Charles been able to speak without his teeth chattering or had he been wearing one of his tailored suits. However, Bill was sitting on a corner of one of the few shreds of costume remaining to Charles, and those shreds departed Charles's paunchy body as he stood. This was not lost on trooper Williams, although it had not registered with Charles.

Williams had never before been lectured on manners, which was gross negligence on the part of his parents, and he certainly had not been lectured on any topic by a naked fat guy standing in the bed of an old pickup. Other things forced their attention on Williams before he could respond.

In the soft moonlight and occasional glare of passing headlights, Charles looked like a naked Pillsbury doughboy. Tires screeched and horns honked as gawking drivers wandered from lane to lane. Children in passing cars asked their fathers why Santa was naked, and one observant little boy asked his father why Santa had two white beards, above and below. Fred, the boy's father, glanced over his shoulder to look at Charles and, inadvertently, turned the steering wheel. The movement sent the car into the ditch.

Sam, the driver behind Fred's car, was on autopilot, absently following the taillights of Fred's car. Sam was driving home from his job flipping burgers. He had worked up the courage to ask Marcy for a date the following night, and she had accepted. Tonight, his attention was on the next day's possibilities.

He'd never kissed a girl, but Sam was an optimist. His mind was on an imaginary amorous wrestling match in the back seat. There is nothing like complete ignorance of a subject coupled to a fertile imagination to produce riveting dreams. Hollywood and political campaigns depend on it.

Sam's libido was in overdrive when he followed Fred's car into the ditch and rear-ended it. Fortunately, as his dream became more and more absorbing, Sam reduced the pressure on the accelerator. The crash didn't cause injuries and barely registered on Sam's mind.

Williams turned to follow the screech of tires, splintering glass, and metallic crunch as sheet metal greeted bumpers. He stood openmouthed as the decibel level soared. Stunned, he staggered backward into the pickup and turned to face Charles. Well, not face him, really. Charles was still standing in the back of the pickup, as startled as Williams by the chaos.

Williams was repulsed by the view of curly white hair and . . . other things that nearly hit him in the nose when he whirled around. It was a mental picture Williams was sure would take years of therapy to shed. He'd been in therapy a few times and had a feel for this kind of thing. It would be years.

In a paroxysm of righteous indignation, Williams barked, "Jesus Christ, you God-damned fool, sit down. Sit down now!"

Charles, finally aware that he was stark naked, was mortified and sat quickly.

Recovering a few shreds of his composure, Williams asked Bill and George, "If you guys are the wise men, where the hell are your camels and where is Jesus?"

Through chattering teeth, Bill said "I ho-hope I n-never see those miserable G-god- damned camels again," and ended in a mighty sneeze.

"I hope they f-find J-J-Jesus soon. The last I saw of him, he was ascending, and, then he was flying. It w-was so beautiful." The innocence and feeling with which George said this gave it the ring of truth, although hypothermia had more to do with it.

Williams assumed this was freaking nonsense.

An ambulance tore past, siren blaring and emergency lights whirling, headed in the direction of the amphitheater. Recovering from his embarrassment, Charles watched the receding lights. "I b-bet they f-found Jesus in the trees. I hope he's o-okay."

Williams called for backup. Turning to Tom, still in the driver's seat, he said, "And you, very slowly, hand me your driver's license." After a cursory exam of the license, he asked, "What's your story?"

Tom was nervous. He had indulged in a beer, maybe three, with his buddies in the parking lot when Elaine wasn't looking. One more DUI and his license was toast.

That was nothing compared to what Elaine was likely to do to him when she found out. He attempted to think, an exercise he always found difficult under pressure. Pictures of a furious Elaine paralyzed his mind. Apprehension, followed by panic, shouldered rational thought aside every time he tried to formulate an explanation. Nothing he could think of sounded credible.

Tom released a long sigh and rested his forehead on the steering wheel before turning to face Williams. "It's just like they said, officer. They are the three wise men; they got caught in a camel fight, and Jesus bungeed to the trees."

Williams felt as though he was in an asylum. Hoping to find a rational explanation for this fiasco, he announced, "Listen up. Each of you will take a breathalyzer test, one at a time. I'll give each of ya one 'ah these." He handed Tom a breathalyzer. "Ya'll will blow into it, when I tell ya, and slowly hand it back to me."

Even Tom passed the test. The men in the pickup were either on the worst smelling street drug of all time or were a group of psychos and deviants. Williams thought "deviant" seemed a good description for three semi-naked men huddling—or was it snuggling—together in the back of a pickup.

Williams turned pale. His minister had warned him of pagans and Satanists who mixed blasphemous versions of Christian rites with deviant sexual practices in their worship. His heart raced, and his mouth was so dry he couldn't swallow. Keeping an eye on the four in the pickup, he backed toward his cruiser and called his dispatcher. "I've discovered a satanic cult. It has all the earmarks: naked perverts, the works."

"Another satanic cult, Earl? That will be three you've uncovered this fall. The other two were a fraternity party and a Boy Scout troop exploring a cave," replied the dispatcher. "Let's complete the investigation before we draw conclusions, shall we, Earl?"

The sarcasm and lack of professional courtesy made Williams indignant, but events were moving too fast for him to dwell on it. The backup arrived, and conferring with Williams, one of the newly arrived officers covered his nose. "What in God's name are these guys on? Have they all been rolling in crap? Jesus, it stinks."

George heard the reference to Christ and corrected the officer. "No, Jesus bungeed out, maybe to the trees."

Williams glared at George while more backup arrived. These officers began checking the condition of people in the ditched cars and worked the traffic to keep it moving.

Williams heard his name on the radio he wore on his shoulder. That radio's reception along this stretch of road was poor, but he heard the department's dispatcher say, "Car 223 . . . identified . . . pick . . . stopped, over"

"Go ahead."

"They . . . Magi . . . camel . . . Jesus found . . . trees. Tell them . . . found . . . pine trees . . . take . . . hospital. All okay. Repeat . . . and Jesus . . . hospital."

The dispatcher had confirmed an impossible alibi. Williams, a man who took everything literally, was shaken to his core. He was already in a delicate mental balance. Aware he was unqualified for his job and with no friends in the department, he had become withdrawn and depressed. Few things are as corrosive to a man's self-esteem as knowing he's incompetent, but Williams found solace in his religion, and he clung to it, ferociously. He looked at his radio as though it were trying to bite him.

Williams gave the shivering Magi a final glance, slowly walked back to his cruiser, and sat in the driver's seat. He didn't look at the other officers or acknowledge them when they spoke. He focused on a distant bend in the highway and began humming, then singing, *Oh, Little Town of Bethlehem*.

The two officers watched Williams. He didn't respond to them, but he didn't appear to be a danger to himself or others. The senior officer asked Williams if he could hold his side arm for him, just to keep it safe. Williams handed it to him without comment, never taking his eyes off the distant road or missing a word of the old carol. The officers turned and walked back to the pickup and the suspects, occasionally looking back at Williams and shaking their heads.

As they walked, the officer who arrived first made his position clear. "I am not putting these stinkers in my cruiser."

"Me neither," said the other, "but you heard the radio. Whatever it was, their story checked out. They seem harmless; we have the license plate number, the driver's ID, and the three old guys look cold enough to go into hypothermia if we don't get 'em warm."

They approached the pickup. Tom spoke for the group. He had time to compose an answer, and these officers seemed willing to listen. "We were at the Living Nativity Pageant. These guys played the wise men. The camels got into a fight and spit smelly stuff all over. These three stunk so bad we had to hose 'em off. I was headed back to the church to get them into hot showers when we were stopped."

"How far to the church?"

"Another mile and we'll be there."

Turning to the men in the back of the pickup, the officer said, "You guys look pretty cold. I'll get a blanket from my cruiser, and you," he added, pointing at Tom, "get these guys in a hot shower when we get to the church. I'll lead in the squad car. We can take them to the hospital if they seem incoherent, but let's get 'em to a hot shower first." The officer took a breath and nearly gagged. "It might take two or three showers to get 'em clean."

That settled the matter, and the sad little caravan headed up the highway.

The officers working the traffic jam and minor accidents soon had traffic moving. As they all wanted to get home at a reasonable hour, they elected not to hand out citations. Sam was the exception.

An officer made sure Fred and his family were not injured before talking to Sam. "Are you okay, son?"

"Huh?"

"I asked if you were all right. Have you been injured?"

"Injured? How?" Sam's mind was only partially in the present. Part of it was still in the future, burying itself in the sweet tresses of Marcy's long black hair. Or was it brown? Sam tried to remember. And it wasn't really long, maybe "medium length" would describe it better, but she did have hair. Sam was sure of that.

"Let me ask the questions, son," the officer said. "Do you have anything against Fred Wilson?"

"No. Who's he?"

"He's the gentleman driving the car you rear-ended."

"Oh." Sam had a sinking feeling this had something to do with why his car was in the ditch.

"If you didn't have anything against him, can you tell me why you left the highway, drove into the ditch, and hit the rear of his car?"

Sam looked at the officer blankly for a moment before moaning, "Dad's going to kill me." He buried his head in his hands, as he realized that tomorrow's date was not going to happen. He wondered if he would die of boredom or virginity first. So far, it looked like a toss-up.

The officer satisfied himself that Sam wasn't drunk or on drugs. Trying to speed the process up, he asked, "Were you distracted by the old guy in the pickup truck that was stopped over there?" He pointed toward the spot where Tom's pickup had been.

"Old guy?" asked Sam.

"Yes, the naked old guy in the pickup."

"You mean somebody didn't have any clothes on?"

"That's usually what the word 'naked' means."

"Where was that?" asked Sam.

It dawned on the officer that, wherever Sam had been physically, he hadn't been anywhere near the highway mentally. Another teenager daydreaming behind the wheel, he concluded, and gave Sam a ticket for inattentive driving.

Chapter 21

The Heirs' Story

Rockburg, 2013

If the wish to be a grandparent is a gentle form of revenge, Doc, Mary, Linda, and Mark would have loved watching their children cope as parents as the heirs and their families gathered at the Westphalia Inn on December 23. The private drive that brought the families to the Inn wound through a forty-acre woodlot of maple and pine. It was a miniature fairyland; green pines were interspersed between maples, black against the previous night's snowfall. The maples' hoarfrost-covered branches and twigs sparkled in the morning light. Even the adults half expected to see elves peeking from under the pine trees.

As they stood in line in the lobby to check in, Wally's sister, Sophie, congratulated herself that her toddler, Betsy, was strapped firmly in a stroller, as was Julie's daughter, Emma. At least these two, the youngest of the kids, were under parental control, or so the adults thought. They hadn't counted on their older boys.

Sophie took her hands off the stroller to adjust the bags she was carrying and turned to ask her husband which room they were in. Julie did the same. Julie's son Danny and Sophie's son Rick each latched onto his sister's stroller and raced down a wing of the Westphalia. Sophie, Julie, and their husbands didn't see the toddlers again for half an hour, although they heard Betsy's happy shrieks and Emma's "faster Danny, faster" several times, always around the next corner in the motel's hallways. The frantic adults caught up with the stroller grand prix at the entrance to the indoor water park.

After a few swats and firm lectures, Danny, Rick, and their cousins had pizza and movies in one of their motel rooms, while the adults recuperated over dinner and drinks at the Westphalia's restaurant. Emma and Betsy were at their sides, strapped into booster seats on chairs without wheels. The group relaxed as Seth's wife talked to the other women, and the word "benign" was whispered around the table.

Seth stood and rapped a fork on his water glass. "It's Christmas. The kids are wired, and none of us are in a mood to work. How many of you have read Dad's book?" He looked around the table. Only Josh and Julie raised their hands.

"How far did you get?" Seth asked.

"I've read through the Nativity, but the 'Doofus' character has me stumped," Julie said.

Josh nodded. "Same here."

Seth nodded. "Yeah, me, too. Would you tell the rest what you mean, in case some haven't started reading the book?"

Josh explained the character of Doofus as best he could, but admitted it made no sense in the context of the codicil requirement. "I have no idea how to take Doofus anywhere," he concluded.

"That's where we're at," Seth said. "We have little to discuss, since none of us knows anything new. I suspect Dad and Linda arranged this vacation for us to visit and reinforce family ties, not to work. I vote we go to church Christmas Eve, like Dad and Linda wanted, have dinner at the house on Christmas, enjoy ourselves, and read the book when we get home." He looked around the table. "Anyone have a better idea?"

"Nope," Jed said. "As hyped as the kids are, somebody's going to drown if all the kids aren't supervised full time."

"Al said there wasn't a time limit," Julie said. "Wally, Josh, is this okay with you?"

"Wally and I are going skiing tomorrow with some . . . new friends." Josh blushed when he saw several of the women at the table smirking. They'd met Wally, Josh and friends in the lobby, and the friends wore spike heels and very tight sweaters.

As the party broke up, Julie whispered to Josh. "Can we talk?"

Josh nodded. "My room, now?"

Josh's door was ajar and Julie walked in without knocking.

"What's going on?" Josh asked.

Julie took a seat at a small table near the window and looked at Josh. "Was there anything odd about your copy of Dad's book?"

"Yeah," Josh grabbed a chair from a nearby desk and sat at the table, "It was a lot longer than I expected."

"Nothing else?"

"Nope. It's not the type of book I usually read. If there's something odd for its genre—"

"No," Julie shook her head, "nothing that subtle." She leaned back in the chair, looked at the ceiling, and bit her lower lip. "I don't know how to say this without sounding . . ." She leaned forward, put her elbows on the table and buried her face in her hands.

Josh put a hand on her arm. "Just spit it out. I'll believe anything after that smell at the bank."

Julie sat upright and folded her arms across her chest. "When I was reading, when I reached the part about the odor, when I reached that part on the page, I smelled it."

"Cow shit?"

"Yeah, ah, cow-flop. I thought it was my imagination. You know, the power of suggestion. I closed the book, and the smell disappeared. I opened it to another page, nothing. I opened it to the page where Dad described the smell, nothing. I read the paragraph about Dad smelling cow-flop, and I smelled it."

Josh shrugged. "So, it was suggestion?"

"That's what I thought, until . . ." Julie buried her face in her hands again.

"Until what?"

"I'd been reading in our living room. I heard laughter coming from the closet by the front door. It was soft, barely audible. Todd wasn't home. I wouldn't have had the courage to look in the closet, but the laugh sounded, well, happy. I can't explain it."

"So?" Josh asked. "What did you find?"

"Coats and boots, and an extra wand for the vacuum cleaner I forgot was in the closet."

"Sounds as though your imagination got the better of you."

"That's what I thought, but when I returned to the book, it was open to a page near the end, and somebody had turned down the page corner to mark it." Julie looked at Josh. "I never do that. Am I going nuts?"

"Was anybody else in the room?"

"Nope. Just me and a book with a mind of its own."

"Did you read the page?" Josh asked.

"No. I freaked out. I went to Emma's room and rocked her. She didn't want to be rocked, but I needed to hold somebody. Todd got home about the time Emma fell back to sleep."

"Anything else happen?"

"Nothing, but I haven't touched the book again, either."

Both were silent until Julie stood. "Maybe I just dreamed the whole thing," she said. "I was exhausted that night. Maybe I fell asleep while reading." She shoved her chair up to the table. "But, if it was a dream, it seemed damned real, and it doesn't explain the marked page."

"Or the odor in the bank closet after the reading of the codicil," Josh added.

The heirs were busy the next day, chatting with each other and chaperoning their children from the moment the water park opened until mid-afternoon naptime. The older kids whined about it, but the naps gave the adults a break and helped when the heirs rounded their charges up that evening and dressed them for church.

The First (and only) Presbyterian Church of Rockburg, the church in which they were raised, seemed smaller than what Doc's children remembered. Little had changed, other than their perspective, and they were just as late for the service as they'd been twenty-five years earlier. Doc and Linda's families took up the first two rows of pews, the only ones open by the time they arrived.

It was a small church, and many of the families had attended the church for more than a century. A succession of pastors tried to update the order of worship, but their parishioners took tradition seriously. Many of them rose at five o'clock to milk cows every morning and worked twelve-hour days. They were half asleep by the time they reached their pew. Changing the service would have interfered with one of their few opportunities for a nap. Thus, little of the service had changed since the heirs last attended. Even Josh, now an evangelical atheist, remembered the responses and hymns.

Doc's children were ambushed that night. Each was surprised by memories of Christmases past, absent family members, and forgotten dreams, as they relaxed into the cadence of the service. Julie remembered Elspeth's best friend who played the organ every Sunday and cried on Julie's shoulder at Elspeth's funeral.

Seth, Josh, and Jed looked at the Christmas tree and then at each other. Seth raised an eyebrow, nodded toward the Christmas tree, and all three smiled. Tears welled up while they remembered the Christmas communion an elderly minister forgot where he was in the Lord's Prayer and started over again. Later, in the same service, a corpulent church Elder toppled the Christmas tree while distributing the communion grape juice.

The falling tree startled the minister out of whatever daydream he was in. He stopped absently munching on the sacramental bread, and aghast, pushed the plate of bread away. Seeing the minister shove the bread away had sent Seth and Jed over the edge. They'd fallen off the pew and collapsed on the floor, hands over their mouths, laughing silently and hiding under the pew.

Remembering that night, Seth leaned over to Jed and whispered, "We wouldn't have caught hell from Doc if Josh hadn't stayed where he was and laughed out loud."

The twenty-year-old memories and Seth's comment started Jed laughing. He pulled out a handkerchief, covered his face, and pretended to blow his nose.

Doc's kids filed out of the church at the end of the service, shook hands with the minister and helped their smaller children with coats and snowsuits. People they hadn't seen in decades—and many whose names they couldn't remember –greeted them on the church steps and on the sidewalk by the church. Each busied themselves with others to forestall tears.

Doc's Manuscript

PART IV

Chapter 22: Jed's Friend

Doc's Manuscript

Rockburg, December 20, 1987

It was the noon rush, and the parking lot was crowded. Crowded, hell—it was full. Couldn't the damned Christmas shoppers eat at home one day of the week?

The morning had been long, and clients with routine calls demanded to be first on my route: three emergency calls on snow-covered back roads, miles apart from each other, and farm driveways plugged with snow. Now I had to circle the full parking lot of a fast-food joint in the town next to Rockburg, searching for a parking place. The only empty slots were the ones the snowplow used to pile snow when they cleared the lot that morning. I put my pickup in four-wheel drive and waddled it into one of the snowbanks.

There, damn it. It was parked. Four-wheel is handy that way.

Patience would have been better. The door wouldn't open because of the snow packed against it. I swiveled on my butt and pushed it open with my feet. The snow topped my boots and packed against my ankles when I stepped out of the truck. Irritated, I was careless as I took my first steps and slipped, fell, and banged my head on the side of the truck.

Way to go, Sherlock. My bare hands hit frozen snow, chunks of ice, and the concrete of the parking lot when I fell, since I had left my gloves in the truck. Now, my head hurt, and my hands were frozen and cut. More careful now, I made it to the back of the truck and bare pavement without further damage.

I swore under my breath as I pried the boots off my steel-toed work shoes, slipped off my coat and coveralls, and opened the back of the truck's Bowie veterinary body. I stuffed the dirty clothing in and slammed the door shut. The insulated underwear, jeans, wool shirt, and hooded sweatshirt I still wore were enough to stay warm.

A kid, maybe eight years old, walked past me, trailing his mother to the Burger King entrance. "Mommy, how come that man can use those words and I can't?"

The lady scowled at me as she opened the restaurant door. "Hush. Just because he doesn't know better doesn't mean you don't. He probably never went to school."

Great. Twenty published scientific papers and I'm a poster child for illiteracy. The day just kept getting better. *Where the hell is Mary? She said she'd meet me here for lunch.*

I normally picked up a burger and fries at the drive-through. I'd eat with one hand, answer the truck radio with the other (clients wondering what was keeping me), and drive with my knees to the next farm. That was the only way I could finish work by seven in the evening from September to the end of December and March through April. The hours were long, the days short, and weekends just two more days to work.

I stood in line at the counter. *Damned lines take forever.* Someone nudged my elbow.

"Where have you been?" I asked Mary.

"Testy today, are we?" She smiled and kissed me on the cheek. "Have you managed to offend everyone in the line already, or do I get to watch?"

Chastened, I apologized and described my day. We ordered, got our food, found a table, and caught up on preparations for Christmas as we ate.

A comment by Mary left me puzzled. "What do you mean Jed didn't want to bring his friend home over break?"

She shrugged. "I think we embarrass him, or he's afraid the family will embarrass him. Who knows what kids think?"

"When does he get home from school?"

"Tomorrow, I think."

I pointed at Mary with a French fry. "You think?"

"It was all I could do to get him to tell me what week he was coming home."

"Some things haven't changed. You'd think we were control freaks." I sat back in my chair and glared at the table. I knew better than to glare at Mary.

"He remembers what you did to Seth."

"That was reasonable. Seth should have known better."

"He was barely twenty."

"And not likely to see twenty-one, if he kept that up. What was I supposed to do?"

"Don't start—"

"The damned fool drove all the way to Fargo through a January blizzard and didn't think to let us know he'd gotten there safely. The Interstate was closed, for God's sake. Three days and nobody at his place picked up the goddamned phone.

Mary leaned toward me and put a hand on my arm. "Keep it down. People are looking at you." She picked up her coffee and held it with both hands to warm them. We were hit with a cold draft every time the restaurant door opened. "I agree with you, but—"

"But he never pulled that stunt again, did he? I wouldn't have called his Department Chair if—"

Mary put her sandwich down, leaned back in her chair, and looked at me as though I had two heads. "Jack! Think how he felt. How would you feel if you'd been pulled out of class, escorted to the departmental office, and told to call your father before the professor got another call at night?"

I steamed, quietly, and thought of my first winter at the University of Wisconsin. I'd been struggling to adjust from a rural high school of one-hundred-seventy students to a world-class university of thirty-five thousand. Used to classes of twenty-five or fewer, I was sitting in lectures with five hundred students, scurrying from class to class, a lemming marching back and forth across a campus two miles long.

That had been twenty-five years ago, but I remembered it like yesterday. It was mid-December and cold, and I was studying between classes in the library of the Dairy Science building, an old brick building on the mall that led to the neoclassical College of Ag Main Hall. The library was small, even for a departmental library, with room for only a few rows of bookshelves and six tables. I loved it, though. Its high ceiling, creaky, wooden floors, and polished oak furniture gave the room character, and the tall, wood-framed windows on the east wall caught the morning light, just as they had in the late 1920s when my father studied there.

I left my coat and books on a library table when I took a study break at the vending machines in the basement. The library door was closed when I returned; a sign on the door said "Faculty Meeting." I'd never felt more lost in my life. I dithered in the hallway, unable to muster the courage to enter the room, and prayed it would be a short meeting.

Fifteen minutes before my next class, I looked at the clock and at the snow outside, and I knocked on the door. I opened the door timidly, poked my head in the room, and asked a group of professors if I could get my coat and books. I wasn't prepared for their reaction.

"Jack, I missed your dad at the Holstein meeting last month. How's he been?" one asked. Another asked how my mother was doing after her surgery for breast cancer. Most of the men in the room were friends of my parents and knew me by name. Agriculture is a small universe. I never felt lost in a lecture hall again, thanks to the kindness of those men.

The way I dealt with Seth didn't compare well to the patience and understanding I encountered during my education. I changed the topic to shopping and holiday parties. We finished our meal and I got back to my farm calls.

I completed my farm calls at a reasonable hour that evening and headed home. As I walked in, I paid close attention to what went on in our household. Seth, a sophomore in college, benched three hundred fifty pounds in his workout. Now, he was down on all fours in the entryway, holding a bone in his mouth and barking at Fang, our thirteen-pound toy poodle.

Julie wandered by, grumbling about an ad on television for a movie starring an actor recently arrested for lewd behavior. She's a sophomore in high school, but I still think of her as my little girl. "Oh brother," she muttered, "the great jerk and his lap puppet coming to a theater near us."

Josh came swinging and leaping down the banister. He careened through the house like a weasel on speed, although I think a weasel would have had better table manners.

I wasn't sure I'd want to bring Mary home to meet these people, and she's their mother—*and* she lives here.

With Seth home from school and the excitement of the season, dinner was rowdy, even for our house. I didn't mind; it was a happy, giggling, joking, and laughing rowdy. I hoped we'd have more meals like that one.

With dinner over and the dishes done, the kids were sprawled on the family room floor, playing Monopoly. Mary was in the living room in a comfortable chair, a lamp behind her. She was knitting a Christmas present for one of the kids, and I was balancing the checkbook at my computer when a loud bang of something dropping came from the garage. Startled, I looked around. No one else had moved. I appeared to be the only one who'd heard the noise. I'd learned that Doofus was nearby and wanted to chat when I heard things that others didn't. It wasn't safe to ignore him when he was making noises that loud, but I didn't want anyone coming out to the garage and see me in an animated discussion with my truck.

I glanced toward the living room. Mary was busy and comfortable. No problem there. The kids? Not a problem. "Hey, anybody want to come out and help me clean up my woodworking space? Seth, I could use some help."

I'd just finished a vanity for our master bathroom. The garage was a mess; wood scraps, sawdust, and tools were scattered all over. Even the kids complained about it.

Seth pretended he didn't hear me. Josh and Julie gave me a quick look and focused on their game. If pretending to be deaf worked for Seth, they probably figured it was worth a try.

Success. None of the kids would come near the garage door tonight. I tried not to look smug as I tossed on a sweatshirt and parka and went to see what twinkle-toes wanted.

Chapter 23: Cost Vs. Price

Doc's Manuscript

Rockburg, December 20, 1987

It was cold in the garage, and I shivered while groping for the light switch.

"Further to yer right, Doc, and a little higher."

"Thanks." I adjusted and hit the switch. Doofus, in a freshly starched tutu with sleigh bells around his waist, leaned against the driver's side of my truck. I can never look at him—western boots, beer belly, handlebar mustache, and pink tutu—without smiling. His scanty costume made me shiver tonight, but he seemed comfortable and happy to see me.

"Doofus, how've you been, buddy? How's your Nativity project?"

"Oh, it's over." He sighed and looked around the garage.

No bragging tonight? "Just curious," I lied. I'd gotten the bare bones account from Mark the day after the pageant—bare bones because he didn't want to talk about it either. "What brings you here?"

"I figured I'd drop by and make sure you was all right, not getting inta trouble by your lonesome or anything. Besides, we have things to talk about, and I've got plenty of time to spend on your projects now. How've ya been?"

"Tired, but okay. The boys are coming home from college and everyone's getting into the spirit." His comment about my projects was unsettling; that was a topic I wanted to avoid. "I've never seen a Christmas pageant with camels. How did it go?"

Doofus avoided eye contact and spoke faster and louder than normal. "They were busy cleaning up when I left. Had a good crowd—hell, a great crowd—and they put on a real show." He looked at his boots and tried to clean the heel of one with the toe of the other. "Boy, they put on a show."

He shook his head and checked his fingernails. I'd never known Doofus to give a damn about his hygiene.

"But ya already know what camels look like and how a Nativity pageant goes." He looked around my garage. "Say, what's all this wood ya got round here? And, whoo-ee, look at the size of this table saw. I been thrown out of bars smaller than the table on that saw. What's this thing-amah-jigger here?" Doofus pointed to a set of precision-machined and calibrated aluminum bars.

"It's a jig to make it easy to cut exact angles."

"Why'd ya need a thing like that?"

"Long story. You probably don't have time for it."

"Nah, go ahead. I love to listen to what ya been up to. It always makes me feel better."

I decided not to think about that comment. "Gee, thanks. You're sure you wouldn't rather talk about the Nativity?"

"Oh, ya seen one, you've seen 'em all. Go ahead with your story."

Doofus relaxed. He was leaning so hard against the truck it was tilting a little. He must have been hitting the brew hard lately.

"Well, last January, I was getting ready for bed, taking off and cleaning my contacts under the tap. The water sprayed rather than flowing smoothly because a screen in the faucet was broken. I told Mary I could fix that. She claimed she'd been after me about it for three years."

Doofus smirked. "Always quick on the uptake, aren't ya?"

"I took another look at it. The threads to hold the screen in place were badly corroded. The faucet had to be replaced, and there were tiny cracks in the sink. The sink was molded into the countertop, so the faucet, sink, and countertop all had to go. Mary never liked the vanity and cabinets, and I knew she'd want those replaced if I put in a new countertop. A 25 cent replacement screen turned into a $4,500 remodeling job, before I made it from the sink to our bed."

Doofus was beaming. "So, it was like most of your projects, huh? This is just the story I needed tonight."

That didn't make me feel better. "Do you know what they charge for bathroom vanities? My God, that was a shock. I figured I could buy a table saw, jigs to get the angles right, and build the whole thing myself for a third of the cost."

"Didn't know you was a carpenter."

"I'm not. Mary encourages me to do woodwork because her father was a carpenter. Heck, I can't pound a nail straight, but cabinets are glued and screwed together. That was all I knew, so I was in a fool's paradise."

"That should put ya in familiar territory." Doofus didn't laugh out loud, but those silly bells he wore tinkled for the next five minutes. It was hard to finish the story.

"Anyway, I knew a store that carried professional-grade equipment. I fell in love with that saw. It was so big it came in pieces. Josh and I had to put it together. The pieces were heavy, but I could stand upright again after a bottle of aspirin and a week's rest."

I walked over to the saw. "Damn, isn't it beautiful? And look at this fence." I couldn't help myself; I ran a hand over the fence, an adjustable guide running parallel to the blade.

"Want me to step out for a minute, Doc? Leave ya alone with your saw?" He snickered and slapped me on the back.

"We could talk about the pageant if I'm boring you."

"No, no. Go ahead. Didn't mean to interrupt. With yer talent, I'm sure disaster is just round the corner."

I was still sore about his comment. "You're sure you wouldn't rather tell me about your pageant?"

"Yup. This is a tonic for what's ailing me now. Being successful all the time can be boring, and your stories are a window on a side of life I don't see often."

That was hogwash, but I decided to tell the story first and get the truth out of him later. "Mary and I argued about how wide the countertop should be while I made the three units that fit under it. None of the units fit the countertop we bought, but I installed the units, with a little shimming here and there. Mary said it looked okay, although it was the first time she'd seen a two-by-four used as a shim."

I wasn't sure Doofus understood any of this, but he looked entranced. That's not a normal response to my stories, so I was happy to rattle on, describing how, when I installed the faucet and knobs, I had to remove the whole countertop to tighten leaky connections because the, ah, shims didn't allow room to use a faucet wrench. For each test, I had to lift the seventy-pound, four-foot countertop onto the cabinets, connect the water lines, find the leaks, disconnect the pipes, remove the countertop, and carry it into the bedroom. I'd lay it upside down on our bed, tighten the connections, pick the damned thing up, carry it back to the bathroom, and put it back on the cabinets. It was like waltzing with a lady wrestler who wanted to lead. I called it the "dance of the never-ending installation."

I was beat by the end of the day, but the sink's drain still leaked. More tightening might have fixed it, but it could crack the sink, too. I stuck a pail under it and went back to the builder's supply store.

The staff all looked like teenagers. I described my problem to the oldest one and asked if I should tighten the connection or disassemble the connections and use more plumber's putty to seal the leak.

The kid looked shocked. He told me plumber's putty would discolor, pit, and corrode the artificial stone of the sink, and my life would become a living hell.

I paused as I remembered that day. The kid hadn't looked old enough to be married, but he sure seemed to understand the institution.

I skipped over the embarrassing parts of the story and cut to the chase. "It took a year to rebuild and reinstall the cabinets, but they're solid oak, beautiful, and exactly what Mary wanted."

"Ya built 'em all over again?"

"Twice. Finally learned how to make a set of cabinets. I was feeling good about the money I saved 'til Mary reminded me that things bought by married men come as sets, His and Hers. Mine was going to be a table saw and sewing machine set."

That seemed to please Doofus even more. Damned if I knew why.

"I complained at the woodworking store that the saw cost me four times the price they quoted. You should have seen their faces. I had 'em going for a while, until one of the guys asked me to explain. When I told him about the sewing machine, he reminded me we had discussed price, not cost.

"I learned three lessons from this fiasco. Wishful thinking isn't planning, and every decision we make has a price and a cost, and they're different. I think those two ideas cover most of the stupid things I've done."

I let Doofus think about that for a second before finishing my thought. "Perhaps they aren't as inclusive for you, with your broader experience in these things."

Doofus got halfway through a shrug, looked at me quizzically, and opened his mouth as though to speak. He stopped, looked confused, closed his mouth, and dropped one hand to his hip. Chin in the other hand, he thought a moment. Apparently deciding, as usual, that it's more important to act than to understand, he stood up straight and announced, "Aww, those ain't much for lessons. Any damned fool should know that."

"Should know it, but wars are started by men who know the price and ignore the cost. All the gold and silver of South America didn't keep Spain from bankruptcy when she tried to carve out an empire in Europe during the seventeenth century, and Napoleon III figured he'd teach Prussia a lesson in 1877 'cause Bismarck hurt his pride. Remember how that ended?"

"Ah, that's ancient—"

"We had a war that was supposed to be necessary for stability in Southeast Asia. Remember the cost? Something like fifty-eight thousand Americans dead, even more were seriously injured, and over a million Vietnamese and Laotian people killed. We lost the war, but the area is still stable and we're happily trading with our former enemy."

"For Christ's sakes, ya can't . . ." Doofus shook his head and looked at the floor.

Neither of us spoke. He broke the tension as the silence became uncomfortable. "And?"

I frowned. "What do you mean, 'And?'"

"Ya said ya learned three lessons. What's the other one?"

"Oh, yeah. Never buy a tool from an English major."

Doofus chuckled. "Would ya build the cabinets again?"

"Mary wants me to work on the kitchen next, but we've wasted enough time on my story. Let's hear about the Nativity."

Chapter 24: Wood Putty

Doc's Manuscript

Rockburg, December 20, 1987

Doofus flinched when I mentioned the Nativity. He covered his reaction with a dismissive wave of his hand. "Oh, nothing to it. Just like every other Nativity."

He picked up a piece of wood and examined it. "Ya know, I always enjoyed woodworking. With a gob 'ah wood putty, ya can fix the little mistakes ya make, like the angles that aren't right or the measurements ya got wrong. I love wood putty. Best tool I had. Hell, I remember projects that were one quarter wood putty by weight, but they looked good."

"Doofus, the Nativity?"

"I'm more interested in that cost idea of yours. I knew a kid who wrote a book about cost when he grew up. The Cost of . . . hmm, Cost of Getting it Right? No. Cost of Doing Good? Nah, that ain't right either. Let's see, maybe, hmm . . .Cost of Discipleship. Yeah, that was it, but I don't remember him doing any woodwork."

"You knew someone who wrote a book on theology?"

"Oh, I've helped out a few, 'specially since they started taking to television, but this was a kid I knew years ago. We were friends 'til he turned eleven or twelve."

"What was his name?"

"It was a long time ago. Ditter or Ditrick something. It'll come ta me." Doofus rested his chin on the palm of one hand, his elbow on the truck.

"Sounds German. Was it Dietrich?"

"Ya, by golly, it was. Did ya know him?"

"Lucky guess. Go on."

"Well, name was ah, Dietrich Barnhouse, or Boneshufler, or somethin' like that. Like I said, he didn't listen to me much after he turned eleven or so, and I gave up trying to help him. Ever notice how some people just won't let ya help 'em?"

Sounded like a smart kid, but I hid my smile and shrugged.

"Anyways, this kid wouldn't listen to me. Came to a bad end, as I remember. He wouldn't stop telling people what he thought of 'em and what he figured they ought to do." Doofus paused in thought. "There was a lot of stuff going on about then."

"Volunteering advice isn't popular," I said.

"Ya know, I think he got himself executed. Yup, I remember now. He got hung."

"Oh, my!" My mind was reeling. "Doofus, was it Dietrich Bonhoeffer?[3] And was that 'stuff' going on World War II?"

"Bonhoeffer, yup, that was the kid's name. Nice kid 'til he got so danged serious."

"Good Lord, Doofus, you knew Dietrich Bonhoeffer?"

"Yeah, so? We didn't talk much as he got older. Last time I talked ta him he tried ta tell me that I had to learn to git stuff right, to do the right thing. He was spouting a bunch a' bull about doing what's right, whatever the cost."

"That sounds like . . ." but Doofus was on a roll.

"He tried to tell me that using wood putty in the shop was like pretending to live right—makes your work look better, or fills the cracks, or something like that. Said it was doing it on the cheap if I used wood putty, took shortcuts, and didn't learn to do stuff right—

3 Dietrich Bonhoeffer, 1906-1945. German theologian and resistance member, executed by the Nazis by hanging in Flossenbürg concentration camp, April 9, 1945.

prissy little bast–ah, kid. He claimed looks weren't as important as what's underneath. Ticked me off, 'cause I take wood putty seriously."

There was a great bang as Doofus brought his fist down on the truck for emphasis. I made a mental note not to criticize wood putty.

"Say, ya got a cold beer and maybe some pretzels? All this yammering on has got me thirsty."

I got us each a cold one and some chips. I couldn't decide if Doofus was clueless or playing mind games with me. Neither subtlety nor guile were in his nature. Bonhoeffer's critique hit too close for me, too. Confused, I tried to get the conversation back on familiar ground.

"Okay, Doofus. What went wrong with your Nativity? No more bull. What happened?"

"What do ya mean?"

"Doofus, I've raised three boys. I've heard every dodge and excuse you can imagine. You can't give me a cock and bull story about your Nativity, ignore every question, and not tip your hand. You'd crow from every roof and shove it down my throat if the pageant went well."

"Well, maybe it didn't go quite like I planned." He avoided looking at me and again spoke rapidly. "The camels didn't get along. They might 'ah spit at each other once or twice, as I remember. The ascension of Jesus could have gone better, I guess." Doofus shuddered at the memory, and his bells tinkled again, "but the crowd sure got a show."

He grimaced, stood up straight, and sucked in his gut. "At least, it wasn't boring, like some stories I've heard."

"So, you'd do it all over again?"

"I guess, well, oh, cripes, look at the time. I'm supposed to be in conference with some guys that really done great with my help."

"Who's that?"

"Oh, long list, long list. Important guys. Some 'ah them radio and television talk shows. Hell, one all-day news channel couldn't get through the day without me. They don't ask a lot 'ah dumb questions or waste time cross-checking facts. I got to introduce ya to those guys sometime. Some of 'em could show ya how to get things done."

He slapped me on the back, thanked me for making him feel better, and gave me a big hug.

"Say, I forgot to tell ya. Remember that second project of yours I promised ya I'd work on?" Doofus looked at me expectantly.

I played dumb. Any help from Doofus scared the hell out of me, and projects I hadn't started were on hold for a reason. He'd already coaxed me into making a fool of myself with Rodgers. I tried to put him off. "I don't remember. I'm not done with the first project. I'll be busy on that until February."

"Yer gonna have to learn to multitask, Doc. I promised ya I'd line up a dairy farm for ya. I got three, maybe four, guys who've raised almost enough cash to buy one. They need a partner with cash and experience with cattle, 'cause they don't know a bull from a steer. I'll bet they'll let ya in as a full partner for only a couple thousand."

I tried not to show interest, but 2,000 would be a steal. One-fifth interest in a big dairy farm in my area could cost 200,000 and up. I bit. "Oh. What type of deal?"

"They don't know it yet, but the partners will call ya right after Christmas. You can use the time to line up the cash."

"$2,000, right?"

"Ya got a great sense of humor, Doc. It'll cost $100,000. A second mortgage and your retirement fund should get ya that, and you'll have to sign a note for another $150,000."

"What! My God, you think—" but he was gone before I could tell him to forget it.

My knees knocked and I stumbled through the garage door and into the family room. He meant well, but his track record was terrible, and I wasn't good at saying no.

Chapter 25: Old Ben

Doc's Manuscript

New Orleans, December 27, 1987

Linda shouldn't have needed Elspeth's advice on how to keep her marriage stable; she had ample opportunity to figure that out, hanging around her father's old horse-showing buddies at the state and county fairs in the 1960s.

Old Ben was one of the more colorful characters who showed horses with the Old Man. Properly lubricated with beer, he was a font of questionable advice and embarrassing stories about the Old Man before he met Elspeth. Ben was rarely seen in anything but old bib overalls. On a good day, when he was dirty, disheveled, and sober, Ben was the archetype of a guy you wouldn't want to meet in a dark alley. That would have been a rare sighting, since Ben wasn't often completely sober during the show season.

Ben had done everything Elspeth warned Linda and Doc against, and he had the scars and tattoos to prove it. He was a good storyteller to boot. To Linda and Doc, this put him in the same league as the Oracle at Delphi was for the Greeks.

Elspeth loathed the man.

How a part-time carney and part-time farmer came to have a barn full of antique furniture was another story. It was enough to know that Sotheby's was delighted to handle his estate sale. After that, "Oh, yeah, but Ben said," became a rejoinder to every serious lesson on life the Old Man or Elspeth tried to drill into the kids and called into question the value of sobriety, discretion, and hygiene.

When she was twelve, Linda was resting on a bale of hay behind the tack trunk on which Old Ben was holding court at the State Fair. It was a hot day, so it wasn't unusual when Doc walked up, took a seat by Ben, and pulled a cold beer out of the cooler beside him.

Ben took it away from him and put it back in the cooler. Doc was stunned. He was a few years younger than the legal drinking age, but that never bothered Ben before. Usually it was Ben who offered him the beer.

Before Doc could register a complaint, Ben looked him in the eye. "Some things you can do at any age. You got better things to do on a warm summer night."

Linda didn't have a clue what Ben meant, but Doc seemed to understand and came back an hour later to announce he had a date with a girl Elspeth had told him to avoid.

The silly grin plastered across Doc's face the rest of the afternoon irritated the living daylights out of Linda. Nothing sticks in a younger sister's craw more than a brother who's delirious over something she doesn't understand. So she asked her mother about it.

Elspeth grounded Doc, arranged a full evening of chores for him for the next week, and had a chat with the Old Man. It was private, but not quiet and was repeated often in tack stalls at the State Fair by old guys cackling around a bottle of Jack Daniels.

Mark and Linda would have been spared all the nonsense of the Nativity had Linda remembered Ben's teachings. She could have figured out the cure for whatever problems she thought she and Mark had, without Elspeth's advice. At least this time, Elspeth and Ben would have agreed. Maybe that was why Linda got it right a few nights after the Nativity.

"But it was funny," Linda said. "What happened to your sense of humor?" She adjusted her pillows and snickered, remembering the stunned look on Charles's face caught in the spotlight as the second wad of camel spit hit him.

She nudged Mark in the ribs with her elbow and trailed a fingernail from his kneecap north along the inside of his thigh. "Maybe you had to be there," she whispered in his ear and giggled again.

Mark brushed her hand away and looked in her eyes. "My sense of humor crashed and burned when Jim broke his arm. He was damned lucky he wasn't killed. No way in hell is that funny." He rolled over, put his back to her, and pretended to fall asleep.

Great magnates and princes once had court jesters to prick inflated egos and speak truths others feared to mention. Their position survives in two forms: the stand-up comics, who do for politicians what the news media should be doing; for the common man who's lucky, it's his wife. Mark was so lucky tonight it nearly drove him nuts.

Linda bided her time, waiting for Mark to relax, a sign he thought he'd won. She decided the time was right, as his breathing slowed and the tension left his shoulders. "Jim's doing fine. Dave got his clothes back. Insurance covered everything but the fractured egos, and the media haven't gotten the pictures—yet."

"Oh, my God, pictures?" Mark sat bolt upright. "What pictures?"

Linda fluttered her eyelashes. "Remember the camera you gave me for my birthday? I didn't have anything to do once we got Jim and the shepherds dressed and made up." She picked up a clutch of eight-by-ten photos on the nightstand next to her and showed them to Mark. "I got the pictures back today. These are some of the better shots. Don't you love the one of our naked angel sprinting, with Charles in the background kissing a calf's ass?" She let Mark get a brief look before switching the pictures to her other hand and holding them at arm's length away from him.

Mark lunged across her, grabbing for the pictures. Linda waved them at him. "How about getting me a cassette recorder for my birthday next year? I'd hate to miss Jim's song again. What did he call it, Handy's Dandy?"

Desperate, Mark took another swipe at the pictures and missed.

"How about paying attention to me for a while? Does Charles look better than me? Do I have to get naked on stage like Dave to get a look?" She dropped the pictures and shifted her grip to what she was really after. "Oh, look! I think we have our own little Handy right here."

Mark knew the difference between win/win and lose/lose. This was a win/win if he was man enough to swallow his pride.

The world looked brighter and a lot funnier the next morning. There's nothing like vigorous exercise to make a man forget his troubles, especially those of the "could have" or "might have" variety that are, at root, self-inflicted. That lesson had slipped Mark's mind, which was understandable, as he'd never had the chance to meet Old Ben.

As daylight slipped through the Venetian blinds, Mark rolled over and kissed Linda. "How come after Thanksgiving you didn't speak to me until you signed me up for the Nativity?"

Linda kissed him back. "You were getting home late and too tired to interact with me or the kids, before and after Thanksgiving. We all felt ignored." She turned away from him, on the verge of tears. "I thought you might be having an affair."

Mark thought he'd been ready for any answer, but this caught him off guard. "What? I was putting in extra time at the office, so I could spend more time with you and the kids at Christmas."

Linda turned to look at him, "But you didn't tell me."

Mark didn't have any answer for that and decided action would be better than words, which always seemed to get him into trouble. They were well on the way to properly celebrating the arrival of morning when it dawned on Mark, preoccupied as he was, that their bedroom door was open, the television was on, and it was turned to a Bugs Bunny program.

He took a guess, "Sophie, did you turn the television on?"

A little voice came from the foot of the bed. "Yes, Daddy."

Linda stifled a giggle.

"Why don't you watch the show on the TV in the family room? The screen is bigger, and you'll have a chair all to yourself," Mark suggested.

There was a rustle at the foot of the bed when Sophie stood. She dragged her favorite stuffed bear to the door. "Should I close the door?"

Linda covered her mouth with her pillow. Mark choked back a laugh. "Good idea, honey."

"Can Bobby come with me?"

There was more stirring at the end of the bed, and Bobby stood. He walked to the door and turned back toward the bed. "Come on, Fang. They don't want you to watch them either."

Fang skulked to the door.

The bedroom erupted in laughter when the door closed, followed by a second round of guffaws when Mark and Linda realized that everything their kids heard would be reported to grandma Elspeth. Life was back on a cheerful track.

Elspeth arrived and was feeding the children breakfast when Linda got to the kitchen. As Linda and Mark had a few days off, they decided to take the kids to a petting zoo.

Elspeth was all for it. "It'll give me a chance to introduce my grandchildren to animals and show them Grandma knows her way around the barn. What kind of animals do they have?"

"Donkeys, ponies, a couple of dairy cows, and a few llamas. They have several camels and, sometimes, they give camel rides," Linda said.

"Camels? Are they the same outfit the church rented their camels from?" Elspeth asked.

"They're nearby. I think they're owned by the same company."

Elspeth picked up a stack of dirty dishes and put them in the sink. "Let's get the kids ready. I'd like to meet this Gladys."

Chapter 26

Where both deliberate, the love is slight:
Who ever loved, that loved not at first sight?
—Christopher Marlowe

Doc's Manuscript

New Orleans, December 27and 28, 1987

It was a warm, sunny day, and with Mark and Elspeth to help her ride herd on Wally and Bobby, Linda was looking forward to a relaxing afternoon. She should have known better. It took all three adults to keep track of the boys at the petting zoo. Elspeth was about to recommend leashes for the boys, but a glance at Linda and she decided to suggest it some other time.

At least Sophie was easy to control. She was a little old for a stroller, but it guaranteed they knew where she was.

The family made it through the calves, chickens, ponies, llamas, sheep, and donkeys without incident. The day turned chilly, and the park was nearly empty by the time they arrived at the camel exhibit late in the afternoon. The camel rides were already closed.

"Mommy, I'm cold," Sophie whined.

Linda wiped Sophie's nose and felt her hands. "Mother, we should go home. Sophie's hands are like ice," Linda waved to Mark and motioned him to round up the boys.

Elspeth was concentrating on the sign by the camel exhibit

and didn't hear Linda's plea. She looked through the names of the camels posted on the outside of the enclosure. Misty, Ophelia, Janice, Gladys—that was the one she wanted to see. Which one was Gladys?

She was still looking for Gladys when Mark corralled the boys and Linda turned the stroller toward the exit. Linda looked for Elspeth, saw her reading the signage by the camel exhibit, and gave an exasperated sigh. She called to Elspeth, "Mother, did you hear me? We should go. Sophie's nearly frozen."

The boys were easier to move after Mark promised to stop for hot chocolate on the way home. When they passed through the gate, Elspeth made a note of the park's address.

Elspeth spent the night at a hotel near the airport, since her flight home was early the next morning and it would have been inconvenient for Mark or Linda to take her to the airport before they went to work. She awoke the next morning to an early wake-up call. The weather forecast for the Gulf coast was warm and sunny, but a blizzard was moving through the upper Midwest.

She showered and was dressing to catch the first airport shuttle when the second call came. Her flight was delayed an hour, then three. By mid-morning, O'Hare and Midway were closed, and Minneapolis International was diverting flights. Elspeth and a few thousand other travelers across the country spent hours trying to find later flights. It was almost noon before she managed to book a ticket—for a flight to leave two days later.

Elspeth called Linda shortly before lunch. Her offer to make dinner was a godsend for Linda, as she had meetings all afternoon and would be home late. Dinner was many hours away, though, and with time on her hands, Elspeth had something she wanted to do.

She arrived at the petting zoo early in the afternoon with a sliced apple and a few fresh carrots in her purse. She didn't know what camels liked, but this was the best she could do.

The camels were separated from park visitors by two fences. The only chance to be close to them was at the rides. Five bucks secured a ride around the paddock on a camel led by a park wrangler. Elspeth bought her ticket and took her place in line.

Pete was stuck leading Gladys on the rides today. That was easy enough, but he also had to answer stupid questions from city kids and keep them from being hurt. Dealing with kids on Christmas break took energy and patience, and Pete was short on both. Neither of his marriages had lasted long enough for him to become comfortable around kids. He detested this job.

He and Gladys were working alone today. Pete was desperate to talk to anyone who didn't have a runny nose by the time he saw the older woman standing in line. *Not a bad looking old girl,* he thought, and the kids in line around her were behaving. He appreciated that.

"Is this the camel named Gladys?" the lady asked when it was her turn for the ride.

Pete couldn't help himself. It was the old habit that had gotten him into trouble so often when he was married; he just naturally turned on the charm when a good-looking woman was near. He tipped his hat, smiled, and softly drawled, "She shore is. And a mighty fine lady, too, just like you."

Elspeth had heard similar lines most of her life. Today, she found herself smiling. She was used to working with men like Pete and recognized the type: men who were naturally charming, but were more interested in their four-footed charges than anything else in their lives. Normally, she steered clear of them, but Pete was refreshing after the men she'd met on her cruise. He was handsome, too, in a worn and weathered way.

"Thank you," Elspeth said. Her voice was warm, almost coquettish; it surprised even her. "I've wanted to meet Gladys. I saw her at the amphitheater a few nights ago. Could I give her a slice of apple or a carrot?"

"Sorry, ma'am. If I let you, every kid in line will want to do it, and feeding animals is against the rules," Pete said. He dragged out a line he hadn't used in twenty years. "I think I could let you give her a little treat if you can wait until the rides are over and she's back in the barn."

Gladys didn't understand a word of this. She understood her nose. Humans fill volumes with poetry about beauty and love and then use corny lines that would embarrass a love-sick horse. Camels sniff.

A mental picture of Pete and the lady in an amorous clinch disturbed Gladys. She snorted, blowing gobs of camel mucus over Pete's shoulder.

She remembered younger wranglers she'd seen in this condition. One was besotted for weeks. Distracted wranglers lost all track of priorities, at least those important to Gladys, chief amongst which was her feeding schedule. A few had completely forgotten to dole out her molasses-drenched vitamin and mineral supplement. And if Gladys felt anything similar to the love and awe humans reserve for religion, it was her passion for molasses.

Gladys listened to Pete's soft tones and started to do a slow burn. She put up with crap from kids and adults—even pretended to like a few, once in a while, if the weather was nice. If she could make a sacrifice like that, was it too much to ask that she be fed on time and get a full ration? Gladys vented her frustration with a rumbling, "Eeeungh."

She looked at Pete again and wondered why Jerry kept a scarecrow-skinny guy with creaky knees around. He could be a health risk, what with the big bald spot he hid under his hat. Could be mange. She looked Pete over closely and decided Jerry should have him put down and sold for dog food. Old Pete reminded her of old bull camels she'd known.

She remembered an all-day tryst she had with an old bull. The old fool kept forgetting what they were up to and wandering off for a drink or something to eat. Their assignation was twenty-three hours and thirty minutes longer than her affairs with younger camels. It wasn't something she cared to remember. And if old men were like old camels, she might starve to death before Pete got over this infatuation.

Gladys turned her head and looked at Elspeth and saw that she was even older than Pete. Gladys couldn't imagine what they saw in each other. Their stupid-looking feet were narrow and would sink in sand, neither of them could chew their cud, they both look starved, and there wasn't a decent hump between the two of them. She shook her head in disgust, sending camel slobber in all directions. This union was a mistake of nature.

Gladys was not a romantic.

She sniffed again and considered her options. Too late to stop it. The only logical option left, Gladys reasoned, was to find a way to speed the proceedings along. Putting them so close together they wouldn't be able to see how ugly they were seemed the best option. She put her head between Pete's shoulder blades and gave him a push. Satisfied she'd done what she could, Gladys turned away with a shudder. She might become nauseous if she saw too much.

Elspeth and Pete didn't collide as planned, but they were closer than either intended, and Pete had to put his hand on Elspeth's shoulder to steady himself. Elspeth found she didn't mind it at all.

Pete recovered first and gave Gladys's lead shank a good tug. "Whoa, you old bat. What's gotten into you?" He turned to Elspeth. "Sorry about that, ma'am. I don't know what got into the old girl."

He was about to say more when teenagers in line behind Elspeth asked loudly if Pete was going to talk all day or do his job. They'd like to get a ride, today. That ended the conversation, at least at the mounting station, although Pete and Elspeth continued bantering back and forth as Elspeth took her ride around the paddock.

To prolong the conversation, Pete slowed Gladys as they approached the platform where riders dismounted. He mentioned that Elspeth could come back to the barn to give Gladys a treat in an hour when the rides were over.

Gladys groaned. If she had to give these rides, Pete could at least get it over with on time. She laid her ears back, increased her speed, and tugged at the lead rope, trying to get Pete to move faster.

At the dismount platform, Pete offered Elspeth his hand. "Can I help you off, ma'am?"

Elspeth took his hand, though with the raised platform right next to her, it would have been easier to get off without "help."

She held his hand longer than necessary. "Thank you for the ride and the conversation. It was a pleasure to meet you, Pete."

"The pleasure was all mine, ma'am. A guy doesn't get to meet a woman as interesting and attractive as—"

"Hey, Tex. Are you going to talk all day, or do we get our rides, too?" a teenager waiting to mount Gladys for his ride asked.

Both Elspeth and Pete blushed a little at that. Pete got back to work and Elspeth stepped out of the way of the next rider. She still wanted to give Gladys a treat and talk to Pete again, but she wasn't about to meet a strange man in a barn—at least, not again.

"Why not?" she heard. The words were said quietly, as though whispered in her ear. "Married most of your life and two good kids; I'd say it worked out well the last time."

Elspeth felt as though she'd touched a live electric wire. She hadn't heard that voice in over forty years. She looked around her, but didn't expect to see anyone. "What are you up to now, you old scoundrel?" she whispered.

Her focus was broken as she took the stairway off the platform, working her way between kids waiting for their rides. She walked toward the exit and paused there, found a pen in her purse and scribbled Linda's address and phone number on a piece of paper. She took a few steps back toward the camel ride. Pete and Gladys were just beginning the next ride as Elspeth reached the white plank fence around the paddock. She waved at Pete as he walked by and handed him the paper. “Dinner with the family is at six thirty tonight. It’s casual. Address and phone number are here,” she said. Turning on her heel, she walked through the exit and out of the park. She caught a taxi at the park entrance and dropped by a grocery store on her way to Mark and Linda’s.

Elspeth spent forty years feeding crews of hungry, boisterous men who worshipped good meals and tormented bad cooks for sport. They insulted good cooks, too, but did it with a smile and knew when to duck.

The boys were put to work setting the table, the roast was in the oven, the potatoes were peeled and boiling, and a bag of frozen vegetables was ready for the microwave when Elspeth left the kitchen and did a little work on the computer. She was back in the kitchen when Pete called.

“Ah, is this, is this the lady I met at the camel ride today?” he asked.

Elspeth had already decided not to give him a chance to back out. “Yes. When will you be arriving?”

“Well, I’m, ah, I’m not sure. You said this was with family?”

“Don’t worry. You’ve met my daughter and her husband. Get yourself cleaned up and be here in forty-five minutes. Pork roast, mashed potatoes and gravy, carrots, and fresh rolls.” She quickly gave him directions to the house and hung up. If a good meal didn’t get him here, he wasn’t the type of man she took him to be.

Not much chance of that, she thought. Her background check had been fast but complete.

Linda was the first to notice the extra plate at the table. She knew her mother could count. “Mom, have you invited someone for dinner?”

"Yes. You and Mark have met him." Elspeth didn't stop moving. There was work to do, and stopping would only give Linda a chance to ask silly questions. She didn't feel it necessary, or wise, to elaborate on where the meeting had taken place.

Linda recognized her mother's ploys and debated whether she should wait and find out who the guest was or try to drag it out of her mother beforehand. She decided she was too tired to interrogate Elspeth, change clothes, and clean the house at the last minute, but she gave it a try. "Who is it?"

"Pete," Elspeth said. "Where do you keep your meat thermometer?"

Linda gave up. "It's in the next drawer down," she said and headed toward her bedroom to change into comfortable shoes.

"Ask Mark to bring up a couple of cold beers, domestic. Don't bother with wine," Elspeth called after her.

Linda's fatigue vanished and she giggled. "Mom has a man coming over? Beer, domestic—so not someone she met at the hotel," she said to herself.

Mark was as bemused and eager as Linda to see who was going to show up. The two of them offered to help, but they knew Elspeth didn't share well in the kitchen. Elspeth didn't stop moving to answer them. "I have dinner under control. Go talk to your children."

Linda and Mark did as they were told, whispering and snickering as they left. Elspeth closed her eyes for a second and wondered if she was really that transparent.

The roast was carved and dinner on the table when Pete arrived. Elspeth showed him into the dining room and pointed to a chair at the table. If this was to grow into something, she had no intention of letting him think he could show up whenever he felt like it and hold up dinner. It would set a precedent for bad habits, and Elspeth believed in starting things right.

Pete felt uncomfortable. It didn't make him feel better when he remembered it was at the Nativity that he'd met Mark and Linda, however briefly. He relaxed when Mark, Linda, and Elspeth began to argue over which of the evening's disasters was their favorite. The first couple of beers helped, but nothing breaks down barriers faster than laughter.

Elspeth was also stiff at first, but she loosened up as Pete joined the Nativity discussion and was leaning toward him and glowing as he described Charles in the camel fight. "The 'smack' was so loud when his face hit the calf's rear end, I thought they'd hear it all over the amphitheater."

No one was interested in dessert, and Elspeth said she was tired after a long day. Pete offered to give her a lift back to the hotel. "It's on my way home, anyhow," he said, which was the second white lie told that night.

Alone in the car with Pete, Elspeth turned serious. "I'm too old to pussyfoot around. I want a man in my life, someone I can care for and share my life with. I'm interested in you if you're interested in me, but I'm not a pushover, and you can expect a fight now and then."

That was the most direct conversation Pete ever had with a woman. He liked it and agreed that he wanted to take this further. They parted at the hotel with a single kiss goodbye and a promise to keep in touch.

Elspeth closed the door to her room, turned on the lights, and flipped the bar for the security lock. "Show yourself, you old rapscallion. What are you up to now?" she whispered as she turned toward the empty room. "Come on, I know you're here, Billy."

The soft voice she heard earlier in the day answered. "I don't go by that name anymore,"

"What do you call yourself then?"

"I go by 'Doofus' now, but I ain't the one that done it."

"Since when do you use substandard English, and if you didn't change your name, who did?" Elspeth demanded.

"Ya ought to talk to your son about that."

"Doc? When did he have anything to do with you? And where are you? Show yourself. I feel foolish talking to an empty room." Elspeth walked through the room and sat in an easy chair by the window.

"Can't show myself. I ain't decent."

"Since when has that bothered you? Show yourself, and be quick about it. I don't have time to play your games."

The air by one of the queen beds began to shimmer, steadied, and Doofus appeared in cowboy boots and manure-spattered tutu.

Elspeth thought she'd been ready for anything, but Doofus in his tutu caught her off guard. She gasped. "Oh, my, what, what in heaven's name is this get-up you're wearing? Turn around, let me see it." Elspeth couldn't help laughing as Doofus turned.

"This warn't my idea. It was Doc's. He's ruined me; I gotta talk like a cowboy and wear this God-forsaken outfit. My social life is ruined." Doofus sat on the bed, tears welling in his eyes.

"Doc did this? My God, I didn't think he had it in him. How?"

"I can't say, and it's not something I'd want to get out."

"But of all people! Doc? He works so hard at being rational; I didn't think you'd ever met him." Elspeth leaned back in her chair, looked at Doofus, and laughed again.

That hurt Doofus. "You know better 'an that. I talk to everybody. Nobody 'doesn't know' me. Like Doc said, all you have to do is watch the news or read the papers to see that."

"Touché, but why are you hanging around me now, and why did you let me know it?" Elspeth squinted, examining his expression for clues.

"I thought I was doin' ya a favor, and Pete's been lonely, too." Doofus didn't want to discuss his motives.

"I can handle my own social life, thank you, and I've seen what your help is worth." Elspeth looked at the clock, a table, any excuse to avoid looking Doofus in the eyes.

"You seemed pretty happy the last time I set ya up. Married to the Old Man for forty years." He paused and spoke softly. "You don't have a whole lot of time to make up yer mind this time."

The silence that followed was awkward for both of them. Doofus pretended to cough, stood, and walked to the door, which made no sense for a fairy. "Just thought I'd give ya a nudge in Pete's direction. He's a good guy."

The room was empty when Elspeth turned to look at him.

Chapter 27: The Nativity's Final Act

Doc's Manuscript

New Orleans, A Week After the Nativity, 1987

When the pastor visited him in the hospital, Jim asked: "Next year, could we donate the Nativity budget to a soup kitchen or give the Nativity back to the kids? Please?"

There was no evidence that Jim asked himself, "What would Jesus do?" but the pastor thought he probably had it right.

Sam, thinking all good things in his life were over, stayed in his room the night after the accident. His spirits revived after talking to Marcy. He called her to let her know he was grounded, and the date was off, but he hardly had a chance to speak once she answered the phone.

She cancelled the date before he did. As he told his friends, his problems were nothing compared to what poor Marcy was going through, with the sudden death of her favorite grandmother.

The next evening, Sam talked to his father as he read the newspaper before dinner. "Dad, how many grandmothers does a girl have?"

John put his paper down and looked at his son, trying to determine if this was an honest question, and if so, how could a kid that naïve get a driver's license? "Two, like everybody else."

"But Marcy cancelled on the date because her grandmother died, and Dave and Rob said she cancelled on each of them for the same reason. How could she have three grandmothers?"

John bit his lip and hid behind the newspaper, until he had his expression under control. "Maybe one was a step-grandmother."

Sam nodded. "She's really been through a lot. Is it okay if I go to the drug store and get a sympathy card for her?"

"Sure, if you walk. It's only half a mile."

John wandered into the kitchen, as Sam left the house. His wife was standing at the sink, peeling carrots. He walked up behind her, put his arms around her waist, and nuzzled her ear. "You know how you worried about Sam becoming sexually active?"

"Yes."

"You can relax."

Charles spent the days following the Nativity sleeping until noon and moping around the house. Amanda, his wife, called him to lunch on the third day. He didn't respond. She walked into their bedroom, opened the blinds, and turned on the lights.

"Amanda, please, I'm trying to sleep."

"Charles, you've had enough sleep for two people. You can't hide from the world, and I'm not serving your meals in bed."

"After what happened at the pageant and then that awful traffic stop," Charles shuddered beneath the blankets. "What will people think? How can I show my face again at the bank? I put so much hope and planning into that pageant. My career at the bank has stalled, and this pageant was going to open doors for me. Instead, I made a fool of myself."

"You did. There's no doubt about it; you made a spectacle of yourself, but I don't think you know how many people have pitched in to help you in the last couple of days."

"What do you mean?"

"Did you watch the news or look at the newspaper?" Amanda asked him.

"No. I couldn't bear to."

"Do it. There was almost no coverage of the pageant. My sister talked to some friends. They saw to it that the police report was buried. The police agreed; the three of you in the pickup were victims, not perpetrators."

"What?" Charles roused himself and sat up in bed. "Betty interceded on my behalf?"

"Yes, Betty. You have many good qualities, Charles, and I love you for them, but you let your pride and eagerness to be in the spotlight get you in trouble. Betty never hated you; she just didn't like the things you did to grab attention. You'd get further if you spent more time helping people and less time trying to take credit. Now, get dressed and come downstairs for lunch."

For once in his life, Charles did as Amanda suggested, but he moved slowly through the rest of the day, depressed and sulking. He learned that Betty and others in the congregation made sure the pageant was given minimal media coverage. The only pictures that made it into the news were those of the trashed Nativity set and a satisfied-looking camel named Gladys. The names of the Magi weren't made public.

At home a few nights after the Nativity, Betty took a platter of hamburgers and sodas down to the family room for Rob and his friends. She'd put together enough clues about what happened to Dave the night of the Nativity to ground Rob for the holidays. She allowed the party tonight only because Dave was invited.

When Betty returned to the kitchen, Rob checked the stairs to make sure she had left the basement and closed the door to the stairway. He returned and with faux solemnity addressed the group.

"Men, we are gathered here to support our buddy, Dave. We didn't know that all the times he bragged in the locker room and called himself 'Long Dong Dave,' he was trying to cover his insecurity. Now we know." Rob handed three pictures around to Justin, Ted, and Steve.

"When I first saw these, I thought you were wearing your football cup," he said to Dave. "Then it hit me. Ever since we started showering together after football practice, you must have been wearing a, what do you call 'em, a, a prosthetic. You poor guy. You didn't need to do that. We would have accepted you just the way you were. None of us would have called you stubby, or tiny, or shorty, or stumpy."

"Ah, Rob, I would have called him 'stumpy,'" said Steve. "I wouldn't be proud of it, and I'd never call him 'dinky', but 'stumpy' has a nice ring to it. If Dave gets his act together on the football team, we could have the cheerleaders chant 'stuuumpy, stuuumpy.' That would get the fans going."

Dave lunged for the pictures. "Oh, shut up and give me those." His anger was feigned, as he had done a little bragging.

Steve grabbed the pictures first. "Geez, this is sad. 'Long dong Dave,' my ass! But don't worry, Dave. We still respect you, kind of, and all the books say that size isn't important. Maybe after church next week you could check with Reverend Smith to see if there are any 'shorty' support groups."

"Come on guys. It was freezing that night, and I was naked," Dave said.

Ted got hold of the pictures next. He held one up. "Gosh. This one reminds me of my little nephew's first bicycle, the kind with those little wheels on the side. That isn't a peter, it's a training dick."

They all collapsed laughing, including Dave. The teasing and wrestling continued until Dave got the pictures and burned them in the fireplace.

Betty reappeared with a pitcher of milk and a plate of fresh chocolate chip cookies as an excuse to check on the boys and see what they were up to. Tonight, they laughed and feasted on burgers and cookies, but Rob and the others knew Dave would make them pay.

The cashiers at the bank thought Charles was quieter than usual, when he returned to work, but none of them heard the full story of the pageant. Four weeks after the Nativity, there was a knock on his office door, and Betty poked her head in. “Hi, Charles. How are you doing?”

He stood to greet her. “Hello, Betty. What brings you here today?” he asked, a note of suspicion in his voice.

“I always thought you were a pompous ass, Charles, but I heard about the scholarship. You did good, kid, you did good.”

Charles flushed a little, but kept his face blank. “I have no idea what you’re talking about.”

“Oh, pishh. You know I have too many contacts to hide this. Keep it up, Charles, and I’ll have to start admiring you. Give my love to Amanda and the girls.”

Betty was gone as quickly as she popped in. Charles returned to his seat, shook his head, smiled, and leaned back in a long, slow stretch. He felt better than he had in a long time.

Earlier that same day, Sheriff Lapham called his wife and told her they were going out to dinner that night, just the two of them.

“Barbeque or fried chicken?” she asked.

“Neither. I was thinking more along the lines of Mediterranean or French. How about Maurice’s or Les Deuxelles?”

“My word! That will be nice. I love Maurice’s, but I know you like Les Deuxelles. Either is fine with me. What’s the occasion? Is the newspaper going to print something nice about the department?”

“Oh, nothing, nothing like that. I just feel good today.”

"My, I'll have to make sure you feel good more often. You're sure there isn't something else?"

"Well, yes, there is, dear, but I'll tell you over dinner."

The *coquilles St. Jacques à la Provençale,* washed down with a glass of *Pouilly Fuissé* was delicious, and the restaurant's signature dish, *jambon braisé Madére, Deuxelles au gratin suisse* was extraordinary. The Sheriff even splurged on pâté before dinner and a good California pinot noir with the *jambon.* As the wine steward opened the bottle, Mrs. Lapham again asked why they were celebrating.

"Well, Earl called me this morning. They're releasing him from observation at the hospital. They said he would be back to normal, for Earl."

Mrs. Lapham put her fork down, leaned forward, and scrutinized her husband's face. "And . . .?"

"Earl told me that after much soul searching and prayer, he decided to leave the department." The sheriff tried to look serious, but his eyes were dancing.

"You didn't force him to resign, did you? We discussed that, and we had an agreement."

"Oh, no, no. I wouldn't dream of it, dear. Earl told me that he spent a lot of time thinking about it and praying over it since the pageant, and he's decided to go back to school to become an arborist."

"A what?" Mrs. Lapham sat back in her chair, dumbfounded.

"An arborist. You know, dear, they trim, prune, and take care of trees. It's a wonderful profession. They work outdoors every day and have the satisfaction of watching things grow. I'm sure Earl will love it."

"He wants to trim trees? Since when? Where on earth did he get this idea?"

"I have no idea, sweetheart. I think it has something to do with his church."

"His church? My God! What in heaven's name does religion have to do with trees?"

"I don't know, dear. You know, I never understood how his mind works."

"You never tried to understand him. Earl isn't a genius, but he's always been kind, trusting, and helpful to me." She drummed her fingers on the table, paused, and glared at the sheriff. "You didn't give him some load of bull to get him off the force, did you?"

"Oh, no, dear. I wouldn't dream of it. I tried to talk him into reconsidering," the sheriff lied, "but Earl was adamant. He said someone set up a scholarship for nontraditional students taking classes in horticulture and agricultural forestry. It sounded tailor-made for him."

"Were you behind this?"

"What? Can you imagine me donating money to fund Earl's latest idea? We've been over this ground before, too." He didn't add that he made a suggestion to a generous philanthropist at the bank, one who recently met Earl professionally. Unnecessary details can so complicate a discussion.

"You've got me there. You're too cheap for that. You rarely even spring for a nice dinner. But why trees, for God's sake?"

"Earl said that he's always wanted to find Jesus, and he thinks the best way to do it is to look in the trees. He handed in his resignation this morning."

The sheriff took another sip of wine, thought hard about the cost of their meal, and made sure he wasn't smiling when he put the glass down and looked at his wife.

Chapter 28

The Heirs' Story

Rockburg, January, 2014

Jed couldn't get to sleep. *Tossing and turning's a waste of time,* he thought. The kids and his wife were asleep, and the codicil nagged him. He put on his robe and went to his desk.

A copy of Doc's password hints sat in front of him. *Boil the water, mother. What in the hell could that mean?* Jed sat back in his chair and looked at the ceiling. *There was something . . . boil the water . . . a story Dad told . . . According to Dad, the Old Man was half asleep by the time he arrived at church every Sunday in the summer because of the brutal hours he worked. He always slept through the sermon. Something woke the Old Man. Yeah, that was it. The minister bellowed something that woke the Old Man, and he yelled back, "Boil the water, mother."*

Jed walked to the kitchen for a cookie and a cup of hot chocolate. *You boil water for hot chocolate, for tea, for instant rice, or . . . if a woman is having a baby at home. Dad said it keeps people busy while they wait for the doctor, and it keeps them from doing something foolish.*

Jed sat back down at his computer. *The minister yelled something he could toss into his sermon to awaken sleeping farmers without it seeming out of place, and it included a name, the name of a neighbor who had a baby at home.* Jed yawned. His cookie and hot chocolate were gone, but they'd done their duty. *Gert, she'll know. Have to call Josh tomorrow.*

Josh's nose detected faint traces of bacon and eggs in the air, almost smothered by the rich aroma of meat loaf and roast beef when he walked into the Coffee Cup Saturday morning. Gert was wiping up tables when she saw him. "Too early for pie, isn't it?"

Josh took a stool at the counter and flashed her his best smile. "How's my favorite waitress? Think I could get a cup of coffee?"

"Why do I think the coffee is going to be the easy part?"

"'Cause you're the smartest lady in town. Cute, too."

"You sure can spread it, kid." Gert brought his coffee and took a stool next to him. "So, what do you need now?"

"We have another password riddle. The clue is, 'Boil the water, mother.' Jed said it had something to do with a neighbor-lady of the Old Man and Elspeth's, a lady who had a baby at home." Josh told her what Jed pieced together about the sermon.

Gert snorted and shook her head. "Your dad and grandpa could take the tiniest scrap of truth and weave a story. After they told it a few times, nobody could remember what really happened." Gert got herself a cup of coffee and sat back down.

"Baby at home, eh? Their neighbor on the west, nah. She was too old. The Jensen's, that was it. Art and Helen Jensen lived to the east. Big family." Gert stared at the counter and absently ran a finger around the rim of her cup. "Art was in the field when her contractions started. Yeah, she was too far along and called Elspeth." Gert slapped the counter top. "That's it. It was the only time I heard of Elspeth being flustered. Too late to get Helen in a car, so Elspeth called old Doc Smith and pretty much stood there wringing her hands after that. She asked Helen if she should get Art from the field. Story was, Helen said, 'Why the hell would you want him. He's already done his damage.'"

"So, what would the password be?"

Gert stirred her coffee. "Let's see, your granddad teased Elspeth about wringing her hands and boiling water. Ahh, Helen named the baby 'Joy.' And she was, let's see, she was their sixth. Yup. It was during the tail end of corn planting and the start of harvesting first-crop hay. All the dairy farmers in the church were so tired, they fell asleep before the sermon even started.

"Old Reverend Wilberts should have been used to that, the way he rambled on, but he looked out at that sea of nodding bald guys and lost his temper. He yelled, 'And Joy, Joy was in the world,' to wake 'em up. Least ways, that's what he usually did when that happened. Anyway, your granddad came to with a start and yelled, 'Boil the water, mother.'"

"I still don't—"

"Christ, kid. Do I have to do it all for you. It was the sixth child, her name was Joy Jensen. Try combinations of six, Joy, Helen, or Jensen, and see what you get." She took a sip of coffee and grimaced. "Darn coffee's cold again. You guys will owe me one of those fancy coffee machines, or at least something to keep a cup hot, when this is done. Now, get out of here and let me get back to work."

There were a surprising number of possible combinations of names and the number six, and it was the next day before Josh tried Helen6Jensen and opened the old e-mails stored on Doc's computer. Most of the e-mails were pedestrian, but one in the "Sent" file looked interesting. Josh forwarded it to Jed.

From: Wilson, Jack <jackwilson3@yaholler.net>
Subject: Idea
Date: July 11, 2009 4:22 PM
To: Linda Grey <lindag553@onthenet.net>

Linda,

It's the damndest thing. In writing this silly book, I've found myself reviewing my life and thinking seriously about much of it for the first time. It's really irritating. There were many lessons I should have learned when I was younger. Now, I understand them, but it's too damned late. I'm retired, and most of my life is over.

Case in point, I joined a church choir when I was in graduate school. Mary sang beautifully, and I liked to sing, but had no talent. The church choir was the only choir desperate enough to let me join and too polite to ask me to leave. Our choir sang for the early service; we only had ten members, and often only eight would show up for a service. Once, only four of us came: Mary, an alto, a tenor, and me.

I figured the director would cancel, and I could sit in a pew and sleep through the service. Instead, he put four microphones in a row next to the pulpit and told us we were a quartet. That scared the hell out of me. I always avoided being near a microphone. Now, I had one so close it was almost in my mouth.

The director liked our performance so much he cancelled one of the hymns the second service choir was scheduled to sing and put us in instead. That was impressive, because that choir had fifty members and a regional reputation.

Forty years later, it's finally soaked through my thick skull that no matter how limited we think we are, we can accomplish more than we ever dreamt we could, if we do our best, listen carefully to each other, work together, and keep our eyes on the director.

All of us censor ourselves. We pass up opportunities because we don't think we can handle them, or we tell ourselves we aren't trained for the job. We restrain ourselves more than parents, teachers, or bosses ever do. I know I did it, and I remember seeing it frequently in very bright people. Fools were full of confidence. They didn't see how far their work fell short, while smart kids saw a gulf between what they could do and what they expected of themselves.

We both have kids who are perfectionists, and all of our kids are bright. We could tell them this, but it won't sink in any better than anything else we've told them. Even Montaigne complained his son didn't listen to him. Why should we expect better?

Can you think of a way to drill this lesson into their thick skulls? I'd hate to have them wake up at seventy and realize they've missed half the opportunities in life. Whatever we do, it will have to force them to learn the lesson by themselves or it won't sink in.

Let's talk this over the next time you're up here.

Doc

Jed sent it on to the rest of the heirs, with a note suggesting they keep it in mind as they read Doc's story and thought about the codicil.

Chapter 29: Jed's Mentor

Doc's Manuscript

Rockburg, January 1, 1988

I talked to Mary on New Year's Day as we tidied up in the kitchen after lunch. Something about the friend Jed didn't bring home for Christmas didn't feel right. "What is their relationship, anyhow? I can't get that straight."

"From what I could get out of him, Cindy is a senior in marketing, engaged to a junior in civil engineering, and she lives in the same dorm as Jed. She helped him get acclimated to college, and he helped her in calculus."

"It's not a romantic relationship, then? She only took pity on a floundering freshman and helped him out in exchange for help on her math?"

"That's what he said."

"I hope you're right, but it sounds like he fell hard for her. That has me worried." I paused in wiping the counter top and shook my head. "I don't understand why an engaged woman, a senior, would devote that much time to help a freshman. She's either a Good Samaritan and Jed misinterpreted her actions, or she's manipulating Jed and her fiancé."

The phone rang and I answered it. It was Cindy. I went down the stairs to the family room where the kids were sitting on the carpet, playing Munchkin on a coffee table in front of the fireplace. They had a fire started. The glass screen was closed, and an electric blower pushed air through the fire grate to distribute the heat. Few things are more satisfying than looking at snowdrifts and icicles with your family from the carpeted floor of a warm room.

"Hah! I attack you with a High Ranking Demon of Great Nastiness," Julie told Seth.

"So what? I defend with 'The Dirty Sheet of Great Stench and Exceptional Thread Count' and counter attack with, hmm, let's see," Seth sorted through his cards. "Yes! I attack with the 'Unnatural Axe.' What're you going to do about that?" Seth sneered.

Seth did a good sneer.

Julie rolled her dice. "Oooh, curses. You lucked out."

"Don't worry, it's my turn, and I've got him," Jed said. "Seth, I attack you with the 'Chain Saw of Dismemberment.'"

I interrupted. "Jed, put your chainsaw down for a minute. You have a phone call."

"Can it wait? Who is it?"

"It's Cindy. I can tell her you're in conference, and she should call—"

"Oh, no, no, don't do that. I'll get it." Jed threw down his cards and raced up the steps to take the call where he'd have privacy.

Julie and Josh waited until Jed rounded a turn on the landing before they asked Seth if he wanted to help them stack the deck or do it himself.

I thought my kids were more honest than that. "Whoa! Isn't that cheating?"

Josh grinned broadly and flipped through the deck. "Sure, Dad, but cheating is legal in Munchkin."

Cindy called Jed three times that day, repeatedly interrupting games. Jed had a long losing streak, but he didn't seem to mind. He came back to the game after each call with a stupid grin and a faraway look in his eyes. I saw a drunken goat with the same expression once. The goat held its head so low it nearly tripped on its tongue, but it almost looked smart compared to Jed.

I pulled Jed out of a game for a few minutes on the pretense of discussing what his mother wanted for her birthday in February. "Your mother's easy to shop for; just get her a gift card from any sewing supply store. Do me a favor though, and see if you can get a card she can't use on fabric. She already has more than she'll ever use, and we don't have room to store more. By the way, Cindy doesn't sew, does she?"

"No, she hasn't mentioned sewing. She's a great girl. She showed me around campus and helped me get through registration. She helped me set up a study schedule and made sure it fit hers. I don't know what I'd do without her. She even took me out to dinner and a movie to show me where I could take girls for a date, and then we, ah . . . why do you ask, Dad?"

I changed my mind. The goat was smarter.

I needed to talk to Mary alone about this, so after dinner, I asked the kids if they wanted to help with the dishes. A box of rattlesnakes couldn't have cleared the first floor of the house faster.

Mary washed dishes at the sink while I dried on her left. "What do you think is going on?" I asked, as I wiped a plate.

"If I'm reading it right, Jed found a woman who felt sorry for him and helped him get used to college. Jed may have—don't put those in the dishwasher, I hand-wash them—misinterpreted her intentions and fell for her. Not there! Serving spoons go in the second drawer, and that's a hand towel, not a dishtowel."

"Could be," I said, "but she's the first mentor I've heard of who calls three times a day, every day, over Christmas vacation."

Mary paused and thought a moment with her hands in the dishwater.

"Ouch, that water's hot." She attacked a bit of crusted grunge on a pot, but soon became distracted and lost in thought again.

Mary came back to life as I opened a cabinet door to put a platter away. "Look at this," she said, pointing to a streak on the platter I dried. "Uggh! How did you get grease on this right after I washed it? Go play a board game with the kids if you can't do it right. I'll wash the dishes myself."

The kids didn't volunteer to help in the kitchen for a reason. On the other hand, my greasy streak gambit still worked. One little streak and Mary expelled me from the kitchen for the week.

The phone rang and Julie answered it as I left the kitchen. "Jed," Julie called. "Pick up the phone. It's Cindy again."

That's how Jed's Christmas vacation went—Cindy called him three times a day, and Jed wandered around like a mentally disturbed goat. Mary continued to insist that Jed misunderstood Cindy, but with a hesitant shrug and a half-octave rise in her voice on the last syllables.

Chapter 30: Back to School

Doc's Manuscript

Rockburg, January 10, 1988

"There's no reason Jed should waste money on a bus ticket. You and I will drive him back to school," Mary said. There was an edge to her voice. This was not a suggestion.

"Why?" I asked. Jed usually took the bus the 200 miles to Owatonna and school, since we couldn't afford to get any of the kids a car.

"Why not? The clinic isn't busy. They can spare you for a day. And we might get to meet Cindy."

Ah, so that was it. There's nothing like maternal concern to get me volunteered for more work. Two can play at that.

"When were you going to take him back?" I asked. I pretended to be watching something in the backyard. Mary is good at reading my expressions, even when I think I've managed a poker face. I knew I wouldn't be able to wiggle out of this trip, but I wasn't going to give in without registering a complaint. I drove up to 250 miles a day in my work. Another seven hours or more on the road on my weekend off didn't appeal to me.

"We, *we* are going to drive him back. I always get turned around leaving campus. Besides, it will give us a chance to talk."

And I had a good idea what the topic would be on the way back, whether or not we would get a chance to meet Cindy.

Jed loaded his luggage into the car, and we headed out early on a Sunday. The roads were nearly empty; but it was overcast, the roads were icy in places, and we didn't make very good time at first. But the glare of sunlight off the snow made me appreciate the overcast once the sun finally came out.

We stopped at a Hardy's at the halfway point. I was hungry and ready for a break, and Mary was concerned that we only had half a tank of gas. That would be enough to get us to Owatonna, but Mary gets nervous about the gas level. I usually don't stop for gas unless a warning light is on or I'm driving somewhere west of the Missouri, where towns and gas stations are scarce.

The point at which a driver becomes concerned about how much gas is in the tank seems to be one of those differences between sexes that irritates women and affords them an excuse to lecture, usually when they are ticked off about something else. It serves to keep a man confused about what it was that got him into trouble, which usually means we get into more trouble. Think of it as an automotive toilet seat that I left up.

I gassed the car up first, in case Mary wasn't sure a half-tank would get us the hundred yards to Hardy's. A young black man, maybe nineteen or twenty years old, stood near the entrance to the restaurant when we arrived. I didn't pay much attention to him, but he was still there as we finished eating. We dumped our leftovers, shelved our trays, and headed for the car. This time I paid attention to him as we walked by.

His coat wasn't heavy enough for winter weather in Minnesota, nor was his cap. He wasn't wearing gloves. He carried a knapsack and a worn book bag sat by his feet, which he was shuffling and stamping to keep warm. *Foreign student from a tropical country headed back to college*, I thought.

I remembered describing Minnesota winters to students from Thailand, India, and Nigeria when I was a graduate student in the twin cities. They were incredulous, their expressions a mix of suspicion—I was thought to have stretched a story once—disbelief and fear. It was innocent entertainment for me and it served a purpose. Somebody had to warn them before the snow flew.

Apparently, no one had done that for this kid. But he was more than cold. We were in a tiny rural community. I'm pretty sure he was the only black person in the county, and he may not have been fluent in English. His expression was flat and his eyes wide, as though he'd been startled, and he averted his gaze when I looked toward him. I've never seen anyone who looked so lonely and forlorn.

We piled into the car. No one volunteered to drive, and we were behind schedule; so I didn't try to talk Mary or Jed into it. I caught sight of the kid again in the mirror as I checked for traffic before backing out of my parking slot. I didn't want to take the time, but I couldn't leave that kid there without finding out if he was okay.

I stopped the car, got out, and walked back to him. "Hello, are you all right?" I asked as I came up to him.

"They just dropped me here and told me to get a bus," he said, rubbing his arms and stamping his feet again.

His English was heavily accented, and at times I couldn't understand him. He had gone on a vacation over winter break with some guys from another school. I couldn't understand the name of the college he was enrolled in or how he'd met the guys with the car, but he'd assumed they were his friends.

On the trip, he was the one who bought the gas, and they'd asked him to buy some of their meals. Vacation over, they'd dumped him at this Hardy's and told him to buy a bus ticket to get back to his school.

The Hardy's doubled as the town's bus station, so he lucked out on that; but the ticket had taken every dime he had. He hadn't had breakfast or lunch, and shortly after he bought the ticket, the management told him to leave if he wasn't going to buy a meal. The bus wouldn't be arriving until late afternoon. He didn't dare leave the place, because he didn't have a watch and couldn't risk missing the bus.

I'm cheap. I was raised on a dairy farm when profits were low to nonexistent, and now I had two boys in college and another getting ready to go next year. That's a time in a man's life when the paycheck never makes it to the end of the month, even if you're self-employed. I fumbled through my pockets and wallet. All I had was a half dollar in change and a twenty dollar bill.

"You do have a ticket to your school?" I asked.

He said he did, although I had to ask him to repeat himself to make sure I understood him.

"Here," I said, and handed him the twenty. "You can't stand here until the bus comes. Have dinner and get a dessert you can stretch for an hour, then get some hot coffee and stretch that out as long as you can. Eat slowly. They have to let you stay inside if you're buying food."

I wished him well and tried not to cry, as I get emotional when it comes to parting with money. His college was in the wrong direction for me to give him a ride, drop Jed off on time, and get back home in time to get some sleep before work tomorrow. I looked at my watch. It wasn't expensive and the finish was worn around the edges. I kept the watch and walked back to the car.

"What was that about?" Mary asked as we got back on the freeway.

I gave her a condensed version. When it came to the twenty, she put the back of her hand to my forehead. She knows my habits.

"No fever," she said. She and Jed talked about my sudden philanthropic urge, and entertained each other for the last hundred miles by making jokes about it.

I didn't care, because I felt good about what I'd done. The only thing that bothered me was that I hadn't given the kid my watch. This shocked me. I'm cheap. I spent the rest of the trip thinking about what it was that made me feel good and likely reasons why. I've learned from experience that what affects me, what I enjoy, fear, hate, and feel, generally affects a chunk of the population, or at least quite a few other men, in a similar way. So why did helping a strange kid make me feel good, and what other things do the same? In effect, how should I, or any man, live his life in order to be content and satisfied?

Others have asked this question before, but like most men, I didn't bother to check the map before I started on this mental trip. Mary and Jed talked and I thought for the next hundred miles.

Besides helping this kid, the things I've done that afforded me the greatest satisfaction were learning and putting the knowledge to work, the love and affection of family and friends, reading literature and poetry, completing difficult and demanding tasks successfully, the respect of my peers, and music—classical, Broadway, and popular. Money, wealth, power, and the possessions they bring weren't as high on the list as the wag of my dog's tail when I got home at night. It shocked the hell out of me.

About then I heard a distant, "Jack," but I didn't let it disturb my thoughts. It came again, more sharply, "Jack, Jack . . . for gosh sakes, stop!"

"Quiet, I'm thinking," I said.

Mary jabbed me in the ribs. "You've driven by our exit and you almost clipped a car. Pull over and let me drive if you can't pay attention."

I pulled over and Jed volunteered to drive; I took his place in the back seat and continued thinking while the denizens of the front seat discussed my driving. I rolled the question over in my mind: Why did these things provide such satisfaction?

A substantial portion of my response to the kid's plight was likely to be nature, not nurture, as all of my upbringing had been to value the dollar. I was cheaper than ever, according to Mary, now that we had two boys in college.

Man is a social animal, or a herding animal, as I prefer to think of it, because those are the animals I work with every day, and herding animals behave that way because it's in their genes. A genetic basis for empathy has been identified and the same is suspected for altruism. That's reasonable, as there would have been selection for herding animals that watched out for each other, especially for the young. The tighter the group, the fewer of its members would be taken by predation.

Social animals compete for food and mates, but the competition is subject to limits that vary by species; stallions and male orangutans won't tolerate another mature male in their area, but wolves, cattle, lions, baboons, and chimps form family groups that include multiple males.

My thoughts followed a new thread: What happens when we try to get respect and affection on the cheap? How does it affect us and society if we substitute possessions for character and braggadocio for accomplishment? I didn't get far. Mary interrupted and invited me to carry Jed's bags up to his room.

When I was in school, two small suitcases held all of my belongings, and I thought myself privileged. Jed had a computer, three suitcases, a cell phone, and up in his room, his own little refrigerator. He carried his laptop and book bag, which he hadn't opened once during Christmas break, and I carried the rest.

Jed headed up the stairs, three floors of them, first and a lot faster than me. My bad knees and I struggled up the stairs behind him. Mary climbed the stairs behind me, whispering that I should watch to see if Jed talked to any girls that fit Cindy's description. That was another thing I couldn't wrap my mind around. When I was in school (is there any other phrase that can make a man sound further out of touch?), I would have been expelled if I had a woman even visiting me in the lounge on my floor after visiting hours. Jed's dorm was unisex, with a shower room for women, one for men, and a unisex bathroom for the undecided.

We'd brought Jed back at least a day too early. There were few students on the floor, and Cindy wasn't among them. I breathed a sigh of relief, since I'd been sure I'd have been ordered to strike up a conversation, during which Mary would have prompted me to ask embarrassing questions I'd never have considered asking in her absence. As it was, I was prompted to think up excuses to stay a few minutes longer, just in case she might show up.

Even Mary took the hint when the conversation lagged for the fourth time and Jed and I were both looking at our watches. We said our goodbyes and left for home. It was not a drive I looked forward to.

But the drive wasn't as bad as I thought it would be. Mary was as lost in her thoughts as I was in mine. That was fine for the drive, but experience had taught me that this was the proverbial lull. Mary's ideas always translated into work for me.

Chapter 31: The Shopping Trip

Doc's Manuscript

Rockburg, January 12, 1988

I didn't have long to wait to find out what Mary had in mind. She interrupted me as I packed Christmas decorations away on a Saturday morning, a week after taking Jed back to school. She spoke slowly, her voice firm. "Jack, I just talked to Jed. I think, well, I think they, ah, they are, intimate."

"What do you mean, intimate?" I tried to look innocent, but I knew what she meant. I was amazed it had taken her this long to figure it out.

"I mean, they are, you know, intimate, and he needs to be careful." The last words were said with vehemence. AIDs was in the news again. "I packed a care package of clean underwear, chocolate chip cookies, and I want to add latex condoms. Jed is at risk, and we are going to protect him."

She glared at me, as though daring me to make a joke at her expense before she continued. "Josh needs to get a job, and Albertson's is hiring. Take Josh down to apply for a job, and while he does that, I want you to pick up a box of condoms for Jed. Remember, make sure they're latex."

"That's insane. They hand them out for free at the student infirmary."

"I know, but he won't think of it. Now get moving, and take Josh with you."

I made a last attempt to insert reason into the discussion. "But, they give them—"

"My baby is at risk! Go! Now!" In a sweeping gesture, Mary pointed toward the door. "Move!"

A man has to set limits, and this was as good a place to start as any I heard of. "They hand the damned things out all over campus," I said slowly. "I will not get involved in something this stupid and embarrassing. That is final. No. Not now. Not later. Not ever."

The morning was bright and below zero, so both Josh and I wore heavy winter coats for the drive to Albertson's. The glare of sunlight reflecting off the snow made sunglasses a requirement for safe driving. It was a nice day for a drive, and Josh was chatty. "Dad, what was Mom yelling about?"

"Your mother wants you to apply for a job at Albertson's."

At fifteen, Josh was a master of the job-dodge; he had no concern about getting his wings clipped. He thought about my answer for a moment. "Nah. She would have been yelling for the last six months if that were it." He paused a moment. "She was pretty loud today. So were you."

"It doesn't concern you."

"But—"

"Drop it. Just drop it. Look, we're here." We arrived at Albertson's as the car warmed up enough to keep frost off the inside of the windshield.

The parking lot was nearly empty this early, and we parked near the store entrance. Albertson's, typical of large grocery stores, was a big, well-lit box, with groceries and household supplies on the interior aisles, and liquor, pharmacy, bakery, and meat sections around the periphery.

Once inside, Josh sauntered off to the Service Department where he would convince them they'd have to be nuts to hire him. I went to look for something in latex.

I hadn't looked for this kind of thing in thirty years. I wandered up and down the aisles, searching for the display. Employees stocked shelves, tidied up, and threatened to offer assistance. All of them seemed to be sixteen-year-old girls. I did not wish to discuss my needs with any of them, so I scooted around them and avoided eye contact. That's not easy when you pass the same ones in narrow aisles repeatedly within a few minutes.

Frustrated, I paused and looked behind me to see if the display might be in that direction. A little blond head ducked behind a display at the end of the aisle as I turned.

Great, the staff was following me. I wore a bulky coat and sunglasses and was acting strangely; they had me pegged as a shoplifter.

I stood for a moment, wondering what character defect, what weakness of intellect gets me into these damned ridiculous situations. I gritted my teeth, shoved my hands in my coat pockets, and heard a familiar chuckle.

"Doofus! Are you behind this?"

"Have ya thought of looking in Feminine Hygiene?" came a voice on my right. I turned. No one was there, but I recognized the voice. I saw the sign—Feminine Hygiene—hanging over the aisle to my right.

"Afraid to show yourself, Doofus?" I asked quietly, as I headed to the next aisle, where I found the condom display.

"No. I just didn't want to upset ya, not with that delicate nervous constitution of yours," Doofus answered. "You were doing so great yourself that I hated to interrupt. Gawd, ya should 'ah seen yer face back there." He started to laugh.

I turned in the direction of the laughter, as I felt my face flush.

Doofus materialized and was laughing so hard that tears ran down his cheeks. He bent at the waist, crossed his legs, and put an arm on my shoulder to steady himself.

"Doc, I gotta find the men's room, and you have a job to do. Get shopping." He turned and hustled down the aisle toward the men's room.

I watched him do a pigeon-toed gallop in boots and tutu down the aisle, bent over with laughter. He clutched his crotch like a four-year-old as the skirt of his tutu bobbed up and down with every step. As silly as he looked, he was laughing at me.

I turned back to the condom display. My God, things had changed since I shopped for these! I stood there, stupefied, my mouth hanging open. I faced a condom display six feet long, three feet high, and with so many brands and types I couldn't see the pegboard behind them.

How in heaven's name am I to choose? Latex, she said. Latex. Right. Lord, I left my reading glasses at home. I squinted at one package after the other, trying to focus. Shoppers stared as they passed. Two young mothers, chest-packing their babies, walked by, nudged each other, shook their heads, and snickered.

I'd still be there if Chuckles the Clown hadn't arrived. "Whoa, Dad. What are we doing here?" came a booming voice from behind me.

Josh had picked up his application forms, crumpled them until they looked like they'd been retrieved from the trash, and scrawled his name illegibly across the pages. Mission accomplished, he'd come in search of me.

In high spirits, he proceeded to give me advice on the choices before me. "How about these Dad, or do you want something flavored, like those over there? How about colors? Which do you think Mom would like?"

I cringed. I did not want to explain my needs to sixteen-year-old salesgirls, and I sure as hell didn't want to take advice from my fifteen-year-old son on how to select a condom. I grabbed a handful of the nearest packages and headed for the checkout lines.

Normally, I take the shortest line, but today I was sensitive to many things I'd normally ignore. Checkout lines end in cashiers. I found a line with a cashier, a lady, who looked older than me. When I put my packages on the moving belt, her expression said, *Who do you think you're kidding, ya old goat?*

"Paper or plastic?" she asked. I stood mute, my mouth open, my mind spinning like tires on ice.

Josh leaned close and whispered, "Dad, she asked a question."

"Ah, ah, latex," I said. I paid as fast as I could and bolted for the parking lot.

Once home, I parked the car in the garage and let Josh go in and tell his mother how he helped me select my purchase. I thought that would forestall future trips like this.

I stayed in the garage to address a bigger problem. "Doofus, how much of this did you engineer?" I asked the empty garage.

The air shimmered in front of me for a second. Doofus stood before me, eyes dancing and the corners of his mouth twitching.

"I wish I could take credit for this one, Doc. If this idea had been mine, I'd brag about it for years. Yer face when Josh started to give ya advice was . . ." Doofus tried to maintain his composure. His face twitched, he hid his mouth with his hand briefly, but a snort led to a giggle that transformed to a guffaw. He collapsed against the car and howled with laughter.

"If this wasn't your idea, how come you happened to be standing next to me when everything went wrong?"

"Doc, on a good day (gasp, snort), anybody who stands next to ya fer more than ten minutes is gonna be there when everything goes wrong." He slapped the hood of the car with his hand and bent over double again. When he could stand, he asked, "How do ya do it? Ya stumble through all kinds 'ah stuff and still come out better than some 'ah the guys I help."

"Thanks. I'll take that as a compliment."

"But we have ta work on that persistence for ya. Tell ya what, I got an idea for a new project, lot better 'an that last one, and I'll let ya help out, you bein' kinda apprentice-like."

"Doofus, you're incorrigible. You bounce from one disaster to the next and charge right into the next one. Don't you ever take a breather or try to figure out what went wrong the last time?"

"Oh, it's only those guys I had help'en me. Not one of 'em could find his backside with both hands. Now, this next project, I'm gonna be real careful and get hombres that will stick to it, the kind of guys you ought 'ah take lessons from. By golly, this next one's gonna be a cracker."

I shook my head in disbelief.

"I have to go, but I'll save a place for ya on this next one, provided ya do okay on the seminar. How's that coming?"

A chill went down my spine. I'd almost managed to put it out of my mind. "I have to put together a veterinary group to listen to Rodgers, pay for renting Ed's pool, rent a room at the country club for the seminar, and find a way to pay for Rodger's speaking fee and airfare. Other than that, I'm all set." My knees grew weak as I thought of it.

"Sounds good, Doc. By God, we'll get ya a set of balls yet, but would ya do somethin' fer me?"

Why not? My life seemed to revolve around satisfying the whims of a deranged fairy, a furious wife, and kids with no common sense. "What?"

"Could ya get some fresh cheese curls for once, and maybe some bock beer, somethin' dark and strong? I haven't had a really good beer for years. Take care, buddy."

Buddy? Good Lord! But damn it, I liked him. He was impetuous, careless, and thoughtless, but his cheerful and endless optimism was endearing, and he was never mean-spirited. I could do worse.

I called Jed a couple weeks later, after his semester finals. I remembered that I always hated having to go back to school after Christmas break to face those. He told me he was surprised by the care package. His affair had already ended when it arrived, but he found a use for the condoms.

"We had a water fight in the dorm hallways after finals, and the condoms made great water balloons, but—"

"Were you guys crazy? What was the temperature outside when you did this?"

"It got up to zero that day, but like I started to say, don't send the lubricated ones again. They really messed up my aim."

I told Mary I will never go on a shopping trip like that again, and if listening to Josh brag about his "help" wasn't enough to discourage her, the following year I wrote it up as a Christmas letter and sent it to everyone on her side of the family. Her older brother loved it.

Chapter 32: The Farm

Doc's Manuscript

Rockburg, Late January 1988

Work slowed from Christmas through February. It did every year, as daytime temperatures hovered around zero and nighttime temperatures dipped to between minus twenty and minus forty-five. It was a welcome respite that would last until temperatures moderated in early March.

I leaned over our receptionist's counter in the morning and looked over the day's farm calls.

"Sheryl, what's this?" I jabbed a finger on a line of the day's log. "What the devil is Wurborg Farms, and why have they asked for me?"

It was too damned cold to wander the countryside looking for a farm I'd never heard of.

Sheryl looked up from filing records. "It came in before Christmas. A guy with a western accent called and asked for you. You were out. He wouldn't give me a name, just called himself Mr. D. He said you'd know who he was."

I had a bad feeling about this. Sheryl found notes she'd taken during the call. The current farm owner was George Dennison. We made a few calls to the farm, but George never paid for the work. He couldn't afford to. He had tripled the size of his farm and added four hundred cows to his milking herd.

George used to compensate for poor management by working

brutally long hours on his farm. There weren't enough hours in the week to do that after he enlarged his farm and herd, and he gradually lost control of the herd's nutrition, reproduction, and health. Milk production dropped, expenses increased, and George floundered in red ink. The banks were going to foreclose within the month, according to rumors.

"We don't go to that farm," I reminded Sheryl.

"Mr. D. said to tell you these are new owners. They want the dry cows examined to verify they are pregnant before they sign the contract. He asked if you can be there between noon and one thirty."

John, one of my partners, came in for his list of farm calls. Tall, bearded, and lean, layered in winter clothing this morning, he looked like a plump sausage in a hurry. I asked what he thought of the Wurborg call.

He metamorphosed into a grumpy bratwurst. "Don't leave without getting the check. Better yet, get cash." Apparently, that said it all, as he picked up his list of calls and went to our storeroom for supplies.

I followed him, "What's going on with that place? Do you know anything about the new guys?"

John looked at me as though I'd farted in church. "It's the Dennison place. I'm in a bridge group with the realtor who handled the sale. He said four investors are putting up three million for it."

"George and a realtor are taking some investors for a ride?" I hadn't credited George with being that savvy.

"Nope. The realtor thought it was such a great deal he gave up his commission to get in on it. He thinks it's a steal."

"Is your realtor friend crazy?"

"I play bridge with him. I didn't say he was a friend. All five of them are nuts. None of them knows anything about farming or cows. Dennison's management was so bad he lost money when milk prices were high. He went from bust to a millionaire over the weekend." John began putting boxes of medication in his truck, and I went back to the receptionist's desk.

John poked his head into the lobby a minute later. "Remember, get cash," he called. "And find out who this veterinarian is that's going to be working with them."

Oh, my God, I thought. *Doofus is Mr. D, and this is the "sure thing" he wanted me to join.* We had accepted the call, and as professional conduct was understood, I was obligated to go. I planned my day to arrive at Dennison's at twelve thirty.

I reviewed what Doofus had already gotten me into as I drove to Dennison's farm. *Disaster, another disaster. Mary will throw me out of the house if I get involved in this, too. Doofus doesn't know a damned thing about farming.*

I still had to put a veterinary group together, find a lecture hall, and find a way to pay Prof. Rodgers. *Sometimes I act as though I'm the Valedictorian of the Stupid School. How do I get myself into these things? Oh, my God.*

A T-intersection was coming up, a quarter mile ahead. I was on a gravel road covered by ice and snow. It glistened in the bright sunlight. That meant the ice was melting and slippery. I touched the brakes as a test.

Nothing. *Damn.* I touched the brakes again, a little harder. The pickup started to skid, coasting sideways down the road. I took my foot off the brake, and the truck straightened out. I was doing thirty-five miles an hour, gradually slowing, and two hundred yards from the intersection.

I called the office on the truck radio. "Sheryl, call Sam Jenkins and ask him to bring a tractor to the T-intersection half a mile west of his farm."

"Why? In the ditch again?" Sheryl loved to bring up my driving history.

"The road is ice, and my brakes have no effect."

"Any damage to the truck?"

"I don't know; I'm not in the ditch yet. Just make the damned call."

I signed off, made sure my seat belt was snug, and moved a few things from the passenger seat to the floor. The snow in the ditch was deep, and the truck slowed enough before it reached the ditch to ease into it gently. I had to shove repeatedly against the door to move the snow packed against it. Sam arrived on his four-wheel drive John Deere tractor as I wiggled out of the cab.

Sam was in a good mood, and he knew we would knock a chunk off his account. The tractor was heavy and had chains on all four tires. Pulling me out of the ditch only took a couple of minutes. I could have thanked him politely and driven on. That would have been sensible.

I had to ask a question, "Sam, what's going on with the Dennison place?"

Sam was dressed for subzero weather, much colder than it was today. He unbuttoned his coat, leaned against my truck, and made himself comfortable. That's when I realized my mistake. This was winter, and with no fieldwork, Sam had time on his hands. Farmers on family dairies spend their days working by themselves, day after day, with no one to talk to but their cows.

Cows do pay attention to the guy with the feed scoop, so they are good listeners. But they never add much to the conversation, and I have yet to hear a cow laugh at a joke. The upshot of this is that many farmers became first-rate gossips, and once they got rolling, it was hard to get away from them.

"Dennison got out barely in time. He spent all day working in the fields from May to October. He ignored the cows, except to feed and milk 'em, and then he wondered why he didn't have enough income to pay his bills."

I wasn't dressed as warmly, and I was trying to keep to a schedule. I tried to get Sam to the point. "I know he sold out. What do you know about the new management?"

Sam was not to be rushed. "Did you know Dennison would strap himself into the tractor seat when he was dragging the fields before planting? He did it so he wouldn't fall off the tractor if he fell asleep. Damned fool worked from four in the morning to midnight. He never figured out the cows were more important than fieldwork, and even managing is work. George is one of those guys who thinks a job isn't work if ya don't get calluses. You know—"

"Sam, I have to get going. I have—"

"Did I tell ya what happened in that old house on what Dennison calls 'the second farm'? Ya see, his oldest boy was a senior . . ."

I took a deep breath. I couldn't shut him up. "Sam, I have to get—"

"Doc, ya can't keep hurrying around like this. I'll just have to drag your sorry ass out of the ditch again. Ya ought to slow down and talk to people more. Be more like your partner's wife. Well, maybe not quite that talkative. Ya know, she was out here with John once. He hardly said anything, but her mouth was going faster than a whippoorwill's ass in chokecherry time.

"Now, where the hell was I? Doc, ya got me off on the wrong track." Sam hitched up his overalls and scratched his chin in thought. Sam wouldn't spend an extra second talking to me in the summer when he was busy with fieldwork, but it was winter.

"Oh, yeah, Dennison's oldest boy was in high school, trying to save money for college, and he needed more money than his old man would pay him for working on the farm. There isn't much to do in winter in Drumley. So small, it ain't even a town. So the kids did what kids have done for fun ever since the first one figured out what an erection's for."

Oh, lord. Get one of these guys talking about sex, and he wasn't going to stop until he finished the story or his wife walked in. There wasn't another car on the road, so I was stuck.

"The kids would meet at the Community Center the town built to keep 'em out of trouble. They'd pair up and look for a place to play.

Dennison's kid saw the potential for income and talked his mom into letting him move into the house. He told her it was so there'd be someone there to check on the cows.

"She believed him, and the first thing he did was rent out bedrooms by the hour. It was only another step to hiring the girls and setting up a brothel on weekends."

This focused my attention. No way were my boys going to any parties in Drumley.

"There were four sisters, from fifteen to twenty-one, who became regulars for him. Anyway, it all ended when one of the girls brought her boyfriend with her. He was sixteen and pretty lively, if you get what I mean. The girls spent the weekend egging him on, as though he needed it, and by Sunday morning he didn't have the strength to crawl out of bed. The cops found out about it when Suzy—that's the youngest sister—called the boy's ma and asked her to come and get him.

"Ma called the cops. The kid was so exhausted the cops had to carry the him down the stairs to get him out of the house." Sam slapped the side of the pickup and laughed.

When a man pulls you out of a ditch twice in one winter, it's wise to laugh at his stories. I smiled, laughed, and managed to break off and head to Dennison's second farm.

It was an old dairy farm, a now empty house, a machine shed, and a traditional red dairy barn about 150 feet long. A path through the snow led to the barn door. Jim McMorrison, the investor's new manager, met me in the barn.

He wore the uniform of dairymen at that time of year: jeans, a flannel shirt, lined denim jacket, and winter cap. In his mid-twenties, he seemed young to be managing a multimillion-dollar enterprise with problems.

We introduced ourselves and got down to work. "What did you want me to do today?" I asked.

"We need to have the dry cows pregnancy checked. Dennison's

breeding records are a mess, and much of the information he gave us doesn't make sense."

"How do you mean?" This was a common story. Men facing bankruptcy and the loss of everything they've worked for often shade the truth, and others—often in politics—do it from force of habit and call it "spin."

A certain amount of flexibility in the description of livestock is condoned, even expected. For example, the term "second-calf heifer" is regularly used in sale barns and auction rings. I, ah, may have used it myself. Translated to urban-speak, it means, "pregnant virgin nursing her two-year-old." And the people who use that term do it with a straight face.

"According to the records, all of these cows are due to have a calf within forty-five days, but none of them looks that close."

Cows have a nine-month gestation period, usually have a calf every eleven to thirteen months, and are "dried off," or stop milking, when they're in their seventh month of pregnancy. As they only produce milk after having a calf, making sure the cows are pregnant within two to three months after calving is critical if a dairy farm is to survive.

Cattle are examined for pregnancy by doing a rectal exam. It's done wearing a glove that reaches from fingertips to shoulder, and you need every inch of it. I examined eighty cows for pregnancy. Jim tallied the results, as I cleaned up. Only half of the cows we examined were pregnant, and only half of the pregnant cows were in their third trimester.

It was worse than I'd ever seen on a dairy farm. "If your investors buy the farm and pay full price for these cows, they'll have an $80,000 loss before the ink is dry. Do you think they'll back out or renegotiate the price?"

Jim shook his head. "The deal's done, and they won't let me sell the cows. I asked that as soon as they hired me. Terms of the land contract require we keep four hundred cows on the farm. The partners can't afford to buy replacement cows, so we're stuck with 'em."

A land contract meant the new investors were buying the farm with a large loan from the owner, and to protect himself, he required that cattle sold had to be replaced. That was standard for land contracts, but I was dumbfounded. "The contracts have been signed and the down payment made? Usually, the herd is examined before the deal closes."

Jim shrugged his shoulders. "They thought the deal was so good somebody else would snap it up if they didn't move right away."

I'd heard that one so often, I won't buy anything if a salesman tries that pitch. It did give me a better sense of the situation. Jim knew what needed to be done, but the partners didn't know anything about the dairy industry and didn't trust his judgment.

"Would you like me to put my opinion in writing for you? The pregnant cows you have are too fat. Many will have difficulty calving. They'll develop foot and leg problems before they calve and metabolic problems after they calve. The cows that aren't pregnant will gain weight and be in worse shape by the time they're bred and ready to calve. Many of these cows will die within a month of calving, and the rest will have health problems. Treatment costs will run in the thousands. It'll cost your partners $500 a day in feed costs while they decide what to do."

Jim nodded. "I know, but they said they couldn't afford to sell them—end of discussion."

"What do they do for a living, and how did they get into this deal?"

"Four of them are chiropractors. They brag that they're making over $250,000 a year, each, and you should hear them complain. They work four days a week and gripe about it."

"I think they've found the cure for their problems." I handed Jim the bill. "Those incomes might almost be enough to support this farm, if their wives are frugal."

I dreaded asking the next question. "The realtor said they had a veterinarian working with them. Know anything about that?"

Jim shook his head. "He talked about it, but didn't mention a name. A guy called Mr. D was supposed to set that up." Jim pushed some straw around on the concrete floor with his foot. "If they hire the vet like they've done everything else, he's probably a dog or cat specialist, someone they met at a party."

Lord, this can't get any worse, I thought. I was wrong.

I waited for Jim to pay the bill, coughed a couple times, and looked at Jim, but he didn't volunteer. I prodded. "We were supposed to be paid today. Did they leave cash or a check with you?"

"No. They said to tell you their accountant would mail the check when he got the bill. That's what I had to tell the driver from the feed mill when he dropped off feed and the guy from the co-op when he brought diesel fuel. I gather you had a different understanding?"

"Right."

I was driving to the farm of a middle-aged bachelor a week later when Doofus appeared in the passenger seat.

"Cripes, Doc. Do you ever clean this cab? There must be a dozen empty soda cans on the floor here and darn near a whole box of used Kleenex. You got anything against neat?"

I'd been looking forward to confronting Doofus. "You don't like it, get a different ride." My kids complained about my truck, too, but why admit it to Doofus?

"What did ya think of the farm? Sweet deal, ain't it?"

I couldn't believe he was serious. "Doofus, that place is a money pit. Your investors will be lucky to avoid bankruptcy."

"Aw, it can't be— "

"It is. I'll be lucky if they pay me for my work today."

"Ya mean, after all my work, you're not going to buy in?"

"Buy in? My God, no. I'll bet you $100 these guys are broke in two years and probably in divorce court. That place is a financial sink hole."

"Well, there might be a little risk, but if a guy like you was to guide 'em, you and them chiropractors could make a bundle in five years. Just give it a chance, Doc."

"They don't have a chance. That farm is the Titanic, and it's already going down. If I buy a farm, I'll settle for breaking even. That isn't a possibility for these guys, and they don't know enough to see it."

"Aw, there ya go again—"

"Doofus, all I want to do is see if I can manage a herd. I'm in it to learn, not make a quick buck," I said, "and I'm wondering about these partners you've found. How can a medical professional make a quarter million a year and only work four eight-hour days a week? These guys aren't neurosurgeons, but they're making more than the specialists at the local clinic. Something's fishy."

I chanced taking my eyes off the road. Doofus was sulking. He caught me looking at him, told me I was a coward, and vanished.

Chapter 33: The Seminar

Doc's Manuscript

Rockburg, January to February, 1988

I called the country club and rented a room for the seminar. It was only two miles from Ed's pool. I desperately needed enough members for the local veterinary group I invented to have a decent audience for Prof. Rodgers and defray the costs. I might survive if I lost a couple hundred dollars, but I couldn't afford to look like a liar and a fool to Rodgers. I asked my two partners if they would attend.

I knew that would be a hard sell. They weren't enthusiastic about getting into new laboratory-based diagnostic tests of body fluids, which falls under clinical pathology. I hadn't been either, when I began practice, but I learned. I finally started our own laboratory, because it drove me nuts to wait twenty-four hours for results from the hospital lab. A younger associate and I saved our clients thousands of dollars a year by having timely lab results. It reduced the number of unnecessary night and weekend treatments, too, and I'm passionate about a good night's sleep.

With that background, I hoped there would be interest in Rodger's talk, even though my partners rarely made use of our lab.

"What's the topic?" asked John.

"Serum enzyme and electrolyte assays, especially those of an enzyme panel he's tested. He's used them to diagnose herd metabolic and nutritional problems. I've heard him before. He's good."

"When is it?"

"Saturday, February 12."

"I'll drop by, if I'm free. How many vets are planning to attend so far?"

I cringed. "Me."

"Sounds like you better get busy."

I knew John well enough to know a "maybe" meant "you couldn't drag me to it." My other partner didn't even feign interest, and our younger associate was taking emergency calls that day and wouldn't be available.

I called our competitors to the North. One of them was an old friend and classmate. He sounded interested and promised to get back to me in a week. Five veterinarians in a practice to our east agreed to attend, after I did some serious begging. I didn't think my self-respect would ever recover, but self-respect was a luxury I couldn't afford. Cranberry bogs, pine forests, and a forty-square-mile swamp bordered us on the south, so my last chance for an audience was a large practice to our west.

I had never met Dr. Warren, the senior partner in the practice. Although relations between practices were usually cordial and professional, there were times when they could be competitive, even confrontational, and we had tried to hire one of his younger associates just a few months earlier.

I doodled on a tablet, wondering if he knew about that. Uncertain of the reception to expect, I avoided looking at the phone on my desk for as long as I could. Exasperated with myself, I finally reached for it. *Oh look at the time. He's probably out for lunch or busy*, I thought. I heard Sheryl, our receptionist, answer the phone at the front desk. *Maybe have Sheryl call him? No, that's obviously a coward's way out, and she'll probably tell him what she thinks of the idea. I need something subtle and cowardly, something I can do tomorrow, or next week.*

Sheryl walked into the office. "Doc, a call for you."

Ah, the perfect excuse. "Who is it?"

"Drew Cincher."

Oh, Lord. Drew could talk all day and not even get to the reason why he called. I grabbed the phone and called Dr. Warren's office. "Tell Drew I'm on another line, important teleconference. Have him leave a message."

Dr. Warren wasn't in, but his receptionist told me she'd forward my message. I hung up, hoping I hadn't sounded as desperate as I felt and praying that Drew wasn't waiting on hold.

It looked like success would be an audience of ten people, with half the cost covered by me. That would take six months of careful tiptoeing to keep Mary from finding out. Nerves, uncertainty, and growing panic gave me abdominal pains most of the day. I finished my last farm call at eight that night and headed home, cold, tired, and doubled over with an aching gut. I was helping Mary clean up the dinner dishes when she handed me the phone. "It's for you," she said.

"Dr. Wilson, this is Jake Ferguson. I'm in a dairy practice in Dane county, but I'm calling for the state veterinary association. The winter meeting will be in your area, in Wausau, in mid-February, but we haven't been able to get a speaker. I heard you might be able to help us out."

I didn't admit it, but I hadn't been to a state veterinary meeting in years. The winter meeting was during our busiest period, and most of the speakers at the summer meeting addressed medical problems of dogs and cats. "How can I help you?" I asked.

"I understand you've arranged for Bill Rodgers to speak at a meeting you've put together on February 12. That overlaps our meeting at the Wilfred Inn in Wausau. That's only fifty miles from you. How about combining your meeting with the state meeting? We'll make you vice-chair of the speaker's committee and cover all the costs."

I was speechless. I'd gone from looming disaster to saving the state association's butt, and they'd cover all the costs. I leaned against the counter and gazed out the bay window overlooking our backyard. Five-foot snowdrifts reflected the kitchen lights, and I could touch the ice buildup along the bottom of the window, on the *inside* of the window. Ice in the kitchen on our triple-paned windows meant it was already minus thirty outside, and it was still early evening.

"Does the Wilfred Inn have an indoor pool?" I asked.

Dr. Ferguson paused, perhaps wondering whether his hearing was going or I was deranged. "Ah, pardon, what was that?"

"A pool, an indoor swimming pool. Does the Wilfred have one?"

"Yes, it has a small pool, mostly for kids to play in. They close it from January through February. It's too expensive to heat. Why do you ask?"

It's times like this that Mary describes me as, "He's stupid and can prove it."

I'd been cold all day, working in an open shed. My chapped hands hurt with every move. It was supposed to be colder tomorrow. "This may sound crazy to someone from southern Wisconsin, but you guys rarely get to minus twenty. It was minus sixty here on New Year's Eve, with a forty-mile-an-hour wind. The wind chill was minus a hundred ten. I saw Holsteins that froze to death. I promised our group we'd have a heated indoor swimming pool available after the seminar. I can't combine the meetings unless you can provide a large, heated, indoor pool, a sauna, and a hot tub, too."

"But this is the Wisconsin State Veterinary Associ—"

"And permission to have alcohol at pool side."

"Nobody allows—"

"I'm sorry, but we're cold up here. No pool, no sauna, no drinks, no speaker. Nice talking to you, Doctor." I hung up, righteously indignant that anyone would ask me to give up an afternoon in warm water—with brandy.

I didn't remain righteous long. My God, I'd done it again. I could have scored points with the state association and handed them the financial risk. Instead, I pissed them off.

"Living dangerously, are we?" Mary asked. "Did Santa leave something extra in your stocking and make you independently wealthy?"

"But, but, it's cold out there," I whined.

With a bang, Mary slammed a platter on the counter. "You'd better break even on this, or it will be cold in here, too."

An hour later, as I stared at my dinner, too tired and dejected to eat, and wondering if I'd still be married next month, Dr. Warren called.

"Hi, Jack, Bob Warren here. How are you doing?"

"Well," I lied. At least this lie was socially acceptable. Maybe I could pull this one off. "How are you this evening?" So far, so good. Two whole sentences and I still sounded sane. Short sentences, I'll grant you, but two. I glanced across the table at Mary. Her expression indicated I was hiding my enthusiasm well.

"They said you called today about a speaker you've lined up and a heated pool. Sounds interesting. What's the story?"

At last, someone who might be interested. I told him the whole sordid story, except for Doofus. My own behavior was hard enough to believe. There was no reason to bring in a chubby beer hound in a pink tutu.

"Man, you've got guts. It sounds like fun. Can you make room for eight, maybe ten if the practice north of us is interested?"

Can I? Saved! Mary claimed I didn't cry, but I felt like crying. "I think we can find room, maybe move a few chairs closer. Rodgers said he prefers small groups, but I think we can squeeze in ten. We'll have lunch at the country club, an hour of lecture, and an hour of discussion with Rodgers. We will spend the rest of the afternoon at the pool. Wives and family are welcome. Mary will make hors d'oeuvres and dessert, and I'll bring the wine, beer, brandy and soft drinks."

Bob reserved places for eight and their families and agreed to the cost per veterinarian. My cost estimate was low, but I didn't want to scare anyone away. Making up a few dollars per veterinarian out of my own pocket was better than paying for half of the total cost myself. Our conversation over, my appetite returned, and my gut felt fine. I wasn't even tired anymore. How could I have questioned my buddy Doofus?

The seminar day was cold and bright. Mary drove to Wausau, the nearest city with an airport, to pick up Rodgers and his wife. She had to drive past the Wilfred Inn. That made me feel even dumber. Fifteen veterinarians attended the meeting, an audience just sufficient to avoid embarrassment. Rodger's talk was interesting, but many of the nutritional deficiencies addressed were due to soil conditions not found in our area, and the data wasn't conclusive for the problems that were applicable to our dairies. It was difficult to see how we could make use of the information.

Rodgers made an odd comment that caught my attention, and I asked him to expand on it in the discussion period. "Bill, you mentioned you'd seen salt deficiencies in dairy herds. That sounds bizarre."

"Never underestimate the ability of well-meaning people to draw the wrong conclusions. Dairy cows require an extra ounce of salt for every thirty pounds of milk produced. That means a cow producing eighty to one hundred pounds of milk a day will need at least three ounces of salt above maintenance requirements. If deficient, they stop eating grain. They continue to eat hay and silage, but milk production collapses. Without adequate sodium levels, water isn't reabsorbed from the distal renal tubules, and urine production skyrockets. It's one of the strangest things you'll ever see."

The party at the pool was fun, but most of all it was warm. The pressure was off, and I celebrated a little too much. Rodgers and his wife seemed to enjoy themselves, and Bob Warren and his group had a ball in the pool; they raced, played water polo, and generally goofed around like a group of ten-year-olds.

I could only see through the center of the hoarfrost-coated patio doors on the south side of the pool. There was something about watching snow gusting from drift to drift, as I basked in the hot tub and nursed a brandy Manhattan that made me feel positively giddy. Two Manhattans and my life was in synch with the world. Even my children looked promising.

Warren took me aside as people were getting ready to leave. "Jack, I want to thank you for setting this up. You did a hell of a job on this. It was scientifically stimulating, and all of my people had a terrific time."

"Thank you. Any kind words are appreciated."

"How much of the cost are you going to have to swallow yourself?"

I glanced around to make sure Mary wasn't in earshot. "I don't have an exact figure yet, but it'll be about four hundred dollars." Truth was, I was afraid to sit down and add it up.

"When you get it figured out, I'll split it with you. We had a great time."

Mary and I drove home, but I could have danced all the way. Mary carried a plate of leftovers into the house, and I tidied up the car, humming and hugging myself. I had a sense I wasn't alone. I continued to straighten up Mary's car and didn't even turn around. "Doofus, what an unpleasant surprise. What brings you here on this beautiful evening?"

"Finally had your seminar, huh, Doc?"

"Yes, and it was better than I'd hoped. Rodgers is a great guy, and—"

"So, this idea of mine turned out okay, did it?" Doofus, hands clasped behind his back, rocked back on the heels of his boots and grinned.

"Not too bad. Scared the hell out of me a few times, and I lost a couple hundred on it, but—"

"Well, then, ya should be thrilled that I'm gonna help ya follow up on it. You could make a bunch of money on it, too." Doofus, apparently in an expansive mood, put an arm around my shoulders and gave me a hug while he gestured broadly with the other hand. "I already have just the partner lined up fer ya: a nutritionist out west. He's got a computer, a program that'll balance cattle rations for a hundred minerals, vitamins, and them other things. Why, working together, you can steer your clients—"

"Doofus, stop right there." It was work to control my temper. "Nutrition scams are more common than mice in a granary. Nobody knows what a cow needs for thirty nutrients, let alone a hundred. This has 'pixy twinkles' written all over it."

"Pixy twinkles?" Doofus looked uncertain whether to be irritated by my interruption or curious if other fairies were working in his area.

"Yeah. It's what I call dietary supplements that salesmen claim can cure everything. 'Sprinkle them on a cow's feed, and all her problems are solved,' they say. It's the nexus of ignorance and greed. Sometimes, it's wishful thinking; usually, it's a con." I didn't add that my partners were easily swayed by these salesmen and frequently recommended supplements of this sort.

"Aw, Doc, don't go all negative on me again. Just wait until I introduce ya to the project. Yer gonna—"

That's when Mary interrupted and complicated things.

Chapter 34

The Heirs' Story

Rockburg, March 2014

Josh walked into the hardware store. He'd forgotten how different the old store was compared to the chain hardware stores he'd become used to. The store, built at the close of the nineteenth century, was high ceilinged, and, like a shotgun barrel, narrow, and long. The entry was also the exit, a single door a little wider than a standard door in a home. The store's floor was wood, made of boards only two or three inches wide, and the center aisle—the entry aisle and widest of the three aisles in the store—was so cramped it could barely hold three people abreast. And they'd better be good friends and all of them on diets.

To Josh's left were shelves, five shelves high, each packed with merchandise. It wasn't a display so much as a clutter of hinges, hammers, pliers, kitchenware, and various types of connections for electronics and plumbing. On his right was a counter running half the length of the store. The one cash register was in the center of the store in front of a display of rifles and shotguns. He recognized one shotgun, a double-barreled eight-gauge that had been in the display rack when he'd been in the store as a kid, almost thirty years ago. The gun had been old then. Sales of eight-gauge shotguns were apparently pretty slow in a state that hadn't had a proper target for that kind of gun since the last mammoth died.

Josh, hoping to talk to Hank, Doc's old friend and proprietor of the store, stood in line behind another customer dressed in jeans, work boots, and a heavy denim jacket. Something about the customer seemed familiar, but Josh didn't recognize the estate's farm manager Jim until he turned to leave.

"Jim, Jim McMorrison?" Josh asked.

"Josh, how have you been? How are you guys coming with your dad's codicil?"

"We've gotten some of Dad's computer passwords and we're working on others, but progress is slow." Josh tried to sound upbeat and optimistic, but the quest for answers was wearing him down.

"Let me buy you a cup of coffee across the street, if you have time. You've met Gert, haven't you?"

The two men jaywalked across the street to the Coffee Cup. The café was empty, except for Gert, who was taking her afternoon nap in one of the booths. She awoke when the bell over the entry door jingled. Jim and Josh took seats at the counter as Gert yawned, stretched and stood.

"Gert, can we get a cup of coffee here?" Jim asked.

"Haven't you two got something better to do than interrupt an old lady's beauty rest?" Gert asked. She walked behind the counter and poured two cups of coffee for the men.

Jim added cream to his coffee and stirred. "You'll have to excuse Gert, Josh. She only pretends to be an old grizzly—hasn't bitten a paying customer in weeks, so they tell me."

"Months," Gert corrected. "Now I just listen to the gossip from the ladies at the hair salon next door and pass it on if certain customers get too mouthy." She put the coffee pot back and put two cheese Danish rolls on a plate. "Either of you guys care for a roll? They're on the house. Be too stale tomorrow."

Jim paid for the coffee, Gert returned to her booth and nap, and Jim asked again how the mystery of the codicil was going.

Between bites of cheese Danish, Josh summarized what he knew. "We haven't figured out what Doc meant by squirrel fishing or the character Doofus," he said. "Whatever Doc wanted to teach us has something to do with the importance of ideas, and it's pretty clear he wanted to instill confidence, or at least teach us not to fear failure. Beyond that, things are pretty hazy."

Jim sipped on his coffee. "Remember what Justin and I told you the night you took us out to dinner. Your dad told me that you have to have a dream, a goal, for the future."

"Vaguely. But how does that fit with what we know?"

"Dreams, goals, and plans are just forms of ideas. If you substitute 'dream' for 'idea' in what you told me, it begins to make sense. Your dad also said that the difference between daydreaming and planning was action. That kind of fits with what you said about fear of failure, doesn't it?"

Josh pulled a notepad and pen from a pocket of his coat, thanked Jim, and made notes on what Jim had said. "You know, I really feel stupid. I had the pieces, but I hadn't thought of dreams being ideas. Once you get past that, it makes sense."

"Glad to be of help. Your dad also said that most ideas are wrong. Let me know if this one turns out right."

"Be happy to. Say, where are you from, originally? I read how Doc met you, and I know you've run the farm for years."

"I grew up in Swanville, Minnesota, on my stepdad's dairy farm."

"Where is Swanville?" Josh asked.

"Just about dead center in the state. It's a dinky place—even smaller than Rockburg. I worked on the farm from the time I was a kid, and Paul, my stepdad, put me through college. He was a few years older than my mother. When I went off to school, Paul and Mom couldn't handle the work and had to cut back. They'd retired and sold the farm by the time I got my degree."

"Was your mother's family from Swanville?"

"Not even close. She'd been raised in Louisiana. I was born there, but my parents divorced about the time I was born." Jim turned from Josh and looked straight across the counter.

"How did you happen to end up in Rockburg? Josh asked.

"An advertisement in *Hoard's Dairyman*. The Warburg farm was looking for a manager, but they weren't willing to pay enough to get someone with experience, so I got the job."

"Warburg farm—that's were Doc met you, right?"

"Yeah. It was my first job out of school. I was only twenty-three, and I was panicking. I'd moved my wife and baby from Minnesota to Rockburg and found out my employers didn't have a clue what they were doing, and they wouldn't listen to me. A million dollar dairy and my job was going down the toilet and there wasn't anything I could do to stop it. There were nights I couldn't sleep, days when I didn't talk to my wife and could barely keep food down."

"Man. Sounds gruesome. How did things turn out?" Josh asked.

Jim took another sip of coffee and finished chewing a bite of pastry. "Best thing that ever happened to me. I got fired six months before the bank foreclosed on the owners. Your grandmother hired me the next day. Elspeth and Doc knew what they were doing and were willing to listen to me when I had suggestions. I enjoyed working again, and I've worked for your family ever since."

Jim finished his Danish and downed the last of his coffee. "Nice to see you again, Josh, but I have to get back to the farm."

After Jim left, Josh was so eager to let the other heirs know what he'd learned that he only paused briefly to say hello to Gert.

Chapter 35: The Speech

Doc's Manuscript

Rockburg, March 10, 1988

Mary put her head in the garage and called me. "Jack, phone. It's the Pittsville High School FFA."[4]

She didn't keep the door open long enough to allow questions.

I took the call in the kitchen, with Doofus sitting next to me. The Ag instructor and advisor to the FFA asked if I could give a talk on bovine mastitis (infections of the udder) to the kids. It would be in three weeks, on a Wednesday evening.

My research in practice was centered on mastitis. I'd set up a bacteriology lab in our office, gone to national seminars on mastitis, even put together a collection of malfunctioning milking equipment that I'd found on dairies with mastitis problems. I was inordinately proud of that collection and what I'd learned, but it would be one more night away from Mary and the kids.

I started to say I wasn't sure I'd be free that night, when Doofus grabbed the phone and clapped a hand over the mouthpiece. "Doc! This is your chance to strut yer stuff, get some credit for all ya know about this here problem. Yer the expert; go show 'em."

I hate to admit it, but those thoughts had crossed my mind. This would be a great way to build a reputation. Doofus handed me the phone, and I accepted the invitation.

4 Future Farmers of America

Pittsville was thirty miles south of our office and on the edge of a forty-mile stretch of swamp. When the teacher started to give me directions to the high school, I stopped him and told him I knew the town. I drove through it every month on my way to one of our clients. A large brick building on the edge of town was visible from the road. It had to be the high school. What else could it be in a dinky little burg like Pittsville?

Doofus clapped me on the back when I put the phone down. "That's the way to do it, Doc. I'll make sure I've got time to go with ya, keep ya on task, and make sure ya don't screw up again like ya done in the past. I can help ya carry that stupid collection 'ah machine parts and hoses ya got. By God, we'll turn ya into a real man yet."

With that, he disappeared. His comments didn't boost my confidence. I had more second thoughts while explaining to Mary why I'd be away from the family another night. I always seemed to get caught in the dilemma of spending time with the family or doing things to keep our clients happy or building our practice. No matter what I decided to do, I risked something important to me.

The day of the talk was busy. I didn't have time to eat dinner or organize my speech. Doofus appeared, as promised, as I was loading the hoses, stainless-steel DeLaval milking bucket, pulsators (vacuum control devices), and other parts of my collection. My hands were full, and a hose dragged behind me as I made my last trip to my truck.

"Here, Doc, let me help you." He picked up the dragging hose and wrapped it around my neck. "There. Wouldn't want you to get it dirty before your talk."

"Thanks. I thought you were going to help me with this?"

"I am. Wouldn't miss it for the world." He opened the door of the pickup for me. "Let's get going. Mustn't keep the kiddies waiting."

Doofus and I talked—or rather, he let me rattle on—as we drove to Pittsville. He didn't complain while I talked about mastitis, bacterial infections, and the inflammatory response to the infection, which often does more damage than the infection. He didn't even criticize my work. All he did was ask me if I needed a map of Pittsville.

Who needs a map for a town of eight hundred?

We found the brick building quickly, but I missed the entry to the parking lot on my first pass. My night vision is bad. It's not something I talk about often, as it makes our insurance agent nervous. So does the number of deer I hit every year.

There were no signs identifying the school. I assumed they weren't lit and I just hadn't seen them in the dark.

I parked the truck and loaded up the milking equipment. As before, Doofus's idea of 'helping' was to wrap the hoses around my neck and shoulders and hold one of the big double doors open for me when we reached the school entrance.

We stood in a high-ceilinged foyer with more double doors in front of us and dark hallways to our left and right. No one was there to greet us. Where the hell was everybody? Someone should have been at the door to at least guide us to the right room. I was swearing under my breath about our host's lack of consideration when Doofus nudged me in the ribs.

"Ah, Doc." He pointed to a picture above the double doors.

The picture was a large oil painting—of Jesus.

Startled, I looked at Doofus.

He shrugged. "Guess this place ain't never heard 'ah the Supreme Court." He looked around the foyer, eyebrows arched innocently, hands clasped behind his back.

Glib and reasonable answers from Doofus made me nervous. I tiptoed to the double doors under the picture and peeked into the next room. There were lit candles all over—and pews. Lots of pews. We were standing in the entrance of a Catholic church on Wednesday night during Lent.

Doofus tapped his map. "According to this here map—"

"Oh, shut up, and help me get this stuff out of here." I stepped outside the church and started toward my truck. I hadn't gone ten feet before I ducked behind bushes and cedar trees between the sidewalk and the church. The sidewalk in front of me was crowded with parishioners coming to the service.

"Ya sure ya don't want to look at that map?" Doofus asked again.

"Shut up," I hissed. "How the hell will I explain this if anybody sees me?"

"You could try, 'the blessing of the milking machines,' or maybe 'the exorcism of defective machines.' You said this stuff didn't work, right?" Doofus pretended to consider the choices. "I like the exorcism best. Ya could tell 'em ya was desperate, 'cause Presbyterians don't have exorcisms." He doubled over with laughter.

I told him to stuff it.

"Doc, I give ya great ideas, and ya twist 'em into disasters. Yer worse 'an some presidents I've worked with, an' you're doing it all on your lonesome. They had help."

I told him what I thought of that, too. A break in the crowd materialized, and I skulked to my truck. We found the high school, and I gave my talk, but my heart wasn't in it. Someone had to have seen me in the bushes. All I could do was pray that nobody recognized me.

Doofus gave me his version of the night, all the way home. "How do ya do it, Doc? Ya got yer nose in a book or looking over records whenever ya aren't workin', then ya turn around and do stuff like this." He talked nonstop until we pulled into my driveway.

It wasn't easier at home. Mary asked me how the talk went, and I lied. "Great. Just great." I stomped into our bedroom and stripped to take a shower.

"Did you get to use your—"

"I don't want to talk about it." I turned on the water and stepped into the shower. "Aahhhg!"

The water was ice cold. I hadn't let it warm up. The evening just kept getting better and better.

I had a rare chance to have lunch at home a couple of days later. The weather was working up to a spring blizzard and farmers were cancelling nonemergency calls. Mary brought up the night of my trip to Pittsville while taking my lunch out of the microwave.

"I talked to Sue at the grocery store this morning. Dan received a call about a disturbance at the Catholic church in Pittsville Wednesday night. Did you hear anything about that?"

Dan, Sue's husband, was a highway patrolman. I could feel my pulse and blood pressure going up. I tried to look innocent. "What? I didn't see anything going on in town."

"Dan said there was a complaint about a person hiding in the shrubbery around the church. People said he looked mentally disturbed. His clothes were dirty, and he was carrying pails and hoses. One of the men thought it might be a skit Father Dan would use later in the service, but Father Dan said he didn't know anything about it. He heard someone yelling in the church earlier, though."

My toes curled in embarrassment.

Mary paused, watching me carefully. She can be awfully suspicious at times. After a tense moment, at least for me, she continued. "Whoever it was could be dangerous. One of the men said he started to walk up to the figure to ask him what he was doing in the shrubbery. He decided not to get close when he heard the guy arguing with one of the trees."

Oh, damn. Other people couldn't hear or see Doofus. I might be able to explain why I was at the church, but no way could I explain Doofus to Mary and not end up talking to a shrink. I bolted the rest of my food, kissed Mary goodbye, and headed back to the office. I needed to get away from questions.

I should have paid attention to the weather.

Chapter 36: Blizzard

Heard the horse whinnying for his corn;
And, sharply clashing horn on horn,
Impatient down the stanchion rows
The cattle shake their walnut bows . . .
—J. G. Whittier, *Snow Bound*

Doc's Manuscript

Rockburg, March 11, 1988

Four hours later, I was trying to keep my practice truck on the road as I searched for the turnoff to Don's farm. Snow whirled around the truck and blasted the windshield. Forward visibility was zero. I held the truck door open, just a little, and watched for glimpses of the yellow centerline. Where the road was snow covered, I watched farther to my left for a fence post or telephone pole to gauge where the edge of the road met the ditch.

"See the crossroads yet?" I asked Ken.

Ken, a senior student in veterinary medicine at the University of Minnesota, rolled the passenger window down and strained to see through the blowing snow and gloom. "Might be past this next telephone pole."

Ken was over six feet, nearly as tall as me, and still looked like the football lineman he'd been as an undergraduate. He was taking his externship with our practice in the spring quarter and had volunteered to go on one last call that day. Don, a dairy farmer who lived ten miles east of town, had called with an emergency just before four.

It was three weeks before Easter and the bad weather this morning had turned into the worst spring blizzard in fifty years. A heavy snow started falling in midmorning, and a northwest wind created whiteout conditions by three in the afternoon. Side roads were impassable by four, and the few open highways were one lane. We were creeping along one of the highways at ten miles an hour, looking for the dead-end road that led to Don's farm.

"Will this guy come out to meet us, if his road is drifted in?" Ken asked.

"I'd better find out." I called the office on the truck's radio. "Don's road will be drifted shut. Can he come out to get us on a tractor or snowmobile?"

Sheryl, the receptionist, answered. "I have him on the other line. He said the weather is awful. He doesn't think he can get to you."

"We noticed the weather. How does he suggest we get to his farm?"

"Just a minute."

"He wants you to hike in. He says it's barely a mile from the highway to his farm."

I told the windshield what I thought of that. "We'll try. It would help if he'd meet us partway. Can he do that?"

"I'll ask. Let me know if you leave the truck."

Ken interrupted. "Here's the side road."

We were in the middle of the intersection. I backed up a few yards to build up speed. We made the turn with enough momentum to bull through a small drift and get another two hundred feet before coming to a drift higher than the headlights of the truck.

I stopped the truck and turned to Ken. "This is it. You can stay with the truck or come with me."

"I'm game."

I called the office. "Tell Don we've hit a drift and will start walking in. Will he pick us up part way?"

"He said he'll try to start his tractor, but the weather is miserable."

Imagine that, I thought. "No kidding."

I left the truck running and the lights on to help us find the truck on our return. We zipped up our coveralls and parkas and opened the truck doors. Driving snow and ice swept through the passenger compartment as we scrambled out of the truck and took our bearings.

We were in a twilight world without color. A black line of trees ahead was the only landmark in a landscape of white and gray, of shifting shadows, sky, and snow. We couldn't see the road we stood on. A glimpse of a telephone pole, fence post, or bush was all we had to guide us.

We slogged forward in silence. Talking into the wind was pointless. Wind cut through coveralls, jeans, and thermal underwear, stinging our legs. Snow hit our eyes like ice pellets. It built up on my eyelashes, partially blinding me.

Leaning into the wind, we walked head down to protect our eyes. That made it impossible to keep a straight course. Chest-deep in snow, we were in the ditch on the east side of the road.

Ditches are deep in snow country, and we had to scramble to get out. I pawed my way through the snow to get back on the road. My wrists burned from the snow, and the wind stung my cheeks and ears. We floundered on another half mile before Ken waved to get my attention. "Hey, hey, Doc, over . . ."

He pointed through gusting snow toward dim lights ahead of us. Don and his tractor came within fifty feet of us before I saw him.

Don braked the left rear wheel and whipped the old John Deere in a tight circle. Ken and I climbed on the back on either side. We each stood on part of the tractor's hitch and held onto a fender and the tractor seat. My feet were numb as Don pulled the tractor up to a cement block milk house next to an old red barn.

Don's herd was small, as was the milk house. Other than size, it was like all milk houses, a maze of stainless-steel pipes just low enough for a tall man to bump his head. A five-hundred-gallon, stainless-steel tank sat in the middle of the room. Ken filled a pail with hot water and Don led us through a short passageway into the barn.

Don hung his coat on a nail in the barn. Fifty cows, each weighing eleven hundred to sixteen hundred pounds, put off a lot of heat. The barn was warm, humid and smelled of hay, molasses, and cows.

We walked onto the center aisle of the barn. The concrete aisle was white with a dusting of crushed limestone, used to improve footing and appearance. A gutter, about a foot deep and a little wider, bordered each side of the aisle to collect manure. On the other side of the gutter, stanchioned cows, facing away from us, stood on a concrete platform bedded with straw and old corn stalks. To a dairyman, the business end of a cow is the rear.

Some cows stood, eating hay in the manger in front of them, while others were lying on the bedding, chewing their cud, and relaxing. With a great clatter of their stanchions, all but one cow stood and turned to look at us.

A fifteen-hundred-pound cow was lying on her sternum. She wasn't moving or responding to stimuli, and her butt was in the gutter, her legs in an unnatural position. Don said she'd calved the night before and looked normal this morning, but she was paralyzed and in the gutter this afternoon, the typical history of a cow with "milk fever"—low blood calcium.

We examined the cow and treated her with intravenous calcium. She became alert, but remained immobile. By brute force, Ken and I pulled her onto the center aisle where we could put her legs in a natural position.

Ken and I washed up as Don started his tractor. We rode back through the blizzard in silence. It was dark by this time, and the glare of the tractor's headlights on the driving snow was nearly blinding.

Don halted the tractor where he picked us up. He could go no farther. Ken and I waded through the snow a couple hundred yards before we could see the truck's headlights through the storm. I tried to pick up the pace, but only managed to trip and stumble the last few yards to the truck.

The driver's side door was frozen shut. Ken was able to open the passenger door, as it was protected from the wind and blowing snow. He clambered into the truck, put both feet against the driver's door, and pushed the frozen door open.

We caught our breath in the warm cab. "Is that cow gonna make it?" Ken asked.

"Unlikely. Her legs have been cramped and circulation impaired for hours. Lactic acid builds up, muscle cells rupture, and the cow becomes a cripple."

I called the office. Sheryl was happy to hear from me, chewed me out for taking risks, and told us to get back to the office.

Ken unzipped his coat. "Man, that was a ride. You're sure it was a wasted effort?"

"Worse. I risked our lives for a cow that was a lost cause before Don called us, and I did it for less than $25. The Three Stooges look like geniuses compared to me."

It took thirty minutes to drive the ten miles back to town. The office had closed early. Ken was able to start his car; he was staying with a friend nearby.

My driveway was drifted shut when I arrived home. Great. I waded through the drifts to the garage and started the snow blower. At least that worked. It took twenty minutes of damned cold work to get my truck into the garage.

Mary reheated my dinner. I barely had the energy to eat. We went to bed as soon as I'd eaten.

The phone rang an hour later.

"Hey, Doc, how ya doin'? This is Paul Hintz out on Highway 55. I have a problem."

I groaned. Paul had a large farm and rarely called us, as he treated his own cattle for routine problems.

"What's that ya said, Doc?"

I should groan more quietly, I thought. "What's the problem?"

"A cow is acting funny. She eats, but I have to prod her to get her to move. When she does, she's slow and throws her head back and forth as she walks."

I tried to think, but all I could come up with was that my bed was warm, and I wasn't going to leave it for anything but an emergency. "How long has this been going on?"

"A couple days. It's a lot worse tonight."

Of course. He could have called yesterday. I asked a few more questions to rule out real emergencies, and the answer came to me. "Which way does she throw her head?"

"Ah, just a second." I heard Paul yell at his son to make the cow walk. The line was dead for a minute as they watched the cow. "To the right, only to the right."

Still sleepy, I tried to think. *She's taking weight off a sore front foot. If she throws her head to the right, the problem is in her left foot. God, I hope this is right. Paul will tell everybody in the county if I'm wrong.* "Paul, pick up her left front foot. Clean the bottom of the inside toe with a hoof knife. There's an abscess between the outer wall of the hoof and the sole."

"What? She's acting crazy, and you think it's a foot problem?"

"Left front hoof, inside toe. Drain the abscess and call me tomorrow, if she isn't better." I hung up and embraced my pillow. There are times when a man loves his pillow more than anything else in life, and tonight was one of those for me.

The phone rang again, a little after midnight. An accented voice spoke slowly. "Doc, this is Aaron Mueller. I have a cow that's real bad. Can you git here right away?"

Too groggy to question what the problem was, I asked for directions and rolled out of bed. I was dressed and headed out the door before I was awake enough to question why the hell I was going on this call. *Mueller, Mueller,* I thought. *Damn, I can't call him back to get more information. He's Amish—used his neighbor's phone.*

There was nothing to do but go to Mueller's and examine the cow.

It was no longer snowing, the wind had died down, and visibility was good. Radio reports said the county snowplows had been pulled off the roads until daybreak. Most north-south roads were impassable, but paved east-west roads were open.

There were only a few low snowdrifts over the highway as I drove west. My pickup easily bulled through these. Twelve miles out of town, I turned south on the gravel road to Mueller's.

High winds had scoured the snow from the road for the first mile, with no trees or bushes along the road to break the wind. Single trees, then groups of two or three, lined the second mile. These became an unbroken line of trees and brush in the final mile to Mueller's crossroads, and drifts across the road became frequent. None were big enough to stop the truck.

A deep drift blocked the road only yards from the crossroads by Mueller's farm. I steered the truck to the side of the road where the drift was smallest and accelerated. The truck started to slide toward the ditch, but the snowdrift on the other side caught the tire, swinging the truck back to the center of the road.

I turned right at the crossroads and saw a dim light, a lantern, one hundred yards ahead. The driveway was easy to spot; sleigh tracks and fresh horse apples marked it. I pulled up to the barn and waited. Aaron, a bearded patriarch, waded through the snow toward me from his house, two teenage sons in tow.

"Hi, Doc. She's in here." Aaron unhooked the latch and swung the barn door open.

The barn was warm and dark. The acrid smell of old urine-soaked straw intermingled with the smell of cows and the slightly sweet odor of horse manure. Aaron led the way with a sputtering lantern, walking down the center aisle of the barn, past the hind quarters of four gold-colored Belgian draft horses standing in their stalls and several Guernsey cows. Hoarfrost on the windows sparkled at the edge of the lantern's light.

The clatter of the stanchions, as the cows turned to look at us, was from an earlier century: cow horns against wooden stanchions. Whittier would have recognized it.

Cows, calves, and horses—all were thin. Aaron pointed to the skinniest cow I'd ever seen. Her spine, shoulders, ribs and hips stood out, barely covered by hide. Her hair was long and dusty, indicating she'd given up grooming herself. There was a deep depression in the cow's belly between the last ribs and her hips.

Aaron hung the lantern on a nail in the wooden beam above the cow. "She stopped eating her ground feed, and now she doesn't even eat her hay."

I stepped next to the cow's rear, inserted a rectal thermometer, and brushed cobwebs out of my hair. Cobwebs in barns like this drape from beams and rafters to the height of the tallest person who works in the barn, and I was a head taller than Aaron or his sons.

"How long has she been off her grain?" I asked.

Aaron scratched his chin. "Ah, let's see. I guess it'd be about three weeks."

"When did she quit eating her hay?"

Chin in hand, Aaron thought a moment. "Thomas, when was the last time she ate her hay?"

The taller of the two boys shrugged his shoulders. "Oh, maybe three, four days ago. She's been ah coughing a lot, too, ya see, for the last month."

I could hear the wheezing in the cow's lungs without a stethoscope, and there was a pause in the inward movement of her chest and abdomen on expiration, followed by an extra push. She had a severe chronic pneumonia. *Great,* I thought. *Another hopeless case. Two in one night.*

Nothing was audible with the stethoscope over a large part of the cow's chest. No air moved in her lungs there. The airways were probably filled with puss and cellular debris. Her lungs would never return to normal.

A greasy coat of gunk covered the hair over her ribs, a residue from a home remedy. I stepped back onto the aisle and turned to Aaron. "She has chronic pneumonia. Most of her lungs are shot. Treatment will be expensive and is unlikely to help. If we treat her, you will not be able to sell the milk she produces for four days or sell her for meat for twenty-one days after the last treatment. I can treat her, or you can cull her as she is. I'd recommend putting her down."

Aaron crossed his arms and looked at the floor. He turned to look at the cow, stroked his beard, and sighed. "Well, yer here, Doc. Ya might as well treat her."

I treated the cow, left medication for several days, and handed Aaron the bill. The trip, exam, and medication came to $28. I hadn't done anything that day that a farm kid with a high school education couldn't do. It was time to review the way we ran the practice or find other work.

It was one thirty in the morning when I wished him a good morning, crawled in my truck, and drove out of the yard. I had to dig my way through a couple drifts on the way home and fight to stay awake during the rest of the drive. At two thirty in the morning I pulled into my driveway.

Paul called that afternoon to tell me the hoof abscess was where I said it would be. Of the three cows I treated that night, the only one that would recover was the one I treated from my bed. Good work, if you can get it, but we didn't charge for advice. I loved veterinary practice, but I was spending too much of my time doing things that didn't help the client or me.

Chapter 37: Romance In Winter

Had we but world enough and time . . .
—Andrew Marvell, *To His Coy Mistress*

Doc's Manuscript

Rockburg, March 11, 1988

"Your mother phoned," Mary called from the kitchen. "She asked if we'd like to have dinner at the farm tomorrow."

It was a Saturday and a rare day off for me. I put my newspaper down and wandered into the kitchen. The Nativity had been a disaster, from what Mark told me, and I was sure Mom helped Linda rope him into it. This could be interesting.

"Did she say what the occasion was?" I asked.

"She wants your advice. Tom is leaving, and she's looking for a new farm manager." Mary was washing dishes and turned to look at me. "She could have called you for that."

Tom, Mom's farm manager, had been looking for a farm of his own for years. "Did she say anything else?" I asked.

"I had the impression there was something she didn't want to say on the phone. She asked if it would be okay if we left the kids at home. That was strange."

"Strange" was an understatement. Mom would usually rather talk to Julie and Josh than Mary and me. She was up to something.

We arrived at the farm shortly after noon the next day. The

table was set and Mom was carving a roast chicken. Mary and I had a beer and helped Mom get the food on the table. Dinner with only the three of us at the table felt odd. There had been children at the table with us whenever we had dinner with Mom for almost twenty years.

The conversation was light at first: how Mark and Linda were doing, how their children were growing, and the Nativity. Then, Mom threw me two curve balls over dessert.

"You know, I've been lonely out here since your father died," she said.

"I guessed that," I said. "Are you thinking of moving into town or renting out the farm?"

"No." She pushed a piece of cake around her plate. "I've met someone. I might ask him to move in with me. I thought I'd tell you so you wouldn't be surprised if I ask him, and if he does. He is a few years younger than me."

I didn't know what to think or say. Mary handled it better. She gushed about how nice it would be for Mom to have a companion, asked about a wedding, and deftly slipped in a questions about how much younger the guy was and where he was from, too.

"No wedding," Mom said. "The gentleman in question doesn't have a stellar record when it comes to handling money. We will keep our finances separate. He's about six years younger than me, I believe. More cake?"

That was vintage Mom: assess potential problems, adroitly sidestep them, and change the subject. We asked when we'd get to meet him and other questions, but Mom said nothing was definite. She just wanted us to know what she was contemplating.

She moved the conversation to her search for a new farm manager. I told her about the Worburg farm and Jim, their manager. "He's already disenchanted with the owners, and it's going to get worse. They seem to be in it to make a quick buck, which proves they either don't know a damned thing about dairy farming or they're running a scam of some sort. He'll bail out as soon as he can, if he's as smart as I think he is. His only problem is a lack of experience. You should give him a call if you're willing to be a mentor for a kid."

Mom's expression became distant, and she stirred her coffee absently. "I'll think it over. You said his name was Jim McMorrison?"

I knew better. If she was interested in Jim, she'd be on the phone calling people who worked with the Worburg farm before Mary and I cleared her driveway. She'd be able to write his resume for him by next week.

Mary interceded when Mom stood and started to clean the table. "Sit down, Elspeth. You and Doc should talk. You hardly see each other anymore. I'll take care of the dishes."

Mary must have suspected Mom wanted to talk to me. Whatever the reason, Mom didn't put up much fuss, which was unusual for her. Mary headed to the kitchen with a load of plates, and we were alone.

Mom leaned back in her chair and smiled. "I hear you've put Doofus in his place. Nice work."

My jaw dropped. I didn't know whether to deny knowing what she was talking about or keep my mouth shut and let her continue. I tried the latter, but she wasn't going to add more and the silence became uncomfortable.

"You and, ah, you've met Doofus?" I asked.

"He's an old acquaintance of anyone with a good imagination. Anybody who claims otherwise didn't recognize it when they met."

"Huh?" was all I could say.

"The raving lunatic and the inspired genius get their ideas from the same well, and sometimes they sound alike. It's always frightened me, and I worried you didn't know the difference."

"I'm not sure I do," I admitted. "I let Doofus talk me into—"

"Recognizing your own fallibility is key. You're doing fine, from what I saw of Doofus." She chuckled, as she stirred her coffee. "He was nearly in tears."

"Where did—" I started, but she wasn't finished.

"The wise question and test their own ideas. Fools and the careless are too busy crowing about their brilliance to worry they might be wrong." She stood and picked up the last few plates. "I shouldn't need to tell you this."

It's embarrassing to be middle-aged and have your mother explain life to you. I followed her toward the kitchen. "I know I shouldn't listen to Doofus, but he—"

Her hands full, Mom turned to back through the door to the kitchen. "Nonsense. Far-out ideas are important. You're the one who said a scientific paper wasn't worth publishing unless it was controversial."

Mary asked me who Doofus was as we drove home. I tried to come up with a believable answer. Fat chance of doing that. I settled for telling her it was family code for someone with untested ideas that fit what people wanted to believe.

"You mean like surefire stock tips and silver mines?" she asked.

Damn. I thought she'd forgotten about those. "Could be." I tried to think of a way to change the topic.

Mary looked altogether too satisfied with how this conversation was going. "Or 'the domino theory of foreign policy,' or 'the wisdom of the marketplace,' or 'trickle-down econom—'"

"Oh, look at the deer," I pointed to a copse of birch and maple to the left of the road. I hadn't seen any deer, but Mary was always afraid I'd hit one. It seemed like a good diversion, and it worked, for now.

Chapter 38: Nutrition

Doc's Manuscript

Rockburg, May 10, 1988

The start of spring is a bad joke in a region with six inches of snow cover until late March. The health of the cattle deteriorated, as daily temperatures started to swing and weather became unpredictable. My partners and I were working twelve- to sixteen-hour days. With April and the spring thaw, the waterlogged clay under the gravel roads thawed, the roads became pliable, heaving and sinking in waves under my truck.

By late April, the Wurborg consortium paid their bill for the exams, and by May, Doofus was 'helping' again. I had another wretched night of emergency calls on lost causes, which put me in a foul mood, but at least I wasn't driving through a blizzard.

I felt much better after a night's sleep and a hot breakfast. At the office that morning, I didn't even quiz our receptionist about the call when she sent me to one of our regular clients, Sam Border. The particulars she provided were bizarre. All the cows were off feed, milk production was down, he was unable to clean the barn, drowning. Drowning? This had to be a practical joke.

The Borders lived in a section that had been logged sixty years ago and divided into four farms. The farm families, with twenty years of backbreaking work, turned the land into fields and pasture. Much of the land was too heavy and wet to farm profitably, but the first generation was too bullheaded to admit their mistakes. They complained endlessly of poor crops and their struggles with tractors stuck in mud, and each year they hoped the next would be different.

Most of the second generation continued the struggle, too set in their ways and sentimental to give up what Mom and Dad started. Their neighbors agreed, privately, that it was convincing evidence that insanity does run in families.

Sam was one of those who couldn't bring himself to leave his parent's farm. He met me at the door to the milk house. A dairyman in his late forties, of medium build, and a bit on the short side, Sam was beside himself with frustration. His baseball cap in hand, he gestured toward the barn. "They ain't milking worth two cents, and they are peeing, just peeing. They're flooding the damned barn. They're, they're . . ."

I'd never seen Sam so upset. "What's going—"

"It's my cows," Sam yelled. He was almost in tears from frustration. "The damned cows. I can't load the manure spreader 'cause it's all liquid. Urine. Nothing but urine. My cows are flooding my . . . I . . . I . . ." Sam ran out of breath and settled down enough to usher me into the barn.

In a perverse salute, every cow in the barn raised her tail and urinated as we entered the barn. I'd never seen anything like it. I had to dance and dodge back and forth across the aisle to stay dry.

The cows looked bright and alert and were eating their hay. They weren't eating their grain ration and milk production dropped in half. Sam was losing money hand over fist, his happy cows were peeing at him, and the center aisle of the barn, where Sam had to walk, was flooding with a yellow tide.

My first thought was, *at least last night I knew what I was doing.* I examined a dozen cows but could find nothing wrong with them. *Urine, where have I heard of something like this?*

I tried an old trick that came in handy over the years. I quizzed Sam about what had been going on, hoping he'd put his answer in a phrase that would remind me of a lecture or seminar from years ago.

When nothing fit the first time, I repeated the questions, phrased differently, and prayed Sam would rephrase his answers and jog my memory. Sam was ready to throttle me by the time we finished the third round of questions.

"Doc, we'll have to swim to get out of here if you ask the same stupid questions again."

Busted. But swim? Seminar? That's where I'd heard about this. Life was good, reason triumphant, and I knew what the hell I was doing. "You do have salt in the ration, don't you?"

"Of course I do. Do I look like an idiot or somebody who'd ask the same stupid questions six times?" Sam said this so loudly all the cows turned to look at him—after they'd taken another group whiz.

I ignored the sarcasm, but I couldn't ignore Sam's red face and clenched fists. I'd better come up with something that would make sense to Sam and do it quickly, or I might be assisted off the farm. "Have you changed the ration lately?" I asked.

"Yeah. I got a new nutritionist and a special vitamin and mineral supplement. Their supplement is damned expensive, but they're balancing my ration for thirty-two minerals and vitamins. Just started with 'em last week."

That sounded familiar, too. Where had I heard that? "You're still giving them free choice salt and minerals, aren't you?"

Sam shook his head. "Nope. They didn't want the cows getting more salt than they needed." Sam's expression went from angry to thoughtful; it suggested a nutritionist was about to get a loud phone call.

It fit. "Sam, nobody knows a cow's requirements for thirty-two nutrients. Put the free choice salt back in the yard and see what happens. I'll submit a few urine samples to the hospital lab. We'll have the results tomorrow."

I headed back to the office, eager to get the samples to the hospital. The nonsense about thirty-two nutrients Sam was talking about bothered me. Where had I heard it before?

I was gulping down a burger for lunch in the back room of our office when it dawned on me where most stupid ideas had come from in the last six months. I had a premonition that a nice day was going bad when Sheryl told me Sam was on the phone, and he sounded upset. He only wanted to talk to me, usually an ominous beginning to a conversation.

"Doc, it's awful. Why are they doing that?" Sam was more disturbed than he'd been that morning.

"Doing what? Who is doing what?"

"My cows. My goddamned cows. I turned 'em out in the lot, they saw the salt feeder, and they've gone crazy. They're rioting, fighting over the salt. They're going to kill each other if they keep at it."

When I suggested he put extra salt licks out for the cows, Sheryl interrupted. Another dairyman was on the phone with a similar problem; his cows were bright and alert, dropping in milk production, and flooding his barn with urine. I told her to ask if he was using a nutritionist who balanced the ration for thirty-two nutrients.

She interrupted me again as I took my second bite of a rapidly cooling burger. Yes, the dairyman was using a new nutritionist. Well, not a nutritionist, the guy was a salesman who worked with a nutritionist in another state.

To hell with the burger, I thought. *Burgers I can have any day. Diagnosing a weird-assed problem and getting it right on the first try comes along once a decade.* I put a little more salt on my fries and relaxed with a silly grin. My blood pressure could take care of itself today.

I was happy as a clam and wanted to talk to somebody about salt. There probably isn't a more exquisite torture than listening to a self-satisfied idiot talk about his ideas, so I don't know why I inflicted myself on Professor Rodgers, but I called him. We reviewed salt deficiencies and the lab results that would be diagnostic. Rodgers was gracious and listened patiently. He seemed happy to hear that his work was useful in the field, almost as happy as when I finally said goodbye.

The lab results made it official the next morning. The cows were deficient in salt.

The diagnosis was easier as other clients called with the same problem. I just asked who their nutritionist was. By the second week of *le deluge doré*, the now-sodden feed salesman dropped by the office and made arrangements to collect urine samples from his client's cows and bring them to our office for submission to the lab. Better yet, I remembered where I first heard about the dairy nutritionist: Doofus.

Never have one of my harebrained ideas turned out as well as the seminar by Rodgers and that wonderful afternoon in a warm pool. That doesn't sound right when I think of the cows at Sam's, but it was a great party. I relished having the goods on Doofus and one of his ideas for the next time he showed up.

Chapter 39: Father and Son

Doc's Manuscript

Rockburg, May 23, 1988

I took a day off to visit Mom late in May. It would take half a day to do the monthly pregnancy exams for her herd, review the vaccination program, and talk things over with her new manager. She finally hired Jim away from the Worburg farm.

A cough from the passenger's side of my pickup interrupted my thoughts as I drove to the farm. "How've you been, Doofus?" I asked.

"I'm fine. Thought I'd drop by and help your mother keep you out 'ah trouble. I figure it will take both of us workin' full time to keep ya in line today."

Oh, Lord, I thought. *More bullshit. What does he have planned for today?* "Why so concerned for my welfare on this trip?"

Doofus tried not to grin. His lips only twitched once or twice, but his eyes gave him away. The skin at the corners of his eyes crinkled, and his eyes seemed to dance. "Oh, nothing. Nothing at all." He turned to look at the fields we were passing to keep me from seeing his face. "I just remembered you're kind 'ah nervous. Ya get jumpy and upset with the least little surprises. Thought I'd better be here in case you went into meltdown again."

"What? What's this 'again' crap? Name one time I've—"

"Doc, it would take a week to recite 'em all. How about the times ya just about hit the ditch when I dropped by while you was driving?

Come to think of it, your driving would put any sane man on edge, but I don't need to quote Mary to ya on that."

That hurt. Mary talked about my driving to anyone who'd listen, but what was Doofus up to? I drew a complete blank.

He wasn't pushing me to start another project; he always got down to business right away on those. I glanced at him again. He was still smiling, still looking at empty fields.

He looked, well, smug. That was unnerving and irritating. He had something big up his sleeve, big and probably unpleasant.

We turned into the driveway of the old homestead. It didn't look old. Dad had a building or remodeling project underway every year I could remember, and Mom kept it up.

I met Jim at the milk house, and we got to work on the pregnancy exams. This was Jim's second week, and he was still getting used to the herd and the record system. He was lucky to have a couple of hired hands who worked for Mom for years.

Veterinary medicine, at least for food-producing animals, has more in common with public health than traditional sick-animal medicine. Jim and I reviewed computer analysis of the breeding records, calf growth records, disease incidence, and how those tied into management decisions and the herd's nutrition program.

No one can have the depth of understanding required in several disciplines. Farms often have consultants on retainer to take care of their nutrition, agricultural engineering (for cow comfort and ventilation), agronomy, and veterinary medicine.

I even had an Amish client with a computer in the barn. An eighth-grade education and a house without electricity didn't prevent him from continuing to learn and to use state-of-the-art equipment in the barn once he had permission from his Bishop. That was my first big lesson when I started practicing veterinary medicine. The formal education a person had wasn't as important as when he quit learning.

It was noon when we finished our work, and Mom came to the barn to invite Jim and me in for lunch. She said she had something to discuss.

Mom tried not to show it, but she gave a little start and almost giggled when she looked toward Doofus. She told me she knew him, but it didn't sink in until she looked at him, raised her eyebrows, and gave me a quick glance. Even I could see she saw him and was used to being quiet about it.

I looked at Doofus. He was whistling and making an exaggerated show of looking over the cows, the sky, and the barn. He looked way too content.

A car drove up to the house while Jim and I were cleaning up in the mud room. We heard Mom greet a man at the door and usher him into the dining room. I looked around the mudroom. There was no sign of Doofus.

If Doofus wasn't with me, he was with Mom and her visitor, probably waiting for me to walk into the dining room. Whoever this guy was, he was the surprise Doofus had for me.

Mom was giving a tall, thin man a peck on the cheek as I walked into the dining room. She wasn't embarrassed when I cleared my throat to announce my presence.

"Jack, I'd like you to meet Pete Williams. He's the gentleman I told you and Mary about some months ago. As of today, this is his home." She put a possessive arm around his waist, and he put his arm across her shoulders.

I introduced myself, and we shook hands. There was nothing pompous or pretentious about him; his face was honest, and his hands hard and rough from manual work. I almost laughed. This had to be a disappointment for Doofus.

Wrong. Doofus was leaning against the dining room wall, looking detached, disinterested, and innocent.

Okay. Pete wasn't the surprise.

Jim walked into the dining room, stopped short, and turned

pale. He recovered and came up to us as Mom introduced Jim. Pete looked uncomfortable, too.

"We've, ah, we've met," Pete said, "although not as often as I wanted," as he extended his hand to Jim.

Jim kept his hands in his pockets. Mom looked as puzzled as I felt. Doofus kept a straight face, but every so often there was a twitch in his cheeks and his eyebrows were arched. He looked like a guy I saw once who had just sold a lame horse with heaves.[5]

Mom never danced around issues, and she didn't now. She looked up at Pete. "Would you care to explain?"

"I'm Jim's father. I did some stupid things, things I'm not proud of, about the time he was born. His mother filed for divorce when he was six months old. She moved up north, and two years later married another guy. I signed the papers so's her husband could adopt Jim when he was six. I kept in touch, as much as I could over the years."

The muscles of Jim's neck were taught, and he stuck his jaw out. "I hardly ever saw you. You sent me, what, a few Christmas cards and a couple birthday cards. You signed them 'Pete,' never Dad or even Uncle."

"Didn't feel I had the right to call myself your dad, and your mother said she wouldn't let you see 'em if I did. That was the deal. I could see you when I could afford the trip, but only if I didn't confuse you about who your daddy was."

"So don't expect to come waltzing in here and claiming to be my Dad now."

"He didn't come here to see you. He's here to see me," Mom said. Her voice was soft but firm. Not even the Old Man had the balls to disagree with her when she spoke like that. "Jim, you are my farm manager. Pete will help you where and when he can, but you will be in charge. I expect both of you to be professional about work."

---

5 Heaves: emphysema in horses, usually caused by exposure to dusty or moldy hay. It can drop the value of a horse to something between dog food and glue.

She turned to Pete. "The same goes for you. You're here because we want to be together. You'll go stir-crazy sitting in the house, so you'll have to find a way to work with Jim, and he's in charge." She smiled sweetly and looked each of them in the eye.

Apparently satisfied that the two men understood her, she looked at Doofus and me. "It's time to eat." She pointed to a chair. "Pete, grab a chair and sit."

She busied herself putting dinner on the table; the noon meal on the farm was always dinner. It fit with the rhythm of the work on a dairy farm. She glared at Doofus a couple of times as she went back and forth from the table to the kitchen, but she laughed, just a little, after he winked and gave her a thumbs up.

I gathered there were a few rocky patches over the next month, but Jim didn't nurse old grievances. He didn't have the chance. His wife and Mom saw to that. No sane manager ever turned down a competent extra hand, especially if it was free, and Jim's wife recognized the potential for dependable babysitters. By the end of the summer, Jim and his family were having Sunday dinner with Mom and Pete and leaving the kids with them for an occasional Friday or Saturday night. Doofus did a good job this time.

Chapter 40: Moving On

Homeward the ploughman plods his weary way,
And leaves the night to darkness and to me.
—Thomas Gray

Doc's Manuscript

Rockburg, April 1988

It was nine in the evening, my night to cover emergencies again—and the first thunderstorm of the spring. Rain hit the windshield in sheets. The windshield wipers couldn't keep up with the rain, and it was difficult to see the road, as I headed home from a late calving problem.

The route home took me past the Cincher farm. It was a small, old-fashioned farm; the Cincher family milked fifty Guernsey cows, raised a few pigs, and periodically sent Drew Cincher, father and husband, off to a clinic to be dried out. Finances were hand to mouth because of Drew, so it was common for them to wait until the last minute to call for sick animals. The lights were on in the milking barn as I drove by.

What? What in daylights are they doing in the barn at this hour? I thought, *Sure as hell, something is sick, and they're dithering about whether to call the vet. If I stop and they don't have anything, they'll keep me there all night doing routine work. If they have something, it'll take Drew all night to describe the problem.*

Screw it. I'm hungry, and I'm going home. He's already six months behind on his bill.

I parked the truck in my driveway, showered, and started eating dinner. The phone rang at ten. I knew who it was before I picked up the phone. "Hello, Drew, how are you doing tonight?"

"Ah, pretty good, Doc. How did you know it was me?

"Wild guess."

"I was wondering if you were going to be out this way tonight."

Typical. Drew wanted to avoid the $5 fee for an after-hours emergency call. "It's ten, Drew. Unless you have an emergency, I'm not going anywhere tonight."

I heard muted discussion in the background and a crash and bang as though Drew dropped the phone. "Well, we . . .ah . . .I've got some little pigs that aren't right."

"How old are they?" I picked up a pencil and started doodling. Drew wasn't accustomed to giving up information quickly.

"About, ah," there was more muted discussion in the background. "Two days. Yeah, they're two days old."

Two days, and he had to ask his kids how old they were. The phone's handset had an exceptionally long cord. I started pacing back and forth in our kitchen. "How long have they been sick?"

"Oh, they ain't sick, Doc. No, they ain't sick." There was a long pause. "They just ain't right."

I broke the pencil between two fingers and picked up another. With effort, I kept a civil tone. "Can you define 'not right,' please?"

"Ah," there was a long silence interspersed with background conversation, "they don't look right, Doc."

I broke the second pencil and pressed my forehead against a cupboard door. "What . . . is . . .wrong . . .with . . .them?"

"Well, that's why I called you, Doc. Aren't you supposed to tell me what's wrong with 'em?"

There was a moment of silence as I digested that. Uncomfortable with the silence, or afraid of more questions, Drew returned to his original refrain. "But they ain't got nothing wrong, Doc. Nothing. They ain't sick."

"Good, then I'll . . ."

"They just ain't right."

I broke two pencils. Mary walked by, looked at the pencil bits and doodling, and snickered. "Drew Cincher?"

I nodded "yes" and broke one of the pencil bits into smaller bits. Were I a swine veterinarian, or if I saw a few hundred pigs a year, I might have been able to make the diagnosis or narrow the problem to two or three likely conditions. If I could have read Drew's mind, I might have guessed that the little pigs were starving because the sow was suffering from MMA (mastitis, metritis, agalactia), but I was a dairy vet who specialized and did research in bovine mastitis. I saw two pigs a year, and if they were lucky, they both died quickly.

We were the only veterinarians within twenty-five miles. I couldn't refer Drew to a swine veterinarian because there were none in the area. Had one been available, he would have expected to be paid, a quaint business practice and often a sore point with Drew. I took a deep breath and dreamt of doing research full time. "The piglets, the ones that aren't right, do they have diarrhea?"

"Oh, no, Doc. If they did, they'd be sick. I told ya, they ain't sick."

"Good, good. Well, if they're not sick, why don't I drop by tomorrow—"

"But, Doc, I'm telling ya, they ain't right."

This went on for another five minutes and a full package of pencils. Drew asked if he should give the piglets any shots. I told him he could if he'd like to, but we didn't have a diagnosis, so I couldn't make any recommendations. That was a novel, if not revolutionary idea, carelessly launched into the little pool of Drew's intellectual universe. The phone was silent as the absurd notion that treatment was related in some mysterious way to diagnosis sloshed back and forth between Drew's ears like a tsunami in a bathtub.

I was about to declare victory and hang up when Drew recovered.

Carefully, as though talking to a simpleton, Drew listed every medication he had on the farm and asked about the dose and how and where it should be injected.

There aren't many places to give a piglet an injection, so the instructions were similar for each medication. After each, I told him the method and site of injection was the same as the medication we had just covered, and for each, he requested that I repeat the instructions again.

Mary, snickering, handed me another box of pencils. She was sweeping up pencil bits when I told Drew I'd be out the next morning and hung up on him.

I was mad but disgusted with my behavior and worried about the future. Small towns don't have secrets, and I heard that Drew was once an intelligent and hardworking young farmer. He crawled into a bottle and experimented with drugs after his brother fell head first into a silo blower. The machine, designed to chop tons of forage per hour into four-inch pieces and blow them sixty feet up metal tubes to fill silos, stopped at his brother's hips. Drew was the one who found him.

It wasn't Drew's fault I was sensitive about my ignorance of swine medicine, and like any father, it scared me to see how easily the life of a man and his family could be ruined. Muttering to myself, I put on a jacket and went out to the garage to clean the trash and empty vials from my truck. I didn't want to talk to anybody until I cooled down and sorted things out in my mind.

The garage was a bad move.

Doofus, startling in a new hot pink tutu speckled with pasture-green cow flop, was leaning against my truck. He must have walked through fresh clover in a crowded pasture to look like that.[6] "Hi buddy. How ya doin' tonight?"

"Oh, for God's sake. Not tonight, Doofus. I've already spent too

6 Cows and yearlings on fresh clover get diarrhea. The cows don't notice it, but it is miserable to work around them.

much time talking to," I caught myself, "to other people. Whatever it is, can't we talk about it another night?"

Doofus smiled. "There ain't time, Doc. That nutritionist I told ya about is looking for a partner, somebody to finance an expansion and introduce him to dairy clients. I tell ya, for a guy—"

Confronting Doofus on this didn't seem like fun anymore. "You haven't heard?" I asked.

He hadn't. I told him about the salt deficiencies and explained, again, that the nutritionist was claiming knowledge no one had, and it cost my clients money.

Doofus objected that his friend did the research and published a paper. Doofus stood to his full height. "Doc, he's got the science behind him."

"Doofus, most scientists have a paper we wished we hadn't published. One paper or a couple of papers by one author mean little. What counts are consistent results from many studies by independent labs and competing scientists. That's—"

"Oh, Lord, not this again."

"—why Pasteur's theory of the microbial cause of disease, Darwin's theory of evolution by natural selection, and plate tectonics are accepted, and why global warming looks solid. You—"

"Aw, come on, Doc." Doofus shook his head and frowned. "I heard a radio talk show host say that global warming studies weren't done right. He said yer supposed to have a theory and—"

"Good lord! You're going to believe a nonscientist who tells scientists that they don't know what science is? Doesn't that strike you as stupid? Did you take the word of the tobacco industry scientists when they 'proved' smoking was harmless? How did that turn out?"

I'd raised my voice, and Doofus figured out that tonight wasn't the time to talk to me. "Shh, take it easy. Cripes, Doc, you'll have Mary out here."

"Hundreds of scientists agree now on something they didn't

agree with twenty years ago. They changed their minds because data collected from all over the world by dozens of their peers consistently supported the theory. After all that, you listen to a blowhard college dropout and politicians funded by the fossil-fuel industries?"

"Shit, Doc, you—"

"What do you think will happen to a nation that lets fools, lobbyists, and politicians define science? Would you let me do brain surgery or write a contract if I read an article about it? Do you think profit or loss changes the facts of nature? Would—"

"You could make a fortune on—"

"Doofus, I consider you a friend because you don't have a mean bone in your body. That's important, but so are facts, knowledge, thinking, and doing work you love. Anybody who puts money or things ahead of truth and people is a sick bastard."

Apparently, Doofus decided I was a lost cause and disappeared. I cleaned out my truck, bagged the trash, and stood by the trash can, lost in thought. Research was what I enjoyed and wanted to do. I could only do that by taking time away from the practice and my family; it wasn't fair to either. This was it. Tomorrow, I'd call my old graduate advisor, make a few inquiries with people in the animal health industry, and start checking the job openings listed in professional journals.

Several months later, I was approached by a company in animal health. They needed someone with my background for a position in R&D. We sold the house, moved to another state, and started a new life. Doofus continued to drop by in the months I was still in practice, after I'd moved into research, and into my retirement, but from this point on, I felt I could handle him.

Chapter 41

The Heirs' Story

Julie's Home, St. Paul, Minnesota, April 2014

Groggy, Julie fumbled in the dark, her head still on the pillow. Her fingers found the phone and picked it up. "Yes?"

"I got it. I finally got it," Wally exclaimed. "We couldn't get past your dad's passwords, but I found a list of Mom's."

Julie rubbed her eyes and looked at the clock on the nightstand. "Great!" She yawned. "What did you find at three in the morning?"

"Everything. I opened all the e-mails between your dad and my mom. It looks like it's got everything. I haven't read all of them yet, but according to the subject lines, we've—"

"What time is it where you are?"

"Three o'clock. Why? Is the power out up there?"

Julie sat up, turned on the light on the nightstand, and reconsidered her opinion of her favorite cousin. "No. That's the time here, too. Imagine that." Reluctantly, she sat upright in bed. "Why don't you settle down, read the fucking e-mails, and send me a summary when you're done. Boil it down to a short, very short, paragraph, and I'll read it over lunch."

"Oh, sorry. I, ah, I forgot about the time, but I thought you'd want to hear about it."

Wide awake, Julie finally noticed the excitement in Wally's voice. He hadn't recognized sarcasm and wasn't taking hints. He probably wasn't even going to hear what she said until he spilled it all. If she hung up, he might just call her back. "What is it you thought I'd want to hear?"

"Mom and Doc's e-mails. I opened them. One of them was about the codicil; another has a short story about squirrel fishing attached. Mom was worried we wouldn't understand what your dad meant. They left some pretty broad hints about it."

Julie toyed with the idea of giving Seth's phone number to Wally. She'd called Seth from college at three in the morning once—only once. Seth's sleep was sacred to him, and his reaction to heresy and sacrilege was medieval.

A cartoon of Seth reaching through the phone and strangling Wally ran through her mind. She giggled. *No. Both of 'em deserve it, but . . .*

Julie looked at the clock again. *Six hours until work. Man . . .* "Forward the e-mails to all of us. We can set up a meeting in a week or so. Include your summary. Goodnight." She turned her phone off, rolled over, pulled the quilt over her shoulders and went back to sleep.

Julie finished putting the kids to bed the next night. It had been near zero when Danny left for school and colder when he returned, exhausted. Kids tire quickly at those temperatures. Even Emma, who was still in day care, went to bed without complaint.

Todd was still working at his computer reconciling their bank statement as Julie checked her e-mails on her laptop on the library table next to Todd's desk. *Here they are, three e-mails and an attachment*, she thought. *Start with . . .*

Todd was startled by a beep from his computer. He opened his calendar. "Damn. Hon, I forgot to tell you. I have a dinner meeting with a client from out of town tomorrow evening. I might have to entertain him the following evening, too, if I can't get somebody else to take him out."

"Oh . . ." *Great,* she thought. "Okay. I'll make arrangements." *I'll have to pick Emma up early and be here when Danny gets home.* "Try to give me a little more warning next time."

Julie opened the first of Wally's e-mails and was about to open the attachment when she heard a thud from the bookshelf on the wall behind her. She turned to look, but Todd was engrossed in his work and didn't notice.

A book had fallen from the shelf, Doc's book. Julie recognized it and looked from the book to her husband. "Todd, will, ah, will you be working here for a while?"

"Hmmm, a couple hours, maybe. Why?"

Julie could tell from the slight movements of his head, back and forth from the screen to the bank statement that he was concentrating on his work.

"Nothing." *I have to read it sometime. Best do it while Todd's here.* "I'll read more of Dad's book if, ah, if you're going to be tied up."

Todd stopped working, marked his place on the bank statement and turned to Julie. "Something the matter?"

"No," Julie retrieved the book and sat in a recliner between the computer desk Todd worked at and the antique library table where she kept her computer.

"That didn't sound very convincing."

Now, what do I say? This is silly, but how do I tell him I'm afraid of a book without sounding crazy? "Things happened, odd sounds, the last time I tried to finish the book." *Might as well go for broke.* "And just now, it fell off the bookshelf as I opened e-mails Wally sent from Linda and Dad."

Todd looked puzzled. "Oookay," he shrugged his shoulders and returned to his work.

Julie turned to the marked page, the one with the turned-down corner and began to read. She finished the page, thought for a minute, turned to the first page of Chapter thirty-six, and read the entire chapter, including Elspeth's meeting with Doofus and her discussion with Doc about inspiration and ideas.

Ya get it now? she heard, as she finished reading. *Ya ain't got nothin' ta be afraid of. Doc said I could help you and Josh on this here codicil, if you got stuck.*

Julie glanced at Todd. He was still working, unaware there was a conversation going on. The voice in her head continued. *Me an old Doc got along fine, 'ceptin how slow on the uptake he was sometimes. He wasn't as sharp as yer gramma Elspeth, but he wasn't too bad . . . leastwise, most of the time.*

"Doofus?" Julie said quietly.

"What's that, dear?" Todd asked, eyes still on the computer screen.

"Nothing." Julie raised her eyes from the book, saw Doofus sitting on the library table next to her computer, and stifled a laugh.

"Best git ta reading that attachment Wally sent ya, 'cause we got a whole bunch to talk about when yer done with that. I got lots of ideas on how we can do those things ya been dreaming about." Doofus nodded toward Todd. "Say, ya think it'll be okay with him if I help myself to a beer?"

Julie nodded and made a note to pick up cheese curls tomorrow.

"Now, about that idea you had. Al still has some farmland, and I know he's looking to sell. There's a little problem with them artichokes, but nothing you and Todd can't handle."

Chapter 42: Squirrel Fishing

The Heirs' Story

From: Wilson, Jack <jackwilson3@yaholler.net>
Subject: Squirrel Fishing
Date: October 24, 2009 11:41AM
To: Linda Grey <lindag553@othernet.net>

Linda,

After you called last week, I reviewed the manuscript, my instructions to Al, and the codicil. You were right: a sane person will need more help to figure out what "take Doofus squirrel fishing" means.

I wrote a story about the day I explained squirrel fishing to Al (attached) and tried to pass it off as fiction in a "creative writing" contest. Nothing in the story was fiction. I even forgot to change the names. Mary was out shopping, and Doofus dropped by with one of his damned-fool ideas.

The story wasn't published. We could add it to the manuscript, leave it where the kids can find it, or give a copy to Al with instructions. I'd love to see Al's face when he reads it.

Let me know what you'd like to do,

Love,
Jack

Attachment

Squirrel Fishing

Jack Wilson

Al set his empty beer can on the table between us, put his feet on a little metal ottoman, and made himself comfortable in the deck chair. "What do you do for entertainment now?"

"You mean other than mow the lawn and bitch about our politicians?"

"Yeah. How are you staying occupied?"

I leaned back in my metal rocking chair. "Ever try squirrel fishing?"

Al did a double take. "What the hell is that?"

"Filling the bird feeder is just chumming for squirrels in our yard. The squirrels dig up Mary's flowers, eat the grapes, and drive the dog nuts."

Al looked into the maple trees towering above us. "Couple tree rats up there now." He took another sip of his beer. "You could take the trees out."

"We're on the west side of the house. We'd fry on the deck without shade from these trees. I put the squirrels to better use. I go squirrel fishing."

Al gave me a curious look. "You can't shoot them in the city limits, can you?"

"Of course not. I fish for them."

"What? With a line and hook?"

"A line, no hooks. I use old fishing tackle, tie an ear of corn on a line, cast into the yard, reel it in slowly—keep it just out of reach of the little bastards. I can drive squirrels nuts all day." I demonstrated, jigging an imaginary fishing rod.

Al shook his head. "Didn't think you were up to it."

"What?"

"Outsmarting a rodent."

I tossed a peanut over the deck rail and watched a squirrel go after it. "I can, on a good day. Besides, the other things that come with it are almost as much fun."

"Such as?"

"Irritating the neighbors." I was out of beer and stood to get another from the kitchen. "Care for another?"

"Yeah, and some pretzels, too."

I returned with beer and snacks and tossed another peanut to the squirrels.

Al pulled the bowl of pretzels to his side of the table. "You're not supposed to eat this stuff, you know. Mary told me about your blood pressure." He opened his beer. "Now, how would we go squirrel fishing?"

"Fresh water squirrel fishing or deep-sea squirrel fishing?"

Al coughed with a mouthful of beer, spewing a fine mist toward the lawn. "How much beer have you had?" he asked once he had his coughing under control. "Did you start before I got here?"

"Half the fun is making the neighbors wonder if I'm crazier than the squirrels. Now, do you want to squirrel fish from the deck, or do you want to get out in the sun, put on a hat, swimming trunks, a life preserver, and sit down there on top of the rose arbor, strapped to that old swivel chair I mounted on it?"

"What in the name of—"

"We use heavier tackle there, and bobbers aren't allowed."

Al craned his head forward and looked toward the rose arbor, five feet below the deck because of the slope to the lawn and halfway down the lawn. "And Mary hasn't had you committed?"

"You can use a bobber, in case your cast goes into deep grass or the day lilies, but if you do, house rules are you fish from the deck with the amateurs and little kids."

"A bobber? Jesus, you're making the squirrels look rational. What have your neighbors said about this?"

"Nothing but praise. At least that's how I took it."

Al looked into the trees and took another swig of beer. "I know I shouldn't ask, but what did they say?"

"The first time I tried deep-sea squirrel fishing, I heard John, the guy who lives over there," I pointed toward a house beyond the rose arbor, "call to his wife, 'Cindy, come look at this. What do you think that crazy son of a bitch is up to now? Call the cops. I think he's nuts.'"

"You were pleased with that?"

"Typed it up in thirty-six-point font and framed it. Even had the officer sign it."

"Officer?"

"Yeah. Cindy called 911 and suggested I be committed for observation. She's a sweetheart. Very protective of the neighborhood."

"They sent a sheriff's deputy?"

"Yup. Wasn't the brightest bulb on the force. Took a long time to explain squirrel fishing to him. I let him cast a few times from the deck." I had another sip of beer and stole one of the pretzels from Al. "He enjoyed it, but had no talent, too damned proud to use a bobber, too. He cast into the day lilies at the back, along the property line, and couldn't keep the corn ahead of the squirrel. Squirrel ate so much corn, he lost interest in the game. Nearly ruined fishing for the day."

I took another sip of beer and readjusted myself in the rocker. "I should have stopped there."

We were both silent for a while, as we enjoyed the shade and a light warm breeze. Al sat upright and looked at me. "No, you didn't put him down there, did you? How much beer did you give him?

"It was a hot day."

Al leaned back and put a hand over his eyes. "You gave him a beer or three and then talked him into getting up on that stupid swivel chair? Jesus!"

"I was careful. He strapped himself in and wore a life preserver."

"There isn't a puddle within half a mile."

"Safety first." I reached across the table to get more pretzels. "You should have seen John's face. I wish I'd taken a picture. Roy really got into deep-sea squirrel fishing."

"Is he still in the department?"

"He was reinstated after the observation period. I offered to drive to the county seat and put in a good word for him, but his attorney told me to stay away from the courthouse during the hearing."

"I'll bet he did. What did Mary think about this?"

"She told the second deputy, 'You know what they say: Give a man a squirrel and he'll think you're nuts, but teach him to squirrel fish and the psychiatric evaluation could get you power of attorney.'"

"She really—"

"Helped him spell 'eccentric,' too."

"Remind me to send Cindy a sympathy card on your birthday."

"That would be nice. She's really a dear, and John gets cranky when I have free time. This year has been hard for her."

Al stared at me for a moment. "You're having fun in retirement, aren't you?"

"Loads."

The sun was warm, and I was comfortable and in a mood to reminisce. "I've been incredibly lucky. I worked in two professions I loved, I was able to dream, and I've spent my entire life learning. Toss in my family, and I couldn't have done better."

Al must have been feeling the same way, or at least he was willing to let me rattle on.

"Of all the things I've done, those that worked out best were the ideas nobody thought would work. I call those ideas 'squirrel fishing.' It took me a long time to learn from that. Of all the ideas I heard others propose, 60 percent of the ones I thought couldn't work did, and several became multimillion dollar products."

Al mulled that over. "So, you didn't learn the bigger lesson?"

"Right. I didn't learn to keep an open mind, until I was too damned old for it to do me any good. You can't judge ideas until you have data. That's the lesson for scientists, and you shouldn't accept or reject an idea because of what you hope or think might be true. We all do that too much."

"It defines politics sometimes," Al said. "Damned frustrating."

A door closed loudly in the house. Mary was out shopping, and Al didn't seem to notice; it had to be Doofus. I was about to excuse myself and see what was up, but Al beat me to it. "You haven't seen the pictures I took at our fiftieth class reunion last summer, have you? They're in my car. Won't take a minute to get them."

As Al left the house to get his pictures, I wandered into the kitchen. A pencil picked itself up and scribbled on a note pad by the phone. The pad floated to me and settled next to my beer. The message read, "Appearance is in the eye of the beholder."

I hunted up more pretzels and some cheese curls from the pantry and retrieved a six-pack of bock beer I'd been saving in the old fridge in the basement.

"Took ya twenty years, but ya finally got it right. Thanks." The air at the end of the kitchen island shimmered, and Doofus materialized, leaning against the island and reaching for a beer.

"Wondering when you'd get here. Will Al be able to see you?"

"Ohh, might as well."

"I can hardly wait to see his face. What did I look like the first time I saw you?"

"Pretty damned stupid, as I recall, but you do stupid real easy. Ya outsmart a couple squirrels, and ya think you're a genius." He grabbed a couple cheese curls. "How has Mary put up with ya all these years?"

"I'll bet Al won't look any smarter than I did when he sees you."

"That's setting the bar pretty low. Ah, did ya read my note?"

"Yeah. What did you mean?"

"I finally got more control over my appearance. You an' Al won't see me the same way."

"We'll see. He's at the door now."

Al let himself in, came up the steps, and walked into the kitchen, holding a manila envelope.

"Al, I'd like you to meet—"

Al extended his hand and walked up to Doofus. "Mr. D, what are you doing here? I didn't know you knew Jack. Is that a new suit?" Al turned to me and winked. "I'm paying you way too much if you can dress like that."

Life is full of surprises. "Ah, you, you know—"

"Al and I have known each other for years. Like you, he calls me Mr. D, rather than try to tackle my surname." Doofus resumed his seat on the stool. His manners became impeccable, his diction perfect. "Al, it's taken ages, but I've finally taught our friend, Doc, to keep bock beer and the appropriate snacks on hand. Has he always been a slow learner?"

"Yup." Al grabbed a handful of pretzels. "He used to be so busy lecturing people he didn't hear what they said. He's changed, almost pleasant to be around now." Al took a stool at the island next to Doofus.

I had trouble collecting my thoughts. "How, how did you, ah, meet Mr. D, Al?"

"Business. Mr. D is my financial advisor. When I saw him here in a suit, I thought he was here to see you on business."

I looked at Al and, ah, Mr. D. Doofus was still wearing his torn pink, manure-spattered tutu, to my eyes. If Doofus was a financial advisor, the history of Wall Street and the stock market began to make sense.

Doofus winked at me and turned to Al. "Al, did I ever tell you how well Doc does 'stupid,' as a facial expression. If you have a camera, we could catch this for posterity?"

Al shook his head. "Don't bother. I have school yearbooks full of that look. Close your mouth, Jack. It's embarrassing. A squirrel could set up house in it." Al handed me a beer and turned to Mr. D.

"How's that artichoke oil extraction plant coming? Will it be ready for me to risk planting Jerusalem artichokes next spring?"

I'd forgotten Al purchased farm land as an investment. This could get interesting.

Doofus looked thoughtful. "Check with me in three months. If it's a go, I can put you in touch with a seed company. You could make a killing on it."

Doofus turned to me. "That's what I wanted to discuss with you, Doc. The consortium building the plant will have an IPO in a month. Give me the go-ahead, and I can reserve a thousand shares for you. Interested?"

I looked at Doofus in disbelief. "Didn't we go through this a few years ago?"

"Yes, but that was a different group. Their financing—"

Al perked up. "You've heard of this?"

I nodded. "Long time ago, before I left practice. A group of Amish farmers bought seed for Jerusalem artichokes and planted almost a thousand acres. Plans for building the oil extraction plant collapsed. The farmers were stuck with tons of artichokes and no market."

I opened a bock beer. "They tried to get their families to eat the artichokes, but the variety they planted was selected for oil production, not taste. They smelled awful and tasted worse when they were cooked. Their kids wouldn't eat them, and the Amish wives wouldn't allow the artichokes in the house a second time. The farmers tried feeding them to their cows, which is how I learned about them."

Remembering the expression on Amos Mueller's face when he told me about it, I had to suppress a giggle. "The cows agreed with the farmer's wives. Milk production cratered, and they couldn't sell what milk they did get because it took on a funny odor and flavor. It almost put some of the farmers out of business."

I glanced at Doofus. He was pretending to ignore my spiel. "The farmers tried composting the tubers to turn them into fertilizer. That didn't work; the artichokes weren't dead and sprouted wherever the compost was spread. That ruined the hay and corn for that year. It was so hard to get rid of the damned things, I think they even tried having an exorcism."

Doofus apparently decided I had enough fun. "That was regrettable, but it was because the oil plant wasn't built. This time we're going to make sure that construction is well underway before fields are planted. We have a person with drive, financial savvy, and persistence in charge now."

"I don't have to commit to buy the seed until the plant has financing, permits, and they've broken ground, do I?" Al asked.

"Right, although Doc here, will have to make up his mind on buying an equity position in the plant within the next two weeks. What do you think, Doc?" Doofus asked, turning to me.

I should have known Doofus would try pushing me on something. "Stocks usually drop after the IPO. What do you think the price will be a month after the initial offering?"

Doofus looked at the ceiling, as though the answer might be floating in the air. "I have no idea, but this time around, the CFO knows how to drive a project. Have I introduced you to Charles? Dynamic, organized, a talented administrator, and team player." Doofus looked at me, "Unlike some people I've had to work with."

This project made squirrel fishing look like an Olympic sport. On the other hand, oh, what the hell. "Okay, Mr. D. If the stock price drops to two dollars a share after the IPO, you can put me down for a hundred shares. It'll be worth the investment just to remind you about it a couple times a year after it tanks."

"You won't regret this, Doc." Doofus smiled. His hands moved, as he took a pen I couldn't see out of a pocket that wasn't there to write a note on a pad only he and Al saw. As he did, he seemed to check a wristwatch I couldn't see either. "Oh, my gosh," he said. "I have to go, already late for another appointment." He excused himself and left.

"Now, there's a guy you could learn from, Jack," Al said. He had a handful of cheese curls and looked toward the door. "When is that Doofus character you talked about going to arrive? Or did you give up on that story?"

"I gave up on it." I started picking up dishes. Al was old enough to handle his Doofus by himself.

"How many acres do you think I should put into artichokes?"

I struggled not to laugh. "I'm out of the advice business. What do you think?"

Chapter 43

The Heirs' Story

Rockburg, May 12, 2014

Julie met the other heirs around Doc's dining room table on a warm afternoon in May. She was scanning through files on her laptop while Jed, sitting across the table from her, worked on a Sudoku.

Josh, sitting next to, Julie, glanced at a calendar in front of him "How much longer can we meet here?"

"Al has it listed with a realtor, and it's on the market," Seth said. "The market isn't very active in Rockburg, and it doesn't cost much to have a housekeeper come in twice a month." He pulled out a small three-ring binder. "However, I have a question about that. I've been cosigning the checks for Al, and I'm getting bills for groceries. Have any of you guys been dropping by the house to work on the codicil?"

Julie looked up from her computer and looked at her brothers. She had an idea where this would go.

Jed put down his Sudoku. "Groceries? You mean, groceries for Christmas dinner?"

"No. Groceries purchased every month." Seth went through the bills. "Some of these are cleaning supplies, but," he pulled out individual receipts and laid them on the table, "here, and here." He looked at the others. "It's every month, without fail. The housekeeper bought a six-pack of beer and a bag of cheese curls."

"Did you ask her about it?" Jed asked.

"No. I thought I'd better check with you guys first in case one of you has been working up an appetite here." Seth looked around the table. "But nobody's been here?"

All the heirs, except Julie, shook their heads no. She sat, chin in hand, thinking.

"Julie?" Josh nudged her elbow. "Julie, have you been dropping by the house and snacking on cheese curls?"

"All this work keeping you guys on track, I get hungry, and—"

Not now, Doofus, Julie thought. "No, I haven't been eating cheese curls. Is the housekeeper the same lady who worked for Dad?"

Seth looked through more papers. "Yup. Same lady. Why?"

"I'll bet . . . I'll bet if you ask her, she'll tell you Dad asked her to keep a six-pack in the fridge and a bag of cheese curls in the pantry." Julie avoided eye contact with her brothers. *Doofus, have you been leaving messages for the housekeeper?*

"Oh, let's see now. I get so busy, have such big questions, big questions, on my mind. Hard to remember everything. Let's see: messages, messages . . ."

Julie glanced at her brothers and Wally. They shrugged their shoulders and seemed satisfied with her answer. Josh, however, looked startled, seemed to think for a minute, and glanced at her.

Josh began shuffling through papers in a way that looked suspiciously pointless. "We're here to answer the codicil questions, not to track down bags of cheese curls," he said.

"Right," Wally said. "I'm only here for three days. My flight leaves four hours after our meeting with Al, so let's concentrate on the codicil. We have the notes your dad left for you in his safety deposit box, your dad's book, two e-mails, and a short story. What do we make of everything?"

"Remember when I said the letters from Dad seemed to fit together?" Julie asked. "I think they fit squirrel fishing, too, as Dad described it."

A voice in her mind interrupted her. *"Now Josh, you help yer sister out on this, okay? I can't do it all by my lonesome."*

Out of the corner of her eye, Julie saw Josh start and turn pale. The rest of the men kept their attention on her.

"Okay." Seth leaned back in his chair and tossed his pencil on the table. "I give up. How do all of those fit together?"

Doofus, Julie thought.

"*Right here*," she heard. "*Don't worry. I got yer back*."

Julie fought the urge to roll her eyes. *I'm not worried. Just shut up while I'm talking*. She glanced at Josh again. He looked like he'd heard a fairy.

Doofus, have you been talking to Josh?

"Oh, no, no, leastways, not until today. Don't worry. I'll ride herd on him."

Lay off, will you? Julie thought. *God, Doofus, just leave us alone for a while*. She winked at Josh and hoped he'd keep his cool. "The notes from Dad could all be comments about ideas and how to evaluate whether the ideas are any good. Remember, Seth's was explicit. There are a lot of ideas and most of them are wrong. The notes to Jed and Josh were about truth and how to test it. The note to me sounded as though it was about gardening, but, 'Weed like hell and thin often' could be code for 'Test your ideas and throw out the bad ones.'"

The men thought about that. Josh looked as though he was about to speak when Jed interrupted. "Your analysis could fit with what Justin and Jim said."

Jed continued talking, but Julie's attention focused on another voice.

"There ain't no bad ideas. Not a one. Least none I gave Doc. There are a lot of clumsy gents who can't scratch both their nuts at once without cutting one off, though, and then, there's some guys without any balls to begin with, like—"

"For God's sake, shut up!" Julie shouted. She stood, picked up her laptop, and stormed out of the dining room and into Doc's old office.

Josh watched her turn a corner and walk down a hall toward Doc's office.

Shaken, Jed tried to finish his thought. "They, they, ah . . . cripes." He glanced in the direction Julie had gone. "They talked about Dad evaluating and acting on ideas, and the book was, basically, about good ideas and bad ideas."

Wally was still looking in the direction Julie left. "What's wrong with her?"

Jed shrugged, "Maybe that time of the month."

"Yer sister have PMS? I heard about women like that." Josh heard. *"Man, she's got a temper. All I said was—"*

Josh ignored Doofus and tried to get the meeting back on track. "Jim talked about dreams. A dream is an idea, one that's important to you." *One more comment, Doofus, and I'll join Julie in Dad's office. Why don't you go talk to her?*

"You sure you can handle this here meeting yerself? Wouldn't want to see—"

Go, Josh thought. *Go talk to Julie, and leave me alone.*

Seth leaned forward. "Let me see if I can put this in the context of the book—"

Doofus continued to jabber in Josh's mind. *"Well, ah, that's kind 'ah the problem, Josh. Women like yer sister, they, ah . . . Why don't I just sit here, quiet like, and wait 'till you're done? Then we'll go see Julie together. I'll be right behind ya. Give ya moral support, don't ya know, in case she gets nasty, or ya can't handle—"*

"Damn it, Doo . . ." Josh hadn't meant to speak out loud.

Seth turned red. "Christ. First Julie, and now you. What's your problem?"

"Ah, a cramp," Josh stood and walked around the dining room table, faking a limp. "You guys keep going. I'll walk it off, maybe talk to Julie."

"You want me ta watch these yahoos and make sure they don't—"

"No, Jesus! Just shut the . . ." Josh realized he'd spoken out loud again. "Damn, this cramp. Aaahh, it's bad."

Seth watched Josh pace for a moment and tried again. "Where was I. Ah, yeah, the squirrel fishing story and the e-mail to Aunt Linda."

Seth paused as Josh took his seat again. "Ah, Dad and Linda wanted us to stretch, to take chances. They wanted us to dream, to come up with ideas, evaluate, and act on them. Squirrel fishing is an oddball idea. It—"

"Deep-sea squirrel fishing sure as hell is," Wally said. "That goofy swivel chair is—"

"Forget the damned chair!" Seth barked. "Won't somebody let me finish a sentence? Now, how does 'Doofus' fit into this?" He looked at the others. "Anybody?"

Josh recognized when Seth's fuse was burning low. Under the table, he tapped Jed's leg with his foot. Jed looked at him and nodded.

"Let's take a break," Jed said. "Seth, you've done a great job summarizing things. Give me a minute to jot down what we've agreed on, and maybe Julie will be ready to join us by that time."

Josh headed to Doc's office and the other men stood and stretched.

Julie worked at her laptop on Doc's desk, and Josh relaxed in Doc's tattered recliner, looking absently at photographs hung on the maple-paneled wall. He sat up and turned to Julie. "Do you remember if Dad put any of his hidden doors in his office?"

She thought a moment. "I don't remember any, but it wouldn't be hard to check." She stood and began pushing gently on the panels wherever two boards in the paneling met, end on. Josh started on the opposite wall.

Three minutes later, a panel under Josh's fingers gave an eighth of an inch, and he heard a click. A small door, the width of the board, sprang open, and Josh found a letter-sized metal box standing on end in the wall. He put it on the corner of Doc's desk and opened it.

Julie looked over his shoulder while Josh carefully removed a tattered newspaper clipping. It began to fall apart as he laid it next to Julie's computer. "What's that?" she asked.

"It's an obituary for Timothy Wilson." Josh tried to smooth the paper out, but it only disintegrated further. "This is the Rockburg Gazette, May 26, the year before Dad was born." Josh examined the rest but couldn't make out any other names in the tattered paper. "There's a picture of a boy, but I don't recognize him."

"Tim?" Julie asked, "Isn't that on the codicil envelope?"

Josh nodded. "And on a tombstone next to grandma's."

Julie left her laptop in Doc's office when the heirs assembled around the table again after the break. Doofus stayed next to Josh, across the table from Julie. Jed looked at his notes. "We were trying to figure out what Doofus was or represents."

"I would interpret him as . . ." Josh looked at Julie. "Near the end of Dad's book, Grandma Elspeth said all ideas come from the same metaphorical well. I'd interpret Doofus as human ingenuity, the well, the source of ideas, good and bad."

"Bullshit! Metaphorical well, my ass. Like I said, I never had a bad—"

Josh glared at an empty chair. "What else did anybody pick up from the book?" Seth asked.

"Motive," Julie said, without looking around the table. "At least in the book, the ideas that worked weren't connected to money or prestige, and the ones that worked very well benefited many."

"Oh, for God's sake. Not that again. Your pa and me went over this once before, an—"

Julie swallowed once, shook her head, and continued. "What worked best benefitted many people, maybe because others were more inclined to pitch in and help out."

Jed nodded. "Good point."

"Aw, shit. I bet yer going to start criticizing wood putty next. Get a grip, girl. I got some ideas that could make a bundle for ya."

For God's sake, shut up! Julie thought.

Seth started to speak, but stopped and looked at Julie and Josh. He continued when neither made a comment, but his eyes shifted nervously from Josh to Julie as he spoke. "To summarize, going fishing with Doofus is to take a chance to follow a dream, an idea. If Doofus represents the idea, squirrel fishing represents putting it into practice, but only after studying it carefully. The farther out the idea seems, the greater its potential value, if it's right. Risks may be less if the benefits are widely spread. Does that cover it?"

All the heads around the table nodded in agreement.

"Good," Julie said. "I'd like to work on a proposal to pitch to Al when we meet him Thursday. Is that okay with the rest of you?"

They agreed, and she carried her laptop into her old bedroom to work.

Josh, his brothers, and Wally went through the e-mails between Linda and Doc again while Julie worked on her proposal,

"My God," Seth said. "Dad was a pack rat. There must be thousands of e-mails here. I should have showed him how to use the delete key."

Josh scratched his beard and looked at the monitor's screen as an endless list of e-mails scrolled past. "Jed, why don't you and I take the ones between seven to five years before Dad died?" Josh asked. "Wally and Seth, you can take the most recent e-mails. If we don't find anything in those, we can check the older ones later."

Josh took a seat in front of his laptop on the dining room table and Jed grabbed a stool behind him. "Let's rank them by oldest to most recent, first," Jed said.

Josh complied. *Doofus, you here?* he thought.

"Figured out ya need my help, did ya?"

"*Ah, yes. I'd appreciate any help.* Josh glanced at Jed."

"Aw, he can't hear me. He's concentrating too hard on the damned computer, like he's never seen a list before. Why do you guys run to a computer first and think later? Ya ain't never gonna get ideas that way. What do ya want me to help you on now?"

Key words for a search. Any advice?

"Let's see . . . Doc was thinking about ideas for his book, for dividing up the bank stock, for setting up the farm for Jim. Try 'book,' 'farm,' or 'codicil.' That should do it."

Josh thought a minute, ranked the e-mails by subject, and scrolled to "I," for ideas.

"Jed, look." Josh pointed to the screen. "Here's an e-mail about an idea. It was sent in October, two months before the codicil was signed."

Doofus, who is Tim?

"Ya don't know? How can ya not know about your uncle? You're like your dad. He wasn't any good at listening either."

"Jed, I think we should take a road trip."

"Right. Cemetery first. You drive, I'll ride shotgun and call the newspaper."

Chapter 44

The Heirs' Story

Rockburg, May 14, 2014

Al no longer maintained an office, but the bank allowed him to use the bank's board room to meet with the heirs. They gathered around the conference table at one in the afternoon. Al again sat at the head of the table, but unlike the previous meeting, Julie sat on one side of the table, and Seth, Josh, Jed, and Wally sat on the other.

Al passed out copies of the codicil and the front of the envelope and placed the originals on the table in front of him. "Seth, you asked me to reserve the room for the meeting. Please begin."

Seth nodded to Julie. "Go ahead."

"Okay. Al, I've—"

"Ah, Al," Josh looked at Julie and Al. "Before Julie presents her proposal, Jed and I have a different proposal to make."

Julie looked surprised, but nodded approval.

Jed nodded to Josh. "Go ahead."

"On the part of all of the heirs, I'd like to return the envelope to its owner."

The day is full of surprises, Al thought. He opened the envelope marked No. 3 and removed the answer. "Please, Josh, continue."

"The codicil envelope belongs to Dad's older brother, Tim, who drowned the year before Dad was born. His grave is next to Elspeth's and the Old Man's. I can leave the envelope at the grave to fulfill the codicil terms, but I'd rather not."

Al checked the name on the envelope and glanced at Doc's answer. *First damned thing that's made sense in this whole fiasco,* he thought. "Your answer is correct, but what would you like to do?" Al looked perplexed.

"I'd like to keep the envelope and invest the money for the next generation. All of us are comfortable. We don't need the money. I'd like to have the next generation go through this exercise in thirty or forty years."

The other heirs at the table looked mildly surprised. Al was more familiar with financial arrangements. *Crap, more complications,* he thought. *This could tie everything in knots. It could take weeks, maybe months.* Al closed his eyes and thought. "A gracious proposal, Josh. As you proposed the answer on behalf of all the heirs, you should discuss this with them. Can we table this until you've had that discussion?"

Josh shrugged his shoulders and agreed.

Al nodded to Julie.

"I've talked it over with my husband, and he says I can go squirrel fishing with Doofus."

"Excellent." Al scanned his copy of the codicil. He was disappointed with what he found. "But the codicil requires that you *take* Doofus squirrel fishing. Declaring your intention to do it does not satisfy the requirements of the codicil. You must do it."

"I know," Julie said. "If I give you a description of how I plan to take Doofus squirrel fishing, can you tell me if the plan, when completed, will satisfy the codicil requirements?

Damn. Doc didn't say anything about this, Al thought. *It'll be a chance to see what he wanted, but I'm sure he didn't want to allow fishing expeditions.* Al drummed his fingers on the table for a minute. *On the other hand, he didn't say we couldn't do it, and it might end this nonsense. I could be done with it by dinner.* "I think we can do it, within these limitations. You describe what you intend to do and why you believe it will satisfy the codicil, and I'll compare your proposal to the answer your father left in the envelope."

"Fair enough. Todd and I plan to quit our jobs and start a nursery and truck farm. We're both interested in horticulture, and we would like to investigate organic farming and sustainable sources of energy, whether wind, solar, or biodigestion. I've been toying with the idea for years, and Todd and I were working on a computer model for this before Dad died. We've identified the conditions needed for the idea to work, and experts at an Ag college have reviewed our plans."

Except for Josh, the others in the room looked confused. Al's brow furrowed, and he reread the codicil. "And what does this have to do with Doofus or squirrel fishing?"

Julie grinned. "I believe Doofus is symbolic for dreams and ideas, and squirrel fishing for taking a calculated chance to act on innovative ideas. Together, they stand for thinking through your ideas, even the ones that sound crazy, and to take a carefully evaluated risk to put your dreams into practice."

"Damn, girl, I got nothing to do with crazy ideas."

Shut up, Doofus, Julie thought.

"That sounds like your dad." Al opened the small envelope labeled, "Squirrel fishing with Doofus." He looked at the answer, wiped his glasses, and tried again. *Oh, hell. You'd think Doc didn't own a printer.* "Julie, it appears," Al smoothed the paper out again and took a small magnifying glass out of his shirt pocket. *At least I was prepared this time.* "It appears," Al put the paper down, "if you do what you've described, you will satisfy the requirements of the codicil. Congratulations."

Al remembered the last meeting and snuck a peek at Seth. *Looks under control so far,* he thought. *All of them seem to be taking the news pretty well. They look relieved, if anything.* Al gathered his notes and the codicil envelope. "Julie has accurately described what Doc and Linda wanted. Unless someone else has a proposal to make,

I believe we are done for the day. Josh, please get back to me when you've discussed your proposal with the rest of the heirs."

As the group walked out of the bank, Al sought out Julie. "Julie, how did you make the connection between Doofus and crazy ideas? And what made you include the, well, the almost due-diligence approach to the idea?"

Julie grinned and turned to Al. "How did your Jerusalem artichoke investments work out, Al?"